D1289605

The Lost Book of Wonders

Chad Brecher

The Lost Book of Wonders

a novel

Chad Brecher

Deeds Publishing | Atlanta

Published by Deeds Publishing in Athens, GA
www.deedspublishing.com

Cover by Mark Babcock

Printed in The United States of America

Library of Congress Cataloging-in-Publications data is available upon request.

ISBN 978-1-944193-86-7
EISBN 978-1-944193-87-4

Books are available in quantity for promotional or premium use. For information, email info@deedspublishing.com.

First Edition, 2017

10 9 8 7 6 5 4 3 2 1

for Sara

"...because there are many great and strange things in his book, which are reckoned past all credence, he was asked by his friends on his death bed to correct it by removing everything that went beyond the facts. To which his reply was that he had not told one half of what he had actually seen!"

— Dominican friar Jacopo d'Acqui, **Imago Mundi**, on the death of Marco Polo

PROLOGUE
Venice
15 April, 1355

A *Piazza San Marco!*

The voices were growing more frantic outside, joined by echoing footsteps across the stone.

Domenico scampered to the window, withdrew the curtain slightly, and peered through the glass. Cloaked forms jostled each other as they passed by the window and made their way towards the bridge. Domenico momentarily caught a metallic glint in the crowd as a man attempted to cover his sword with his cape. A parade of torches filled the courtyard with orange and red.

There isn't much time, Domenico thought with alarm as he retreated from the window and crawled across the wooden floor until his fingers found the edges of the oversized rug. As the torchlight cast menacing shadows against the far wall, he struggled to push aside the heavy fabric.

The floorboards beneath the rug were newer than the surrounding wood. Finding the edge of a strip of wood, Domenico drove the tip of the metal rod under the plank and eased the fulcrum to the floor with a grating sound. The plank suddenly released with a snap, sending two nails skipping across the floor. He reached down, his fingers finding the back side of the adjacent plank. A scream from outside caused him to hesitate and glance back at the front door.

It is all unraveling!

Domenico gripped the piece of wood and pulled upward with

all his strength. The second plank gave way with a crack. Able to right himself, Domenico tossed the piece of wood aside.

This is taking too long, he thought anxiously as he looked down at the small hole. His hands searched in the darkness until his fingers found the hatchet resting on the floor beside him. Gripping the ax, he began to swing it repeatedly against the wooden floor, splintering the planks. He stood up, raised the heel of his boot, and drove it hard into the floor. The wood disintegrated beneath his foot, nearly sending him toppling forward into the darkness before he was able to regain his balance.

He dropped to his knees with urgency, lowered his torso to the ground, and extended his arms into the blackened pit. His hands explored the darkness until he was able to locate the metal chest. With his muscles straining, Domenico withdrew the chest from the hiding place and, with a final grunt, set it safely on the floor beside the hole.

Domenico stared at the ducal coat of arms as he caught his breath. The throng outside was growing more raucous. Springing to his feet, he lifted the chest and made his way towards the back door. As his right hand found the handle, the front door swung open with a bang. The cacophonous voices from the mob immediately filled the room. Domenico froze, his hand instinctively gripping the handle of the dagger he had slid under his belt.

Isabel stood in the doorway, nearly out of breath. She looked at Domenico with confusion and alarm.

"It's the Doge!" she cried out, her eyes wide with concern.

Domenico sighed, relieved to see that the intruder was his wife. "I know, Isabel. I know!" He pulled at the knob and opened the back door.

Isabel stared with apprehension at the shattered wooden planks haphazardly piled beside the gaping hole in her floor.

"What is going on? What is this all about?" she asked.

"Close the door!" Domenico barked back. "You will get us both killed."

Isabel reached for the door and closed it as if in a trance. Behind Domenico, the opened back door revealed the flickering water of the canal. Domenico maneuvered down a small series of stone steps, teetering precariously as the weight of the chest threatened to topple him into the water. With a final heave, he hoisted the chest into the small flat-bottom boat.

He looked back at his wife before climbing into the boat. "I have something I must do. Do not speak of this night ever. If all goes well, I will be back soon."

"Where are you going?" Isabel begged as she ran to the steps.

Domenico pushed off with the edge of a paddle, sending the boat floating slowly away from the back of his house. He peered over his shoulder a final time, spotting his wife's form still on the landing. *The less she knows, the better,* he thought sadly, regretting that he had unwittingly dragged her into danger. Domenico looked down at the black water as his paddle broke the surface with a ripple.

We waited too long! he thought. *We will be lucky if any of us survive this night!*

Domenico silently navigated through the mazelike canals as the sounds of panic echoed across the city. When the boat passed under a stone bridge, he watched as his fellow Venetians scampered across the bridges towards the piazza. He felt a sense of sadness at the thought that they would probably never know what this night was truly about. *What lie will they create to mask this night?* Domenico wondered. As he continued to row, the noise from the crowds grew fainter until it was a mere rustle. The waterway grew tranquil, the moonlight giving the black water a silvery glow.

I must get to the Arsenal, he thought desperately. A boat would be waiting to secret away the chest—far away from Venice—to safety. *What had the Doge said?* Domenico asked himself.

"Domenico, they must never take possession of this chest. Never."

Domenico could see the masts of ships looming over the buildings. He allowed himself to sigh with relief. *Not much farther!*

Domenico drew the boat alongside a wall that lined the waterway to prevent detection. The sound of whispering and the flap of footsteps against stone broke the silence. Withdrawing the paddle from the water, he allowed the boat to drift with the current. Domenico stiffened his body and listened. An eerie quiet settled in, interrupted by a faint, rhythmic *splish-splash* noise, like waves meeting the shore and then retreating.

As he turned the boat down the canal towards the docks, he froze with horror. A human form hung from a bridge, swaying to and fro. As the boat neared the body, Domenico could see a man with hands bound behind his back, his chin dipped down towards his chest as if he were asleep. The man's feet were partially immersed in the water, allowing the current to lap at them periodically. A sign was suspended from the man's neck with scarlet red wording:

THIS IS WHAT HAPPENS TO TRAITORS

Domenico maneuvered the boat under the bridge, avoiding the hanging man. As he passed by, he looked up at the face and whimpered. *The Captain!* This was the man he was supposed to deliver the chest to. This was the man who was going to spirit away the box and its contents before it was too late. Domenico moaned.

He slowed the boat and brought it up against the wall of the canal. In the distance, he could see that all the outlets to the lagoon were blocked by men dressed in black, holding torches. There was no escape. The secret was out. They had been betrayed!

His mind raced as he tried to weigh his options. He could try to evade the boats, but he knew that was futile. He recognized what these men were capable of. He had witnessed the torture, heard the screams echoing from the inquisition chambers, seen the entrails coiled across the stone floors, smelled the feces, bile, and blood. If caught, one thing was certain—a horrible death.

There are better ways of dying, he thought as the boat bobbed up and down.

He slowly advanced the paddle into the water and directed the boat backwards until he was out of sight of the lagoon. Gripping the chest, he lifted it up. The boat teetered dangerously, threatening to send both him and the chest overboard. Domenico spread out his legs, regained his balance, and planted the chest on the edge of the boat. He looked down at the box a final time. The ducal coat of arms was exquisite—a wedge of yellow in the upper left, a wedge of black in the upper right, and a semicircle of beige on the bottom. The chest had been sealed with a resin, as instructed for ocean travel. There was still hope.

They must never take possession of this chest. Never.

Domenico rested his palms against the side of the chest and pushed. The container dropped into the dark water with a splash, sending the boat bobbing back and forth. He watched as it slipped beneath the surface and disappeared.

The boat began to drift away with the current towards the lagoon. In the distance, a darkened form on another vessel yelled, "You, come forward. We must inspect your boat on order of the Council of Ten."

Domenico fell backwards into the boat with exhaustion. His hands searched his pockets and pulled out a flask. He uncorked it, brought it to his lips, hesitated, and smiled. The apothecary had looked at him with a mix of suspicion and devilish amusement when he had bought it. "How big a rat, you say?" the man had asked. Domenico drew his hands far apart and muttered, "It's for a very, very big rat."

The liquid tasted bitter and he fought to keep it down. He threw the paddle over the side of the boat and lay down upon the wooden deck. As the boat floated slowly and serenely towards the lagoon, Domenico looked up at the stars and the moon.

There are better ways of dying.

Rome, Italy
1998

Father Italo Marconi felt sick.

It was not the sickness that accompanied a cold, but a more sinister illness that had crept into his body and dug in deep, wrapping itself tightly around his core, his soul. It had only gotten worse since he crossed the Tiber River and left Vatican City behind.

His legs felt rubbery as he slowly made his way down the center aisle of the bus. He avoided the stares of the passengers while his trembling hands gripped each metallic ring suspended from the ceiling, one after another. The priest could see the impatient eyes of the bus driver following his measured movements in the mirror until the driver caught the white of Father Marconi's collar poking out from under his overcoat, made the sign of the cross, and looked away with embarrassment.

An elderly woman in the front seat suddenly reached out and gripped his wrist. "Father, you do not look well."

The priest managed a crooked smile and nodded in silence, gently breaking the woman's hold. He momentarily caught his reflection in the mirror and was horrified to see the ghostlike pallor of his skin.

He took the steps one at a time until he was left standing alone beside the bus. Father Marconi watched as the bus hissed like a vicious snake, pulled away from the curb, and sped off down the street, leaving behind a black cloud that slowly dissipated. He looked down at the archival tubing that he clutched firmly against his body. Although weighing just a few ounces, it felt as heavy as lead in his hands.

The priest glanced at his surroundings. A billboard showed a bare-chested man looking intently at a gold watch. Several tourists sat at small tables pushed up against the storefront of a café, flipping through a guidebook. Beside the café was a lingerie store with scantily clad mannequins in the window.

Rome.

He wished he were back across the river and not in such a place of decadence. For a city of so many churches, Father Marconi could not help but feel a sense of dismay at the spiritual depravity of the modern city of Rome. And now, he was being sucked into its vortex.

He grimaced and walked a short distance down the street, finally stopping in front of a bank with elaborate Roman columns and a domed roof. He glanced down at the address written in his shaky handwriting and tried to muster enough saliva to swallow, but found his mouth unbearably dry.

What am I doing?

Father Marconi had worked for over thirty years as the chief librarian at the Vatican Central Library. He was the entrusted gatekeeper of information, the organizer of a seemingly infinite collection, and the protector of secrets long since buried behind the stone walls. He had no doubt that his betrayal would go unnoticed. There were, after all, levels of secrets. Some secrets were hidden until they were ultimately forgotten as the generations passed and bled into the centuries. No, there would be no grand discovery of its absence, no formal trial. In any event, he could deal with the repercussions of this world. It was the next world that weighed profoundly on him—his spiritual salvation. He was now a sinner.

Father Marconi pushed open the glass-paneled door and entered the bank. The noise of the busy street disappeared and was replaced by the hushed silence of the interior. The modern space contrasted sharply with the classical exterior. The bank was empty except for a teller, a guard, and a receptionist. He walked past the guard and approached the young woman behind a desk of frosted glass.

"Mi scusi, signora. I am supposed to give this to you," Father Marconi said. He unfolded a piece of paper and handed it to the woman.

The woman examined the paper and smiled at the priest. "Yes. He has been expecting you. Please follow me."

Father Marconi followed the woman down a narrow hallway. They arrived at a metal door. A guard rose from a desk and approached the door. The priest watched as the woman withdrew a key, placed it in the keyhole, and waited as the guard did the same in another keyhole a distance away. After simultaneously turning the keys, the metallic door opened.

The woman motioned for Father Marconi to go forward. As he advanced, the door was fastened shut behind him. He could hear the woman say, "Father, this bank is very discrete. Please go to room eight and knock."

The priest found himself in a large vault with an endless number of silver safe-deposit boxes that made up the walls. There were several doors labeled with numbers. He found room eight, brought his knuckles against the door several times in quick succession, and waited. Soon thereafter, a man opened the door.

The man was in his late thirties, with tightly cropped, jet-black hair. He wore a smart, black Armani suit that was fitted to his muscular frame. His eyes, as dark as his suit, were calm and controlled. *This is the man behind the voice*, the priest thought. It seemed so long ago that he was first contacted after leaving the hospital.

"Father, please." The man directed Father Marconi to sit down on a silver, metal chair. As he sat down, the man walked to the opposite side of the black table and sat down himself.

"You are the man I spoke to on the phone?" asked the priest.

"Yes. I am Jonas," the man replied nonchalantly.

"Are you him, the man who can make things happen?" The priest started to ask more, but stopped after realizing how confusing his statement sounded.

Jonas chuckled briefly. "I think I know what you mean. No, I am not him. He is...how shall I put it...a patron. I make things happen for him...and you for that matter. I am here to ensure that our transaction is completed. If you fulfill your side of the deal, you will only see me today and never again. Do you have it?"

The priest looked below the table, aggrieved. He leaned down, retrieved the tubing, and slid it across the table. Jonas lifted the tubing, popped off the top, and put on acid-free gloves. Reaching into the container, he withdrew the contents. He smiled, uncurled the parchment onto the table, and examined it closely. Satisfied with what he saw, he re-curled the document, slid it back into the tubing, and set the cylinder aside on the table.

Jonas straightened his back and pulled the chair close to the table.

"You are not the best dealer. What would prevent me from taking this tubing and leaving you with nothing? Always have the other person show their cards first. You are in the driver's seat. Or were," Jonas said.

"I am a priest...I am not a dealer," said Father Marconi. He was aghast.

"A pity. Don't worry, Father. We are not evil. Quite the contrary," the well-dressed man replied. "GBM," he added matter-of-factly.

"Scusi?" replied the priest with a look of annoyance.

"Glioblastoma Multiforme. It's what you have. It's the most aggressive form of brain cancer. The glial cells that compose part of your brain have decided to divide and grow uncontrollably. There is no cure. You will be dead in three months."

"But a cure?" The priest looked around the room desperately.

"No cure, I'm afraid. But I do give you hope." The man reached into his jacket pocket and withdrew a blue vial. He held it up between his right thumb and middle finger. "I'm holding a sample of RD-485. It's not available on the market now and may not be available for some time. You will be long dead before it receives a proper name and graces the pages of magazines and television commercials. We are making this available to you in a limited, advanced engagement. This medication is designed to specifically target your tumor."

"It is safe?" asked the priest.

"Three months, Father. Three months is all you have without treatment. I believe it is safe to say that you are beyond the concern for safety." Jonas ran his hands through his hair. "You must take these pills four times a day. On the first Monday of each month, a new supply of medication will be left in this safety deposit box." The man patted the black metal box at the edge of the table. Father Marconi made a mental note of the number of the box. He looked down at the table as Jonas pushed a key across it.

"You'll need this," Jonas added.

"It will work…yes…it will work, the pills?" implored the priest.

"We will see. I guess we will have to have something you already know quite a bit about…faith."

"How can I contact you?" asked the priest.

"You won't be able to. All contact will be severed today. You will get the pills as promised. That is our deal. I will follow through on my side as you have followed through on yours." The man got up from his chair and placed the tubing under his left arm.

He extended his hand and helped the priest to his feet. "Good luck, Father. I know this was a difficult thing for you to do, but you have done a good thing—something that will help the world one day."

The priest shot the man a perplexed look. Jonas winked,

turned away from Father Marconi, and walked slowly to the door, then paused.

"Good luck, Father," Jonas muttered again, before pulling open the door and walking out.

The priest could hear the door snap shut behind him. He looked down at the palm of his hand. The blue vial felt cool. There was nothing written on it, no name, no instructions. He had heard of people given placebos—sugar-pills—in scientific experiments without their knowledge. *What if that is the case? Have I been duped?* It was too late. The man had already left.

Faith?

The priest sat down on the chair and cradled his head in his hands. He hadn't cried like this since he was child.

Mosul, Iraq
2005

Ellie felt ridiculous. The oversized blue flak jacket dug into her thighs as she reached up to steady her helmet. The Armored Personnel Carrier had temporarily come to a halt before suddenly lurching forward, nearly catapulting Ellie from her seat. White-knuckled, she clung to the metal frame underneath her as she fought to steady herself and keep the growing nausea at bay.

"It's like *Heart of Darkness*," Gordon muttered, wiping beads of perspiration from his brow with the black and white handkerchief tied around his neck. "To think, you fought tooth-and-nail to come with me. Two hours in a windowless tin can. Not a heck of a lot of glory. Having any second thoughts?" Gordon cocked his head, slightly curling his lips into a wry smile. It was a smile she had become familiar with over the past couple years.

Ellie brushed back a strand of blond hair and poked Gordon in the chest, shooting him a look of false indignation. "Gordon, my dear, don't forget that Hamzi is *my* contact. MART would still be searching the cellars of the Iraq National Museum without me. I think I earned this, don't you? I'm not a schoolgirl."

Gordon nodded as he rubbed his brown beard, allowing the smile to temporarily reappear. "Dr. Griffin, one thing I learned quickly is that you are definitely no schoolgirl, and there is no convincing you otherwise once your mind is made up. You are as stubborn as they come."

'Stubborn', 'recalcitrant', 'pig-headed', and 'fixed-in-your-ways' were all things she had heard before during her days at Oxford.

She had secretly enjoyed terrorizing the ancient, white relics who filled the Antiquity Department. Tenured and mired in old-fashioned ideas and theories, these tweed-wearing academics would invariably cross paths with the seemingly demure five-foot-four Brit and make a monumental miscalculation. Once challenged by Ellie, they would be left to putter around the university, greeting her entrance into a room with uncomfortable coughs and averted eyes. Such was the legacy of Eleanor Griffin.

When she was recruited to join the Mesopotamian Antiquity Recovery Team, or MART for short, she was chosen precisely because of her passion for the field of antiquities, as well as her uncompromising drive. It was a fire in her that immediately attracted Gordon and terrified him at the same time. She could be a force of nature, remarkably beautiful and unpredictable.

He had seen countless young academics come his way through the years. As a minor celebrity in the field of Mesopotamian archeology, Gordon had the opportunity to teach many of them in the classroom and on archeological expeditions throughout the Middle East. But Ellie was special. This fact was unmistakable. She had a gift for the field. Perhaps it was genetic — Ellie was after all the only child of the late-great Harold Griffin, world-renowned Egyptologist. The more time he spent with Ellie, the more Gordon was confronted with a feeling that rarely surfaces in the life of an accomplished academic: the uncomfortable realization that a student's career will inevitably eclipse one's own. Staring at her in the stifling heat of the APC, he quickly computed the ratio in his head... nine parts pride, one part jealousy.

A rhythmic clanging echoed through the vehicle. Ellie's eyes drifted away from Gordon and caught the glare of a soldier in desert fatigues hunched over the barrel of an M-16. With sunken cheeks and dark eyes, the soldier scowled and continued to rap the butt of his gun against the reinforced steel floor.

"Will you quit it, Macowski? Jeez," piped up a soldier beside Ellie who had remained silent, seemingly comatose, since they left the base. He now squirmed uncomfortably in his seat as the vehicle slowed.

Macowski stopped, laid the barrel of the gun across his lap, and leaned back. Ellie felt uneasy as the soldier's eyes followed her own. "Hey Sarge…why we risking our lives for a piece of pottery? Shit. I didn't ship over to this hell-hole, and I mean freakin' hot-as-balls hell-hole, to get shot up so we can find Queen Who-Gives-A-Shit's clay dildo."

"Shut it, Macowski. I'm sorry we had to drag you away from the PlayStation at the base, but you got a job to do. I don't care if you don't like it," snapped Sergeant Rafferty. It had not taken Ellie long to realize that this sergeant ran a tight ship. His loyalty lay with the mission and keeping the soldiers under his command, many of whom were fresh out of high school, alive. He was ruggedly handsome with gray hair and faded blue eyes and carried himself with a calm confidence that somehow seemed to keep the wheels from falling off the wagon. Ellie could imagine him joining the ranks of the military analysts that were spreading across American newscasts—delivering good or bad news with a matter-of-factness that allowed the viewer to finish dinner. The sergeant nodded to Ellie as if to apologize.

Ellie could feel Macowski's eyes searing into her and she began to resent how uncomfortable she felt amongst the men. She pushed her helmet back off her forehead and leaned forward. "You know, it is more than just a bunch of clay pots. These artifacts are thousands of years old. They've withstood earthquakes, floods…" she motioned around the vehicle "…wars, and it would be criminal to just write them off. These items are older than the Bible, for Christ's sake. Some of these items are the oldest artifacts produced by mankind still in existence. I'd say that it is worth our lives to find them."

Macowski rolled his eyes. "Speak for yourself," he mumbled under his breath and looked away.

Ellie could feel Gordon's hand slide into hers. His lips brushed against her ear momentarily. "Well done. I hope they don't decide to leave *us* here."

Here...where exactly is here?' Ellie thought, feeling increasingly claustrophobic in the APC.

The last year was a blur. The images of Iraqi's celebratory toppling of statues of Saddam Hussein had long faded from television sets across the world, replaced by questions about faulty prewar intelligence and an increasingly deadly insurgency.

The looting of Iraq's vast collection of Mesopotamian artifacts had become emblematic of mistaken priorities and served as an embarrassing black eye for an already beleaguered American administration. The international press lambasted the military's defense of the oil ministries while widespread ransacking of the nation's heritage was tolerated. Prominent figures in the field of antiquities were already labeling it as one of the greatest calamities in history—a cultural Chernobyl.

To counter this criticism, the United States government had organized a motley assortment of task forces, mixing together FBI and customs officers, ex-special forces, and even New York City detectives. Interpol, for its part, had expanded investigations into international rings specializing in the illicit acquisition and trade of Mesopotamian antiquities, but with only lukewarm results. Several of the most famous pieces had resurfaced predominately intact, including the Lady's Head from Warka and the Bassetki Statue. The Warka Vase, dating from 3000 B.C., was eventually located but had not fared as well—it was broken into numerous pieces. Thousands of other items had not been recovered.

Conspiracy theories inevitably began to swirl as the media filmed empty but intact display cases and storage units in the National Museum in Baghdad. The robberies seemed focused and deliberate. The questions mounted. Were the thieves organized? Were these inside jobs? Some even argued that the American military itself had systematically emptied the museums.

In this atmosphere, MART was well-positioned. As an NGO, or non-government organization, MART was attractively "independent." Amply funded by private, often anonymous donors, MART was seen by the government as a bargain as the financial costs of the occupation continued to soar. As Iraq increasingly slipped towards civil war, the government readjusted its priorities and happily passed the baton into Gordon's hands.

Gordon Russell had been a professor at the Oriental Institute at the University of Chicago for over a decade before the war broke out. He enjoyed the unique status of being one of a handful of American scholars permitted into Iraq during the Baathist regime to help supervise several archeological expeditions in Umma, Nippur, and Lagash. Under seemingly constant surveillance by Saddam's security minders, Gordon was able to navigate a political tightrope, successfully arranging for cultural exchanges even in the midst of seething hostilities.

It was in Nippur that Gordon first encountered Ellie. At the time, she was squatting in an excavation pit holding a nearly intact water vase.

Gordon had knelt down beside her and said, "Now there's a find. May I?" Ellie smiled and handed over the jug. She watched as Gordon peered at it from every angle, finally holding it aloft against the desert sun before handing it delicately back. "I can already see it on the cover of *Biblical Archeology Review*. What do you think, 2000 B.C.?" Gordon asked with a smile.

Ellie grinned back, shielding her eyes with her hands. "Try 2000 *A.D.*" Ellie tilted the jug precariously in her hands; "...probably made in China. I bought it from that bloke selling postcards over there. I thought my aunt might like it. But something tells me you knew it was a fake."

Gordon chuckled briefly, shrugged, and extended his hand. "I'm Gordon Russell."

Ellie placed the vase down on the sand beside her and rose to her feet, her hands finding the small of her back. She accepted his handshake and replied, "I know who you are, Dr. Russell. I've read all your work on the Great Ziggurat of Ur. Your book *Excavating Ur* was a bit long-winded for my taste, although I did cough up fifteen pounds or so for it. The way I see it, you owe me a cup of Turkish coffee at that price. It was highway robbery, if you ask me. I much preferred your earlier work on religious iconography in early Babylon when you were still at Columbia."

Gordon scratched his head in amusement. "Well, you seem to know all about me. Other than the fact that you are spot on about my book—I could have used an editor with a very large chainsaw—I know nothing about you."

"I'm Eleanor Griffin from Oxford. I'm your new assistant. And I wasn't kidding about the coffee."

Ellie flourished in Iraq. She organized several excavations on the outskirts of Nippur, uncovering an ancient Jewish settlement built upon Babylonian ruins. Unlike many of the expatriates who tended to gravitate towards each other socially, Ellie intentionally pulled away from her colleagues and immersed herself in Iraqi culture—making friends and contacts in the small but active local antiquity community. It was through these contacts that Ellie found herself one weekend in Baghdad on a private after-hours tour of the National Museum with Hamzi.

Hamzi Hussein, although unrelated to the Iraqi dictator, had enjoyed the benefit of the doubt in pre-war Baathist Baghdad. He grew out the regulation Saddam moustache and slowly clawed his way to the coveted position of security chief at the National Museum. He knew every hall, display case, and storage closet better than the faces of his own children. He boasted that he probably knew more about the museum collections than even the curator.

During their private tour of the museum, he directed Ellie through the Sumerian gallery. Pausing periodically to admire a cuneiform tablet, he suddenly pulled her aside and whispered that he had seen many wondrous, secret artifacts hidden in the vaults of the museum, items that even Saddam himself did not know about, items of great historical importance. When pressed about the nature of these items, Hamzi grinned devilishly, brought the tip of his index finger to his lips, and shook his head disapprovingly.

"I should have never spoken of this. If you speak too loud, they can come one night and..." Hamzi frowned, dragging his finger across his neck. "...zippp...you and your family. This is a strange country and even stranger times. Yes, let's go. There is more I wish to show you."

Knowing all the chambers in the museum turned out to be very useful. When the smart bombs began to fall and the Americans pushed into the city, Hamzi was set to act. The time was ripe. He knew the right men for the job and most importantly, he knew the right exits.

After the fall of Saddam, Hamzi vanished into the chaos. When Ellie returned to Iraq as a member of MART, she immediately began to track the shadowy figure through black market channels and successfully made contact one afternoon in a Baghdad restaurant. Feigning illness, Ellie left Gordon and the team at the hotel, slipped the hijab over her head, and melted away. At the restaurant, she listened as Hamzi spoke of tablets, ancient maps and seals, and of artifacts unseen for centuries.

Hamzi drew a white napkin across his mouth, temporarily letting his fingers run across the smooth spot beneath his nose where his moustache once sat. "I want you to know that it is not all about money. I, too, love these artifacts, this history...just like you. You understand? I have many suitors, unscrupulous people who would offer quite a lot. I like you. I always have. I want you to keep it safe, you see. It is not all about money, but I am a businessman, too. I have a family and you must see, there are no heroes in Iraq. Do you understand? Do you trust me?" Hamzi brought the cup of tea to his lips and paused.

Ellie pulled the hijab taut against her head and whispered, "I trust you."

Hamzi smiled and jotted down a number on the napkin, pushed it across the table, and stood up stiffly. "When the time comes, it may be necessary for me and my family to leave this country, and I will need your help. Ellie...it is good to see you. Be careful in all this madness."

Ellie watched as Hamzi retreated towards the door and out to the street.

"This is it!" barked Sergeant Rafferty. He tightened his helmet strap beneath his chin and watched as his soldiers filed quickly out of the APC and into the searing yellow sunlight.

Ellie and Gordon followed the soldiers, nearly stumbling out of the vehicle as they tried to shake off the heaviness that had seeped into their legs during the trip.

Mosul was a maze of narrow streets—a city where mosques, churches, and ancient fortifications were interspersed with stores and marketplaces. As one of the most ethnically diverse Iraqi cities, simmering sectarian divides were threatening to erupt into violence. As much of central Iraq slipped into disarray, the City of Two Springs seemed to be bracing for the inevitable fall.

As the sergeant conferred with another soldier beside an armored Humvee that had pulled up alongside the APC, Ellie watched as the remaining soldiers crouched with the barrels of their guns directed towards the surrounding windows and rooftops.

"Over here!"

Ellie and Gordon turned to see the soldier who had confronted Macowski squatting behind the bumper of the APC. He motioned to them with the wave of his hand and a look of exasperation. As they pushed their bodies against the steel frame, the soldier quickly glanced back and said, "You're going to get yourself killed. There could be snipers, IEDs, god-knows-what…jeez." The soldier looked away, training his gun on the empty street.

The street was unpaved and trash lined its edges. Boarded up storefronts framed the road. In the not too distant past, Ellie imagined that the street was probably the center of a thriving marketplace where fabrics, rugs, and produce were sold. Now it was empty and eerily quiet.

The soldier scratched nervously at the back of his neck and mumbled, "I don't like this. This doesn't feel right. I don't like this."

Gordon shot Ellie a tense look, unable to hide his sudden concern. Ellie squinted, seemingly unfazed by the soldier's comments. *Why did I agree to let Ellie go?* Gordon asked himself. *This isn't a game. This is all too dangerous. I shouldn't have put her life at risk.*

"O.K. Our target is there," the sergeant explained as he knelt and pointed at a store diagonally across from them. The store was nondescript—boarded up windows, chipped and peeling paint, and faded Arabic above the doorway. Ellie studied the writing: Al-Faiha…*The Paradise.*

"Let's go," commanded the sergeant, waving at two soldiers.

Ellie watched over the sergeant's shoulder as the two soldiers darted across the street with their rifles clutched against their chests. Sergeant Rafferty turned to Ellie and Gordon. "O.K. You two…let's go. Follow me and stay close."

They made their way quickly across the street and paused beside the soldiers who flanked the doorway. With a nod from the sergeant, the two soldiers pushed open the door and entered. The sergeant turned away momentarily as he relayed information into his phone back to base. Ellie could feel her heart begin to race in anticipation while a tingling sensation spread across the nape of her neck. As if in a trance, she inched forward.

"Ellie, what are you doing?" Gordon whispered, crouching by the storefront as he tried to maneuver past the sergeant.

Sergeant Rafferty, catching Ellie's movement in the corner of his eye, tried to reach out, but his fingers only grazed the edge of her flak jacket.

"Dr. Griffin…wait! It is not secure!" the sergeant roared, watching helplessly as she pushed forward and disappeared into the store.

The room was a muted purple as her eyes struggled to adjust to the darkness. When light streamed in from the opened front door, she emitted a gasp. The store was filled with several rows of shelving units all containing rows upon rows of artifacts. Approaching the first line, Ellie smiled wildly—it was more wondrous than she could have ever imagined. *Hamzi was right*, she thought. A nearly intact statue of a gold bull adorned with lapis lazuli rested against the wall. Several stone tablets were stacked on a shelf, engraved with scenes that appeared to depict royal ceremonies. Beside the tablets was an open box containing ancient scrolls. A small dagger with a golden sheath of meticulous craftsmanship rested at eye level next to a damaged but beautiful bronze helmet. Ellie nearly ran alongside the artifacts, unable to contain her excitement.

"Dr. Griffin! I'm in charge of this operation. Me! The welfare of you and my troops is in my hands and frankly, I'm two seconds away from having you sit in the APC. I knew it was a bad idea having civilians on site for this operation," bellowed Sergeant Rafferty, his eyes ablaze. "I'm sorry, Sergeant," Ellie apologized, hoping to placate the soldier. "I really am. You're in charge. I don't want to do anything that could endanger this mission or your men…or myself for that matter." Ellie gave a guilty smile and then quickly turned her attention to Gordon, who was wide-eyed scanning the shelves beside her.

She squeezed Gordon's shoulder. "Gordon…my God. It's incredible. It's more than we could ever have dreamed of," Ellie nearly giggled. She stopped in front of an irregularly shaped stone tablet. "Look, Gordon. This may be the lost compendium to the Hammurabi Codex you wrote about. Think of what impact this will have on the field, on your research! We could spend days just inventorying these items. Sergeant, I think we are going to need more trucks." Ellie laughed and twirled around.

"Sergeant…I think we have a problem."

Ellie stopped her search and peered back over her shoulder. Macowski had emerged from an adjacent room with a grim look. "I don't want to ruin the party but I found something you should take a look at."

While the sergeant made his way into the adjoining room, Ellie and Gordon followed closely behind. The interior was sparse, with a bare table pressed against the far wall and a large basket resting on the floor in the corner. Several broken vases and statues rested against the wall. In the middle of the room lay a man with his gaze fixed upon the ceiling, his arms awkwardly splayed out beside his body. A pool of blood silhouetted his head. A small dark hole was centered on his forehead, with the hazy gray-black rim of a powder burn.

A look of concern flashed across Sergeant Rafferty's face before he could suppress it. Several other soldiers had arrived and looked down at the dead man with a mix of curiosity and uncertainty.

The sergeant turned to Ellie and asked, "What the hell is going on here?"

Ellie could feel a tightness forming in her abdomen. The sergeant's eyes went from the man to Ellie. "Where is this Hamzi fellow?"

Ellie dropped to her knees and cradled the dead man's hand. Staring at the lifeless face, she muttered, "You're looking at him. This is Hamzi."

Ellie's hand rose and cupped her mouth. She had never seen a dead man before, at least not one that had not died thousands of years ago. Macowski knelt beside Ellie and roughly gripped the dead man's arm. "This man hasn't been dead for long," the soldier said.

The room grew silent. Ellie studied Hamzi's face, seemingly frozen with fright. A creaking noise suddenly broke her trance, nearly causing her to jump.

The creaking lasted only a second, but it was long enough for Macowski to pinpoint its origin. Lifting his index finger to his lips, he drifted backwards until he stood over a woven basket in the far corner of the room. With the tip of his M-16, he pushed aside the lid, allowing it to land on the floor with a dull thud. He quickly jabbed the barrel of the gun into the basket like a bayonet and peered into the darkness. Frightened eyes stared back with wide pupils and bright white sclera. Ellie watched from the distance as two small, trembling hands poked out of the top of the basket. In one hand was a rectangular object.

"No shoot! No shoot!" pleaded a voice from inside the basket.

"Out! Out!" Macowski commanded, forcefully jiggling the basket with the barrel of the gun until it teetered precariously and suddenly tumbled to the floor. A boy, no older than eight, quickly crawled out. Macowski bent down, grabbed a fistful of shirt, and roughly dragged the scrawny boy to his feet. The boy shook as his eyes scanned the room, finally settling on Hamzi's lifeless body.

"Baba! Baba!" the boy wailed mournfully, struggling to free himself from Macowski's grip. His slender form only bounced backwards as if tied to a rubber band, and he landed hard on his knees.

"Let him go, please," Ellie pleaded, looking up at Sergeant Rafferty to intervene.

The sergeant nodded to Macowski, who begrudgingly obliged by pushing the boy forward, sending him stumbling towards the feet of his father.

"Where is the interpreter?" barked the sergeant as he surveyed the group of soldiers who had gathered in the room.

A thin Iraqi stepped forward, wearing oversized camouflage fatigues and a flak jacket. He had an uneasy look.

Macowski began to pace around the room, muttering, "He's a freakin' terrorist."

"He's a scared little boy for Christ's sake," Ellie responded curtly. She watched as the boy clutched at his father's pant legs and whimpered.

"Don't be so sure. He's a terrorist," Macowski shot back, giving her a venomous glare.

"O.K. Quit it," interrupted the sergeant. He turned to the interpreter and said, "I want you to ask this boy what happened here and tell him that unless he wants to go to prison, he better tell us the truth."

The interpreter paused and translated. The boy stropped crying and looked up, as if surprised to hear Arabic. He listened silently for a moment and then began to speak rapidly, glancing around the room as if searching for support.

"He says that it is fault. He says that *he* got his father killed. Men came here for the box but his father did not have it because *he* stole it and hid in the basket. He says he was scared, scared of the men, scared of what his father might do if he found out. When his father said he did not know where this box was, they killed him." The boy grew morose, muttered several more words in Arabic, and was silent.

The interpreter looked around the room. "He says that he got his father killed. It was his fault."

Ellie studied the boy's face as he clutched a wooden box tightly against his body. She could see the familial resemblance to his father, the dark eyes, jet-black hair, and olive skin. She felt profoundly sorry that not only did the boy lose his father, but that he also felt responsible for this loss. It was a brand of grief she knew well.

"Who killed this Hamzi fellow?" Sergeant Rafferty interjected and waited as the interpreter translated.

"English," the boy uttered under his breath.

"Yeah, bullshit," Macowski blurted out. "BULLSHIT! This kid is a liar and he's a goddamn terrorist. I can't believe we are listening to this crap."

The boy looked away from Macowski and continued to talk, his eyes filling with tears. He reached out suddenly, pushed the wooden box into Ellie's lap, and released it with a look of relief.

The interpreter paused and appeared to be thinking about how to best translate the boy's words. "He says take the box. He does not want the box anymore. He says the box is cursed. He says that *he* is cursed."

Ellie stared down at the item in her lap. The box was constructed out of a pale brown wood that appeared almost white. Symbols and figures were meticulously carved into the surface. It was truly beautiful, a treasure of master craftsmanship. *No wonder the boy couldn't resist taking the box*, Ellie thought as she ran her fingers across the surface, as if reading Braille. She could see Gordon's eyes open wide at the sight of the box. A grainy voice in the distance interrupted her analysis. The voice was speaking Arabic, chanting over a loud speaker. The expression on the face of the interpreter grew grave.

"This is no good," said the interpreter, his eyes darting around the room as if looking for an exit. "That voice is not a call to prayer. It is a call to arms. They know we are here and they are coming for us."

Sergeant Rafferty marched into the front room and swung around, his face inches from Gordon's.

"Doctor, you better grab what you can and do it right quick."

"Sergeant, Sergeant!" urged a soldier kneeling in the corner of the room. "Check this out."

The sergeant leaned on one knee and looked down with alarm. A rectangular device of white clay, wires, and a timer sat casually on the stone floor. The timer display flashed neon blue. *Fourteen minutes*. The numbers continued to count down.

"What the shit!" Sergeant Rafferty exclaimed, instantaneously quieting the room. The unraveling of the sergeant sent a sense of uncertainty through the unit. "Those are military grade explosives." He had been in Iraq long enough to know that this wasn't the M.O. of the insurgents. The sergeant rubbed his chin. "Do you think you could disarm it?"

"I don't know…probably. It's fairly sophisticated. There's a trip switch and I think a backup module. But, Sergeant, it's worse than this." The soldier paused to wipe sweat from his brow with the back of his sleeve. "I found five more of these explosives. Someone knew we were coming."

"It's a freakin' ambush. I knew it," Macowski growled.

Sergeant Rafferty looked around the room at his men and nodded. His mind was made up. "O.K. That's it. We're out of here."

"Fuckin-A," applauded Macowski, temporarily relinquishing his grip on the boy. Seizing his moment of freedom, the boy twisted away from Macowski and sprinted towards the door. Macowski raised his gun and placed his finger against the trigger. The sergeant pushed the barrel up at the ceiling.

"Just let him go," Sergeant Rafferty sighed. The boy disappeared into the street, the pitter-patter of his footsteps growing faint. The sergeant made for the doorway but Ellie blocked his exit.

"Sergeant...what about the artifacts? What about the mission?" Ellie pleaded.

"After the dead guy and the bombs, the mission just changed. Screw the artifacts," replied the sergeant with a scowl. He pushed passed Ellie and into the sunlight.

Ellie looked desperately at Gordon. Gordon held the wooden box and was examining it intently. "We can't leave these artifacts. They are going to be destroyed." She ran to the shelves and looked with frustration at all the artifacts, trying to decide what to take. Grabbing a box from the floor, she began to quickly place several of the smaller artifacts into it until it was nearly full. Gordon bent down and lifted the bull statue, feeling the muscles in his back tighten with pain. Straining, the two exited the store and stumbled slowly across the street. They climbed up into the APC and deposited their haul on the floor. Ellie looked back at the storefront. *The Hammurabi Codex!* Everything was so frantic. *I should have taken it,* she thought. *There was so much to choose from.*

Ellie turned to Gordon. "I'm going back," she said with a look of determination.

The first explosion was deafening and disorienting, sending Ellie hurtling towards the ground. She landed in a spray of pebbles and dust. A soldier beside her had sustained the brunt of the explosion and rolled on the ground in pain as his uniform smoldered with molten shrapnel. Above the ringing in her ears she could hear a desperate call for a medic. A long train of machine gun fire erupted as the other soldiers dove behind the vehicles and returned fire wildly.

Ellie suddenly felt herself pulled off the ground as if she were weightless and dragged back against the side of the APC. Gordon brought his face close to hers, his beard coated in dirt with a trail of blood at the corner of his lips.

"You all right?" he screamed as the gunfire continued to echo across the street, ricocheting off the ground and against the armored plating of the vehicles with a mix of thuds and pings. A whizzing noise cut through the air. A soldier screamed, "RPG!" but it was too late. A storefront was blown out by the rocket-propelled grenade and two soldiers were sent tumbling through the air. Ellie turned to see the sergeant screaming into a walkie-talkie as he pressed his palm tightly against his right ear.

Ellie began to feel strangely calm as she looked into Gordon's blue eyes, the whites tinted pink from smoke. "Gordon, listen to me. I'm going back in there. I'm not leaving here without the Hammurabi Codex." She turned away and tried to rise, but Gordon held her shoulders.

"Ellie, please! It's not important. It's not worth your life," Gordon pleaded.

"I can't believe you are saying this. It's going to be destroyed." Ellie twisted herself free from his grip and stood up, her back flush against the APC. Gordon quickly reached out and tightly caught her left wrist, bringing her close.

"Ellie, please. I'm begging you. Get into the APC. There isn't time." Gordon looked into her eyes. They were ablaze. Her face was taut with determination. She shook her head slowly.

"No, Gordon. I'm not leaving without it."

Gordon knew what must be done. "I'll get it," he said and pushed her back towards the APC.

Ellie watched as Gordon took two steps forward. An immense explosion shook the street as the Humvee burst apart, sending hot metal into the air. Ellie fell backwards onto the ground. A searing pain shot forth from under her left armpit. Her fingers found the space below her axilla, where the flak jacket hung limply, and felt warmth dripping. Her vision turned red and she struggled to stay conscious. Every breath was a battle as she fought to get air in. She tried to stand up but only fell forward, managing to prop herself up on her knees as if in prayer. The staccato rhythm of gunfire continued to reverberate around her.

Through the black smoke, Ellie could see Gordon take several steps forward, suddenly stumble awkwardly, and crumple to the ground in a cloud of dust.

Ellie tried to scream but nothing came forth. Gas that had spilled from the smoldering Humvee erupted in flames. Ellie watched in disbelief as Macowski rolled frantically on the ground as flames engulfed him. She fell forward into the dirt in a heap. Several feet away, she could see the undersurface of Gordon's boots and his motionless body.

"Gordon!" she attempted to scream but wasn't sure if anything came out.

She tried to move, but the pain was excruciating. Her cheek on the dirt, she could see that the boy's wooden box sat within a puddle of burning gasoline. As the chaos swirled around her, she found herself strangely fixated on the box. The flames lapped at it but were seemingly driven away. *The box isn't burning!*

"Gordon, the box isn't burning! Gordon!" she pleaded with frustration.

Somewhere above her, she could make out the *thump-thump* of helicopter blades cutting through the gunfire, sending the black smoke swirling in the air. Propped up on both elbows, the rest of her body limp, she crawled slowly towards the box until she could feel the heat of the flames against her face.

"Gordon! The box!" she screamed and reached towards the fire, her hands stinging with pain. She hesitated for a moment and then plunged them through the flames. The agony was unimaginable.

FOURTEEN MONTHS LATER

I
Venice, Italy

Venice is sinking.

Pietro Zeno looked down at his rubber boots as he sloshed through the thick mud. What was to become of his beloved city, he asked himself as his fingers searched through the pockets of his pants, finding a loose cigarette. He brought the cigarette to his lips, cupped his hands around the flame, and lit it with a long puff.

Desponsamus te mare — we wed thee, Sea!

Founded in the fifth century by settlers fleeing for their lives, Venice took comfort in the surrounding sea and waterways as a barrier to certain death from the encroaching barbarians in the North. These ancestors pounded long poles into the solid substance of the marshes, the layer of *caranto* — the hard clay foundation — and over the centuries constructed an elaborate city of watery tributaries and bridges. Every Ascension Day, the Doge would commemorate the bond Venice had to the sea by throwing a wreath into the waters to celebrate this "marriage." Venice, for better or for worse, was linked inextricably to the water.

Of course, it was precisely this connection to the sea that enabled Venice to become the world's supreme maritime power in the fourteenth century. Every Italian school kid had this engrained in his little skull since grade school. Pietro was no different. But the days of Venetian dominance had long passed, replaced by the ascendancy of tourism as the lifeblood of the city. Tourists filled the piazzas, restaurants, museums, and music halls.

Venice was romantic, a dreamlike, magical, seemingly impossible city, but Pietro knew better. There was an undersurface to the city, and it was rotting. As the gondoliers sang, navigating through the narrow canals with couples in tow, the boats rode ever so higher each year against the historic palaces.

The water was rising, and the city was sinking.

Pietro was only ten when a storm surge from the Adriatic slammed into the sea walls and flooded the city. Even then, he was used to the daily ebb and flow of the tide and even the winds that periodically buffeted Venice: the *Bora* from the northeast and the *Sirocco* from the Sahara. But that storm was monumental and left the city a soggy mess, flooding stores and churches and creating a toxic cocktail of raw sewage and dead pigeons.

Since then, the populace, at least that portion of the population that did not leave permanently for the mainland, learned to live with periodic flooding, particularly during the winter months. The raised wooden walkways, or *passerelles,* would routinely be laid out and tourist and local alike would navigate the city like rats in a maze. If nothing was done, Venice would inevitably be lost to the sea like a modern-day Atlantis.

Engineering school in Sienna prepared Pietro well for his job with the Magistrato Alle Acque, or Venice Water Authority. His seniority had elevated him to a supervisory role in the defense of the city. It seemed like yesterday that the Consorzio Venezia Nuova (CVN) was created in 1984. The CVN was an amalgamation of Italian engineering and construction firms united by the common goal of rescuing Venice from the sea. But nothing was simple in Italy. There was plenty of bureaucracy and everybody wanted a piece. Fortunately for Pietro, the Venice Water Authority was granted the lead.

Pietro walked down the emptied canal, examining the exposed foundations of the buildings. The stone walls were cracked, eroded, and covered in a thick green-black slime. The decay was more advanced than Pietro thought. Much had lain hidden beneath the murky waters. *Out of sight, out of mind,* Pietro thought with a shake of the head.

"Why is Venice sinking?" the fat politician in an Armani suit had asked Pietro years before as he sat next to his bleach-blond "secretary."

How best to explain it? Pietro wondered. "It's complicated, Signore. You see, the city of Venice is sinking approximately 0.5 millimeters each year. The sediment that the city was built on is subsiding. It is also an issue of plate tectonics."

The politician's eyebrows rose with bewilderment. His secretary tilted the notebook she had been taking notes on and showed it the politician, uncertain as to the spelling. The politician shrugged.

"You see, the whole earth is changing. Slowly, no doubt…but changing. Land masses are gradually moving. Italy is being driven under the Alps. But, who are we fooling, Signore? Much of what is happening is from our own hand. We've extracted groundwater without any regard for what impact this will have on the composition of the land, we are destroying the salt marshes that flush toxins out of our city at an alarming rate, and we are melting the polar ice caps, elevating the global level of the sea. If nothing is done, Venice will be lost."

The politician rubbed his bald head and tightened his belt. "I have two more questions, Signor Zeno. What do we need to do to fix this and how much will it cost?"

Progress had been made. MOSE offered hope. Modulo Sperimentale Elettromeccanico was an ambitious project to protect the city from the Adriatic Sea. Consisting of moveable steel barriers, these floodgates were envisioned to serve as a protective barrier shielding the three inlets into the Venetian lagoon. During times of storm surges, air could be pumped into the gates, which would slowly rise from a horizontal position on the floor of the Adriatic until they were standing upright, rising out of the sea like a steel sea wall. Pietro liked to call it Project Moses. The gates would part the Adriatic Sea.

Unfortunately, everything in Italy took longer than it should and needed more money than planned. The completion date of MOSE was still uncertain. Until then, Pietro was left to dreg the canals and evaluate the local impact of the tributaries on the surrounding buildings. It was not a glorious job, but it was a necessity.

With the tide at its lowest, a temporary barrier had been erected, damming a segment of the serpentine channels. High-powered pumps worked overtime to displace the water into a catch basin. This week he was working on an unnamed canal off Rio di Si San Zulian beyond the Piazza San Marco. Due to the proximity to the lagoon, as far as he could determine, it had never been dredged in the past. *Technology is a wonderful thing*, he sighed as he struggled to free his boot from the mud.

Pietro looked around. He felt like he was in a large trench. Ancient buildings loomed above him. It was eerily quiet, the only sound being that of the squish of his footsteps. The canal was removed from the typical tourist locations, an area beyond the edge of the maps provided for free by the Venice Tourism Agency. Tomorrow the refuse team would come and begin a lengthy process of hauling away centuries of junk that had collected on the floor of the canal. He had a lot of work still to do.

Pietro withdrew a clipboard and examined the foundation of a fifteenth century building. The stone exterior crumbled upon touch, sending white flakes onto the ground. He jotted down the findings on his paper and backed up, attempting to gain a view of the building at street level. As he did this, the heel of his boot struck a hard object. He attempted to regain his balance but overcompensated and went flailing onto his back with a splat.

"Perfetto," Pietro muttered as he stared up at the sky, the cigarette hanging precariously from his lips.

He slowly pulled himself up and wiped the mud off his palms with his shirt. *Where did the clipboard go?* he thought as he examined the floor of the drained canal. A dull silvery object caught his attention. Pietro squatted and pushed aside centuries of mud, revealing a metal chest. He stared at for a moment with curiosity. Pietro pulled a water bottle from his coat and cleaned off the chest as best he could, revealing elaborate gold engravings and a large tricolor crest. The chest was less than a meter in length and had a latch with a lock that had decayed. Pietro tugged at the lid, which initially resisted before suddenly releasing with a sucking sound. The lid flipped backward and Pietro peered inside.

"What do we have here?" he asked aloud before he realized it. His heart was racing.

2
NYC

"You sure you can't come, Alex?" April asked as she dropped the notebook into the trashcan and pushed it down with the ball of her hand.

Alexander Stone glanced up from the golden crucifix long enough to watch April walk towards the door, precariously balancing a stack of books on her outstretched arms and a loose leather satchel across her shoulder.

Alex returned his gaze to the back of the cross, finding a series of hatch marks etched into the metal. Flipping through the pages of the catalogue, he stopped at the section on French crucifixes and rubbed his eyes.

"I would love to come, but I really can't. I have so much more work to do. Graham's been breathing down my neck for weeks to finish organizing this exhibit," Alex replied, running his hands through his light brown hair. He pushed the metal chair away from the workbench with a screech. The exhibit "The Passion of the Cross" was scheduled to open in September. He had thousands of crosses from museums and private collections all around the world to categorize and create a running narrative about.

April paused in the doorway and pushed out her lower lip in disappointment. Alex knew that the disappointment was not feigned. Ever since Alex's lips had semi-accidentally found April's last New Year's Eve in a drunken haze, the what-ifs floated awkwardly around their shared workspace. April was smart, attractive, and caring. However, a relationship would only be a distraction from his work and would inevitably poison their friendship. Besides, he had been down that road before. A week at April's family's vacation home in Maine was enticing, but an opportunity to make extra money tonight was even more alluring. It was tough living on a graduate student's salary in New York City and even a catering job was welcome.

"You know, Graham is an ass. He doesn't appreciate one-tenth of the work you do for him. He jets around the world giving lectures and having fancy dinners and leaves you here to do all the work. He doesn't even credit you ninety percent of the time. He's getting props for *your* ideas," April added as she dropped the books one by one into the book return.

Alex shrugged and watched as April twirled around. "Last chance..." she offered. Alex sighed, shook his head reluctantly, and gave a half-hearted wave. April frowned and slipped out of the room, allowing the door to snap shut. Alex could hear her footsteps on the concrete floor trail away as he looked around the coffin-sized research room hidden away in the bowels of the Metropolitan Museum of Art.

He suddenly felt very lonely.

When he was granted the Carrington Fellowship under the tutelage of Dr. Kenneth Graham to run concurrent with his graduate schooling at Columbia University, he was in a select club. After all, few had come before him. Those who had completed the coveted fellowship went on to become leaders in the field of antiquities with several occupying high positions at respected universities and at least two serving as presidents of the Society for Antiquities.

Yet, for such a prestigious fellowship, the facilities were far from grandiose. Instead of a sophisticated research library with bookcases of leather-bound volumes, mahogany ladders, and plush chairs, he was confined to a tiny, windowless room nestled between a utility closet and the kitchen in basement of the museum. The office was adorned with a strangely out-of-place periodic table hanging on the wall, two ancient wooden drafting tables, a broken pencil sharpener fastened to the wall, and a file-cabinet that was filled with an endless assortment of research notes on the use of the color green in Nicolas Poussin's works from 1637-1647.

April, to her credit, had attempted to improve the working environment, relocating an ancient cathode ray tube to the warehouse, hanging up a travel poster of the Greek isles, and even purchasing a small refrigerator that they tucked away in the corner and used to house bottles of water, yogurt, and the occasional beer. After complaining loudly about the lack of Internet access in their office, two computers miraculously appeared after one weekend, a donation from an anonymous patron. The office was slowly becoming a workable environment.

Despite the relatively frugal accommodations, it was hard for Alex to complain. Above their heads was one of the greatest museum collections in the world and they had unparalleled access to the research archives and collections. The price to be paid was working with Dr. Kenneth Graham.

A leading medievalist, Dr. Graham was an obnoxious, self-centered twit. Born in Ohio, he somehow developed a British accent while studying at Oxford and gained greatest fame for his seminal work on religious cults in the Middle Ages. This work was enough to land him a tenured position at Columbia University. Although he was never able to replicate the success of his initial research, Alex was amazed to see how long Graham could ride this wave of early achievement in academia. As he became more interested in the lifestyle of a globetrotting lecturer, Graham began to rely more and more heavily upon underpaid research assistants and graduate students to continue his intellectual pursuits. April was right. Kenneth Graham certainly had pushed the limits of ethical conduct over the past two years. Alex had been forewarned about Graham's penchant for abusing interns, but was willing to put up with it for the opportunity to work at the Metropolitan Museum of Art.

Alex stared at the cross resting on the table. Constructed out of gold, the crucifix was framed by a silver rim with an ornateness that suggested that it was the property of a Parisian aristocrat in the eighteenth century. He laid the cross upon a white sheet of paper and withdrew a digital camera from his bag and snapped a photo. On a small index card he jotted down a description of the cross, including the likely year of creation, country of origin, and source of acquisition. *Just two hundred and eighty five more,* Alex moaned internally, depositing the cross within a protective case.

When he had made the decision years ago to pursue a career in antiquities, he had envisioned a Hollywood existence—a world of Indiana Jones and Alan Quartermain. In this world he would travel through deserts and jungles, discover ancient tombs and lost artifacts, dodge poisoned blow darts and evade elaborate booby traps. Instead, his life was reduced to an oppressive monotony—endless hours of kneeling in dried-out riverbeds brushing dirt from pottery fragments, flipping through mildewed archives in the deep recesses of libraries, and, most painfully, preparing lectures for Graham to deliver to colleagues who had long ago abandoned any hope of intrigue and adventures in their careers.

Yet, it was still his one true love. He was so committed to the study of antiquities that romantic relationships and friendships had inevitably suffered through the years. In college, he would spend his weekend nights holed up in the library and his weekdays filling out paperwork for school-sponsored archeological digs in places like Crete, Petra, and Nemrut Dagh. He studied foreign languages in order to read the original texts, becoming well versed in Latin, Greek, and French. Lately, he had begun to focus more on medieval studies, influenced by Norman Cohn's book on millennial groups in the Middle Ages, *The Pursuit of the Millennium.* The truth was that his appreciation for antiquity spanned time and place.

He could remember the sense of awe he felt when he first wandered through the Egyptian Gallery of the Metropolitan Museum of Art as a child. Then, he was enthralled with the mummies and could stare for hours at the gleaming armor of medieval knights. He dreamed of being accidentally locked in the museum late at night and left to explore the passageways, push aside the beautiful death masks of the sarcophagi, and look inside. The museum was a magical place filled with wondrous items and glimpses into ancient cultures long since gone but not forgotten. It was more than just a voyeuristic thrill at peering into the inner workings of societies that had passed into history. He did not wish to be a mere student of antiquity. He wanted more than anything to impact the field, to discover artifacts that had been lost to history, to provide a fresh view of past civilizations. Much had been discovered through the centuries, but this was only the surface. There was much more that remained untouched and undisturbed. As modern society chugged on, tearing up the ground and paving it over with asphalt, it was a race against time to reclaim the past.

Time! Alex thought, abruptly snapping himself out of his day-dream. He tilted his wrist to reveal his watch. The gala was to start shortly. He had planned to go up early in order to leisurely stroll through the exhibit before the guests arrived. He looked back over his shoulder and spotted his tuxedo hanging from a misshapen pipe protruding from the wall.

Even great archeologists started from the ground floor, Alex told himself with a smile. *Sometimes, even the basement.*

3

The immense banner announcing "Paradise Lost, Paradise Regained: The Recovery of Mesopotamian Antiquities" hung stiffly from the façade of the Metropolitan Museum of Art, flanked by two huge sets of Corinthian columns. Ellie walked down Fifth Avenue clutching a thin jacket against her black evening gown. It was an unseasonably cool March night and a series of stiff breezes sent the two American flags in front of the museum flapping wildly. Behind her, taxi cabs zipped by with periodic screeching and the blare of horns.

Ellie found the first step and carefully climbed the stone staircase towards the entrance. Her legs felt wobbly and several times she nearly lost her footing before reaching the top of the staircase.

I'm drunk, she thought with a mix of embarrassment and annoyance. She could not face this night of all nights without the help of the two martinis she had downed at the lobby bar of the W Hotel around the corner from her apartment. It didn't help that she had not eaten anything all day—*just a touch of nerves*, she had told herself. Add in the two-inch heels and the loose evening gown, it was a miracle she hadn't tumbled down the stairs and ended up face down on the concrete.

As she stepped onto the top platform and approached the three tall doors that greeted visitors to the museum, she could feel her legs grow heavy and the breath escape her body as if a fist had unexpectedly been driven into her abdomen. Her legs quivered as her eyes settled on a large placard resting on an oversized easel beside the far doorway.

In Memoriam
Dr. Gordon Russell
A *Life Remembered*

Gordon stared back at her.

This is all too soon, she moaned internally, feeling her heart race. She instinctively ran the tip of her thumb against her index finger and found the sensation dulled, as if her hand were covered with a glove.

Gordon looked much younger than when she had known him. In the photo, he seemed filled with life. He was dressed in a khaki shirt and shorts and stood beside a large Babylonian statue. A giant smile ran across his face. This Gordon had yet to write *Excavating Ur.* He had not helped unearth ancient settlements in Nippur, had not formed MART, and most importantly, had not met Ellie. He had so much potential…so much life, and Ellie had taken this life away. *For what?* She could feel the tears begin to well up. *A piece of a bloody tablet, now incinerated into a billion pieces.* She pushed her hands into the oversized bag she held over her shoulder, withdrew a tissue, and dabbed at her eyes, taking care not to smear her black mascara. She fought the tears, feeling her face tighten. Her fingers found an errant strand of blond hair set free by the wind and flicked it aside. She turned away from the placard. *It should have been me*, she thought.

Ellie pushed the tissue back into her bag and withdrew the wooden box. She remembered what the boy had said. *It is cursed.*

As she examined the box in the moonlight, it looked more beautiful than ever. She had stared at it for so many sleepless nights that she wondered if she was losing her mind. *What is it? What does it mean?* She was smart enough to realize that this was a fool's errand: that there was no more meaning in this box than in Gordon's death. *What had Gordon said that day?* she asked herself.

"It is not worth your life."

Her fingers clenched the box. She had purposefully arrived at the museum early. *This needs to be settled.* Her fingers searched blindly in her bag as a stiff wind blew across Fifth Avenue. She had been given a contact by a research colleague. This man was an expert in the field, she was told. And if it was not fate, then what could it be? He had an office at the museum and was going to be at tonight's gala. She would meet with him before the gala and settle this once and for all.

Ellie pulled out a ragged piece of paper and unfolded it. The ink glistened in the moonlight.

Dr. Kenneth Graham, Department of Medieval Studies.

4

The exhibit hall was quiet and serene. The darkened interior was lit by strategi-
cally placed lights that cast the sandstone pillars and golden statues
in a wondrous yellow glow. The doors to the museum had not yet
opened to the guests and Alex took this opportunity to casually
stroll through the hall, periodically pausing to examine the contents
of a display case or to read a blurb fastened to the wall describing an
accompanied artifact. Down in the foyer, he could hear the bustle of
the party staff moving tables and chairs and a call for staff to man
the entranceway in anticipation of the arrival of the guests.

The security for the evening was unusually tight for the invi-
tation-only affair. Not only were the usual New York City Upper
East Side crowd and mayor expected to attend, but the event
also promised to have an international flair. The Iraqi ambassa-
dor to the United States and his American counterpart, several high-ranking members of the military, and even the Secre-
tary-General of the United Nations were going to be present.
Alex had to have security clearance to even work for the museum's catering service.

As Alex studied the Lady's Head from Warka, he sensed the
arrival of another person. Turning slightly, he could see a woman
silently steal into the hall. The woman was beautiful with blond
hair spilling out over her black evening gown. Her blue eyes were
wet with the whites slightly pink as if she had been crying. She
stood before a golden statue of a bull and turned her back to Alex
and a security guard who was discreetly positioned in the darkened corner of the room.

Alex had seen the woman approximately a half-an-hour before, sitting across from Kenneth Graham in his office. As he approached the office, he could hear the woman plead with Graham. "Please, Dr. Graham. Take a closer look at the box."

Graham's response was typical, abrupt and condescending. "Look Miss, I'm not sure who this Arab lad was, but I suspect you've been had. Although well-crafted, this box is probably a tourist knickknack. The symbols on the box are a hodge-podge with no rhyme or reason. As for the business with the flames, I think you would have better luck with the pimple-faced kid behind the counter at the hardware store for an explanation. I don't want to put you out, but I have a flight to Paris tomorrow morning, a million phone calls to make, and I have to chit-chat with a bunch of one-hundred-and-ten-year-old blue haired women from the museum's support committee tonight at this gala. I suggest you do as I intend to do—find the nearest waiter and drink yourself silly."

When Alex left the exhibit hall, the woman had not moved, continuing to stare at the statue with a look tinged with sadness and familiarity.

Alex felt uncomfortable in the tuxedo as he navigated through the foyer of the museum. The spacious room that greeted the everyday tourist had been transformed into a wonderland of silver and gold. Elegantly dressed patrons milled about, picking off flutes of champagne from his tray as he wandered around the room. In the corner, a string quartet entertained the guests as they gathered around elaborately decorated tables filled with a wide assortment of food from caviar to oysters.

Dr. Graham, dressed in a crisp tuxedo and dark-rimmed glasses, appeared to float across the floor, periodically stopping for a handshake or kiss on the cheek. Upon spotting Alex, he stopped, grinned broadly, and swaggered over to where Alex stood.

"Why am I not surprised you found your way into this party. Catering? I could have gotten you a ticket for Pete's sake. People will talk, say we don't pay you enough," Graham said with a chuckle. He reached forward and removed the last of Alex's champagne flutes from his tray. "Now Alex, I'm off to the South of France tomorrow. I'll be co-hosting the conference on medieval studies in Cannes."

"When will you be back?" Alex asked, relieved to be suddenly free of his mentor.

"Probably three weeks or so. A little business and pleasure. I trust you can manage on your own. There's the crucifix exhibit…" Graham put his index finger to his chin and tapped it as if in thought. "…and I have to give a talk to the undergraduates when I get back on the Black Death. It would be great if you can whip up something. There are slides on my desk…" Graham's voice trailed off as he made eye contact with an elderly, grayhaired woman across the room. He nodded to her with a smile before turning quickly back to Alex. "And Alex, try to get out. Have some fun. It's New York City, for Pete's sake. Enjoy yourself. Cheerio."

Before Alex could respond, Graham trotted off in pursuit of the gray-haired lady, calling out, "Sonia, Sonia…it's so good to see you again."

Alex fought the urge to whip his empty tray at Graham like a frisbee, imagining it whizzing over the heads of the patrons and hitting the back of his head with a *ding*. Alex smirked and made his way to the bar.

As Alex refilled his tray with long-stemmed glasses of champagne and returned to the foyer, he could see the director of the museum, Constantine DeFillipo, standing at a podium. The crowd quieted in anticipation.

"As you know, this is a very exciting day for the Metropolitan Museum of Art. In 1870, the museum received its first acquisition, entitled "70.1", denoting the year and identifying acquisition number. The item was a magnificent Roman sarcophagus from Tarsus created in the third century of the Common Era. Since then, the museum has relocated from its humble origin to this magnificent edifice and in the process expanded its collections to become one of the most comprehensive museums in the world. We have prided ourselves as being the protector of artifacts and works of art from around the globe and throughout history.

"Currently, there are hundreds of conflicts across the globe that threaten ancient artifacts, archeological excavation sites, and museum collections. The war in Iraq has not only been devastating from a personal and financial perspective, but has put some of the most incredible and important artifacts at risk of obliteration. When it became clear that these rich cultural treasures were in danger of being lost forever, I know I felt a mix of indignation and despair. Some said it was hopeless. Indeed, I believe many of us never envisioned this night would be possible. I am pleased to announce the opening of the exhibit 'Paradise Lost, Paradise Regained: The Recovery of Mesopotamian Antiquities.'"

A wave of applause swept through the crowd. As Alex watched the director lift his hands and begin to clap, the blond woman from the exhibit hall stumbled into Alex, nearly causing his tray to launch from his hands. He balanced the tray with one hand and attempted to steady the obviously drunk woman. She smiled giddily at Alex, bringing her face close to his. When she spoke, the volume of her voice was far too loud, leading several other guests to cast over looks of displeasure.

The woman glared back at the guests. "What are you looking at, you bunch of cows?" she blurted out, causing two women to look at each other in horror and turn away with a "did you ever?" The blond-haired woman turned back to Alex and reached forward in an uncoordinated fashion, depositing an empty glass on his tray upside down. She grabbed a new flute of champagne.

Alex steadied the woman and asked, "Are you O.K.?"

The woman smiled back at Alex. "You're sweet. Actually, no, these bloody heels are killing me. Do have any idea how hard it is to walk in these buggers?" She extended her arm, gripped Alex's shoulder, lifted her legs one after the other, and removed her shoes, holding them by the straps. She was instantly reduced in height. In front of them, Alex could hear the director ramble on.

"Many agencies came together to make this night possible. I want to thank the State Department, the Iraqi government, and the generous donations from the private and public sector. I would specifically like to recognize the generous contributions made possible by Clay Pharmaceuticals and its Antiquity Recovery grant." Another round of applause spread through the room.

"Although this is a celebration, the acquisition of these items was not without loss. We are also here to pay tribute to a great archeologist and friend of the museum, a light in the field of antiquities...the late Dr. Gordon Russell, who lost his life attempting to save these very precious items. I have asked Dr. Eleanor Griffin to say a few words about her colleague and friend. Dr. Griffin?"

The director looked around the room with confusion. The woman next to Alex put the flute of champagne down on his tray. "That's me," she slurred and made an awkward move towards the podium, but stopped suddenly and swung around. "Maybe you should hold onto these," she muttered and deposited her shoes on Alex's tray, nearly knocking a glass over the side in the process.

Alex watched with concern as Ellie stumbled forward, not so delicately parting the crowd. The patrons glanced over their shoulders with looks of amusement and bewilderment. The museum director smiled upon spotting Ellie emerging from the crowd and motioned for her to join him by the podium.

Director DeFillipo leaned into the microphone. "First a few words about Dr. Griffin." Ellie tried to shoo away the museum director. "Dr. Eleanor Griffin graduated from Cambridge University with honors and completed her graduate studies in antiquities at Oxford University. If that was not enough, she was the recipient of the prestigious Middleton Fellowship for Oriental Studies and has published widely in the field of Biblical and pre-Biblical archeology. Most recently she has been a part of the Mesopotamian Antiquity Recovery Team responsible for the acquisition of many of the artifacts collected in the exhibit hall above. We are delighted to see that her period of convalescence has been swift. Without further ado...Dr. Griffin." The director gave her a paternalistic pat on the back and brought the palms of his hands together to spark another round of applause.

"*Dr. Eleanor Griffin,*" Alex muttered to himself. He wondered if she was related to Harold Griffin, the Egyptologist. He made a mental note to look it up after the gala.

Ellie gripped the edges of the podium, her right hand finding the microphone and pulling it down to her height. Ear-splitting feedback echoed through the foyer.

"Whoo! I think that woke everyone up! I know it woke *me* up. Thank you, Director DeFillipo. I doubt that many of you had the opportunity to know Gordon Russell, that is, really *know* Gordon Russell. For that matter, I suspect many of you know more about caviar than Mesopotamian archeology."

Several of the audience members sniggered. A crooked smile formed on the museum director's face, uncertain as to the benignity of the comment. Alex brought a flute of champagne to his lips when no one was looking and took a quick sip. *This is going to be interesting*, Alex thought, staring briefly at the high heel shoes resting on his serving tray.

"Where does one start? Gordon Russell was a brilliant man. He was a scholar whose works on Mesopotamia have revolutionized the field and whose teachings have helped create a new generation of young archeologists. He was committed to preserving the past for humanity and insuring that ancient artifacts would be protected."

Alex watched as the director, who had clearly taken a whiff of the alcohol on Ellie's breath, lowered his shoulders slightly with relief, hoping that Ellie would continue with a short and lucid speech.

"There are three things that I am certain of. The first is that I could really use another drink. The second is that I would like very much to use the loo." Ellie smiled and leaned to her right. Her elbow nearly slipped off the podium, threatening to send her hurtling to the floor. She managed to catch the microphone with her outstretched left hand. A screech erupted from the speakers. Director DeFillipo's eyes opened widely and several of the older guests' hearing aides responded with piercing echoes. In front of Alex, a white-haired gentleman leaned to his wife and whispered, "I think this woman is completely sloshed or out of her mind, or both."

"The third is that the world was a better place with Gordon in it. As I see all you elegant gents and ladies wander through the exhibit hall, I cannot help wonder if you get more excited browsing through the museum gift shop than seeing these artifacts. There was a soldier in Iraq who was frankly a pain in the ass. He asked me an insightful question. He wondered if saving these precious pieces of pottery and gold was worth getting killed for, I believe it went something like, to save 'Queen Who-Gives-Two-Shits' or something like that's 'clay dildo.'"

The room grew suddenly silent. The director DeFillipo looked mortified and several older women raised their hands to their mouths.

"Now, I assure you that we did not recover a clay dildo, but you get the point. I wish this pain-in-the-ass soldier were here to correct me, but unfortunately I had the pleasure of watching him burn to death. I can still smell it, the smell of roasting flesh."

Alex could see there was an impending breaking point fast approaching. He was drawn towards the podium, fixated on the seeming self-destruction of a tortured soul. Her eyes began to fill with tears. The museum director sprung forward. Ellie grabbed the microphone a final time and blurted, "I just wish that Gordon were here giving this eulogy about me. I'm sorry."

The room descended into complete silence, except for the clanging of silverware by the serving staff immune to the drama at hand. Alex watched as Ellie drifted back away from the podium and the director maneuvered forward to snatch away the microphone. Ellie melted into the crowd, her head bowed as if in defeat. Alex followed her through the throng, weaving with his tray held aloft above the heads of the guests. Director DeFillipo, having assumed the podium, stood tensely with a slight quiver at the corner of his lips and began to recite this month's upcoming lecture series as if Ellie's speech had never occurred. As Ellie pushed through the crowd towards the coat check, several guests peered at her with looks of horror.

Alex found an empty stand in the corner, deposited his serving tray on it, and grasped the straps of the woman's shoes awkwardly in his hand.

Ellie recovered her jacket from the woman at the coat check, silently handing over her claim ticket before dropping a dollar into a woven basket. After slipping on the gossamer covering, she quickly made for the exit. She instinctively reached into her bag, her fingers exploring the inside until they found the edges of the wooden box. Ellie grasped it, pulled it out of the bag, and clutched it tightly against her breast. Unable to catch her breath, she pushed open the door and darted out of the museum into the night. The cool air felt refreshing and she found herself slowly able to regulate her breathing. Covered in only thin stockings, her toes curled as they touched the cold stone staircase. She sprinted down the stairs towards the street and a line of waiting taxicabs.

As she neared the first cab, she could hear a labored voice exclaim, "Wait!" Pivoting around, Ellie spotted the waiter she had bumped into earlier running down the stairs with her shoes dangling from his fingers. The surreal image caused Ellie to hesitate momentarily. Her left hand blindly explored the cab's door until her fingers found the handle. The waiter stood in front of her, panting. *In another life, this Cinderella moment would have brought a smile to my face, but not tonight*, Ellie thought. She reached out suddenly and snatched the shoes away with boiling anger, sadness, and disgust at her behavior. As she turned back to the cab, the wooden box slipped from her grip and tumbled to the ground.

"Are you going to be alright?" Alex asked as he bent down to retrieve the box from the pavement.

"I don't know," Ellie responded with a heartfelt honesty that made her head swirl. She stared with intensity at the box in Alex's hands for a moment before jumping into the backseat of the taxicab. She gripped the door's handle and pulled the door towards her. Alex sprung forward, catching the edge of the door before it snapped shut.

"Wait, your box!" Alex exclaimed, struggling to keep the passenger door open.

"It was never mine to own. Please, keep it," the woman moaned through the window, tears returning to her eyes. "It's nothing." The despair in Ellie's voice caused Alex to release the door and retreat a step backwards. The door slammed shut and Alex watched through the cloudy window as Ellie muttered something to the driver. The cab pulled away from the curb.

Alex watched the taxi cab drive down Fifth Avenue, turn, and disappear behind a building. His fingers ran across the box's surface. Looking down, the box was exquisite in the moonlight.

5

The door squeaked as Alex pushed it open. Probing the wall in the dark, his fingers found the light switch and flipped it on. He hesitated as the fluorescent lights emitted a buzz, flickered, and filled the room with a greenish-yellow glow. Alex could hear the faint hum of the refrigerator in the corner competing with the metallic clanging of an old radiator.

The office seemed even smaller than usual this night. Up above, the guests had long since departed, leaving the staff to restore the foyer of the museum to its previous state.

Alex felt exhausted, his shoulders sore from holding aloft a seemingly endless number of glasses. The arches of his feet pulsated with a dull ache. As he closed the door behind him with a click, his thoughts drifted to the beautiful and tragic woman and the strange events that had transpired this night.

Dr. Eleanor Griffin.

Alex maneuvered through the office space, stepping over a satchel and winding past a tower of books, before depositing the wooden box on his workbench. Reaching beneath the desk pushed against his workbench, he pressed the computer tower's power button and glanced at his watch. It was nearly midnight and he responded with a yawn. *Another midnight at the museum,* Alex contemplated as he pulled off the tuxedo jacket and laid it over the back of April's chair.

The computer screen whirled to life, the background an ink schematic of the Roman Coliseum. His fingers found the knot in his bow tie, which he tiredly tugged at until it suddenly released and unfolded, hanging limply across his neck. He brought up a search engine with a single stroke of the mouse button from his left hand as his right hand unbuttoned his dress shirt. He quickly changed into the pair of jeans and tee-shirt that had been crumpled on his chair in a ball before settling himself in front of the computer. Alex grabbed a half-empty bottle of water sitting on his desk, took a sip, and deposited it on the edge of his work-bench.

The cursor blinked impatiently in the search engine box. His fingers found the keyboard and he quickly typed in "Eleanor Griffin." A long list of entries appeared and he sifted through them, ultimately finding a link to the New York University web-site. Clicking on this entry, Alex was directed to the Department of Ancient Near Eastern and Egyptian Studies. A long directory of faculty ran down the screen, an eclectic assortment of schol-ars studying anything from zooarchaeology to gender studies in ancient Syria. Alex found Eleanor Griffin's name and photo at the bottom of the list, followed by a description of her academic training and accomplishments. Her areas of interest were list-ed as "Hebrew Bible, pre-Biblical archeology, and ancient Near Eastern studies."

Alex gripped the mouse and returned to the search engine. *What was that Egyptologist's name?* Alex asked himself, trying to think back to a class on Ancient Egypt he'd taken as an under-graduate. *Henry...no, Harold Griffin.* He typed in the name and found a similar, apparently infinite list of websites. Alex squeezed his chin as he navigated through the entries, discarding one after another until he arrived at a link to *The Journal of Egyptology*.

Like many academic journals today, prior issues had been dig-itally scanned into a database and were available over the inter-net. Fortunately, Alex had access to the journal through a shared account at the MET and with a click of the mouse, he was redi-rected to a lengthy obituary on Dr. Harold Griffin. The obituary was an impressive recollection of the many great achievements of Dr. Griffin, from his role in excavations at Giza and Luxor to his contributions to elucidating the complex world of hieroglyphics. The final paragraph reflected on the archeologist's untimely death, apparently from a car crash in which his wife also perished. The last sentence stated that he was "survived by his beloved, only child, Eleanor."

Alex did the calculations in his head. The journal dated back to nineteen seventy-eight. He figured that would make her around eight to ten when she was orphaned. He couldn't say that he had a spectacular relationship with his parents. They never approved of his decision to pursue a career in antiquities. His parents would much preferred that he follow a more "responsible" and "predictable" path, like many of his childhood friends—pursue a "real profession" such as medicine, law, or investment banking. Alex was sad to say that they remained in a state of denial, holding out hope that one day Alex would snap out of his latest daydream, as if he were still a child enchanted with pirates or space ships. However, through all of it, they were at least there in case he needed them.

Alex thought back to the way the woman had stared at the statue of the bull in the exhibit hall, the way in which her body language simultaneously conveyed a sense of impenetrability and fragility. Then later that night at the taxi stand, he watched as her eyes fixated upon the wooden box as he retrieved it from the ground, with a mix of guilt and…*What was it?*…relief.

The box.

He had nearly forgotten about it. Alex dragged his chair from beside his workbench, turned on a small desk lamp, and grabbed the lamp's moldable, swan-like neck. Bending the silver frame downward, he focused the yellow light upon the box. Lifting the object with both hands, he began to examine the box with the attention a jeweler might give to a precious diamond.

The box was constructed out of a brown wood that was so pale, it was almost ivory. He estimated that it was approximately 6 x 2 ½ x 2 ½ inches and seemed heavier than expected for a box of that size. He brought the box up towards his ear and gently shook it. Nothing rattled inside, and he lowered it again to the table. Each of the surfaces of the box except the bottom had an intricate carving. These carvings were raised from the surface of the box like bas reliefs. The surrounding surface was a silky, smooth canvas without a single blemish or defect.

His attention was first drawn to the top of the box. There was an elaborate carving of a cross with flayed and blunted ends, like the bottom of a pedestal or the base of a grandfather clock. The cross appeared to sprout from a cloud-like structure that flowed around the foundation. Each end of the bars that formed the cross had three small circles with a central dot affixed to it. At the junction of the bars, there were three similar circles. Alex was intrigued by the image before him. He had never seen such a cross during his studies and preparation for the upcoming exhibit on crucifixes. The three circles conjured up a fairly typical Christian motif of the Holy Trinity, but the cloudlike structure was an unusual added feature.

Alex turned the box onto its side. There was a crest carved onto the long side of the box. The crest was a relatively simple design, with three birds walking single-file against a flowing-ribbon. The birds had prominent beaks, wings tucked down by their sides, and stick-like feet. On the opposite side of the box, there was an identical crest.

Alex turned the box on end and examined the short sides. The first side he examined had a conventional cross that one might see at any Roman Catholic Church. Unlike the Greek cross, which had four arms of equal distance, the vertical component of this cross was longer than the arms. There was a simplicity to the cross that seemed strangely out of place when compared to the complex imagery on the top of the box.

The opposite short side had another cross that was distinctly pagan in origin. The top bar of the cross was looped back on itself, forming the appearance of a head sitting on the body of a person. Alex recognized it as an ancient Egyptian symbol but could not remember the significance of it.

He could see what made Graham so exasperated by the box and why he dismissed it as easily as he had. The symbols seemed to be arranged without a unifying theme. It almost appeared to be doodles of woodcraft. Yet, Alex remained intrigued by the piece. After all, some craftsman had clearly devoted a tremendous amount of time to its creation.

Alex looked beyond the symbols, exploring the edge of the box in the hope of finding a way to open it. Disappointed, he could not find even a hint of a gap in the wooden frame to suggest the presence of a lid that could be lifted. *Perhaps this is not a box at all,* Alex thought. He assumed, based on its shape, that it was, but maybe it was a wooden block. He had seen images of old printing presses that employed wooden blocks that, when dipped into ink and pushed against a piece of paper or parchment, left an imprint. If this was the case, the shape was certainly unusual. The block would not have been used, as there was no trace of ink on the surface.

Alex placed the wooden object back onto the table and stretched. *What had Dr. Griffin said before departing in the cab?* Alex wondered as he squinted, eyes once again drawn to the box.

It's nothing.

It rang of mournful deception.

Alex reflected momentarily on the stack of material on the Black Death that undoubtedly sat on Graham's desk, waiting to be sifted through. Any distraction was better than being Graham's lackey, Alex concluded. It did not hurt that Graham had so callously dismissed the object as insignificant. *It would be nice to prove him wrong*, Alex thought and smiled. He would just have to take it one symbol at a time. He would give it one night, and then back to the slave mines.

Alex retrieved a blank piece of paper and sketched out the sides of the box as if it were unfolded into two dimensions. He would start from the top—the unusual cross rising from the cloud. Reaching across his workbench, he gripped the binding of an oversized volume on Christian iconography resting horizontally on a shelf. He quickly realized he had miscalculated how heavy the book was, and his right elbow tried to lock to counter the weight, but instead it gave way. His elbow struck the half-empty bottle of water and knocked it on its side. The cap rolled across the workbench, followed by a rapidly increasing puddle of water. He attempted to grab the wooden box before the water reached it, but he was too late.

Holding the box in the air, Alex cursed himself for being so clumsy. *How could I be so careless leaving a bottle of water in my work space!* Alex groaned to himself. *What if it was a priceless piece for the exhibit? My career could be over.*

Alex shook his head as he held aloft the box, water droplets falling to the floor. He trotted over to the corner of the room and grabbed a wad of paper towels. Returning to his workbench, he peeled the saturated paper he had used to sketch the sides of the box from the surface of the table and placed them aside. He then used the fistful of paper towels to mop up the rest of the water. Covering the workbench with dry towels, he placed the box on its side, and retrieved a cotton towel he used to polish the metallic crosses. As he brought the towel to wipe off the bottom of the box, he froze. The towel dropped to the floor as he stared in disbelief at the box and then at his schematic of the six sides of the box.

It's been a long night. Am I just overtired? Alex wondered.

He could have sworn that the bottom of the box had been blank.

6

*Ellie could feel a warm tide of anxiety sweep over her as she neared the Met-*ropolitan Museum of Art, the scene of her most recent embarrassment. After her very public meltdown, she had retreated into a cocoon of self-loathing, seeking refuge in her tiny, closet-sized apartment. Interrupted only by periodic visits from food-delivery people, she found a sense of peace in her separation from the rest of humanity. Indeed, Ellie was truly amazed at how easy it was to never have to step foot outside her apartment in New York City.

The cell phone had rung nearly ten times before she threw aside the comforter that was wrapped tightly around her head and wedged the phone between her ear and the pillow. The voice on the other end sounded tentative. He apologized for disturbing her and explained that he had gotten her phone number from her secretary at NYU. Ellie silently cursed Gail, the angelic secretary from the Department of Ancient Near Eastern and Egyptian Studies, who, undoubtedly concerned about Ellie's deep descent into isolation, must have decided that any contact with the outside world was better than none at all.

The caller identified himself as Alex Stone, a graduate student working at the MET. He hesitated, as if suddenly realizing that he had woken Ellie at one in the afternoon. Ellie listened as he explained that he had examined the wooden box she had given him and would like to meet with her as soon as possible to discuss his findings.

Ellie groaned. *The box! What is it with this box?* she asked herself as she pushed her upper torso off the bed with her elbows, her curiosity piqued. It was like a bottle that the tide just kept bringing back to shore.

She tried to think back to the wine-filled gala, but her mind was cloudy. "Are you the waiter?" Ellie wondered.

There was a brief chuckle on the other end of the line. "I would say part-time waiter, full-time student. I'm actually a graduate student working with Dr. Graham." The voice trailed off, allowing an uncomfortable silence to settle in. "...and yes, Dr. Graham is a complete ass."

Ellie smiled. There was something pleasant and unassuming in the student's voice that disarmed her.

"What have you found?" Ellie asked as she looked across the room and caught her reflection in the mirror. Her hair was a wild mess of blond. She ran her hands through it with displeasure.

"I'd rather just show you. It's hard to explain over the phone. Could you come by the museum?"

Ellie rubbed at the dark rings below her eyes and scanned the apartment that had become her prison. "When?"

"Would tonight be too soon?"

Ellie pushed open the door and made her way into the grand entrance hall of the museum. She was happy to be rid of her high heels and evening gown. Ellie could easily blend into the throng of tourists milling about. Dressed in sneakers, jeans, a faded tee shirt, and hooded sweatshirt, Ellie adjusted her Yankees cap and scanned the room in search of a familiar face. A cacophony of hundreds of different conversations filled the expansive space. Visitors spilled out of gift shops, trotted up the marble staircase, and circled around the large information desk.

"Dr. Griffin..."

Ellie turned and tried to place the origin of the voice. She could see the waiter-cum-graduate student weave through a group of

Japanese tourists. He was taller than she remembered, with light brown hair, dark brown eyes, and a boyish smile. Dressed in khaki pants, brown sneakers, and a button-down light blue shirt, he immediately reminded her of a younger Gordon.

"Dr. Griffin…" He extended his hand and Ellie took it with some embarrassment, thinking back to her behavior at the gala.

As Ellie's hand slid into his, Alex could not help but notice that her palm was unusually smooth. Ellie quickly withdrew it with a look of self-consciousness. Alex caught a glimpse of the palm of her hand, pink and glistening, before she brought her hands together.

"…Alex Stone. Thanks for coming on such short notice." He caught her blue eyes under the lid of her cap and let out an awkward half-cough. "It's pretty remarkable."

Ellie raised her eyebrows.

"The box, that is. The box is remarkable," Alex added, maneuvering her towards the information desk. Ellie could feel the faintest touch of the palm of his hand gently behind her right shoulder blade.

Arriving at the information desk, Alex smiled at an elderly lady behind the counter. She pushed a laminated card with the word VISITOR in blue across the countertop. Alex retrieved it by the string and passed it to Ellie, who looped it over her head and peered down with amusement at it swinging from her neck.

"I don't get one of those fancy tin buttons to snap on my lapel?" she asked with a grin, noting a troop of rotund women wearing fanny packs happily snapping the tin MET buttons onto their shirts after handing over their "donations."

"Where we are going, the tin buttons won't get us in. The basement is not very glorious, but few people get the pleasure of being *under* one of the most impressive collections of art and culture in the world. Consider yourself lucky. Not to mention that's where my crypt, I mean, office, is."

Alex motioned for her to follow. They walked across the entrance hall until they arrived at a nondescript tan door in the corner. Ellie watched as Alex removed an ID card secured to his belt and slid it through a card reader. The door emitted a crisp snap. Alex held the door open as Ellie slipped through the opening. She glanced at her surroundings.

They were in a stairwell lined by concrete walls. Somewhere below there was the *drip-drip* of water. The stairwell was not dirty, just sterile and industrial, a far cry from the ornate interior of the museum. Alex began to walk down the stairs, halted, and turned back to Ellie.

"Hey, even the *Titanic* had steerage," he muttered with a grin.

Ellie smiled back and ducked slightly to avoid hitting a dangling PVC pipe. After walking down several flights of stairs, they arrived at another tan door. A small surveillance camera was perched in the corner above the doorway. Alex once again slid his ID card through a card reader and pushed the door open.

The hallway beyond the door was dark with long fluorescent lights along the walls. A guard sat by a desk and smiled upon seeing Alex.

"Hey. It's my Main Man A," teased the guard.

"Hey, Cyrus," Alex responded with some embarrassment. "I have a visitor with me."

The guard scrunched his chin and nodded as if in approval. "You know the drill, my Main Man. Sign on the dotted line." Cyrus tilted a clipboard towards Ellie, who obliged. As she bent down she could see the guard give a thumbs-up sign to Alex. Straightening, she could see that Alex's cheeks were flushed and he was shaking his head with dissatisfaction.

"Thanks, Cyrus," Alex mumbled and led them further down the hallway. He looked over his shoulder at Ellie. "They store many of the artifacts not on display down here. There's also a restoration laboratory, a couple of conference rooms, a kitchen…and last but not least…" Alex paused by a warped door with peeling paint. "…my office."

Alex slipped a key into the lock and shoved the door open with his shoulder. "It sticks a bit," he remarked, pushing it open with a grating noise. He reached in and flicked on the lights.

Ellie followed Alex in without a word. The office was about one-fifth the size of her office back at NYU. It was more akin to a storage closet than a workspace. The windowless room with exposed lead pipes and crumbling paint immediately transported Ellie back to Iraq, her ill-fated trip in the APC, and the overwhelming claustrophobia she felt. It was a memory she had fought hard to suppress for some time.

"This certainly isn't the healthiest of working environments. Ever have this checked for asbestos or radon?" Ellie joked.

"It's probably best to not find out. I'm clearly not too high on the totem pole," Alex replied as he reached over his workbench and flicked on a lamp.

"Welcome to graduate student life. It's a thankless existence," Ellie muttered, grateful that her days of being the underpaid engine of academia were over.

Ellie could see the wooden box illuminated in the center of the workbench. Suspended from a corkboard with thumb tacks were a series of sketches, photographs, and photocopies of different types of crosses. A small pile of hard-covered books sat on an adjacent desk. Ellie bent slightly to examine the titles of the books whose spines faced outward: *Christian Iconography, The History of the Cross, Woodworking, Ciphers*. Her father's final book, *Decoding the Afterlife: Egyptian Hieroglyphics and the Next World*, rested askew on the top of the pile. Her fingers instinctively found the binding and righted the book. Ellie turned to see Alex disappear beneath a cabinet.

"Can I get you something to drink?" Alex inquired as he returned with a plastic bottle of water and set it down on the edge of the workbench. Ellie shook her head and pulled aside a chair to sit on. The sight of the wooden box on the workbench unsettled her.

Ellie straightened her shoulders and the chair squeaked back in protest. "Alex, you should know that this box has been an intolerable burden. I would sooner forget I ever saw it. It has brought me only bad luck and pain." Ellie's voice trailed off. Alex watched as she brought the palms of her hands together and wrung them nervously.

Alex broke eye contact and awkwardly mumbled, "I'm sorry. I never intended to make things difficult for you. I thought by coming here you…it's just such an amazing finding…"

Ellie glanced up and peered into Alex's eyes. She could see that he was almost bubbling over with excitement and it pained her. Several years ago it was she who enthusiastically embraced her work. Her passion for the field of antiquities was well-known. She was the first to arrive at the excavation site and the last to finally wrest herself away to bed. She would often toil alone under the moonlight and the yellow glow of battery-powered lamps long after the rest of the team had retired. It was at those moments that she felt most whole, felt closest to those who came before her, the civilizations and cultures that rose and fell and were long buried beneath the ground. *What had Father said?*

There are secrets in the past…mysteries that have yet to be uncovered. Somehow the world is incomplete without understanding where we came from.

Ellie could feel her insides begin to burn. Whatever was there as she traveled through Mosul was dormant, but it had not died with Gordon. *How could she turn her back on everything she had devoted her life to?* It was in her blood. She looked down at the cover of her father's book with a feeling of nostalgia and loss. She fought the urge to rise from her chair and flee from this office, from Alex, from the box and its mysteries.

Alex watched as Ellie lifted her eyes from her father's book and looked at him with resolve.

"What's so amazing?" she asked.

Alex smiled back and maneuvered a chair beside the workbench such that he could face Ellie. As he sat down, their knees nearly touched. Alex appeared to be measuring how to start.

"I have to be honest, at first I did not know what to make of the box. I know that you met with Graham about it. I overheard part of your conversation and have to admit that I couldn't disagree with him. It's beautiful to be sure, a work of incredible craftsmanship. Someone spent a considerable amount of time meticulously carving these symbols. But at first glance, the symbols did not make a whole lot of sense to me. It was like a school kid doodling on a piece of paper, you know, unicorns, stars, hearts, smiley faces. But why *these* symbols?"

Alex stopped and looked at Ellie. *What am I saying? She probably knows this and more. What's a graduate student doing trying to teach someone as accomplished as her?*

"Dr. Griffin…" Alex stuttered.

"Ellie," she responded with a smile.

Alex paused. "Ellie, the last thing I want to do is bore or offend you. This may all be very basic for you."

Ellie shook her head. "Alex, please. Assume I know nothing… that I'm some bright-eyed freshman."

Alex nodded his head with approval. He was thankful to be free to brainstorm.

"The overriding, unifying theme of the box is the image of the cross. What do you think about when you see a cross?" Alex asked with an earnest look.

"Christianity, I suppose," Ellie replied with a shrug.

"Sure, who wouldn't? Like most things, however, it is more complicated than that. Have you ever realized how many forms of crosses there are just in the Christian religion? Each cross means something a little different." Alex reached across the workbench, retrieved a manila folder, and opened it. He withdrew a crisp, white sheet of paper with a cross drawn on it and placed it on the table next to them.

Ellie studied the image and found it to be a simple cross.

"This is an image of the Latin cross, or *crux ordinaria*. Note that the horizontal bars of the cross are shorter than the vertical bar that runs through it. The horizontal bar is elevated above the midpoint of the vertical bar. It is certainly a more anatomic cross. After all, a crucified man's arms are shorter than his legs. From a simply utilitarian standpoint, it made sense for the Romans to construct a cross in this manner if the purpose was to execute an individual. To a Christian, this image conjures up the *True Cross* and reminds the faithful of the sacrifice Jesus made for the sake of humanity. Quite simply, it is a symbol just like the Star of David or the crescent. This cross is most commonly displayed in the Roman Catholic denomination. The form of the Latin cross found its way into many parts of medieval society. For example, many churches were constructed in the shape of this cross."

Alex withdrew another sheet of paper from the folder and slid it over the first. Ellie peered down. Another cross was depicted in black. Instead of bars of different lengths, this time the arms and legs were of equal length.

"This is a Greek Cross, also known as the *crux immissa quadrata*. Unlike the previous cross, this is not an 'anatomic' cross. The first thing I'm sure you noted was that the arms and legs are of equal length and the point at which they cross is in the center, producing an image of symmetry. What we know is that the Greek Cross predated the *crux ordinaria*. The significance of four equal length arms depends on who was using the symbol. For early Christians, it represented the four directions of the earth towards which the gospel of Christ would be spread."

Ellie pointed at the cross, feeling the need to interrupt. "Alex, it was also a symbol with deep pagan roots." She could see Alex smile as he sunk slightly backwards into his chair. He was glad that she had been hooked. "For some it represented the four platonic elements: Air, Fire, Water, and Earth. In ancient Babylon, the cross symbolized the sun-god Shamash. There's an Assyrian cross from 3000 years before Christ! Religion has always been in the business of co-opting prior symbols and rituals and reinventing them as it sees fit. In one of my classes I refer to a wonderful quote of St. Augustine, who said that, 'What is now called the Christian religion has existed among the ancients, and was not absent from the beginning of the human race until Christ came in the flesh.' This is nothing new. People have been writing critically about this for a long time."

Alex held up a finger. "This will all fit into place. Please, just bear with me. Now if we look at the side of the box, we see our first symbol—the Greek Cross." Alex retrieved the box and faced the side towards Ellie. Ellie could see the cross symmetrically carved into the side of the box.

Alex twirled the box until the opposite side was directed toward Ellie. "Now I'm sure you are familiar with this symbol," Alex said as he withdrew a schematic of a cross not unlike the Latin cross, but with the top portion of the vertical line folded upon itself.

Ellie's finger traced the cross before speaking. "It's called the Ankh Cross. My father wrote at length about it. I grew up seeing representations of it all around his office. The Ankh Cross is an ancient Egyptian hieroglyphic. The meaning is debatable but most people believe that it was a symbol of immortality. When an Ankh Cross was placed under the nose of a newly deceased pharaoh, it was supposed to confer access to everlasting life. My father, however, believed that it was more complicated, akin to a ying-yang symbol; it represented both life and death in eternal balance. The symbol is associated with Egyptian medicine and is sometimes called the 'Key of the Nile.' Imkotep, the famous physician to the pharaohs from 3000 B.C., is most closely associated with the symbol."

Alex nodded. "Some have said that the looped portion represents a head and that it is a female form representing fertility. If one makes the head of the cross round, fill it in with a symmetric cross, and leave a neck …" Alex withdrew a paper depicting this image. "…it becomes the *crux ansata* or Coptic cross."

Alex placed another paper on top of the pile. The image was very similar to the Coptic cross but the rounded head had a short stem elevating it from the cross, like a stick figure. "This image is from alchemy and represents Venus, returning to its connection to fertility, life, and rebirth."

Alex pulled out a blank piece of paper and a marker and drew out the two crosses: the Greek Cross and the Ankh Cross. "So we have two of the crosses from the box. Now to the third and most complex." He tilted the box, exposing the top. Ellie leaned in.

The cross at first glance appeared to have the most in common with the Greek Cross. The cross was symmetric with equal length arms. The arms, however, were flared out. There were three circles attached to each arm and a circle at the junction point of the four arms. The cross appeared to rise out of a cloud-like structure.

"This cross perplexed me. I had to search for a similar example, but eventually I found it. It's called the Lotus Cross." Alex removed a photocopy of a stone monument with Chinese symbols on the tablet. At the top of the tablet was a nearly identical cross.

"This is an image from a monument that was discovered by Chinese workers at Hsian in the Shanhsi Province in 1623. It had been lost for nearly a thousand years and commemorates the 'Propagation of the Syrian Luminous Religion in China.' It depicts a cross arising from an opened lotus blossom."

"Are you saying that the cross was created in China in 600 A.D.?" Ellie asked with some surprise.

"Actually, probably 700 A.D. It is a little known fact that after the death of Jesus, there were many competing groups vying to continue his legacy. They each had a different slant on the teachings of Jesus. To this day we have the Roman Catholics, Greek Orthodox, Russian Orthodox, and Coptic Christians, just to name a few, not to even mention all the denominations after the Reformation. One group that was particularly important in the early years after the death of Jesus was the Nestorians.

"Nestorius was a Syrian priest who became the Patriarch

of Constantinople in 428. He believed that Jesus had two na-tures—one human and one divine. It was his belief that Mary, mother of Jesus, was not divine and gave birth to a very mortal Jesus. Later in his life, Jesus became divine. Central to this view was that appreciation of the human side of Jesus was key—his trials and tribulations, sufferings, and temptations. For the fol-lowers of Nestorius, the so-called Nestorians, there was no Trin-ity. The Nestorians were merchants and missionaries who spread their gospel eastward into the Middle East and as far as China. Pursued as heretics by the Roman Catholics, the Nestorians were the face of Christianity for much of the Eastern world in the cen-turies after Jesus' crucifixion." Alex drew a picture of the Lotus Cross under the Ankh Cross.

Ellie's fingers found the box and she lifted it up. She turned the box slowly in her hands and paused at the image of three birds on the side of the box. "What about these birds? What do they mean?"

Alex held out his hand and accepted the box from Ellie. "It's a crest. Three birds against a ribbon. There's an identical crest on the other side. I think I found out who this box belongs to. I'm getting there, but there is something else I need to show you first. It's the fourth cross."

Ellie looked perplexed. She gripped the box and turned it over and over, looking at each side. "I think I'm missing something. I've stared at this box for hours on end and only saw three crosses." She watched as Alex grinned and reached across the workbench to retrieve the bottle of water. His hands found the handle of his desk's drawer, opened it, and withdrew a sponge. He unscrewed the cap of the bottle and proceeded to pour the contents onto the sponge until it turned a dark color. He positioned the box in the center of the workbench and flipped it so that it rested on the top side with the Lotus Cross. The blank side of the box faced them.

"This is the best part," Alex mumbled under his breath. He

brought the sponge to the surface of the box and hesitated. "What do you see?"

"Nothing," Ellie responded with suspicion.

She watched as Alex brought the saturated sponge up against the surface of the wood and ran it across it with a single motion.

"What are you do…?" Ellie asked but her voice trailed off with amazement. As Alex lifted the sponge from the surface of the wood, the blank canvas was suddenly filled with yellow words set against a brown background. As Ellie brought her nose nearly up against the box, she could also make out an unusual symbol.

The symbol was composed of a circle, and within the circle was a vertical line that transected the circle, dividing it into halves. A second, shorter, horizontal line divided the right semicircle into half like a T on its side. Extending from the circle was a long line with two hatch marks like bristles of a toothbrush. To the left of the symbol were several lines of text.

"I wish I could tell you that I discovered this through genius and curiosity, but in reality it was a complete accident. If you look close enough before you wet the surface you can faintly make out the hidden message." Alex pulled down a detailed photograph from his corkboard and passed it to Ellie. It was digitally magnified to the point that one could almost see the texture of the wood. The grains of wood were faintly visible and appeared to have been altered to produce the series of words and the symbol.

"The words are written in Latin," Alex noted. "It translates loosely as:

Adam's Staff
Eastward Go
Illuminated Path
Where King Interred"

"This is bloody amazing, Alex!" Ellie whispered in awe. "What does it all mean?"

Alex frowned. "I hope this isn't too anticlimactic, but I'm not entirely certain that I know, but I do have some ideas. Frankly, I was thinking that you might be able to help decipher this hidden message. I started with the symbol, but haven't found anything that matches it. At first I thought that it was an alchemy symbol, but after reading through book after book, I haven't seen anything that looks like it. Have you ever seen a symbol like this, maybe in the pre-Christian era?"

"I would have to research it as well. It doesn't look like any hieroglyphic I've seen and certainly not in any Mesopotamian culture I am familiar with," Ellie replied. She bit down on her lower lip in thought.

"I think that the words in the bottom right corner may be a clue," Alex said. He removed a magnified photo of the area and traced out the letters. "It says 'M. Paulo.' You asked me before about the birds on the box and their significance."

Alex rose from his chair and began to go through the pile of books on his desk, rearranging them until he came away with a soft-bound, baby-blue covered book. Ellie craned her neck as Alex opened the book and began to flip through the pages. She could see that it was the Yule-Cordier edition of *The Travels of Marco Polo*. Ellie was embarrassed to admit that despite its notoriety, she, like most people, knew the general story of Marco Polo but had never actually read the traveler's account.

Having found what he was looking for, Alex bent the binding back so the book remained open and pushed it towards Ellie. There was a similar crest of three black birds walking in a single file across a winding ribbon, or possibly a road.

"This is the crest of the Polo family," Alex explained.

"*M. Paulo...Marco Paulo...Marco Polo!*" Ellie interrupted.

"Exactly! It all fits together. The choices in crosses veer away from traditional Western European iconography and flirt with both the Eastern world and paganism. One, the Lotus Cross, even conjures up the Far East and China. Polo traveled to the East at a time in which few risked such a trip. He lived for decades away from the world of Europe. In his travels, he also writes about his encounters with Nestorian Christians. I think it is possible that what we have in front of us is the lost property of Marco Polo." Alex's face was pink.

"I don't know if that argument would stand up in a court of law or academia for that matter, but it is an enchanting thought. But what is this box for?" Ellie inquired.

Alex picked up the box and brought it up to eye level. "I think the more important question is: what's in the box?"

The room grew silent. The radiator began to make a snapping noise and something behind a cabinet hissed.

"We need to find a way to open the box without damaging it," Ellie concluded.

"I have an idea of how to find out what's in the box without even touching it," Alex replied with a smirk.

7

*Ellie hated hospitals. She hated everything about them — the smell of disin-*fectant, the whirl of gurney wheels, the white-coated doctors that looked like they had just graduated high school, and the idle chatter of staff juxtaposed with the enormity of death. If she ever had the guts to actually see a shrink, he would probably seize on her childhood experience with the death of her parents as a catalyst for these feelings. For years after, she had recurring nightmares of an overturned Mini Cooper pressed up against a tree, the rain falling through the shattered windshield, and the reflection of red brake lights on the wet, black asphalt. The scene would fade into her sitting in an empty waiting room wearing a pink tutu for her ballet recital, seeing her uncle enter the room. His face tried to convey a sense of strength but was twisted by an unbearable horror that frightened her then and continued to haunt her to this day. She would wake up in a cold sweat, the sheets stuck to her skin, her heart racing.

Her three-month stay at Ramstein Air Force Base in the burn unit only served to reinforce her dislike of hospitals. She knew that she was one of the lucky ones. She got to leave with a scar between her ribs where the chest tube was shoved in, a reddish patch along her hip where the skin donor site was, and her hands delicately wrapped in gauze to protect the pink skin grafts. But she got to leave on her own two feet and with her faculties intact, which was more than she could say for many of the other poor patients.

"You O.K.?" Alex asked.

Ellie continued to look through the oversized window at the Hudson River below, and New Jersey beyond it. She dabbed at her eyes with the sleeve of her shirt before swinging around with an overcompensating smile and a nod. Alex was not fooled and looked at her with concern. As he was about to speak, he was suddenly interrupted by a bear hug from behind by a young man in khaki pants and a blue scrub top.

The man deposited Alex's feet back on solid ground and shook his hand.

"Alex. Alex Stone. It's been a long time," exclaimed the man.

"Ellie, I want to introduce you to Josh Weinstein. We went to college together," Alex explained.

Josh delicately shook Ellie's hand with a giant grin. "Hello."

Ellie studied Josh. He looked like the prototypical fraternity brother who probably found it "cool" to be premed and ultimately satisfied his parents' expectations by becoming a physician.

"I'm pre-call, so let's get a move on. This should be interesting. I've heard of it being done to look at mummies. I saw some documentary on it on cable a couple of weeks ago," Josh said before turning around.

Ellie and Alex followed him down a long corridor. Josh turned his head around as he walked like a tour guide. "Alex Stone... man! I was wondering what the hell happened to you after college." He looked at Ellie and poked Alex in the sternum. "This guy was the smartest kid I ever met. We used to call him 'Professor.'" He glanced back at Alex and smiled. "Everyone thought it was such a waste for you do the archeology thing. I mean, I liked the Indiana Jones movies, too—except maybe for that second one...that was pretty bad now that I think of it...especially when that Indian dude rams his hand through that guy's chest and pulls out his heart and it's still beating. But you must make shit money in archeology."

They arrived at a door. Josh pushed it open and held it for

them to enter. As Alex and Ellie filed in, Josh inquired what Ellie did.

"I'm afraid that, like Alex, I'm wasting my life away in archeology," Ellie replied with a good-natured grin.

"Shoot. I should just stop talking. My girlfriend says I talk way
too much and all I do is end up putting my foot in my mouth."

They were in a small control room with multiple computer
screens. Through a large window was a white donut-shaped ap-
paratus with a long, thin table suspended in the hole. A petite
blond sat behind the console with a look of boredom.

"This is Debbie." The woman gave a half-hearted wave. Josh
turned to them. "I may be a radiology resident, but I could probably fly a 747 better than I could figure out how to work this
machine. They teach us to read the images, not make them."

"What is it?" Ellie questioned as the woman made selections
on the touch-screen with her long painted fingernails.

"It's a CAT scan—Computed Axial Tomography. I'm sure
you've heard of x-rays. Well, think of this as a fancy x-ray. See
that donut over there? All along the inside of the donut are detectors. Radiation is shot through the patient—or whatever is
on the table for that matter—as it moves through the donut.
The detectors pick up the information and make a picture with
cross-sectional images like slices of a loaf of bread. This one is a
sixty-four-slice detector. It's pretty quick."

The technician looked up at a clock on the wall. "Josh, we
really need to move this thing along. I have a patient coming any
second. As it is, we could get busted for this."

"Yeah, you're right," Josh responded. "The mysterious box,
please," he asked and extended his hands.

Alex withdrew the box from his bag and handed it to Josh,
who examined it like a tourist looking over some curio. "Interesting. What is it?"

"That's what we're trying to figure out," Alex responded and followed Josh into the adjacent room where the CAT scanner sat. He watched as Josh placed the box on the table and, with a touch of a button, advanced it into the core of the donut.

Having returned back to the control room, Josh asked the technician to scan the item. Ellie and Alex watched as Debbie pushed several buttons. Beyond the window, the table swept through the donut and the machine buzzed. Josh leaned into the console and examined the images. He sighed.

"What is it?" Ellie asked with concern.

"I'm afraid that this is not going to be too helpful to you guys," Josh answered. He clicked a button and brought up an image on the screen. They stared at a white rectangle. "This is a scout. It's basically a two-dimensional x-ray. Things that are this white on x-ray are made out of metal. When you get the third dimension with a CAT scan it will look like this..." Another click of the button showed images of what appeared to a white rectangle with white beams shooting out of it like a star. "It's what we call in the radiology world, 'streak artifact.' It's caused by 'beam hardening.' To the layman, the x-rays do not penetrate the metal."

"Metal? It's made of wood." Ellie responded.

"It must be filled with metal or have an inner lining of metal for it to look like this," Josh countered.

"Is there anything else we can use to see into this box?" Alex asked as Josh lifted the box off the table.

"Not here. An MRI at best wouldn't help out. At worst, it might heat up or stick to the magnet. That's all the tricks I have up my sleeve." He looked down at the box and shrugged. "Why don't you just go to the hardware store and saw it open?"

Alex and Ellie looked horrified by the suggestion. "We can't just destroy it! It is a historic artifact!" Ellie cried out.

Josh held up his hands defensively. "Sorry. Just trying to help out." He could see the disappointment in his visitor's eyes. He patted Alex on the back. "Hey, if anyone can figure this thing out it's you. All those late nights in the library while I was partying must have been worth something." He gave a mischievous grin.

Alex was not amused and extended his hand, palm up, towards Josh. The radiology resident returned the box. He gave Alex a firm pat on the back.

"Gotta get back to work. Good luck."

"Thanks for trying," Alex muttered. He looked at Ellie with disappointment. "I guess we need to think of something else."

"First, I think we both could use a drink."

8

Somewhere in the back of the small, dark bar, Alex could hear the thump of a bass and the blare of a saxophone. A waitress dressed in black wordlessly arrived and roughly placed a bottle of beer on the wooden table in front of Alex. He watched the condensation drip down the label of the microbrew as the waitress slid a cocktail to Ellie and left.

"I think dirty martinis have become my new favorite drink," Ellie announced as she twirled the olive speared by a toothpick between her thumb and index finger. "I've been doing my fair share of drinking since…" Ellie's voice drifted off. She smiled at Alex and glanced down at the table. "Let's just say that I've been doing my fair share of drinking of late."

Alex hesitated, uncertain if Ellie's comment was an invitation to pry into the sordid details. He tried to study her face but the flickering light of the candle positioned in the center of the table only provided intermittent, shadowy glimpses. Although he had only recently met Ellie, Alex could not help but feel that some kind of protective layer had unwittingly peeled away from her back in his office. Exposed was a raw passion for uncovering the mysteries of the past. He recognized a kinship in such quixotic pursuits. Alex lifted the bottle by its neck and tried to act nonchalant as he brought it to his lips.

"It seems like you've been through a lot," Alex said.

"That's an understatement," Ellie tersely replied. She brought the glass up to her mouth, flicked the olive to the side with her ring finger, and took an extended drink.

Although Alex tried to be discrete, his eyes were drawn to the pink glow of the skin on her palm as she held aloft the glass. Cognizant of Alex's interest, Ellie self-consciously deposited the glass back down and placed her hands palm-down on the table-top.

Alex gritted his teeth with embarrassment. He was immediately upset with himself for being so callous in his invasion of her personal space. All he could muster was a stuttering "I'm sorry...I..."

Ellie looked down at the top of her hands and thought of how best to respond. She peeked across the table at Alex who was nervously swigging from the bottle of beer. Ellie turned over her hands like she was visiting a fortune-teller. The skin graft on her palms glistened in the candlelight.

"It's OK. Really, it's OK," she said as much to convince herself of this fact as to comfort Alex. "They're skin grafts, if you couldn't figure it out. The doctors at Ramstein are quite adept at putting people back together. There were a lot of soldiers a lot worse off than me. I'm the lucky one. I guess I had it coming. It's what you get for plunging your hands into a raging fire in order to retrieve a wooden box. Now that is out in the open, you might have a better understanding about my misgivings about our mysterious box."

Alex watched as Ellie turned her head in the direction of the jazz band. He took it as a sign that any further discussion on the subject was off limits. *There's more to this story,* Alex surmised. *What exactly happened in Iraq? It's wrong to force the issue,* Alex decided.

"Where do we go from here?" Alex asked, his voice nearly drowned out by an impromptu saxophone solo.

"Do you think that it could really be a possession of Marco Polo, THE Marco Polo?" Ellie wondered.

Alex shrugged. "Wouldn't it be amazing?"

Ellie appeared to be deep in thought. "I don't know about you, but I'm not quite ready to give up on deciphering this box. If you think that there may be a connection to Polo, then I could make a phone call to someone who would be intrigued by the prospect. He's practically an uncle. I could see what he thinks."

"Who did you have in mind?" Alex asked, his interest piqued.

"His name is Bernardo Gozzi."

"You know Bernardo Gozzi? His book on Marco Polo's travels is a classic."

"I haven't spoken to him for a while. I guess he's a part of a past I thought I had moved on from."

"Will he help?"

Ellie brought the martini glass to her lips and finished the contents. Her face emerged from the shadows.

"He'll help."

9
Cape Town, South Africa

Solomon Haasbroek groaned as he sat bare-chested on the edge of the bed. An excruciating pain radiated through his skull, like a leather belt tightening against his temple, until the roots of his hair tingled. He squinted and blindly reached over to the bedside table until his fingers found a pair of sunglasses. He slid them on with relief and forced himself to a standing position. Bright white light streamed in through the glass doors leading to a small plunge pool.

Solomon stretched and loosened up some phlegm with several coughs. He tightened the strings on his pajama bottoms, reached into a bowl of biltong, and withdrew a handful of the dried beef strips. He popped them in his mouth and removed a beer from the refrigerator. *South African breakfast of champions,* he thought, and passed through the opened sliding doors and onto the patio. The robotic pool cleaner explored the bottom of the plunge pool, dragging a long hose behind it that produced ripples across the surface. He leaned up against the railing, slid the pistol between his pants and the small of his back, and stared down at Camps Bay. The ocean looked particularly rough today and undoubtedly freezing, as usual.

He could see a group of black boys walking across the beach lugging large wooden statues from the Ivory Coast that they hoped to unload on tourists.

This place has gone to the dogs, man.

He had served his time for God and country in the SADF,

the South Africa Defense Force. He had fought in the brutal cross-border campaigns in Namibia, Angola, and Mozambique. He had seen and done horrible things that would give nightmares to even the worst of killers. This was all before – as he put it – Nelson Mandela trotted out of prison like Jesus reborn and gave the country to the kaffirs once and for all. But every setback ultimately breeds opportunity, and he had skills for this new age. He had done quite well for himself serving as a mercenary, or as the Americans like to sugar-coat it, a "contractor." He, after all, had done well enough to purchase a swanky flat overlooking the Cape Town beaches and beneath the shadow of Table Mountain. But the truth was that it was more than just money that attracted him to his job, it was the freedom of being nationless, extralegal, and independent.

The cellphone vibrated in his pocket. He brought it up to his ear.

"Howzit?" he answered.

The voice on the other end was deep and had an accent. He tried to place it—Italian? Portuguese? He had not heard the voice since just after his ill-fated mission to Iraq. His client had paid well, despite the fact that the box could not be located. The mysterious patron had explained that despite his failure, he would be kept on retainer in case any new leads arose.

Iraq, Solomon snorted to himself. *Iraq is a zoo. A complete freakin' disaster.* His lips curled at the corners. *At least I added some madness to the mix before departing.*

"Mr. Haasbroek, I hope you are well."

"I'm alright."

"I have another job for you if you are interested…" The man's voice trailed off.

Solomon pulled the pistol from his pants and held it by his side. "I'm listening."

"I need you to go to Venice. I will send you all the details when you are on your way."

"No hint of what the job will entail?" Solomon asked.

"Your discretion and the special skill set you have developed over the years. You will need to arrange a team. Will this be a problem?"

"It can be arranged for the right price."

"Money is not a problem."

"Good. When do we leave?"

"Tomorrow."

10
Venice, Italy

The telephone call had interrupted an otherwise monotonous day. Dr. Bernardo Gozzi laid down his wire-rimmed glasses upon his desk and rubbed at his eyes with the balls of his hands. The three years since he had assumed the directorship of the Biblioteca Nazionale Marciana were a blur. Plucked out of the world of academia, Dr. Gozzi was gradually being transformed into what he despised most — a bureaucrat.

There were the endless meetings on cataloguing and *re*-cataloguing the thousands and thousands of maps and manuscripts that comprised the library's enormous collection. Then there was the massive project of creating a greater European research database to compliment the new political and economic realities of the continent. And if that was not enough, there was the battle against the Anobidi — the dreaded woodworm.

Oh the woodworm! Dr. Gozzi moaned to himself. Who would have thought that he would have become such an expert on the mating patterns of the tiny insect? The woodworm threatened to turn many of the most fragile and irreplaceable works within the library into piles of sawdust. To combat this beetle infestation, Dr. Gozzi had elicited the help of several high-tech companies. The vulnerable volumes were digitized and then hermetically sealed in special bags. The ambient oxygen was progressively driven from the bag until the concentration was below that in which an aerobic organism like the woodworm could survive. This had succeeded in limiting the damage and saving the library, but at a steep financial cost. It was a cost the library would have to recoup with a successful exhibit and with generosity from both the public and private sectors. Dr. Gozzi painfully recognized that this meant fundraising, and a lot of it.

Dr. Gozzi placed the glasses back on the bridge of his nose and wound the wires around his ears. He peered at the computer screen. A long list of emails ran down the screen. He had only recently and reluctantly learned to "surf" the internet and send electronic mail. He missed the days of academia when it was just him and a pile of moldy, leather bound books—volumes that you could put your fingers on and smell the musty scent of. He devoured books with an insatiable appetite like...like a *bookworm*. Dr. Gozzi smiled and stretched.

The phone call had come at the end of a meeting on acquiring two rare maps of Venice from a private collector. His secretary had silently slipped into the room and whispered in his ear that there was an urgent phone call from Pietro Zeno. Dr. Gozzi watched as the lawyer and collector politely nodded farewell and slipped out of his office. *Is the library sinking?* Dr. Gozzi wondered with alarm.

Dr. Gozzi pressed the blinking hold button and brought the receiver to his ear. "Pronto?"

Pietro's voice seemed pressured. The nervousness and excitement on the other end of the phone startled the director as he pushed aside the paperwork on his desk.

Pietro was a well-known figure in Venice—a blue-collar celebrity of sorts. As a city engineer, he was routinely consulted on the flooding issues that plagued the city. Sitting at the southwest corner of the Piazzetta San Marco across from the Doge's Palace, the library was on the front line—a stone's throw from the Bacino di San Marco, the major basin at the mouth of the Grand Canal. More recently, he had been hired to help supervise the elaborate construction of a wooden ramp that was to serve a dual role of protecting the stone entranceway into the library as it was being renovated and providing wheel-chair accessibility. Not yet completed, the ramp was going to ferry visitors for the upcoming exhibit celebrating Cardinal Bessarion's initial donation of codices, manuscripts, and books in 1468, which served to turn the library into a truly public forum for research and discourse. Dr. Gozzi had high hopes for the exhibition.

Dr. Gozzi listened as Pietro muttered about having acquired several items of historical importance from a recently expired uncle. Due to the potential lucrative nature of these particular pieces, he was inquiring if Dr. Gozzi would discreetly examine them and offer an opinion as to their worth. Dr. Gozzi exhaled, thankful that the library was not at risk of being flooded before the exhibition could begin.

He suggested that as he was not an appraiser; perhaps Pietro would be better served by contacting an antiquity dealer. Pietro was quiet for several seconds before responding that he trusted Dr. Gozzi's opinion above all others and that he, more than anyone, may appreciate the "uniqueness" of this find. Succumbing to a mixture of boredom and intrigue, Dr. Gozzi invited him to come by the library after it had closed and the staff departed.

Dr. Gozzi glanced down at his watch and shook his head. It was almost nine p.m. Pietro was already a half-an-hour late. The director sighed and strolled around the library, his hands loosely clasped behind his back.

The library felt eerie. The street lights cast jagged shadows against the walls and the *tap-tap* of his shoes against the marble only seemed to reinforce his solitude. He paused at a marble column framing an arched passageway and bent forward until his nose nearly touched the surface. Dr. Gozzi ran his finger across the marble and his fingertip came away with a thick coating of gray dust. The director withdrew a handkerchief from his pocket and began to clean the column. *What would Titian think of this mess?* Dr. Gozzi wondered, reflecting on the artist whose paintings graced the ceiling of the library.

In the distance, he could hear the clunk of heavy footsteps slowly moving up the wooden ramp and the front door creak open. Dr. Gozzi made his way to the door and arrived just as the darkened form of Pietro emerged from the doorway, holding a chest against his body. Pietro's face glistened in the yellow light as he struggled forward, gripping the chest tightly.

"Are we alone?" Pietro questioned with a sudden look of paranoia. His eyes darted around the room.

Dr. Gozzi nodded and motioned with an outstretched hand for Pietro to come forward and deposit the clearly heavy chest on one of the many long wooden reading tables. Pietro inched up the table, set the chest down with a final grunt, and wiped the sweat off his forehead with the sleeve of his jacket. Before Dr. Gozzi could speak, the engineer retreated back to the front door, poked his head through the opening, and scanned the Piazzetta. It was empty except for a handful of wandering tourists. After a moment of inspection, Pietro silently pushed the front door closed with a clunk.

"Signori, this may appear odd, but I would feel better if we could lock the door," Pietro uttered with a bashful look of concern, like a child asking for a nightlight to be turned on before going to sleep.

"Yes, of course," Dr. Gozzi replied. He shuffled over to the door, slipped the oversized key into the lock, and turned it until a *clunk* was emitted that echoed throughout the library.

Satisfied, Pietro stumbled back to the table and sat down on a chair with a look of exhaustion.

"You never realize just how big the Piazza is until you have to lug around something this heavy," Pietro mumbled with a pained smile and motioned with his chin to the chest resting on the table.

The director responded with an awkward grin and mechanically extended his hand. Pietro grasped it tightly. The grip made Dr. Gozzi suddenly uncomfortable and he withdrew quickly, finding the palm of his hand wet. "How are you, Pietro? You seem a bit flustered. I must admit, when my secretary came into my office and told me there was an *urgent* message from Pietro Zeno, engineer to Venice, I frankly assumed the worst. I was afraid that the Adriatic was getting ready to swallow up the library."

"No, Signori. It is nothing like that. But it is something that can't wait," Pietro replied. Dr. Gozzi shot a puzzled look at the engineer.

"Now, I must say, this is all very mysterious—the nighttime meeting, locking the door, a curious chest. This is much too much excitement for an old librarian."

Dr. Gozzi inched forward until his generous belly spilled onto the table and brushed up against the chest. "How very interesting," Dr. Gozzi muttered under his breath as he hunched over the chest. He pulled his glasses further down the bridge of his nose and squinted.

Though the crest on top of the chest had seen better days, it was still spectacular. The oval crest was framed by an elaborate, ornate decorative flare that appeared to be painted in gold. The central crest was divided into three parts. The paint was chipped, peeled, and in places bubbled upwards, but it was still vibrant. In the top left, there was a wedge of yellow. In the top right, there was a wedge of black. The bottom half of the oval was a tan color.

Dr. Gozzi looked at Pietro with surprise. "Do you know what this is? Do you know whose family this crest belongs to?" the director asked with excitement.

"Not right away, Signori. I could tell you the tidal patterns of the lagoon by heart, but this is far out of my comfort zone. I did do a little research, however. It is amazing what one can uncover on the internet these days if you search hard enough," Pietro responded with a devilish smile. "I was able to find a drawing of a similar crest from an article *you* had written many years ago."

"You should know that it was an article that was disparaged throughout the academic community. I wouldn't give it too much weight..." Dr. Gozzi's voice trailed off as if in a trance. He continued to stare down at the crest. The name dribbled out between his lips before he was even aware of it. "Falier."

Pietro responded with a nod. Dr. Gozzi's thoughts drifted.

Marin Falier was a unique figure in Venetian history. His tale was taught in history classes throughout Italy with some relish by teachers who would whisper the sordid account as if reciting an old ghost story. Falier, the infamous Doge of Venice, was the only Doge in the history of the Republic to be executed for high crimes against the state. He was a Venetian Guy Fawkes of sorts, without the bang of explosives.

The conventional teaching was that Marin Falier, hungry for absolute power, crafted a devious plot to overthrow the Republic in 1355. At the time, Venice was a Republic primarily controlled by the powerful nobility who ruled through the Maggior Consiglio—Great Council—and through a special division of government called the Council of Ten. The Council of Ten consisted of nobles with the mission of providing security for the Republic and battling threats against it from outside and within. As such, they served as a powerful intelligence organization.

Elected by the Great Council, the Doge was chosen for life, typically as a reward for prior service to the Republic. The position was purely decorative. The Doge would entertain foreign dignitaries and paternalistically preside over councils. Monitored closely by six Counsillors, the Doge was ultimately under the control of the Venetian nobility that had placed him there. So limited was the power of the Doge that he could not even leave the plush Ducal Palace without the permission of the nobility and an escort. The grand Ducal Palace was little more than a gilded prison.

As the traditional account is told, Marin Falier was enraged after a noble who insulted his wife's reputation went unpunished for his slander. Convinced that he must subjugate the elites, Falier crafted a scheme to lure the nobles to the Piazza San Marco under the pretense of an impending Genoese invasion. Once the nobles had clustered in the Piazza, armed men loyal to the Doge would come to the "defense" of the Doge and massacre the nobles. With the nobles annihilated, Marin Falier would be named Prince of Venice and the Republic would come under his control. As it was told in the history books, Falier's plot was leaked to the nobles before the plan could be set in motion. The Doge was arrested and later executed for these crimes.

Dr. Gozzi was intrigued by the story of Marin Falier. As a historian with a tendency to support unconventional views, he was convinced that the whole story of the ill-fated Doge had not been told. He was determined to investigate why such a distinguished man with a lifetime of service to the Republic would want to overthrow what he spent decades protecting. The orthodox teachings all seemed too *convenient* for the director. He was reminded that, "history is written by the victors," and had wondered, *Why was Marin Falier really deposed and executed?*

He began to wonder what truly happened on April 15, 1355 when the plot suddenly unraveled. While researching his seminal work on the life and voyages of the great Venetian explorer, Marco Polo, a clue to the mystery surfaced. Obsessed with Polo's travels throughout the East, Marin Falier began to quietly collect as many manuscripts and artifacts related to his voyages as he could find. So vast became his collection that Falier dedicated a room in his palace specifically for it. On that fateful night in 1355, there were rumors of missing items from this room. There were stories that circulated among the Venetian populace of seizure of the Doge's property and frantic searches by the Council of Ten and their hired goons through palace grounds. Several letters suggested that the Doge was interrogated and tortured for days within the deepest recesses of the prison without result. Dr. Gozzi became convinced that the standard story of Falier's betrayal was ultimately concocted by those in power trying to hide a deadly secret. In the end, there remained as many questions as answers. *Who was ultimately behind the Council of Ten? What were they looking for? What became of it? What was the connection to Marco Polo?*

Dr. Gozzi had decided to revisit the story of Falier in a long article. Having recently written the well-received work on the life and travels of Marco Polo, he was somewhat insulated from being seen as a mere academic hack. He advanced the theory that the Doge was forced from power and executed, not for any plans against the Republic, but because he possessed something so valuable that powerful people were willing to stage a coup and murder for it. What this item—or items—was, Dr. Gozzi could only speculate, but it possibly could have been connected to the equally enigmatic figure of Venetian history, Marco Polo. The article was initially met with raised eyebrows and shakes of the head by his academic colleagues. Some questioned if Gozzi had finally gone off the deep end, allowing his own obsessions with Falier and Polo to get the best of him. The article was quietly put in the category of speculative history, the depository of wild theories without concrete evidence, and ultimately ignored.

Pietro's voice broke through the director's recollections.

"Open it," Pietro urged.

"I must admit that I'm afraid of what I may find. I hope it isn't Falier's skull," Dr. Gozzi whispered back.

"Open it, Signori," Pietro reiterated.

The director reached out, gripped the lid, and swung it upwards. He found himself uttering the only words he could find.

"It is true...it is true."

Pietro looked into Dr. Gozzi's wet eyes. "I guess I found the right man."

II

Dr. Gozzi stared in silence at the opened chest. Is it possible? *he thought* with excitement.

"May I?" asked the director, pointing to the items in the chest. Pietro nodded his approval and watched as Dr. Gozzi retrieved a long piece of acid-free paper. Stretching it across the length of the table, he weighed it down with two discs of stainless steel. He then disappeared for several minutes deeper into the library and returned with a pair of archival gloves that he used for examining rare manuscripts. Reaching into the chest, he proceeded to delicately remove the contents and place them on the table before them. With the chest finally empty, the director silently circled the table, periodically bending down to more closely inspect an item before shaking his head and snorting with satisfaction. Pietro's eyes followed the director's movements as he analyzed the contents.

Dr. Gozzi finally broke away from his inspection and turned to Pietro.

"Do you realize what you have?" the director asked, seemingly exasperated with the find.

"Is it valuable?" Pietro asked.

Dr. Gozzi snorted like a bull. "I'd say it is priceless. What do you know about Marco Polo?"

Pietro shrugged. "The usual, I suppose. He was an explorer who left Venice and went to China. When he finally returned to Venice after a long time away, he wrote a book about his travels."

"That's the basic storyline, at least the one that has been taught

99

in school. What if I told you that there are those who do not even believe that Polo ever journeyed to the East, that he never reached China? Now I always love a great conspiracy theory, but this one did not make a whole lot of sense to me. What was he doing during those seventeen years if not traveling? When he died, he was said to have left items from his trips. These have been searched for but none have been found, at least until now."

Dr. Gozzi walked around the table and faced Pietro. "If I may..." The director pointed to a thick fur-lined blanket lying at the corner of the table. "This is bedding, no doubt of Mongol workmanship." He then pointed to a single feminine sandal. "And over here is a sandal from China, or as it was called in Polo's time, Cathay. And next to it is a beautiful silk brocade, richly woven with gold and silver thread. Polo visited Tenduc in China during his travels and writes about such woven fabrics." Dr. Gozzi continued to walk around the table. "And over here is a Buddhist rosary."

Pietro rose to his feet and peered at the wooden beads.

"It's called a japa mala, or mala for short. This was probably made from a sacred wood in Eastern cultures, the Bodhi tree. If we count the beads, I bet it will have 108 beads—one for each human passion." Dr. Gozzi emitted a short chuckle.

The director maneuvered towards the end of the table and paused in front of an elaborate silver girdle from a Mongolian knight. Beside it was an exquisite headdress adorned in silver and peals. "These two items must have been gifts: the first, the gilded girdle of a Mongol warrior and the second, the headdress of a woman of great stature." Dr. Gozzi stopped in front of a foot-long tablet of gold emblazoned with a gerfalcon. A hole was bored through one end, likely to accommodate a metal chain that could be hung around the owner's neck. This item evoked Pietro's greatest interest.

"And this?" Pietro asked.

"It's called a Paiza or tablet of authority. During the Mongol dynasty, the great Khans had these tablets fashioned out of gold and given to men of great importance. When these individuals traveled through Mongol-controlled territory, these tablets were symbols of power. If that person needed food, a horse, or a place to stay, merely displaying this tablet would send people running to help. The tablet was an extension of the Great Khan and the Great Khan was all-powerful. It was a magnificent thing to have, because in those days the Mongol Empire was massive. Few seem to know it these days, but at the height of their civilization, the Mongols controlled an area that stretched from Korea and China through the Middle East and India and even into Eastern Europe. In fact, if it wasn't for infighting within the Mongol tribes, most historians believe that all of Europe could have fallen to the Mongols. So powerful were they that the Roman Catholics wondered if demons had escaped from hell to annihilate all civilization."

The two men were silent for a minute as they stared at the items on the table. Dr. Gozzi finally broke the silence.

"These are important historical items. They prove that Marco Polo did indeed travel to the East, that his tale was not a work of fiction."

"What about the last item?" Pietro queried and pointed at a leather bag. Dr. Gozzi had not paid it much notice, enraptured by the stunning silk and jewelry.

"I skipped right by it, imagine that," Dr. Gozzi replied. He lifted up the leather pouch and pulled out two items. The first was an object constructed out of metal in the shape of a flower. It was the size of his hand. The second was a long, thin metal rod with a black bird at one end and an elaborate set of hatch marks at the other.

Pietro leaned over. "What is it, Signori?"

Dr. Gozzi continued to look at the items closely. "I don't know what these objects are."

The director felt a wave of tiredness wash over him and he sat down in a chair by the table. "Pietro, I feel obligated to ask you this. Where did you get this chest from?"

Pietro hesitated. "My uncle...he passed away and gave it to me."

"Where did he get it?"

Pietro sighed. "Signori, I cannot lie to you. I did not get this from my uncle. I found it in a drained canal behind San Marco. It has been underwater for a very long time."

Dr. Gozzi looked over at the chest. He stood up and examined the chest more closely. The craftsmanship was extraordinary. There was an inner lining within the chest and a resin-like material that sealed the chest from the inside. *Centuries under the canal and not a drop of water!* It was either a miracle or an engineering marvel. The chest had certainly been prepared for the elements.

"There is something else I must tell you, Signori. You were not the first person I have shown this to. I regret this very much. I showed it to an antiquity dealer, Girolamo Paolo. He was very excited about the finding and urged me not to tell anyone of it. He said that he could find a patron who would pay a considerable sum for the items. He said we would both be rich. Two days later he was found dead, murdered."

Dr. Gozzi had heard about the murder of Girolamo Paolo in the local newspapers. He was found floating in the canal, his throat slit. The preliminary stages of investigation by the carabinieri revealed that Paolo had strong ties to the black market trade in antiquities and interacted with many unscrupulous individuals. The general feeling was that Paolo was a victim of his work.

"Signori, I am afraid that whoever killed Paolo is now after me. I went back to my apartment and found it turned upside down. Now every street I walk down, I sense that I am being watched and followed."

Dr. Gozzi frowned. "You must go to the carabinieri."

"What will the carabinieri do? They will find out that I found the chest in the canal. It will be taken away from me. You know how the government is about protecting antiquities. They will call me a grave robber, a looter stealing items of Italian cultural heritage. This is my ticket to a better life. Day in and day out I have slaved to protect this city. I was meant to find this chest. It is my reward."

The director squeezed his chin. "What can I do?"

"The library has money. Buy it from me. You are a good man. I trust you to do the right thing."

Dr. Gozzi thought about it. He looked over at the table. He would have to convince the Board of Directors as the merits of such a purchase. This should not be too difficult. After all, prior exhibits on Marco Polo were always anticlimactic because so few artifacts could be shown that were connected to the man. Indeed, in 1954 for the 700th jubilee of Marco Polo's birth, the celebration displayed only several of Marco Polo's books in French and Italian and maps of the world that were made long after his death. This was one of the most incredible findings during Dr. Gozzi's career. It belonged in the library right beside Marco Polo's last will and testament. There was no way the Board would say no to his request. He just needed proof that these items were authentic.

"I will see what I can do. In the meantime, I would like very much to study these artifacts further to ensure that they are what I think they are. This takes time. I promise to keep them safe," Dr. Gozzi replied.

"Yes, Signori. It is safer here with you. I will be leaving Venice for the time being. I will return in a week. Hopefully, by then we will have an answer."

Pietro walked to the door and waited as Dr. Gozzi unlocked it. Turning back, Pietro smiled. "Life is strange, how things turn out. This canal wasn't even scheduled to be drained originally. It's fate."

Dr. Gozzi returned the smile. "Pietro, be careful."

Pietro looked out the door, the smile disappearing. "You too."

12
NYC

The knock at the door startled Alex, stirring him from sleep. He raised his head off his workbench and groggily stretched his neck so he could peer over the top of two stacks of books piled high beside him. He could see the doorknob slowly turn. The dilapidated door responded with a rattle and finally opened with a sudden pop. He could see Ellie's head poke through the opening with a smile. She scanned the narrow confines of the office.

"Anyone home?"

Alex gripped each of the piles of books and spread them apart so she could see him.

"There you are. Hiding?" Ellie bounced into the room with a bag slung over her left shoulder. In her right hand, she held a stuffed white plastic bag. She raised the bag higher in the air so Alex could see it. "I brought some Chinese food...a little tribute to Marco Polo. By the way, Cyrus says hello."

"Some security he is. He'll let anybody in," Alex smiled and stretched his hands above his head.

"And to think all it took was two fortune cookies and a spring roll." Ellie cleared off a space on top of a file cabinet and began to remove the white paper cartons. She glanced over her shoulder at the pile of books on his workbench.

"What are those for?" she asked as she ripped open the red chopstick wrapper and broke apart the wooden chopsticks.

"The books?"

"That's right."

"It's Graham," Alex replied and rolled his eyes. "He needs a canned lecture on the Black Death for when he comes back."

Ellie handed Alex the chopsticks and returned to looking through the plastic bag. "Damn it. They forgot plates. I hope you don't mind just eating from the cartons. I got Chicken Lo Mein, spring rolls, and beef with broccoli."

"I don't mind. I was inoculated for cooties when I was five," Alex said with a smirk as he accepted the distinctive paper carton from Ellie. "This is a great surprise."

Ellie drove her chopsticks into the carton of Chicken Lo Mein and tweezed out a bundle of noodles.

"I have some news," Ellie announced mid-chew. Alex's eyes peered up from the carton of beef with broccoli.

"Hum," he responded.

"I got in touch with Bernardo. He only wanted to see an image of the box so I took some photos and emailed them to him. Let's just say that he was very excited by the box. He said that he had recently come in possession of other articles that may be connected to Marco Polo and was eager to examine the box."

"That's great…except for the distance of course."

Ellie pulled aside a chair, sat cross-legged on it, and balanced the carton of Lo Mein on her lap. "That's the crazy part. He wants us to come to Venice with the box. And he wants us to come as soon as possible."

Alex shot her a skeptical glance. "Us? Go to Venice?" Ellie nodded her head. He looked at the two towers of books on his workbench and a paper with notes jotted down on the Black Death.

"Ellie, I have all this work to do. There's the Cross exhibition coming up, Graham's going to be back soon and will want this lecture completed, and not to mention the biggest issue, I'm broke." Alex lowered his shoulders with disappointment.

Ellie grabbed Alex's knees and swiveled his chair until he was fully facing her.

"Do you really want to be Graham's lackey?"

"I could lose my fellowship," Alex answered and placed the Chinese carton on his workbench.

"Maybe. Heh, you're the one that sucked me into this mystery. I was perfectly happy to wallow in my own misery. Besides, we could try and get back before Graham returns. It might be a nice distraction. When's he due back?"

"A couple of weeks…I'm not exactly sure."

"That's plenty of time," Ellie pouted.

Alex squeezed his chin and shook his head. *There is something special about the box. I need to know what.*

"Even if I could sneak out of here, I couldn't even scrape up enough to buy a ticket. They're so much when you buy them just before you leave."

"I'll take that as a conditional yes," Ellie responded with a devilish smile. She leaned back, twisted her hand into her bag, and removed an envelope. Ellie handed it to Alex and resumed eating her noodles.

"What's this?" Alex asked as he flipped the tab of the envelope open and peered inside.

"I forgot to tell you the best part. Bernardo was so excited by our finding, he sent us two plane tickets to Venice."

"When?" Alex raised his eyebrows.

"Tomorrow. Better get packing," Ellie replied with a devilish smile before popping a piece of broccoli into her mouth.

13
Venice, Italy

Dr. Gozzi felt like he hadn't slept for days. His office was quickly becoming a disaster zone with books piled high, threatening to teeter over and collapse in a heap onto the floor. The items from the chest were splayed out on a large canvas stretched across the floor of his office. He scratched nervously at the stubble on his face and stood with his arms folded, looking down at the canvas.

Venice was on edge. Two high-profile murders within one week of each other had the carabinieri working overtime. First, there was the antiquity dealer, Girolamo Paolo, found floating with his neck slit in a canal, and last night, to Dr. Gozzi's dismay, the civil engineer, Pietro Zeno. He could remember the uncertainty and fear in Pietro's eyes as he departed the library that eventful night last week. A store clerk had found Pietro's body slumped over in an alleyway, his carotid artery severed. Pietro's paranoia proved to be well-deserved, which meant that Dr. Gozzi was likely next. He didn't have much time: not much time at all.

The last week was a blur. He felt closer than ever to unwrapping the mystery of the chest. A clue came from an unlikely and unexpected source, a figure from his past. Pietro had earlier questioned if it was fate that he discovered the chest after all these centuries buried under water. Dr. Gozzi was not a superstitious soul but if the return of Harold Griffin's daughter into his life after all these years was not enough, her apparent discovery of a box related to Marco Polo was well…miraculous to say the least. He was not a religious man, but this past week was almost enough to send him back to the folds of the Church. He glanced across the room and caught the image of the box Eleanor discovered still displayed on his computer screen and grimaced.

When she had contacted him about the box several days ago, he could barely contain his excitement. And when he saw the symbols on the box, he was captivated by it. He urged Eleanor and her colleague to visit him as soon as possible so he could examine the box in person. Now they were on their way to Venice and he had unwittingly exposed them to danger. Pietro was now dead. Whoever had killed him most certainly now knew that he possessed the chest's contents. Dr. Gozzi peered down at the items on the canvas again and allowed his lips to curl into a smile. *Not all the contents,* he thought to himself. He had made sure that the mystery would not die with him. He looked down at the ducal crest and felt a kinship to Falier that spanned the centuries. *What were the words Lord Byron placed in Falier's mouth as the axe was falling?* Dr. Gozzi asked himself.

Strike as I struck the foe! Strike as I would
Have struck those tyrants! Strike deep as my curse!
Strike — and but once!

Dr. Gozzi could hear footsteps against the marble floor outside his office. *They are here already!* He quickly made his way to the chair behind his desk, sat down, and moved the mouse across the computer. He typed in the email address, skipped the subject, and quickly typed in a message. The footsteps grew louder. He wished he could write more. He hoped she would understand. After he had sent the email, he brought up his recent correspondences one by one and sent them to the trash bin. With a click of the button, the virtual trash bin was emptied.

He swiveled his chair around and stared at the door. The doorknob silently turned. With a creak, the door swung open.

Dr. Gozzi brought his hands together and rested them on his lap. He looked at the figures standing in the doorway.

"What took you so long?" he asked with the faintest smile.

14

Ellie couldn't help but grin as she emerged from the Stazione Ferroviaria Santa Lucia, the main train station in Venice. She slipped on a pair of sunglasses and watched as Alex dragged two small suitcases behind him towards the vaporetto. To her left she could see the exquisite columns of the Scalzi Church on the bank of the canal, providing a stark contrast to the modern exterior of the neighboring train station.

She felt at home.

Some of her earliest and fondest memories were of Venice and of 'Uncle Bernardo.' One of her father's oldest and dearest friends, Bernardo Gozzi, would host her family for weeks during the summertime after the university had let out. They would wander through the narrow alleyways and along the canals for hours with Bernardo acting as an impromptu tour guide. He would point out some of the lesser-known facts about the ancient city one would not find in a guidebook. Each decaying palace, archway, and church had a story, and Bernardo reveled in telling these tales with a bravado that enraptured Ellie when she was a young girl.

Several years after her parents died, she spent the summer in Venice at Bernardo's flat. She had yet to go to college and was a fairly typical teenager filled with angst and uncertainty about her future. It was a pivotal summer for her as she fought the demons from her past and emerged at the end a stronger and more focused woman. She spent hours exploring the city on her own, creating charcoal sketches of the wonderful architecture, and staring silently at the gondolas bobbing up and down in the Grand Canal. Bernardo seemed to recognize that Ellie needed something that only she could provide herself and gave her the space to do so. By the end of that summer, the timelessness of Venice had seeped into her soul and had helped heal her. And like a chick hatching, she left broken pieces of shell behind.

Ellie had not seen Bernardo since that summer. She had been consumed by her dedication to the field of antiquities and found her interest stretch away from the European continent to the Middle East. Bernardo always remembered her birthday and never forgot an important event such as a graduation, but he, too, had gotten wrapped up in his work. *It will be good to see Bernardo again*, Ellie thought as she took the stairs two steps at a time.

Alex waved to her as the water taxi neared the pier. Once the flat-bottomed boat was moored, they boarded and made their way to the railing. They waited as a throng of tourists lugging oversized suitcases crammed onto the boat. The motor began to croak, sending reverberations through the vessel. Alex and Ellie leaned over the railing as the boat pulled away and made its way towards the next stop.

"It's amazing that you know Bernardo Gozzi," Alex said as he looked sideways at Ellie. Her hair was golden in the brilliant sunlight, her eyes a turquoise blue. "His book on Marco Polo is a classic. If anyone can help us out, it is him."

Ellie nodded. Her eyes followed a small, motorized pleasure boat as it traveled rapidly down the canal, sending a small wake towards their boat. The water taxi rocked back and forth in response. "I can't wait to see those items in the chest. Between those items and this box, Bernardo is on his way to arranging a phenomenal exhibition for the library. You know, it's a little embarrassing to admit it but I never read Marco Polo's *Description of the World* before this trip. After reading through it on the flight and the train ride from Milan, I have to admit, Alex, that it is not all that good of a read."

Alex stared down at the water. "I know what you are saying. It's a criticism that has been leveled at the book ever since it was published. It can be dry and boring. Sometimes it seems like just a catalogue of different cities and local customs. But you have to put it into the context of the times. When Marco Polo set out for the East in search of fortune with his uncle, Maffeo, and his father, Nicoló, in 1271, he was fifteen. He had spent his entire life in Venice. Although there had been trade with the East for some time, the East remained alien to most Europeans.

"The Europeans considered themselves heirs to the great empires of the past like the Romans and Greeks. And Venice considered itself at the time to be the rising superpower of Europe. It had gotten rich providing maritime travel during the Crusades and controlled a large share of the wealth of Constantinople. The Venetians felt that their world had to be the most advanced and enlightened civilization. Imagine what it must have felt like when Marco Polo traveled across the East into the Mongol empire and to China only to discover the varied cultures out there. These cultures were not only wondrous and exotic but had even *greater* wealth, scientific achievements, and social order than anything in Europe at the time. It must have been a real eye opener.

"What is even more extraordinary is that Marco Polo, after spending the next seventeen years in the East at the service of the great Mongol ruler, Kublai Khan, survived the trip back to Venice to tell his tale. Imagine the perspective he had on the world. He was not a writer and probably never had a formal education. In fact, as you know, the legend is that the book was written by the ghostwriter, Rustichello of Pisa, while the two of them were imprisoned in a Genoan jail in 1298. In the end though, there is nothing magical about *The Description of the World*. It is not a fantasy story like *The Arabian Nights*. There are no genies in bottles or flying carpets. Marco Polo was a merchant who traveled East and simply lived to tell of what he saw. He was merely helping to define the world."

Ellie was quiet. She folded her hands on the railing and rested her chin on it. She tilted her head towards Alex. "Maybe I'm a romantic, but I'd like to think there is more to the story of Marco Polo—that maybe there is a little magic. There seems to be so little known about the man, after all. It's almost like he disappeared for seventeen years in the service of the Khan, returned to Venice to write the tale, and promptly fell off the face of the earth until he died. There's just so little known about him."

Alex smiled and patted his satchel. "Maybe this box might just help clear up some of the mysteries. I can't wait to see what Dr. Gozzi thinks of it." The water taxi slowly zigzagged across the canal. Along the horizon, the sun was beginning to set, creating mesmerizing silhouettes. The buildings of Venice stood like darkened facades against a backdrop of oranges and reds.

15

Alex folded the wooden shutters back and stared out the window of the hotel at the street below. Ellie sat on the edge of the bed and tried to flatten a piece of paper, which repeatedly curled itself again on the bedside table. She retrieved a pen provided by the hotel, recopied the phone number on a new piece of paper, and lifted the phone to her ear.

Alex looked around the room. It was nearly identical to his room several doors away, even down to the small bed in the center of the room and a painting of a gondola passing beneath the Ponte di Rialto. He felt a sense of impatience welling up inside his body. It was a feeling he commonly got when traveling—an immediate desire to drop off his bags at the hotel or hostel and begin to explore the city. He pushed his head out of the window. Warm air blew against his face. He could hear the laughter of a couple strolling arm-in-arm below.

"This is strange. I've tried Bernardo's number and nobody is answering. He knew that we were coming in at this time. This is very unlike Bernardo not to be here for a grand welcome. He would always greet my family with a big basket of wine, cheese, and salami. When I was a child, he would bring me a tin of that black licorice with colored fillings. And, I know he is dying to see the wooden box." Ellie gripped the receiver against her chest in thought. Alex watched as she bit her lip with frustration. In the little time he had spent with Ellie, he had quickly become acquainted with her quirky mannerism—the slight curl of her lips when she was embarrassed, the squint of her eyes when she was getting mad but had not yet exploded, and of course, the nibbling of her lip when she was bothered.

"Maybe he forgot when we were coming in or something important came up. I'm sure he'll call," Alex offered and slumped down into a plush chair. He nonchalantly flipped through a magazine highlighting the museums of Venice. He stopped at an advertisement for the Museo Archeologico.

"Yeah maybe…it's just not like him to forget." Ellie rummaged through her bag and withdrew her cellphone. She turned it on and began to navigate through the commands until she was able to bring up her email account.

"There's an email from Bernardo," Ellie said with a touch of relief. A look of confusion prompted Alex to rise from the chair and kneel beside Ellie. The email message lacked a reference line. The message was a jumbled mess of letters:

VSMHMCBUYMSBLAVSMYJPRHANDM

"Well, that's not much help," Alex snorted. "It looks like the message got corrupted or something."

"It was sent last night," Ellie added. She stared at the screen, her chin scrunched up against the ball of her hand. "I guess we'll meet up with him tomorrow at the library." She shook her head as if to refocus her thoughts. "What do you think about getting out of here and grabbing some food?"

"I could be dragged," Alex responded. He had not been in Venice since a backpacking trip in college across Europe and was eager to explore the city again.

Ellie squeezed the cell phone into her pocket and watched as Alex grabbed a coat and made for the door. She lingered momentarily on the edge of the bed, trying to suppress her anxiety. *Something is wrong.*

16

The Piazza San Marco was abuzz with tourists as Alex and Ellie emerged early the next morning from Calle Cavalietto and entered the large expanse. A flock of pigeons suddenly sprung skyward as a small child wildly charged at them with a squeal. The flap of the wings echoed across the open space, temporarily drowning out dueling pianists performing at the edges of the outdoor dining sections of the Caffé Florian and Gran Caffé Quadri.

Although it was not the geographic center of the city, the Piazza San Marco was truly the core of Venetian life. It had existed in some form since the ninth century and as the city's prestige increased through trade, the architecture grew more elaborate and eclectic.

"It's just so refreshing to be free of cars and trucks. It feels like New York is a million miles away," Ellie said with a smile.

The ban on motorized travel within the city-limits was truly liberating to Alex as well. He slowly spun around to marvel at the Procuraties, the three interconnecting buildings that served as the north, south, and west perimeters of the square. To his left, the Procuratie Vecchie stretched towards the grounds of the Basilica di San Marco. An elaborate building composed of archways, the Procuratie Vecchie had been transformed into a commercial arcade selling everything from watches to coffee. The Procuratie Nuove was located directly across the square from the Procuratie Vecchie and was constructed in a more classical style with graying columns and black-framed windows. Alex turned back to see the Napoleonic Wing of the Procuraties bridge the two buildings along the western perimeter. The two-story wing displayed a large red banner advertising the Museo Correr that was housed within it.

Ellie squeezed Alex's arm and motioned to the Basilica ahead. "The Basilica always takes my breath away. I spent days sketching that building when I was a teenager."

The Basilica di San Marco sat at the eastern side of the piazza. This seemed only appropriate to Alex. Unlike many of the cathedrals that were constructed on the European continent during the Middle Ages, the Basilica combined both gothic and Byzantine elements. It was a testament to the duality of Venice, a western city-state with close Eastern ties.

Alex nodded his head. "I couldn't agree more. Now when I look at it I can't help but think how 'Venice' the building is. It reminds me that Venice was the perfect city for an individual like Marco Polo to come of age. I can see a fifteen-year-old Marco Polo waiting for the return of a father who left for the East before he was born. I can see him staring at the boats returning from the East filled with wondrous spices and crafts and imagining what these exotic lands were like." They walked in silence, taking in the square.

"Not to harp on the whole cross thing again, but the floor plan of the Basilica is based on the Greek cross," Alex added as they strolled across the piazza. Ellie watched as he traced out the design across the palm of his hand with his finger. "Each of the arms of the cross has a dome associated with it. The fifth dome is at the point in which the arms meet. It has a similar design to the Hagia Sophia in Istanbul and the Church of the Holy Apostles that was constructed by Constantine, the first Roman Emperor who embraced Christianity. The Church of the Holy Apostles apparently held many relics of the early Christian apostles, like the skull of Saint Andrew. It was unfortunately destroyed and looted during the Fourth Crusade. Some of the relics ended up in Venice and in the Basilica."

Ellie couldn't help but be impressed by Alex's knowledge, especially for a graduate student.

"Isn't Saint Mark's body in the Basilica?" Ellie asked as they instinctively ducked to avoid being captured in a tourist's photo of Saint Mark's Campanile, the bell-tower that loomed over the piazza.

"It's an interesting story and makes you wonder even more what Marco Polo could have brought back from his trip. The legend goes that Venetian merchants stole relics related to Saint Mark from Alexandria, Egypt—some say the actual remains of the saint. In order to get them out of Muslim territory, the relics were hidden in a barrel of pork. Needless to say, it got past inspection as no Muslim guard was willing to come in contact with the pork fat. When the merchants returned to Venice, the relics were installed in the church for safe-keeping. Venice's patron saint was changed from Saint Theodore to Mark. There's a mosaic in the Basilica that depicts the whole sequence of events."

They walked past the bell-tower and turned into a smaller courtyard in front of the Palazzo Ducale, the Doge's Palace. The palace had a faintly pink and white color and was constructed of archways on the ground floor. A series of columns composed the façade of the second level, capped by a series of Greek crosses. Once the seat of power for the Venetian republic and the home of the doges, the palace was now a well-maintained museum.

Across from the Doge's Palace, there was a considerable amount of activity in front of the Biblioteca Marciana. A group of carabinieri mingled around in front of a wooden ramp leading into the library. A barrier had been erected in front of the entrance. Alex could hear a police officer explaining to a woman clutching a camera in broken English that the library was closed and he did not know when it would open.

"What's going on?" Ellie asked rhetorically and pushed her way up against the barrier. Alex tried to stay close.

"Scusi," Ellie interrupted as she popped her head up in front of the officers. "The library is closed?" The officer nodded and tried to push her away from the barrier. Ellie glanced back at Alex with confusion. She tapped the officer on the shoulder who looked at her with growing anger. "We are here to see Dr. Gozzi...Bernardo Gozzi...the director of the library. He is expecting us. It is very important." The officer's demeanor seemed to change all of a sudden and he looked at Ellie and then Alex with a sober expression. "Please, wait here."

"This is strange," Alex muttered under his breath as he watched the officer retreat into the building. After waiting five minutes, a man wearing a dark suite walked down the ramp and approached them. His hair was oiled back and his skin was pockmarked from acne as a child. As he neared Ellie, she could smell a sour scent of cigarettes clinging to his clothes. He silently nodded to both Alex and Ellie and appeared to be sizing them up.

"You say you are here to see Dr. Gozzi?" the man asked with a squint.

"Yes. What's all this?" Ellie asked, motioning around her.

"I'm Inspector Calvino. Would you please come with me? I would like to ask you some questions in a more discreet setting." He pushed aside the wooden barrier slightly with his hip, allowing Ellie and Alex to pass by.

As they followed the Inspector up the ramp, Ellie asked, "Is everything alright with Bernardo?" The Inspector looked back over his shoulder, appeared to begin to speak, and decided against it while outside.

Once inside the library they were directed into a small coatroom. The inspector closed the door and asked them to sit behind a cheap folding table. He slowly withdrew a Mont Blanc pen and a notepad from his pocket, placed it on the table, and sat down across from them.

"Who are you?" asked the inspector.

Ellie and Alex looked at each other with uncertainty. "I'm Eleanor Griffin and this is Alexander Stone. We are visiting from the United States. Bernardo Gozzi is a close family friend. We just recently arrived."

The Inspector wrote on his pad in silence and slowly raised his head and looked at Ellie without emotion. "I'm afraid that Dr. Gozzi is dead."

"What?!" Ellie blurted out. A look of dread spread across her face. "Dead. There must be some mistake." Alex instinctively reached out and gripped her shoulder. Ellie's eyes began to fill with tears.

"I'm sorry, but he is very much dead. He was found wrapped in a rug and beaten to death."

"Who would do this?" Alex asked

The inspector crossed his arms, pulled out a cigarette from his pocket and lit it. "It's hard to say. We have a bit of a crime wave in the city. This is the third homicide in the past two weeks. It's not good for tourism, not good for the city. Did he say anything to you recently that may have seemed unusual? Did he indicate any concerns for his safety?" inquired the inspector.

"No, he was very excited to see us. He was elated about the discovery of the chest with the artifacts of Marco Polo," Ellie responded.

The inspector peered up from his notepad. "A chest?"

"Yes. He was studying items recovered from a chest. We were going to show him…"

Alex interrupted Ellie. "…what we thought." Alex nudged Ellie's knee under the table. She gave him a suspicious look.

"We have not found a chest. This is interesting," replied the inspector. "What was in this chest?"

"We don't know. We never saw the chest. He thought it contained artifacts related to Marco Polo's trip," Ellie answered.

Inspector Calvino looked down at his notepad and began to

write in it. He held the pad at an angle that prevented Alex and Ellie from seeing what he was jotting down. After some time, he glanced up.

"Marco Polo, you say? The explorer?" muttered the Inspector.

Ellie nodded her head impatiently. She gave Alex a sideways glance filled with uncertainty and despair.

The corners of the Inspector's mouth curled up into an unnerving smile. "Interesting."

The Inspector pulled out a business card from his wallet and slid it across the table. Ellie was taken aback by the suddenness in which the interview had ended.

"Thank you for taking the time to speak to me. Here is my card. Please do not hesitate to call me if you think of anything that may aid in this investigation. We will be in touch if we have any more questions. I am sorry for your loss."

"Who did this?" Ellie asked mournfully.

Inspector Calvino flipped his wallet shut and slipped it into his suit pocket. His fingers continued to explore the contents of the pocket until he came away with a cigarette. He held it in his hand like a pencil and tapped it against the tabletop.

"Who can say?" he shrugged. "Let us worry about it."

17

"*I'm cursed. Everybody I love seems to die. It's all pretty Shakespearean, really.* You may not want to stand so close to me. A meteor might stream out of the sky and hit us," Ellie muttered and gave a pained chuckle.

Alex stood stiffly behind her, uncertain of what to say. He watched silently as Ellie crouched beside two stone pillars on the quay of the piazzetta staring blankly across the water at the Isola di San Giogio Margiore. Alex positioned himself next to her and peered down at the rippling water of the basin. An iridescent film of oil clung to the surface.

"Why didn't you let me tell the inspector about why we are actually here, about the wooden box?" Ellie asked.

"I don't know. It just didn't seem right. I got this vibe that the inspector wasn't being up front with us, especially about the chest that Dr. Gozzi was studying. Whoever killed Dr. Gozzi probably stole the chest and the items within it. In fact, maybe Dr. Gozzi was killed *for* the chest. If so, maybe we shouldn't be broadcasting about the existence of a compendium piece. We could be next."

"What if telling them about the wooden box might aid them in their investigation and help them catch whoever did this to Bernardo?" Ellie asked. She picked up a small stone and tossed it into the basin.

"You could be right. We can always contact the inspector. He left us his card. I just wonder if Dr. Gozzi was trying to tell us something with the email you got—if he was attempting to convey a message to us. What if he was hurt when he wrote the email and didn't have the faculties to type it properly?" Alex wondered aloud.

Ellie pulled out the cell phone from her pocket and turned it on. She brought up Dr. Gozzi's final email. Ellie stared at the jumbled series of letters, trying to make sense of it. They appeared to be arranged with no rhyme or reason.

Alex leaned over her shoulder. "Does any of it make sense? It's like a different language."

Different language, Ellie thought. *Could it be?* She turned to Alex with a look of urgency.

"Alex, could you grab a pen and paper from my bag. Quickly, please! See if there is a book for me to lean on."

Alex rummaged through her bag pushing aside the wooden box. He finally located a booklet containing train schedules, a pen from the hotel, and a small pad of paper. He passed them to Ellie who snatched them up and sat Indian-style on the stone surface. She began to feverishly write letters vertically along the left side of the paper. Alex could see that the letters that stretched across the paper like Chinese characters were simply in alphabetical order. Ellie began to create another column of letters beside the first column. Unlike the first column, the letters were not in alphabetical order but did contained twenty-six characters.

AP
BY
CR
DA
EM
FI
GD
HS
IB
JF

KH
LJ
MK
NL
ON
PO
QQ
RT
SU
TV
UW
VX
WZ
XE
YC
ZG

Ellie paused and looked back at Alex.

"When you said *it was like a different language*, it got me thinking. When I was a little girl, my family used to visit Bernardo every summer. He was the best—he was like an oversized kid. You have to understand; I was one of those precocious kids that desperately wanted to be sophisticated. I was mad about James Bond at the time. In fact, I wanted more than anything to be a spy traveling the world, engaging in espionage, and decoding secret messages. Bernardo entertained this and had the idea of creating a language that only we could understand. I thought it was the most brilliant idea in the history of ideas. I haven't thought of it for a long time, but I think I remember it."

"It's actually a very basic cipher. In fact, he based it on a substitution or shift cipher that was made famous by Julius Caesar during his campaign in Gaul. All Caesar did was create a cipher that shifted the alphabet a predetermined number of letters. For example, in a four-shift substitution cipher, the letter 'a' would be replaced with 'e' and 'b' would be substituted with 'f,' and so on until each of the twenty-six letters had a corresponding replacement letter."

"Now our cipher was a bit more complex than Caesar's. We used a keyword, actually two keywords, that only we knew. These keywords served to shift the alphabet." Ellie pointed to the second list. The keywords are composed of non-repeating letters and are located at either end of the list. The first keyword we used was in tribute to my father: 'pyramids.' The second keyword was my initials: 'ECG.'"

"If we use the ciphered alphabet as the template…

VSMHMCBUYMSBLAVSMYJPRHANDM

Becomes…."

Ellie hummed softly as she substituted each letter with a corresponding letter from the ciphered alphabet.

THEKEYISBEHINDTHEBLACKDOGE."

Ellie drew slashes across the message.

THE/KEY/IS/BEHIND/THE/BLACK/DOGE

"The key is behind the black doge," Alex read off the paper. He glanced back at the beautiful loggia of the Doge's Palace. His eyes drifted up to the balcony of the Waterfront façade that overlooked the quay and back down to the stone statue of a fallen Eve, holding aloft the forbidden fruit in her right hand.

"What does it mean?" Ellie asked, her eyes suddenly wide with wonder.

Alex extended his hand and helped Ellie up. She brushed pebbles off her pants and grabbed her bag.

"You probably already know this, but the doges were the ceremonial leaders of the Venetian republic entrusted to provide fatherly wisdom to the governing body and to entertain visiting dignitaries. The first doge, or dux, as he was known in the Venetian dialect was installed in the seventh century and the last doge ruled through to the late eighteenth century. During this time span, there were a ton of doges—some more influential than others. We're only steps from the most important building in the doges' lives."

Alex pointed towards the grand building across from the Biblioteca Marciana.

"The doges ate, slept, and worked in the palace. They rarely were permitted to leave the building. Some have called the palace a gilded cage in that the doge was very much controlled by the representative council of nobles."

"Who was the 'black doge?" Ellie asked.

"I've never heard the term before. I don't think any of the doges were black in the sense of skin color."

"What if 'black' refers to a quality of the doge—like an evil nature," Ellie offered.

"It's an interesting thought. There were two dark periods of Venetian history. The first was when a Venetian noble named Bajamonte Tepielo tried to overthrow the Venetian government and the doge. The second was when a doge named Marin Falier tried to stage a coup of his own to overthrow the republic. It failed and he had his head chopped off not too far from here. If there ever was an evil doge, most would probably say it was Falier."

"I've heard this name before. Bernardo used to talk about him, especially when he used to take us on tours through the city," Ellie responded.

"It's got to be Falier that he is talking about in his message. But what does he mean that the key is behind Falier? One thing is certain, Dr. Gozzi felt that it was important enough to pass a message to us and convey that message in a code that no one but *you* could translate."

"My God, Alex. Bernardo must have known he was in danger!" Ellie scanned the piazzetta suspiciously. She suddenly felt profoundly guilty. Bernardo was dead and instead of feeling depressed, she was buoyed by the excitement of deciphering the message. The mystery of the chest, the box, and Bernardo's secret message were all consuming and she felt intoxicated by the prospect of running full-speed ahead into this quest.

"Where do we start?" Ellie asked.

Alex slid his arm under Ellie's and began to walk towards the Porta del Frumento, the seventeenth-century gateway into the palace along the waterfront that served as the modern-day entrance to the museum.

"If you are looking for the doge, let's start at the top."

18

"*It's all here...sort of,*" *Martin said. He impatiently scratched the back of his* neck and then flicked the tip of his index finger across the stubble on his cheek. The glow of the computer screen reflected off his glasses and mixed with the smoke rising from the cigarette precariously perched on a makeshift ash-tray.

"I can always count on you, my boy," Solomon smiled and patted Martin on the shoulder.

He had come to rely heavily on Martin's computer expertise of late and considered him to be a crucial member of the team. Martin couldn't fire a gun for shit (he would probably blow off his foot before he could lift it). His nervous tics were distracting, but he was a wizard with technology and technology was the name of the game these days. Why blow down a door with C4 if you could delicately unlock the same door with a string of keystrokes. With all the money that was floating around in the ether and the ghostly world of wire transfers, Martin was a great insurance policy to certify that they all got paid at the end of the day.

He had a lot of faith in his team. They had been through a lot over the years. There were many dangerous missions and close calls — some failures but even greater successes. Solomon peered over Martin's shoulder and beyond the screen of the laptop. He could see the massive form of Ox sitting next to a small table dutifully cleaning his revolver. Picked off a farm in the *Gamadeoulis* as a teenager, Ox had served with distinction in the South Africa Defense Force during the dirty war in Rhodesia. What he lacked in keen intellect was more than compensated for by an unholy love of weaponry and an impossibly muscular frame. Behind him was Pieter, sitting upon a dilapidated sofa as he flipped through a local newspaper. Pieter was a product of the South Africa Defense Forces elite special ops unit. He was a soldier through and through—stealthy, reliable, and deadly. The two remaining members of his team, Bryce and Fredrick, were the youngest of the group. Although Bryce looked more like a professional surfer than a mercenary, he had been trained by the Australian Special Air Service Regiment, where he gained a great aptitude in jungle warfare. Finally, Fredrick was a humorless German from the Kommando SpezialKraefte, whose skills as a sniper were essential for several prior missions. His words were few and his gunshots even fewer.

"Who would have thought that old guy was such a sneaky S.O.B." Martin blurted out, disturbing Solomon's thoughts. "Gozzi attempted to erase a series of email messages about thirty-seconds before we busted into his office."

"Attempted?" Solomon asked, realizing Martin was once again sucking him into one of his patented "ta-dah" theatrical performances.

"Nothing really *disappears* from the internet. There are always trails and ghosts. If you know where to look, you can dig up the bone, so to speak. It seems that Gozzi was engaging in an email correspondence with a certain Eleanor Griffin and Alexander Stone."

Solomon watched with arms crossed as Martin retrieved a series of emails. Solomon read through the emails as Martin clicked through them.

"This attachment from Eleanor Griffin may interest you." Martin brought the arrow of the mouse to the attachment icon and clicked on it. A digital image of a wooden box appeared on the screen.

"Son of a bitch!" Solomon muttered through clenched teeth.

It's the Polo box! He nearly laughed. The events in Mosul were as close to a disaster as possible. To begin with, one of his men got trigger-happy and plugged the Arab antiquity dealer too soon. Then the Americans arrived much quicker than his well-paid intelligence predicted. They were lucky to get out of there with their lives. He did think it was a nice touch to booby-trap the store and draw in the insurgents for a fireworks show. It allowed for a tidy exit. Phillip, his mysterious patron, was livid with the outcome but did agree to transfer funds to cover the cost of the mission.

"There's more. The last message that Gozzi sent looked like this:

VSMHMCBUYMSBLAVSMYJPRHANDM."

Martin grinned. "Looks like verbal vomit, huh. Well I had a hunch and ran it through your basic military grade decryption program that I had lying around from that Caspian pipeline thing we did a while back and you get several permutations each with different weights of confidence."

Solomon stared at the screen and saw a series of rearrangements of the letters, most of which still did not make much grammatical sense.

"The computer predicts with a 99.985% confidence that the message Gozzi sent says:

THE KEY IS BEHIND THE BLACK DOGE

"O.K," Solomon answered, uncertain of what the message meant. He ran his hand through his hair. He quickly switched into mission mode. "Martin, we need to find out who this Eleanor Griffin and Alexander Stone are. We need to locate them."

Martin smiled and scratched his cheeks with both hands. "One step ahead of you, boss. I took the liberty of tracking them down. Eleanor Griffin is a professor of Mesopotamian history at

New York University and incidentally a member of MART. She might not be too fond of you."

Of course, Solomon thought. *She found the Polo box! She was in Mosul that day.*

"There's not much on Alexander Stone. He's just some graduate student from Columbia University. But, the best part is that we don't need to hop on a plane to New York because they are on their way to Venice."

"They're already here."

Solomon pulled the pistol from his holster and leveled it at the intruder. The man did not flinch at the sight of the gun and gave an amused smile. He had the look of omnipotence that only a man in law enforcement has, especially the corrupt ones. *Smug bastard*, Solomon thought. *We will take care of him in due time. Rule number one is never to leave loose ends behind.*

"Inspector," Solomon nodded and returned the pistol to his holster. Solomon motioned to Bryce and Fredrick, who having accompanied Inspector Calvino, hesitated by the door before leaving.

Inspector Calvino sauntered around the dilapidated apartment room, nodding his head. "I could find you better accommodations."

"This will do," Solomon replied, trying hard to mask the venom in his voice.

The Inspector sat down on a chair, crossed his legs, and attempted to straighten out the pleats in his pants. He removed a notepad from his pocket and flipped it open. "I had a delightful visit with Eleanor Griffin and Alexander Stone over an hour ago at the Biblioteca Marciana…"

Solomon's cell phone began to vibrate vigorously and he raised his finger to silence the Inspector. He walked into the adjoining room, shut the door, and brought the phone to his ear. He looked out of a window onto the canal below.

"Howzit?"

The voice was impatient and gruff. "I have reviewed the photos of the items from the chest you sent me. It is incomplete. There are missing items. In fact, the most important items are gone!"

Solomon felt immediately frustrated. "Why don't I go ask Dr. Gozzi what he did with it? Oh, I can't because he is dead. I killed him like you wanted me to. How about giving me some clue of just what I am looking for? It might just help both of us out. None of this secret shit."

The line grew silent and Solomon wondered if his patron had finally tired of his failures and hung up. "It is a key...a key that opens a box...the box you couldn't find for me in Mosul."

Solomon began to pace. "A key you say? Well, this is interesting. What if I told you that I might be able to get your box after all? What if I could get the key at the same time?"

"I would say my people have been waiting for a man like you for centuries. You would be well compensated for such a feat."

"Phillip, I may need your help to point me in the right direction. I believe Bernardo Gozzi hid the key before we got to him. He left a message saying, 'The key is behind the black doge.' Does it mean anything to you?"

The line grew silent again. Solomon strained to listen. It almost sounded like laughter. "More than you will ever know."

Solomon listened as Phillip spoke. When he hung up, he lingered by the window, watching a gondola stream by with a couple cuddling in the back of the boat. He instinctively patted the gun in his holster and made for the door.

Inspector Calvino and Martin looked at him as he re-entered the room. "Inspector, I need you to get us into the Doge's Palace for a private viewing."

"When?" the Inspector asked, his eyebrows raised with curiosity.

"Tonight."

19

*Alex pushed the Euros across the counter, slipped the book out of the trans-*parent bag, and retreated to the corner of the gift shop. He had searched through the limited selection of books in hope of finding either a work focusing on general Venetian history or, even better, on the history of the Venetian doges. He was disappointed to find such works absent from the gift shop's collection and settled on a glossy paperback on the history of the Doge's Palace. Alex was immediately frustrated to find that the book was little more than a guidebook geared towards the visitor desiring a self-directed tour. Small vignettes were devoted to each of the rooms that comprised the palace and schematic diagrams mapped out possible itineraries. Alex searched in vain for an index.

"Find anything useful?"

Ellie had quietly sidled up to Alex, rested her chin on his shoulder, and peered down at the book.

"It's hard to say. The palace is a pretty unique building, combining the living quarters of the doge, administrative and governing chambers, and even prison cells." Alex continued to scan through the book, stopping at a portrait of an austere looking man dressed in a pink and gold robe with an aquiline nose and sunken cheeks. The ceremonial como ducale, the bejeweled, horn-like ducal hat, sat on the camauro, a white linen cap, that was snuggly fitted to the man's head. The figure held a long strip of parchment in his left hand, listing his accomplishments during his tenure as doge.

"Is that Marin Falier?" Ellie inquired.

Alex read the fine print in the caption. "It's a portrait of

Doge Mario Babarigo by the painter Domenico Tintoretto. I'm not sure if there will be much on Falier here," Alex pronounced. "Maybe we are headed down the wrong road. I think Falier had a palace that has been converted into a hotel somewhere in Venice. Maybe that's the place we should start. Hell, who knows if the 'black doge' even refers to Falier in the first place."

"Look Alex, the way I see it is the museum closes in about two hours." She produced two tickets and waved them in front of Alex. "We already bought the tickets. I say we see what we can find on Falier here. At the very least, we might see what the guy looks like. I wonder if he is as creepy looking as, what's his name? Doge Mario Babarigo," Ellie smiled as she read the name off the page. She reached out and took the book from Alex's hands and made for the entranceway to the palace.

As they handed over their newly purchased tickets to an elderly woman by the entrance, Ellie folded back the book and showed the woman the portrait of the doge.

"Scusi. Do you know if there is a portrait of Doge Marin Falier?"

The woman squinted at the page, reached into her pocket, and slid reading glasses on. "Falier? No portrait of Falier."

Ellie could hear Alex sigh with disappointment. Ellie thanked the woman. As they began to walk away, they could hear the woman say, "No portrait, just nero, nero."

Alex gripped Ellie's elbow, halting her progress with the pressure from his fingers. He swung around and approached the woman again. "Nero? Black?"

"Yes, yes, black, only black…no picture," the woman stuttered.

"Where signora?" Ellie eagerly questioned as she pushed up against Alex's side.

"In the Sala del Maggiore Consiglio of course…but it is closed." The woman pointed to a placard by the entrance apologizing in multiple languages for the scheduled closure of the Sala del Maggiore Consiglio due to a restoration project.

Ellie glanced over at Alex and watched him scrunch his nose in thought. Alex thanked the woman and directed them into the Museo dell'Opera. Ellie looked around at her surroundings as Alex feverishly flipped through the book in search of the Sala del Maggiore Consiglio.

The Museo dell'Opera housed archeological artifacts from earlier incarnations of the Doge's Palace such as large capitals and columns that had been located along the waterfront arcade. The palace, as Ellie understood it, was a composite version, the piecemeal creation of numerous artists and patrons through the centuries. The palace had been destroyed so many times through its tortured history from civil disturbances and fires that many of the great works that had adorned the interiors of the buildings had been lost and recreations or replacement pieces had been placed to fill the voids.

"I found it," Alex remarked. "We need to go through the court-yard. It is on the first floor above the loggia. It's the room with the balcony overlooking the basin."

They left the Museo dell'Opera and entered the large central courtyard. A series of archways crowned the perimeter. In the center of the courtyard were two large, octagonal well-heads cast in bronze by Allbergeto and Nicoló dei Conti. An oversized, or-nate marble staircase, the Scala dei Giganti, led down from the East or Renaissance wing of the palace, which housed the doge's private apartments. Flanking the sides of the top of the stairs were two large statues of Mars and Neptune, symbols meant to conjure up Venetian land and sea dominance. One of the gilded domes of St. Mark's Basilica towered high above the stone and marble arch dedicated to Doge Francesco Foscari at the base of the staircase.

"This way." Alex reached out, delicately gripped Ellie's hand, and led her across the courtyard to a marble staircase, the Sca-la dei Censori. Ellie could feel Alex's excitement transmitted through her body and found herself periodically looking down at their hands entwined. She felt a sense of exhilaration and freedom she had not experienced for some time.

They walked up two flights of stairs and reached the level of the loggias. As they traversed the covered, arched arcade, they could see the courtyard below through the airy, expansive openings. Built into the inner walls of the loggia were stone faces of lions known as bocche di leone. In the past, Venetians would deposit accusations and complaints on folded papers into the lions' mouths for collection by the appropriate magistrature or government department.

Alex followed the map to the Scala d'Oro. The Scala d'Oro or Golden Staircase was an elaborate staircase decorated with white stucco and gold leaf that sparkled in the late-day sun. As they crossed under the archway at the foot of the staircase, Alex pivoted back to see the ducal crest of the commissioning doge, Andrea Gritti, surrounded by cherubic angels. A large, arched window loomed tall at the top of the landing. As they arrived at the first floor above the loggia, Alex turned towards the right and steered them through the old governing chambers until they were in the Liagó, a long hallway where the nobles gathered during meetings of the grand Council. Two doors led from the Liagó into the Sale del Maggiore Consiglio. Both doors had red velvet ropes stretching across the openings with signs reiterating that the chamber and adjoining rooms were closed to the public during the period of restoration.

Alex and Ellie inched as close as possible to the rope barrier and looked into the massive room. Alex brought out the book and located the section on the Sala del Maggior Consiglio.

"It says here that the Sala del Maggior Consiglio was the chamber where the legislative body of Venice met to deliberate. The Maggior Consiglio or Grand Council was composed of nobles and was presided over by the Doge and the Signoria. It was the central seat of power in Venice until the legislative power was transferred to the Senate. In 1577, a large fire destroyed much of the chamber and many works of art were almost completed damaged. The chamber was then reconstructed and filled with artwork, mostly depicting military victories of Venice."

Ellie looked around the room. There were multiple large windows along the walls of the chamber covered with thin white tapestries that allowed the sun to stream. Created out of dark wood, the walls were adorned with many prominent canvases of complex, busy paintings. The colors of the paintings were a mix of blacks, oranges, and reds and portrayed elaborate episodes of Venetian history such as a maritime battle with thousands of fighters. A balcony to the left was roped off. Several ladders were erected around the perimeter of the chamber, no doubt part of the restoration project. The ceiling was covered in its entirety by a complex arrangement of paintings enclosed by ornate, gilded frames.

"Below the ceiling is a frieze consisting of portraits of the first sixty-six doges, from Obelerio Antenoreo to Francesco Venier painted by Jacopo Tintoretto and his son, Domenico."

Ellie could see the ducal portraits running along the perimeter of the wall beneath the ceiling. There were two portraits per canvas with the neighboring doges facing each other. The canvases were separated by gold frames. The portraits ran along three of the walls. The wall closest to them did not have any portraits. Instead, Tintoretto's massive painting of *Paradise* was displayed.

Alex found a small blurb on the corner of a page and read excitedly, "It says here that 'the portrait of Doge Marin Falier who was executed for a conspiracy against the state was covered by a black curtain with the inscription: *HIC EST LOCUS MARINI FALETHRI DECAPITATI PRO CRIMINIBUS* (THIS IS THE PLACE OF MARIN FALIER, BEHEADED FOR HIS CRIMES)."

"The black doge!" Ellie exclaimed. "You were right!"

Alex smiled back at her. He scanned the portraits. "But where?"

Ellie pointed. "There, I think!" Alex squinted. In the far left corner of the room, the penultimate ducal portrait was absent. Instead, the portrait was painted over with a curtain-like swatch of black. Alex fought the urge to climb over the barrier and get a better look at the painting. A worker moving a ladder eyed him suspiciously.

"It still doesn't answer what Bernardo meant by '*The key is behind the black doge*,' Ellie offered.

"What if Dr. Gozzi hid something behind the portrait. He probably had free access to the palace. There's a ladder right next to it!"

They both grew quiet, trying to comprehend the significance of their discovery.

"Assuming you are right and there is something hidden behind the portrait, what are we going to do about it? Go to the police? We can't just waltz up to it, pull the ladder over, and take it down," Ellie noted.

"When does the museum close?" Alex asked, glancing at his watch.

"Pretty soon."

"Ever since I was a little kid, I've always wanted to sleep over at a museum," Alex muttered. Ellie eyed him skeptically.

"What are you saying, Alex? Get caught doing that as a kid, they send you back to your parents for a spanking. Get caught doing that as an adult, it's an entirely different matter."

Alex looked at the canvas where Falier's image should have been and back at Ellie.

"Well, I guess we better find a good place to hide and not get caught."

20

The wooden floor felt cool against her skin as Ellie shifted her body. Her knees pushed against the small of Alex's back. Alex responded with a grunt and inched forward slightly under the raised wooden platform that served as a prisoner's bed. He clenched the penlight between his teeth and tried to direct the light onto the pages of the guide book in an attempt to memorize the maps of the palace.

"How much longer do we have to stay like this," Ellie whispered with a tinge of annoyance. The footsteps of the museum staff had not been heard for over an hour. Alex pulled the penlight out of his mouth.

"Not much longer," Alex replied and rotated the penlight until it went off.

"Did you have to choose a prison?" she complained.

"It seemed like the best place to hide. Nobody has found us, have they?"

Ellie glanced at her surroundings from under the bed. The light that had streamed through the iron bars of the window had long since disappeared, replaced by the muted, silvery moonlight. A single small light fixture fastened to the stone wall above the opened cell door provided a limited, yellow glow, partly illuminating the stone ceiling. Ellie could see graffiti from earlier imprisoned souls carved into the stone walls.

They had crossed over from the Doge's Palace to the Prigioni Nuove, the New Prisons, shortly before the museum closed. It had gained its name to distinguish it from the old prison cells that were a part of the palace grounds. They had taken the narrow

Ponte dei Sospiri, the so-called "Bridge of Sighs," the notorious bridge through which prisoners would peer through a small window at Venice and sigh that it would be the last time they would lay eyes upon the city. The Prigioni Nuove had not had a prisoner since the 1930s and had been converted into a museum where visitors could get a taste of the oppressive nature of confinement during the time in which it functioned.

Alex looked at his watch and pulled himself up from under the wooden bed and extended his hand to Ellie. Ellie stretched in pain.

"We need to be quiet," Alex urged as he led them from the prison back to the Ponte dei Sospiri. The bridge was eerie in the dark but they managed to reach the Sala dei Censori. A small light provided a modicum of illumination as they navigated under the austere portraits of magistrates painted by Tintoretto. They crept through the Sala dell'Avogaria, Sala dello Scrigno, and Sala della Milizia da Mar, stopping periodically to listen intently for any sounds of security. They heard nothing and scampered up to the first floor. They quietly retraced their earlier path, crossing into the Liagó until they stood once again in front of the scarlet rope barrier blocking entrance into the Sale del Maggiore. There were four small lights in each corner that provided enough light to see the corners of the rooms, but not much more. Moonlight shined through the veneer, white drapes causing the small stones composing the floor to sparkle brilliantly. Two fire-extinguishers were positioned against the wall in glass cases emanating a red, neon glow.

"It's beautiful…and creepy at the same time," Ellie whispered and climbed over the barrier, followed silently by Alex. They walked to the distant corner and stared up. Alex directed the light from his penlight towards the portrait but the beam barely reached it.

"We need to move that ladder over here," Alex whispered to Ellie. She nodded silently, circled a tall ladder that was fully opened resting some distance from the portrait, and gripped two of the legs. Alex grabbed the opposite two and they carefully moved it to a position beneath Falier's blackened portrait. Alex planted his foot on the bottom rung and began to climb as Ellie steadied the ladder. The ladder squeaked, sending an uncomfortable echo reverberating through the vacuous chamber. Ellie looked nervously backward, expecting to see a security guard rushing in. The room once again was plunged into silence.

Alex reached the top of the ladder, glanced down at Ellie, and smiled. In front of him was the portrait as it was described in the book. A black curtain was painted across it with the proclamation of *damnation memoriae*. Alex directed the pen light at the edges of the portrait. There was an elaborate gold frame that ran around both the covered portrait of Marin Falier and a neighboring doge who shared the same canvas. His fingertips found the edge of the frame and he leaned his body precariously to the right in an attempt to see behind the frame. Alex suddenly lost his balance and fell forward. He reached out wildly to right himself. His hold on the frame prevented him from toppling off the ladder. As his legs quivered in response to the moment of panic, he could feel the frame loosen from the wall and release. He looked down and could see Ellie staring at him with concern as she tried to steady the ladder with her torso.

Reaching up he lifted the frame off its support and clutched it tightly to his chest. The frame was remarkably heavy and he teetered at the top of the ladder. Alex slowly descended rung by rung with the portrait resting between his chest and the ladder. He sighed with relief as his feet finally made contact with the floor. Ellie helped steady the frame against the ladder.

"You did it," Ellie whispered and tenderly squeezed Alex's shoulder.

The key is behind the black doge.

Alex wiped the sweat from his forehead with his shirt and kneeled by the portraits. "Let's turn it around."

They cautiously rotated the portraits, careful not to scrape the golden frame against the floor. Ellie let out a gasp. There was a metal cylinder and leather bag taped to the back of the portrait. Alex teased the cylinder and bag from the portrait and placed them on the floor in front of them. He shined the beam of the flashlight on them but could not find any indication of their contents from the outside.

A noise from beyond the room made them both freeze. They could hear faint footsteps and voices.

"Someone's here! What do we do?" Ellie cried.

"We have to hide," Alex responded, his eyes darting around the room. He passed the cylinder and leather bag to Ellie and grabbed her hand. Ellie resisted.

"We need to put the painting back up."

"There's no time," Alex responded and pulled her towards the way they had entered the room.

"What about that room?" Ellie asked, pointing to a door near them.

"There's no way out through that room. It's a dead end. We need to go back the way we came."

They ran across the room and reached the roped barrier. Stepping over it, they peered down the Liagó. They could see flashlights bouncing around in the distance and hear footsteps walking up the stairs.

"Which way?" Ellie wondered aloud, her eyes wide with fright.

"This way." Alex pulled Ellie forward across the Liagó and into an adjacent room. They found themselves in a small chamber opposite the Sala del Maggior Consiglio. As they frantically searched for a place to hide, the voices grew louder. Finding a small desk at the far end of the room beneath a large window, they dropped to their knees and crawled across the room. As menacing shadows stretched across the doorway to the room, they pushed themselves behind the desk at the last moment.

21

The voices were at first hard to discern but grew clearer as the men approached.

"The Sala del Maggiore Consiglia is this way. Do you want me to send some carabinieri to pick up this Eleanor Griffin and Alexander Stone?"

Ellie looked at Alex with alarm at the sound of their names. The voice was familiar.

"No need to, Inspector. I've already sent one of my men to track them down. I suspect we will have this whole affair wrapped up very soon. First, let's deal with the Gozzi matter. Where is this painting?"

Alex brought his lips close to Ellie's and whispered. "I think these guys are the people who killed Dr. Gozzi. We need to get out of here. That Inspector seems to be in on it. It's only a matter of time before they realize we're here."

"What should we do?"

"Come on," Alex responded and raised Ellie to her feet. They maneuvered in the darkness along a bench running the length of the wall, careful not to step into the center of the room. As they neared the doorway into the Liagó, they crouched along the wall and looked out. They could see a small group of men dressed in black pass into the Sala del Consiglia. Ellie gasped at the sight of the barrel of a pistol held by one of the men. "They have guns," she whispered.

Alex nodded gravely and slowly nudged his head beyond the doorframe and peered down the hallway. The Liagó was empty.

Seizing the opportunity, they silently crept into the hallway and quickly made for the closest stairway. Behind them, they could hear a commotion emanating from the grand chamber and the static of a walkie-talkie. *They found the painting!* Alex thought.

They sprinted up the staircase, realizing too late that the acoustics were unfavorable. The clack-clack of their shoes echoed down to the first floor. They maneuvered into a small room next to the staircase. Alex twirled around in hopes of finding his bearing. Ellie clutched the cylinder and leather bag to her chest. It was unnervingly quiet.

"We need to make it back to the Golden Staircase," Alex whispered and directed them into a larger, ornate adjoining room. "This should be the Sala del Consiglio dei Dieci where the Council of Ten met. The staircase shouldn't be too much further." As they left the room and maneuvered down a narrow corridor, the sound of static ahead caused them to freeze. They could make out a beam of light moving in the darkness within a large room ahead of them.

"We can't get out that way. We need to go back the way we came," Alex urged and gripped Ellie's hand tightly. They passed through the chamber for the Council of Ten and back into the smaller room adjacent to the staircase that lead up to the second floor. Alex looked around the room. *We're trapped,* he thought with terror.

"I think this is the Sala della Bussola," Alex whispered. "I read about it in the book. If I'm right, there is a secret passage in this room." Alex made for a large wooden compass with a statue of Justice in the northwest corner of the room. As Ellie watched Alex disappear behind the wooden compass, she felt a pressure against the side of her head.

"Don't even think of running." The voice was tinged with annoyance.

Ellie turned her head slightly, gaining a glimpse of the silver tubing of the silencer attached to the gun.

Fredrick brought the walkie-talkie to his mouth. "I caught one of them…a girl. She looks like she's got the stuff. I'm going to bring her down."

The man turned Ellie around and leveled the gun at her face. Fredrick stared at her with a sour expression, his eyes a dark black, like the cap pulled tight over his head.

"Where's your friend?" he barked at her.

Ellie nervously locked her lips and hoped that Alex had managed to find an exit to safety. She only wished he had taken the items they found behind the painting and her bag with the wooden box. *Now these men will get what they are looking for*, she thought with dismay.

"Not going to talk? We'll make you talk soon enough," Fredrick growled menacingly. He pushed her forward toward the stairs down to the Liagó. The shove knocked her off balance, sending the cylinder from her hand. It rolled across the floor and into the corner. She needed to escape! But how?

"Pick it up," Fredrick ordered behind her.

As she slowly made her way to the corner of the room, her eyes darted around in hopes of finding a way out of her predicament.

22

Alex maneuvered through the hidden passageway. He found the narrow staircase leading to the Piombi, the notorious prison cells within the Doge's Palace from where Casanova had made his famous escape. What was he going to do?

Just moments earlier he had found the secret passage behind the compass in the Sala della Bussola. He had thought Ellie was just behind him but suddenly found himself alone within the passage. He returned to find Ellie at gunpoint and ducked back behind the compass. His skin began to tingle as he frantically tried to think of how he could rescue her. He was the reason they were here this night. It was his idea to stay in the palace. He was the one that put her in danger.

Alex wound his way through the corridors in search of a weapon. He entered the Sala dei Tre Capi, the hidden antechamber in which prisoners were kept before being brought in front of the dreaded Council of Ten. He passed through the Sala degli Inquisitori and into a series of interconnected rooms that composed the armory for the palace. In front of him was a seemingly infinite assortment of weapons from maces and crossbows to swords and muskets. There was even a slender cannon perched on two wagon wheels in the center of one of the rooms.

I'm an academic, not a soldier, he thought as he desperately ran through the armory, searching for something he could use. If he didn't get back to the Sala della Bussola before they left, he feared all would be lost. *It may already be too late.*

He stopped at a halberd that was fastened to the wall and

pulled it off with a grunt. The weapon consisted of a long wooden pole that was topped with a frightening axe and enormous spike. Gripping the pole, he ran back through the secret corridor.

23

Ellie dropped to the floor, clutching the leather bag and her satchel close to her body. She reluctantly collected the cylinder off the ground and slowly rose from the floor.

Ellie was suddenly yanked back to her feet by Fredrick. The man roughly pushed her forward with his knuckles towards the nearby staircase.

"Hurry up. I don't get paid by the..." Fredrick's voice trailed off, suddenly distracted by motion behind them. Ellie could feel the pressure of the gun against the small of her back disappear as her captor turned around with surprise.

The crack was earsplitting. A wooden pole whizzed through the air and struck the man across the side of his head. The man grunted and was sent tumbling to the floor with a thump. The gun flew out of his hand and skidded harmlessly across the room.

Ellie turned to see Alex awkwardly holding the halberd. He stared down at the unconscious man bleeding from a large gash across his head with a mix of surprise and pride.

"That was pretty crazy. None of us saw that coming, especially him. Now what? How do we get out of here?" Ellie asked. They could hear a voice on the walkie-talkie ask if everything was all right and state that they were coming up. The sound of people running reverberated from downstairs.

Seized by a wave of adrenaline, Alex and Ellie ran hand and hand through the palace rooms. "We need to get back to the Golden Staircase," Alex urged as they entered the Atrio Quadrato, a small chamber next to the doge's apartment. As they turned the corner, they could see the familiar staircase in front of them. They took the stairs two steps at a time and reached the loggia level. Footsteps echoed closely behind them.

"This way," Alex pleaded and pulled her to the right. The wind blew through the archways of the loggia as they sprinted across the arcade. Ahead of them, they could see the statues of Neptune and Mars. They hesitated at the top of the stairs and carefully scaled a security barrier. As the two cleared the barrier, a ping ricocheted next to them, sending shards of marble from Neptune's beard onto them. Turning back, they could make out a crouched, darkened form on the loggia aiming a gun at them.

"Someone is shooting at us!" Ellie protested.

"Duck!" Alex yelled and pushed her head down below the marble railing just as several additional pings rang out. They quickly descended the stairs, careful to remain concealed behind the railing. Alex and Ellie paused at the bottom of the staircase, realizing that the railing would no longer provide any barrier to the gunshots. Another security barrier blocked their exit.

"If we go any further, we are going to be out in the open. It's suicide," Ellie moaned.

Alex looked ahead at Foscari's arch, mere feet from where they crouched. If they could pass under it, they would be shielded.

"We need to get to the arch. It's our only chance," Alex replied, trying to catch his breath.

Ellie stared ahead and nodded. "For the record, if we don't make it, thanks for coming back for me."

"It's either this or getting hit by a meteor, right?" Alex smiled.

They ducked under the security barrier and tensely ran to the arch, expecting to hear the bang of a gunshot, which never came. They made their way towards the Porta della Carta, the main exit to the Piazzetta San Marco. Ellie could feel her lungs burn as they reached the massive iron door. They lunged for the door and removed a long metal locking rod and sent it clanging to the ground. Taking hold of two large rings, they pulled with all their might. With a creak, the door reluctantly swung open a small amount. It was large enough for them to slip their bodies through. As they exited the palace grounds, Ellie looked back a final time and could see the darkened form of a man standing between the statues of Neptune and Mars, looking menacingly towards them.

A sudden sense of relief swept across Ellie as they squeezed through the Porta della Carta and fled into the piazzetta. The piazzetta was crowded with pedestrians enjoying a nighttime stroll, and Alex and Ellie took advantage of this opportunity to blend into the mass of people. The music of Vivaldi filled the square from hidden speakers producing a surreal environment as they turned towards the San Marco bell-tower and the piazza beyond it.

"We should go to the police," Ellie concluded as her heart rate slowly returned to normal.

"I don't know. That Inspector seems to be wrapped up in it…" Alex's voice trailed off as he scanned the square ahead. He could see two men on either side of the Piazza tilt their heads against their shoulders as if to hear something more closely, speak into the air, and begin to anxiously look through the crowd.

Alex grabbed Ellie's elbow and in one swift motion quickly turned her around. He wove them through the crowd.

"Ouch," she protested and pulled her elbow away from Alex's grip. "What are you doing?"

"Don't look back but there are two guys searching through the crowd. I think they're looking for us," Alex muttered through the side of his mouth.

"I don't want to head back towards the palace," Ellie complained. She could not resist taking a peak and nonchalantly brought her chin against her shoulder in order to glance backwards. At first, all she saw was a throng of tourists. Suddenly she could see a man wearing a dark sweatshirt and jeans begin to move rapidly through the crowd towards them. He raised his hand above the crowd and pointed in their direction.

"Crap. I think they spotted us," Ellie spat out. They began to quicken their pace and rapidly made their way towards the quay. As they approached the large columns of Venice's patrons, San Marco and Saint Teodoro of Amasea, Alex began to frantically debate which way they should travel along the waterfront. He nervously peered up at the southern façade of the Doge's Palace, which appeared ominous after the most recent events within its halls. A line of gondolas bobbed up and down at the Ponte della Paglia.

Finally making up his mind, Alex maneuvered them to the left along the Riva Degli Schiavoni beside the basin. Just then, Ellie was startled by a gondolier who jumped in front of them, blocking their path.

"Gondola ride. Only eighty euro. You take the lady. It very romantic at night," the gondolier offered, extending his hands widely to prevent them from walking on. The man wore the standard black and white striped shirt and black pants of all the gondoliers. He pointed to a black gondola with a red satin seat cushion at the back of the craft.

Alex pushed the man's hand aside, annoyed to be suddenly distracted. He looked back towards the piazzetta with alarm. The two men were rapidly making ground. "No, we are in a rush," Alex barked. The gondolier appeared to feint backwards but suddenly sprung forward. Reaching out with his right hand, he grabbed a handful of Alex's shirt and drew his face close to Alex's.

"Look, Mr. Stone, listen to me and listen carefully. You do not have much time. Those men chasing you are going to catch you and when they do they will take the items your girlfriend has and then they will kill you. You have a choice. Get in the gondola now and live or you can walk away and…who knows? If I were you, I'd get in the goddamn boat."

Alex looked at Ellie for some guidance and then at the boat. The man released Alex's shirt and backed away towards the gondola.

The gondolier stopped and looked back. "Are you coming?" he asked.

Ellie reluctantly nodded to Alex and they silently boarded the gondola as if in a daze. The gondolier sprung into the boat and maneuvered to the back of the vessel. Alex and Ellie slumped into the seat and waited as the gondolier stood behind them and pushed off with a long wooden pole, sending the boat floating away from the pier. They searched the crowd on the waterfront and could no longer see the men pursuing them. Suddenly they could see the crowd part as one of their pursuers roughly pushed aside a pedestrian who glared at him with disapproval.

The gondolier leaned over them. "This is romantic. It would help if you are two lovers. You may want to kiss," the gondolier muttered as he struggled to send the gondola further away from the pier.

Ellie looked at Alex with uncertainty and leaned in just as the gondolier swept a black blanket over them. Alex peered out from behind the blanket and could see the two men unite by the edge of the water. They searched the pier, running along it for a short distance. After consulting with each other, they split up, each traveling down the waterfront in an opposite direction.

"That was close, my friends."

The boat rocked side to side as they drifted further into the basin.

"Not romantic? That is too bad. This is Venice." The gondolier frowned and then laughed.

"Who are you?" Alex asked.

"Who I am is not important. I am here to help you. That is all you need to know now. All will be revealed in time."

The night grew dark the further they drifted away from San

Marco. They could see Isola Di San Giogio Maggiore grow closer. The sound of a motorized engine broke the unnerving silence of the night, and they turned to see a boat dock alongside the gondola.

"I'm afraid there is only so far I can push this gondola. If you please, we will be transferring to another boat. The helicopter is waiting on Isola di San Giorgio Maggiore and then a plane flight."

Alex attempted to stand up but toppled backwards. "Helicopter? Plane flight? What is this all about? We're not going anywhere with you?"

The gondolier shook his head back and forth and looked at the pilot of the motorized boat. "Not very grateful, I'm afraid. I can understand your reluctance but..." Ellie watched as the gondolier withdrew a pistol and kept it by his side. "...I must insist that you come with us. It is imperative. I was hoping I wouldn't have to do this."

"Do what?" Ellie asked, as she turned towards the gondolier. He suddenly crouched down, withdrew a canister from his pocket, and with one quick motion sprayed Alex and Ellie in their faces.

Ellie looked at Alex with horror as the bitter taste of the spray stung the back of her tongue and burned her throat. She could see Alex's face twist as he coughed desperately. Ellie pulled her satchel and Dr. Gozzi's items protectively against her chest and reached out for Alex's hand. She struggled to focus but found her vision blur and dim. Ellie tried to speak but found her jaw locked in place. The stars above began to swirl wildly as she tried to stand up but felt completely disconnected from her body. She flopped onto her back and stared up at the sky. She struggled to keep her eyes open. The world went black.

25

*The muffled sound of knocking echoed through her head as if she was sub-*merged underwater. Her eyelids slowly parted revealing a fuzzy image. As her eyes gradually focused, she could make out the blades of a ceiling fan slicing through the air above her. Ellie struggled to raise her head but found it unbearably heavy. *Where am I?* she wondered, hoping to escape from the fog that filled her head. She groaned and pulled herself up to a sitting position on the bed.

She caught her reflection in a large mirror positioned above a dresser across from her. A skirt and blouse was carefully laid out upon the dresser top. She looked down and found herself clothed in fine, white and blue toile pajamas. Ellie forced herself to her feet and stood unsteady for a moment by the side of the bed, her hand gripping the edge of the mattress in order to right herself. Her toes curled against the cold, rust-colored tiles. She stumbled over to the window, her head throbbing with pain. Drawing aside the wooden shutters, she looked out of the window upon a lush landscape of rolling hills. Below her was a stonewalled courtyard and beyond that a large vineyard and garden.

As she stared out of the window trying to collect her thoughts, she realized that the pounding in her head was coming from the wooden door of her room. She staggered over to the door and tried to turn the knob but found it locked. She could make out voices arguing beyond the door. Ellie could hear a key roughly being inserted into the lock and feel the doorknob twist in her hand. She released the knob and apprehensively backed away.

The door swung open. Alex stood in front of the doorway dressed in light blue pajamas next to a man carrying a ring of keys. As she stared at the man, she realized it was the gondolier that had "saved" them. The memories from the events in Venice suddenly began to stream back to her.

"Are you O.K.?" Alex asked with concern.

"She's alright, see," muttered the man beside him. "Our intention was never to hurt you. But, you didn't give me much choice. We had to move quickly. Time was of the essence. Now that you have been reacquainted, breakfast is being served downstairs. Unfortunately, your luggage had to be left behind in Venice. Our staff has left out clothes for you. Dr. Clay is eagerly awaiting your arrival." The man bowed slightly and disappeared down the hallway.

Ellie looked at Alex with confusion. "Alex, what is going on?" Ellie asked as she rolled the ball of her hand against her temple. "I have a splitting headache."

"I think we were drugged or gassed, or something," Alex replied, glancing down the now empty hallway.

"Where are we?" Ellie asked as she smoothed out the front of her shirt.

"I'm not sure. Not Venice," Alex answered and modestly averted his eyes from Ellie's low cut pajama top.

Ellie suddenly hugged herself. A look of panic flashed across her face. She glanced around the room. She had an odd feeling of nakedness. "My bag! The stuff Bernardo hid behind the Doge's portrait, they're gone! What do we do now?"

Alex was silent for a moment as he leaned heavily against the doorframe. He had wished for a life of adventure and intrigue and now that he was in the midst of it, he felt overwhelmed and unsure. The Metropolitan Museum of Art and Dr. Graham seemed to be distant memories.

"I don't know if we really have much choice. I say we change and see what this Dr. Clay wants from us. My guess is that if he wanted to get rid of us, he probably would have done so already."

Alex and Ellie walked single file down the stairs. Ellie's pants and blouse fit perfectly and were clearly an expensive make. She watched Alex descend the stairs dressed in a linen, blue dress shirt and khaki pants. She could not help but notice how nicely he could clean up.

At the bottom of the stairs, they were greeted by a servant who politely directed them through white-trimmed French doors onto a large flagstone patio. Men in dark suits hovered around the perimeter of the patio, silently monitoring the area. A long rustic wooden table was in the center of the patio under a wood-framed canopy. There was a wide assortment of foods on the table. There was a large cheese plate with fruit elegantly arranged along the edges. Carafes of different juices and milk poked out from an immense stainless steel ice bucket. There was a pitcher of coffee. A basket of freshly baked breads and cakes rested beside the cheese and fruit platter. Alex and Ellie could feel their stomachs twist in response to the bounty in front of them. One thing was clear, they were famished.

"Please, help yourself. Everything is organic here. Our chef is preparing fresh eggs as we speak. I hope poached eggs will be acceptable. Dr. Clay will be along shortly. He wishes you bon appetite," said the servant who bowed and left them to eat.

Ellie grabbed a white plate and began to pile on food. She buttered a piece of bread and popped it into her mouth. "I'm starving," she mumbled with a full mouth. Alex joined her and began to feast on the offerings. They sat across from each other as the servant returned with two plates of poached eggs. Ellie reach for the salt and pepper and flicked a fine coating of each upon the egg. She slid the egg onto a piece of toasted country bread. She smiled as she began to chomp on it, the yolk dribbling down her chin. "So good." She nearly laughed.

"Please, continue to enjoy your meal." They turned to see a man walk up to the patio from a large garden at the edge of the vineyard. He appeared to be in his mid to late sixties, fit, with faded blue eyes that complemented his gray hair. He was dressed in casual khaki pants and a loose-fitting white linen shirt. Gardening gloves hung from a back pocket of his pants. He approached the head of the table, reached for a crystal pitcher of water, and filled a glass halfway. He looked at each one of them for a moment with an air of amusement before sitting down.

The man held up a brown-gray ball and passed it to Ellie. She cupped it delicately in the palm of her hands. The ball appeared to be composed of a tangle of withered and brittle branches.

"You have to excuse me, but I was just gardening. I find that it allows me to reach an inner peace. You are holding *Anastatica hierochuntica*. It is also known as the Rose of Jericho or as I prefer, the Resurrection Plant. After the rainy season has passed, this plant has an unusual survival mechanism. It shrivels up and dries into the odd structure you are holding. It can stay that way in a state of hibernation until it is finally awakened by the drops of life-sustaining water. It's almost poetic."

Ellie passed the plant to Alex who juggled it briefly in his hands before returning it to the man. The man took the plant, dropped it into the glass of water he had just poured, and pushed it aside.

"Allow me to introduce myself. I am Redmund Clay, and you are guests at my estate here in Tuscany."

Redmund Clay? Ellie wondered. The reclusive pharmaceutical mogul. He was one of the richest men in the world. He had estates across the globe.

"Do you drug all your guests?" Alex asked sarcastically. He could see a guard walking towards a security booth beside the long driveway stretching away from the property. A sleek, black submachine gun was tightly slung over his shoulder.

"I have to apologize for that. Jonas is a loyal employee, but he is admittedly heavy-handed at times. He always completes his job, at any cost. I can assure you that you are not prisoners here. You are free to leave at any time you choose. I can have a car take you to the airport or train station or wherever you choose to go."

"Where is the wooden box I had and Bernardo's items?" Ellie questioned, unwilling to consider leaving without them.

"Safe, I assure you." Clay smiled at her in a grandfatherly way. "Dr. Griffin, you are a very impressive young lady. I expect great things from you. It was why *I* requested that Gordon recruit you for MART in the first place and sponsored the endeavor. Gordon's loss was, well, devastating. He was a great scholar and loyal employee."

Hearing Gordon's name filled her with foreboding. *MART? What does this have to do with MART?* Ellie wondered. *Gordon never discussed his relationship with Clay. 'Loyal employee?' What else did Gordon not tell me about?* she wondered. Her mind frantically replayed conversations she had with Gordon for any clue to the veracity of Clay's claim. Ellie found herself running her fingertips across the smooth skin grafts on her palms.

"Before you get too jealous, Mr. Stone, you are also quite a marvel yourself. You are a precocious graduate student. You have a bright future ahead of you."

Alex could feel himself self-consciously blush.

"Before you decide to leave this estate, I would like to tell you about a passion of mine. My company, Clay Pharmaceuticals, has created many drugs that have prolonged and improved the quality of life for millions of people. Our new class of lipid lowering drugs provides for the most dramatic and sustained decrease in death from a cardiovascular incident. New compounds we are currently working on will someday eradicate the beta-amyloid plaques that are deposited in the brains of Alzheimer's disease patients. Our new anti-malaria cocktail promises to decrease the death toll on the African continent by nearly twenty-five percent over the next decade. We have developed a new class of antimicrobials that will treat increasingly resistant bacterial strains and have made considerable inroads into the treatment of HIV. My company is in the business of saving lives, but it is not enough. Science can only go so far."

"What does this have to do with us?" Ellie interrupted.

Clay smiled, unfazed by the outburst.

"If you would kindly humor this old man, I would like to tell you my story. You might find it odd but I was never much a man of science when I was younger. I gravitated towards history, Edward Gibbons and the like. I was captivated by how civilizations rose and fell. I was preoccupied by the thought that our civilization was destined to ultimately fail. I was a lost soul. It was the sixties and the world seemed to be spinning wildly out of control and I, like many at the time, was desperately searching for a purpose. I considered the religious fold but found it too claustrophobic, too confining. I knew I wanted to help people, but there were so many ways and so many people who needed help. There was such an abundance of suffering it was...immobilizing.

"One day I picked up a book about Louis Pasteur and the discovery of Penicillin. Imagine treating bacterial infections that killed millions with a common household mold. Then I learned about Johannes Salk and the discovery of the vaccine for polio. I knew at that moment I had found my calling. A single doctor may help cure a small number of people over the course of his or her career. I had the opportunity to help millions.

"The production of medicines is a complicated process. The first drug my company developed was derived from an ancient herb that grew in the peat bogs of England. I realized early on that not all answers could be found in the sterile atmosphere of the academic laboratory. Recombinant DNA, telomeric decay, and nanotechnology are all very sexy topics with great practical promise, but I found that God had left many small miracles scattered throughout this planet. There were wondrous secrets hidden in ancient cultures and the natural world. In short, the world was my laboratory and I made it my mission to explore it fully. I scoured the globe, researching witch-doctor remedies that were passed down orally through the generations. I employed ethno-botanists who hacked their way through the South American rainforests in order to study exotic species of plants for medicinal properties. I had scholars pore through ancient Egyptian, Greek, and Mayan codices for lost therapeutic treatments. I knew if I just searched hard enough, I could find a cure for all our ailments. The more I searched, however, the more this holy grail eluded me. That was until I stumbled upon a shadow I have been pursuing ever since: Marco Polo.

"Polo?" Ellie asked.

Clay ignored Ellie's question, rose from his chair, and began to slowly pace back and forth by the end of the table.

"What are we to think of the Bible? Is it a work of fiction? Or is it an historical account? Maybe it is truly the words of prophets. 'The Lord God planted a garden in Eden, in the east; and there he put the man whom he had formed. Out of the ground the Lord God made to grow every tree that is pleasant to the sight and good for food, *the tree of life also in the midst of the garden...,*" Clay recited with his eyes closed.

"...and the tree of the knowledge of good and evil," Ellie interrupted. "It's from Genesis. What does this have to do with Marco Polo?"

"You are one to get to the point. Do you flip to the back of the book just to see how it ends? Patience. I heard you speak at an antiquity forum in Dubai many years ago. You talked about how many of the elements contained within the Bible had historical roots—that there was a perpetual narrative being written as cultures came and went. You discussed the *Epic of Gilgamesh* and how the great Sumerian poem had parallels to the story of Genesis. Specifically, the description of the garden of the gods and Gilgamesh's search for a life-giving plant were echoed in the pages of the Bible despite these topics being written before it."

"What you are talking about is 'Creation Mythology.' Many scholars have made careers out of it." Ellie looked across the table at Alex. "It is a known fact that there are many cultures spread out geographically and temporally who have legends of a Great Flood that ravishes the earth. Similarly, there are many cultures that have myths about marvelous gardens and magical trees. Some scholars have argued that the fact that these stories keep appearing in varied cultures raises the possibility that there is some historical *truth* at the core of these tales—that there was in fact an extraordinary flood and a wondrous garden. I would argue that cultures borrow from previous and coexistent cultures, incorporate legends, and transform them to suit their needs. History is organic. Everything we are today has roots in the past, whether we realize it or not."

"At some point these legends appeared for the first time," Clay interjected. "What if there is truth in them? What if these things whispered throughout history actually existed in some form? You yourself said that there is enough truth hidden beneath the sands to search forever and still not feel complete."

Clay picked up the glass with the Resurrection Plant floating in it and positioned it in the center of the table. The shriveled ball bobbed sadly in the water. The man motioned for them to follow.

"I have something to show you, something remarkable."

26

Alex and Ellie followed Clay across the courtyard towards a small building attached to the main house by a covered walkway. As they strolled along, Ellie could see workers picking grapes along the rows of vines and depositing them in woven baskets. A stiff breeze blew down through the valley, rustling the leaves on a nearby tree.

They crossed onto the covered walkway and arrived at the building. Clay paused in front of a large, wooden door and turned to them.

"This is more your area of interest, Mr. Stone. Many people believe that the Age of Exploration that stretched from the fifteenth through seventeenth century was driven by economic forces—that Bartholomeu Dias reaching the Cape of Good Hope, Ferdinand Magellan circumnavigating the globe, and Christopher Columbus' discovery of the New World were merely about establishing trade routes and procuring spices. I don't doubt for an instant that these were in fact important motivating factors contributing to travel, but they only tell part of the story. It is a lesser-known fact that one of the greatest impetuses for exploration was religion. I'm not just talking about missionary work and conversion of the natives, but *rediscovering* our common religious heritage.

"The Crusades served to remind Europeans that those sites discussed in the Old and New Testament *actually* existed and that one could physically visit them. Imagine what it must have felt like for these Christians to walk in the footsteps of Christ in the Holy Land or see the site of his crucifixion. Perhaps it would be possible to rediscover sites described in the Old Testament: the ruins of Sodom and Gomorrah, the Tower of Babel, and even the Garden of Eden. In fact, when Christopher Columbus traveled to the New World on his Third Voyage he was convinced that he had found the Garden of Eden in what is now Venezuela. In his *Book of Prophecies*, the increasingly religious and apocalyptic Columbus believed that certain requirements were needed to be met prior to the return of Christ: Christianity must spread throughout the world, a supreme Catholic emperor would rule the world, the Holy Land would be freed from the Muslims, and *the Garden of Eden would be found*."

Clay opened the door and held it as Alex and Ellie filed past him into the building. Both of them nearly gasped at the sight before them.

They found themselves in an enormous library that rivaled many of the most prestigious university libraries. The building was rectangular in shape. The first floor had numerous wooden tables positioned across a large atrium. Thousands of books filled mahogany bookcases that stretched along the perimeter of the room. There were cabinets with artifacts from ancient sandstone tablets to iron weapons. The ceiling was constructed out of a seemingly infinite number of glass panes with a fenestrated drape that allowed one to see the clouds in the sky without the brilliant glare of sunlight. At the far end of the room was an ornate staircase that wound its way to the second floor. The second floor looked down upon the atrium with rows and rows of additional bookcases. Several doors on the first floor remained closed. Alex read the gold placards beside them: *Map Room, Rare Books, Restoration Room.*

"This is amazing," Alex mumbled as he tried to take in the magnitude of Clay's private collection. He felt like a child in a candy store and fought the desire to immediately run through the aisles and examine the collection more closely. He cast a sideways glance at Ellie and detected a twinkle in her eye that conveyed a similar sentiment.

"Please, this way," Clay urged and directed them to a long table in the middle of the room. On the wooden table was a piece of parchment paper contained within a protective laminate covering. Alex could see that it was written in Latin and appeared quite old. The parchment was a pale yellow and was frayed at its edges. Its illuminated script was in the convention of medieval monks.

"You asked me before what Marco Polo has to do with all this. As you know, sometime around 1250 or 1260, no one knows for sure, Niccolo and Maffeo Polo, the father and uncle, respectively, of Marco Polo left Soldaia in the Crimea to trade jewels in the Mongol Khanate of the Golden Horde. During their travels to the East, they were invited to meet Kublai Khan—the 'Lord of the Tartars over all the earth, and all the kingdoms and provinces and territories of that vast quarter of the world.' Marco Polo recounts in his book that the Great Khan gave his uncle and father letters which asked the Pope to send him a hundred men skilled in the seven liberal arts and oil from the lamp housed in the Church of the Sepulchre of Christ in Jerusalem. The Polos were given a paiza, the golden tablet that provided safe-passage through the Mongol-controlled lands. They eventually arrived at Acre, the Christian controlled city in the Holy Land, sometime around 1269, only to find that Pope Clement IV had died and a successor had not been chosen. While waiting for the papal interregnum to resolve, Niccolo and Maffeo Polo decided to return to Venice.

"According to Marco Polo's account, he was fifteen years old when his father returned from the East. They waited for two years in Venice and still no Pope had been chosen. Niccolo and Maffeo decided it was time to return to Kublai Khan even if they could not deliver the letter to the Pope. They took young Marco with them and returned to Acre where they conferred with Archdeacon Tedaldo Visconti who encouraged them to obtain the requested oil from the lamp at the Holy Sepulchre. When they returned from Jerusalem, the Polo's learned that Visconti had been chosen as the next Pope—very convenient for everyone involved. He, of course, became Pope Gregory X. With his blessing, the Polo's were sent back to the court of the Great Khan. The rest is history, of course.

"It is, however, not the *whole* history. Haven't you ever wondered what the Polos were really doing? And who was Marco Polo anyway? Who were Niccolo and Maffeo Polo, for that matter? Were they merchants? Missionaries? Explorers? We know Marco Polo wasn't a writer. His *Description of the World* was after all penned by a ghostwriter, Rustichello. Somewhere along the way, I became obsessed with Polo. I began to track down many of the manuscripts of his travels to the East."

"You are the one buying his manuscripts?" Alex asked incredulously. It was well known in the antiquity community that an anonymous, private collector was quietly scurrying away the many different versions of Marco Polo's *Description of the World* that existed. There were approximately one hundred and fifty manuscripts that had been altered through the centuries by innocent errors in translation to purposeful embellishments. The original, unadulterated manuscript composed by Rustichello and Marco Polo in a Genoese jail had never been located.

Clay looked at them with a maniacal intensity that unnerved Ellie. "Manuscripts *and more*. What you are looking at is the only known document outside of Marco Polo's *Description of the World* that evidences that a meeting between Tedaldo Visconti, soon to be Pope Gregory X, and the Polos ever took place!"

"How…where did you get this?" Alex asked with disbelief, his eyes running over the document with palpable excitement.

"It was not easy. The Vatican holds its secrets tightly to its chest. Let's just say I have my sources." Clay folded his arms and stepped back, allowing Alex to lean over the document.

"I would love to work on a formal translation. If this is real, it is a truly historic find," Alex muttered as if in a daze.

"Oh, I assure you it is real," Clay replied.

Ellie nudged closer to the document. "Alex, my Latin is a wee rusty. Do you know what it says?" She wished she had paid more attention during her Latin classes when she was younger.

Alex remained silent as his eyes ran across the lines of text.

"I would have to spend more time on it but a lot of this is the usual floral writing that you see in papal documents during this time period. It talks about how the papacy will finance the Polo's return to the court of the Great Khan. While there, they are to gain the Khan's confidence and report back to the papacy with news of the Mongol culture and political and military objectives. They are also instructed to search throughout the East for any sign of the…" Alex looked up from the document, peered at Ellie, and then back at Clay.

"What does it say?" Ellie asked, impatiently prodding Alex with her shoulder.

"…the Garden of Eden," Alex finished.

"Spies *and* explorers," Clay announced from behind them. "I know what you are thinking: so what? Many people during the Middle Ages were convinced that if one traveled to the lands to the East, they would ultimately stumble upon the Garden of Eden just like many people believed that Columbus was doomed to fall off the edge of the world if he traveled west. I have drawers full of medieval maps that attempt to provide a location for the Garden of Eden. They are frauds. The difference about this case is that I believe *Marco Polo actually found it.*"

Clay's words hung in the air. *This guy is crazy*, Alex thought. He cast Ellie a dubious look.

"You think I am crazy. I don't blame you. Honorius of Autun wrote in the twelfth century that paradise "was a place…in which trees of different kinds had been planted that met all possible needs; for example, a person ate the fruit [of one of them] at the right time his hunger would be satisfied, if another, his thirst would be slaked, if of still another, his weariness would disappear; finally, if he turned to the tree of life, he would escape old age, sickness, and death.' This is a fairly appealing thing to search for. It was not lost on those who suspected that Polo had completed his mission. Shortly after Marco Polo died, a doge in Venice began to aggressively collect his manuscripts and procure his personal items."

"Marin Falier," Ellie interrupted. Clay nodded and continued.

"Before his death, Marco Polo left clues to the location of the Biblical Eden. I believe that Falier came closer than anyone to solving the mystery. He had tracked down many of the artifacts Polo had returned with from his travels to the East. He was searching for a wooden box that Polo hid a key to deciphering the puzzle. Before he could assemble the pieces, he was betrayed and killed."

"Like Bernardo," Ellie moaned.

"These items were thought lost until you rediscovered them. Now we are on the verge of uncovering the greatest mystery in history and you two have made it possible!"

Alex squeezed his chin in thought. Whether Clay was off his rocker or not, it was clear that there were people willing to kill for these items.

"Who were those people trying to kill us?" Alex nearly whispered.

"There are people who, like me, have searched the ends of the earth to decipher Polo's final secret. They have been seeking centuries for these items. With these most recent discoveries, they have been stirred from the shadows of history. They are a mysterious lot and, to be honest, I cannot be certain of who they are. They probably are a splinter group from the Order of Christ."

"The Order of Christ?" Alex asked.

"Who are they?" Ellie echoed.

"I'm sure you've heard of the Knights Templar, the warrior-priests during Crusader times who obtained great power and wealth during the Middle Ages until they were viciously suppressed in 1312 by King Philip IV of France," Alex offered.

"Yes. These Knights Templar blokes seem to be behind every conspiracy these days. You can hardly go into a bookstore without seeing some paperback on them," Ellie replied.

"Well, after the Knights Templar was suppressed, many of the members went underground fearing for their lives. Yet King Denis of Portugal could ill afford to lose the help of the Knights Templar in his kingdom. He desperately needed their expertise during the Reconquista, the epic battle against the Moors and Muslims for control of the Iberian Peninsula. He reinstituted the Templars in a different guise and called them the Order of Christ."

"It's funny, I've never heard of them," Ellie noted.

"You've probably heard of their greatest Grand Master: Prince Henry the Navigator."

"Sure, who hasn't? He was the guy who set up a school in Portugal to train explorers. I learned this in grammar school."

Alex nodded his head. "Yes, but Prince Henry was more than just a school master. He was a zealot. He made exploration a religious mission and the primary focus for the Order of Christ. During his tenure as Grand Master, a new generation of sea-faring explorers-cum crusaders came of age. His caravels of Christ, a flotilla of specially-designed boats, engaged in a concerted effort to spread Christianity into Africa and the Middle East. He was also consumed with discovering the Sinus Aethiopicus, the mythical waterway that cut across Africa and led to Prester John's empire."

Clay gently took Ellie's hand and led her to the door labeled, *Map Room*. He punched in several numbers on a keypad and the door opened. The room was moderately large with a long table in the center of the room. Several cabinets with long, thin drawers lined the walls. Clay made for the closest cabinet, pulled out the top drawer and flipped through the contents. He returned with an antique map and laid it out carefully upon the table. Ellie and Alex leaned over the edge of the table. The map showed several large landmasses that were not immediately recognizable. There were pictures of men sitting in tents upon the landmasses. Sailboats were positioned upon the oceans and navigation lines crisscrossed the map.

"I'm not fortunate enough to have the real thing. This is a reproduction of the fifteenth century Catalan World Map. This waterway is meant to depict the Sinus Aethiopicus," Clay explained. Ellie could see a crescent-shaped body of water nearly transecting the misshapen African continent.

"Who is Prester John?" Ellie asked.

Clay nodded to Alex and stepped slightly back.

"During the twelfth century there was a rumor of the existence of a powerful Christian king known as Prester John who lived somewhere in the East. Prester John reportedly ruled over a realm filled with gold, precious gems, magical trees, and fantastical creatures. There was debate as to the precise location of the land of Pester John—some argued that he lived in the East as far as China, others felt that he resided in Africa. Needless to say, he was a fictional creation of a Christian Europe desperately hoping for an all-powerful ruler. At the time, Europe was under intense military and cultural pressure. The Muslims had regained much of the Holy Land and the Mongols were spreading through the East. There was genuine fear of the unknown. Out of this fear rose a legend of a Christian king in the East who would ride to the aid of his brethren in the West and rid the Holy Land of the scourge of Islam."

"The land of Prester John sounds a lot like paradise," Ellie responded.

"Exactly," Clay piped up. "Our young Alex is neglecting to tell you that the land of Prester John reportedly bordered on that of Eden. The water that runs into Prester John's realm has healing properties. Prince Henry and his minions were not only looking for a Crusader ally. They were looking for much more—a pathway to paradise on Earth. His mistake was that he became convinced that it could be found in Africa when he should have looked further east. His followers would not make the same mistake."

The room grew silent and Clay appeared tired. He looked at his two guests with some seriousness. "I mentioned before that you are guests here and you can leave whenever you choose. I meant every word I said. Next to here is *The Restoration Room*. There you will find the long lost box of Marco Polo and the items the late Dr. Gozzi recovered. I have devoted much of my recent life to this search for Eden, but the truth is I need your help solving this mystery. I, however, will not stoop to coercion to get it. I desire only willing colleagues. I also cannot lie to you. Those men who chased you will stop at nothing to find you. It won't take them long to realize that I now possess these items. They will be tracking me down in no time. We do not have much time to spare. If you decide to leave, I'm afraid that I cannot allow you to depart with these items. But if you stay, I am offering you nothing less than a chance to join me in the search for the greatest treasure on this planet."

Alex stared at Clay, dumbfounded. The glint of craziness faded from Clay's eyes and he seemed to return to a grandfatherly form once again. Alex reflected on the recent events and the world of mystery Ellie and he had been plunged head first into. One of the things he had learned early in his studies of great discoveries in archeology was that the greatest revolutionaries in the field were those willing to pursue some of the most outlandish beliefs. Maybe Clay was eccentric, possibly insane, but there was something intriguing about his hypothesis. Alex was desperate to see what Gozzi had hidden behind the painting and what was in Polo's wooden box. And besides, the work at the Metropolitan Museum of Art and Dr. Graham could wait.

Ellie's thoughts drifted to Gordon. She could not shake a sense of betrayal. Clay's ideas seemed ludicrous and improbable but Gordon was not a stupid man. He was brilliant in fact. *What had he seen in Clay? If Gordon had trusted the man, should she?* She looked down at her hands, evidence of what she had unwittingly suffered already for the sake of Clay's quest. She could feel a bubbling up within her that was driving her towards Clay. It was what drove her to Alex that night he called. It was the insatiable desire to make sense of all this—to answer the mysteries once and for all.

Alex could see Ellie nibbling at the bottom of her lip. He could instantaneously tell what her answer was. She gave a mischievous smile and nodded to him.

Alex looked at Clay. "What are we waiting for?"

27

Ellie's fingers found the edges of the wooden box as she glanced around the Restoration Room. The room was larger than the neighboring *Map Room*. In the center was a table lined with archival paper. Against the wall, there were canisters of compressed air and brushes housed within a metal cabinet. Advanced scanning equipment was positioned in the corner alongside a computer. At the end of the room was an isolation chamber completely enclosed in glass with pipes and exhaust ducts emerging from the top of it. A small table constructed out of black marble was centered in the middle of the booth with several ancient scrolls resting upon it. A magnifying lamp emitting an eerie blue light was suspended from the ceiling. Clay had clearly invested a considerable sum into the construction of a state-of-the-art restoration room.

Ellie's eyes drifted away from the chamber. She listened as Alex explained to Clay his interpretation of the significance of the crosses carved into the box. Clay appeared captivated by Alex's explanation, nodding his head with each revelation. Alex extended his hand to Ellie who mechanically passed the box to him. With the bravado of a seasoned magician, Alex proudly wiped the bottom of the box with a wet towel.

"Amazing," Clay uttered as he reached out for the box, bringing it closer to his eyes. The bizarre symbol and message faded as the liquid quickly dried in the dehumidified room. "What does it mean?"

"The message translates roughly to...

Adam's Staff
Eastward Go
Illuminated Path
Where King Interred

"Interesting. I haven't heard of 'Adam's staff.' Have you?" Clay wondered aloud. He looked at Alex who shook his head and then turned to Ellie, who suddenly appeared uncomfortable. She was reluctant to say anything that might affirm Clay's outlandish theories on the existence of an actual Garden of Eden. "What do you know that you are not telling?" Clay asked.

"O.K. Everyone here knows the traditional story of Adam and Eve. Eve is tempted by the serpent, eats the fruit from the tree of knowledge of good and evil, convinces Adam to do likewise, and they are summarily kicked out of paradise. Well, there are many variations to the Adam and Eve story. For example, there are apocryphal texts of the Old Testament that argue that Adam had a wife before Eve, called Lilith, who interestingly is derived from Sumerian legends of storm spirits.

"Another story popular during the Middle Ages tells not of the birth of Adam but of his death. In that tale, Adam is somewhere around 800 to 900 years old and he is dying. His son Seth decides to embark on a quest to relocate the Garden of Eden, hoping to find oil from the tree of mercy. During his search, he encounters the Archangel Michael who explains to Seth that Adam cannot be saved from his sins until Jesus arrives and leads Adam ultimately to the tree of mercy. This story illustrates my contention that this mythology has been metamorphosed through time to suit new cultures. This is a blatant attempt to assert that the New Testament is the legitimate heir to the Old Testament.

"Another example deals with the wood from the Tree of Life. There are many legends about the wondrous properties of the wood. One legend states that the staff of Moses was derived from wood from the Tree of Life. Another tale tells of a branch of the Tree of Life floating in the pool of Bethesda conferring curative properties to the water. Lastly, there is the so-called Legend of the Cross. This legend states that wood from the Tree of Life was used to make the cross upon which Jesus was crucified. A portion of this cross was believed to have been discovered by Helena, the mother of Constantine I, the Roman emperor who made Christianity the state religion of the empire. Some call this piece of wood 'Adam's Staff.'"

"Magical wood," Alex muttered.

Ellie thought back to Mosul and the image of the wooden box harmlessly engulfed by flames. She remained silent.

Clay clapped his hands happily. "I knew it! Marco is sending us clues through time. Eden is to the east…where Prester John is buried."

"Mr. Clay, that conclusion may be a bit premature, don't you think?" Alex asked.

"Please call me Redmund, both of you. O.K., let's proceed with your analytical ways. What about the symbol on the box?"

"I'm not sure," Alex answered. Clay appeared disappointed and the two of them stared across the table at the metal cylinder and leather bag Dr. Gozzi had hidden for them behind the portrait of Marin Falier back in Venice. "But something tells me those items might help out."

Clay reached across the table, gripped the metal cylinder, and handed it to Alex. With all the excitement in the Doge's Palace, Alex did not have any time to inspect it. The tube was long and slender, measuring approximately two and a half feet in length. There was a cap fastened to the end with a clasp. Alex slipped his fingers under the clasp and flipped the clip back with a snap. The cylinder made a faint sucking sound as the cap sprung back to reveal a darkened interior. All three of them crowded together to peer into the lumen in anticipation, finding the edge of a rolled-up piece of parchment.

Alex extended his fingers into the cylinder and slowly eased the document out. He flipped the cylinder over and gently tapped the opposite end until the parchment slid delicately onto the table. Ellie helped to straighten out the piece of parchment upon the table and stared down at its contents.

The paper was worn and faded. Upon it was writing composed of miniscule script with the letters flowing into each other. There was no obvious punctuation or paragraph formation. Alex squinted, trying to decipher what language it was. He was lost.

"I know I've seen this before," Ellie piped up with excitement. She placed the tip of her index finger against her lips in thought. "Recently, in fact!" Her eyes were wide as she explored the recesses of her mind. She suddenly turned to Clay. "Do you happen to have the Yule-Cordier edition of Marco Polo's *Description of the World*?"

"Yes, of course," Clay responded with a stutter, taken aback by her outburst. "I'll go get it. It won't take much more than a moment." Clay retreated to the door and disappeared into the main atrium of the library.

Alex looked at Ellie with amused pride. Her eyes twinkled.

"I've seen a photograph of this document in the book you lent me. I can't remember what it was, but it had something to do with Marco Polo."

Alex nodded, reached across the table, and retrieved the leather bag. He guiltily looked back at the door and found it closed. "I've been dying to see what's in the bag." He untied a leather string that kept the top of the bag cinched together and gazed inside. He could make out two unusually shaped metallic items. Alex reached in and removed the artifacts, carefully placing them upon the archival paper.

The first item was a long, thin rod constructed out of a dull gray iron. The tip of the rod was irregular, with jagged edges. The other end of the rod had a figurine in the shape of a bird, identical to the ones carved into the side of the wooden box.

"Alex, it looks like a key," Ellie offered. What was the message that Bernardo had left for them? *The key is behind the black doge.*

Alex laid the rod on the table and lifted up the second item. It was constructed out of black metal and was in the shape of an eight-petaled flower. Each of the petals was hollow with a single hole at the tip of each petal. In the center of the flower was an empty chamber. The back of the flower was flat and rested on the table like a paperweight. On the back, inscribed in Latin, were the words *First footsteps.*

"What is it?" Ellie asked. Alex shrugged and turned back as the door behind them slid open. Clay entered carrying worn copies of the two-volume version of Marco Polo's travels. He hesitated upon seeing the metallic items resting upon the table.

"Wonderful. It's the first volume if I am recalling correctly," Ellie said and accepted the blue-covered paperback. She flipped open the book. The Yule-Cordier edition of *The Description of the World* was in many ways the most definitive English version of the text as translated and dissected by the venerable Polo scholars, Colonel Henry Yule and Henri Cordier in the late nineteenth and early twentieth centuries. The version had extensive footnotes analyzing everything from Marco Polo's description of cities to the flora and fauna of Mongolia. It also had a comprehensive prologue that explored the lives of the Polos and the origins of the book.

Clay watched as Ellie quickly flipped through the introductory section of the book, pausing periodically at several black ink drawings. She passed by a drawing of the three-bird crest of the Polo family and reproductions of old photographs of Venice. She suddenly stopped, sucking air between her pursed lips. Bending the binding backwards, she slid the book beside the piece of parchment. The book displayed an exact photographic duplicate of the parchment.

"It's the last will and testament of Marco Polo," Ellie pronounced.

"Well, Dr. Gozi would have had easy access to it. It is…err *was* housed at the Biblioteca Marciana," Alex replied. He suddenly felt both an immense sense of guilt and fear. They had unwittingly stolen a priceless document. What if something happened to it? Luckily, his despondency was short-lived.

"The symbols!" Ellie exclaimed.

She pointed to the end of the will. On the last row were three symbols displayed vertically like Chinese characters.

"My God!" responded Clay.

Alex turned the wooden box over and placed it upside down on the table. He positioned the metallic flower above it and wiped the wooden box with the wet towel once more revealing the hidden symbol. They were a match.

"It's called a Tabellionato," Alex said. He could see that both Ellie and Clay had never heard of the term and switched comfortably into his didactic mode. "It's a fancy monogram that notaries used to sign important documents during Marco Polo's time. Each person had a unique brand. Instead of providing a signature, they would doodle some symbol, or symbols in this case."

"Who does this Tabellionato belong to?" Clay asked.

Alex turned the page of the book and found a translation of the will into English. "This Tabellionato belongs to 'John Giustiniani, Priest of S. Proculo.' I can't say I've ever heard of him or San Proculo, for that matter."

"If it's a code for something, we seem to be missing the third symbol—the circle with a dot in it thing," Ellie sighed.

"Dr. Gozzi left us this for a reason. These pieces must fit together some way. This can't all be a coincidence." Alex ran his hands through his hair with frustration. "We have a lot of work to do if we are going to ever make sense of this."

"How can I help?" inquired Clay.

"We need some time and space," Alex answered.

"You will have both. The last thing you need is me hovering over your shoulders. I have employed many great scholars through the years who have toiled in my library. I know how grumpy you academics can be when it comes to your work. I will have my staff deliver food to you. I will make myself scarce."

"Thank you," Alex replied and returned to looking at the will.

Before leaving the library, Clay turned back and said, "And, Ellie, I know you think of everything I have said as an impossibility—that my head is in the clouds. I just ask you to have an open mind and believe in Marco Polo."

"I don't know what Polo found—but it wasn't paradise," Ellie responded.

28

"I just don't get it," Alex complained. *"The will is just so...ordinary. It talks* about paying tithes and bequeathing money to this monastery or that convent. Other than the symbols, I don't see anything unusual about it." He plopped his head down on the table with exhaustion.

They had moved from the *Restoration Room* back into the atrium of the library. The day had galloped away. The sunlight had given way first to a purple dusk that filled the atrium with a fantastical glow. The library was now dark except for several desk lamps positioned around their work area and the light from the monitor of a laptop computer Clay had provided them. Above them, they could see the stars through the glass ceiling. Ellie put the weight of her chin upon Alex's shoulder, pulled herself away from trying to decipher the writing on the wooden box, and read through the translation of the will again.

"It's not totally ordinary. He did free his Mongol slave, Peter. Not everyone had a Mongol slave, huh." She continued to scan through the page. "It's nice to see that he left some money to his three daughters: Fantina, Bellela, and Moreta. At least he wasn't a deadbeat dad. I guess three is the magic number when it came to Marco." She emitted a faint snort.

Alex tilted his head, amused by her unladylike snort. Ellie chin slid off his shoulder. "What do you mean by three being 'the magic number'?"

"I wouldn't make much of it. You know...*three* daughters. There are *three* symbols that compose the Tabellionato on the will. There were three Polos that set out for the East—Maffeo, Niccollo, and Marco. There are two witnesses that signed the will in *addition* to the notary. There are the *three* birds that make up the Polo family crest. *Three.*" Ellie shrugged and returned to the notes she had prepared on 'Adam's staff.'

Alex laid his cheek down on the table and glanced sideways at the wooden box. "Actually there were five people who set out for the East. There were Maffeo, Niccollo, Marco, and two friars sent by Gregory X: Friar William of Tripoli and Friar Nicolas of Vicenza. The friars turned around and ran back to the West at the first sign of danger." He closed his eyes and slowly reopened them. He could see the crest of the three birds carved into the box before him. *West!* His head sprung up, startling Ellie.

"What is it?!"

Alex gripped the box in his hands. He turned it over, examining both crests. "You're a genius!" Without thinking he reached out and placed the palms of his hands against each of Ellie's cheeks, brought her lips against his, and kissed her. Ellie's eyes opened wide with astonishment. Alex pulled away with equal surprise and gave an awkward smile.

"Sorry about that," Alex muttered as Ellie's cheeks flushed. Alex attempted to change the subject and showed Ellie the box. "These two crests aren't the same. I can't believe that I didn't see it until now, but on this side, all three birds are walking to our right—East. On the other side..." Alex flipped the box over. "... the first two birds are walking east. The final one is walking west! This can't be an accident. If my hunch is right...

"Ellie, hand me that paperclip, please." She passed it to him and watched with intrigue as he straightened it out. Alex brought the tip of the now straightened paperclip to the head of the bird facing west and advanced it. A small door pushed backwards as the tip of the paperclip disappeared into the box. It traveled a short distance before meeting resistance.

"It's a keyhole," Alex pronounced with a smile. He lifted the metal rod with the matching image of the bird from the table and removed the paperclip from the hole. Alex held aloft the key and brought it flush against the center image of the bird. The key slid effortlessly into the hole. Meeting resistance, he turned the key clockwise and watched as the lid of the box sprung backwards like a music box. Together both Alex and Ellie gripped the box tightly and tilted it towards themselves, held their breath, and peered inside.

29

In the center of the box were two large diamonds, secured in separate metal baskets. Alex reached into the box and plucked one of the jewels out of its casing. It was easily the largest diamond he had ever seen. He held it up to the desk lamp. As the light struck the gem, it sparkled wondrously, sending refracted beams of white light throughout the atrium. Alex twirled the diamond between his fingertips and watched as a seemingly infinite number of dots shimmered, dancing on the walls, tables, floor, and bookcases. They twinkled like stars on the ceiling.

"They're beautiful," Ellie pronounced, mesmerized by the magnificence of the jewels. "They must cost a fortune." Alex handed the diamond to Ellie, who delicately cupped it in her hands. He retrieved the second and held it up to the moonlight. It appeared identical.

"It reminds me of a story most academics have come to consider as an apocryphal tale." Ellie broke away from inspecting the diamond and peered at Alex. "It involved the return of the Polos to Venice after decades in the East. As the legend goes, the Polos returned to Venice after over twenty-five years away, dressed in traditional Mongol clothing. Having been absent for so long and dressed in such strange attire, they were not recognized by their family and friends. When these apparitions attempted to tell about their marvelous journey to the East, they were accused of being charlatans and frauds. As the story goes, the three men withdrew knives and cut away the lining of their coats. Precious jewels spilled out onto the floor. Needless to say, their story became instantaneously more believable. Maybe the legend was not too far off. The Polos, remember, were primarily traders of jewels."

The two of them sat in silence staring at the diamonds.

"Is there anything else in the box?" Ellie asked.

"You mean more than just freakin' huge priceless rocks," Alex joked. He tilted the box, allowing the light from the lamp to shine into it. There were two lines of writing between the two baskets. Both were written in Latin. Alex transcribed it onto a yellow legal pad and studied the words.

"It says…

Escaping Diocletian Wrath
Not Eternal Sin

"Another riddle," Ellie complained. She reached for the laptop computer with wireless access to the Internet. "Diocletian was the Roman Emperor famous for the baths…let's see." Alex watched as she typed his name into a search engine.

"It says here that he was the Roman Emperor from 284 to 305 AD. He enacted military and economic reforms…blah, blah, blah. It says here the he presided over the mass persecution of Christians. His 'Edith Against the Christians' ordered the destruction of Christian places of worship, assemblage, and texts. Over three thousand Christians were killed. This included Pope Marcellinus, Saint Doimus, and Saint Sarah."

"Saints? Look up…" Alex swiveled the Yule-Cordier version of *The Description of the World* in his arms. "…Saint Proculus."

Ellie keyed in the name and pulled up a reference. "It says that Saint Proculus was the Bishop of Verona who was persecuted by Diocletian but managed to survive the 'Edith Against the Christians,' ultimately dying of natural causes in Verona in 320 AD."

"*Escaping Diocletian Wrath,*" Alex pronounced.

"…*Not Eternal Sin,*" Ellie finished. "This must be referring to the Biblical sin of man…the legendary fall from grace. Adam and Eve succumbed to temptation and ate the fruit from the tree of knowledge. They were banished from Eden and lost their immortality."

"We need to see if the Church of San Procolo still exists." Alex pulled the laptop away from Ellie and started a new search. He sifted through numerous listings that were not helpful, finally settling on a site with a directory of Christian churches in Verona. Navigating through the material, he stopped at a link to the Basilica San Zeno. "It says here that there is a small Church housing the remains of Saint Proculus attached to the Basilica San Zeno. It was built in the sixth or seventh century and was rebuilt after the 1117 earthquake. It's in Verona. It would have been around during Polo's lifetime. This has got to be where Polo is leading us! The third symbol must be there!"

Ellie looked over Alex's shoulder as he scrolled through the screen. He brought up a map of Verona and located the Basilica San Zeno near the west bank of the Adige River. Ellie turned the page of the legal pad she had been using to take notes on and drew a rough map of Verona. She made a small sketch of a church with a cross and marked it *C. San Proculus*, and circled it. Ellie flipped through the legal pad, surprised by how many notes she had taken over the last couple of hours.

"I don't trust Redmund," Ellie declared as she placed the legal pad on the table.

"Neither do I, but he may be onto something here—something of great historical importance. People do not take elaborate steps to hide a secret unless it is significant."

"Are you trying to say that Marco Polo found the Garden of Eden?" Ellie asked incredulously.

"I'm not a religious person. What I do know is that Marco Polo was gone for a long time. Most of this time remains a mystery. I would love to find out what he was doing during this time and why it was such a secret. I don't think it is too far-fetched to believe he could have searched for the Garden of Eden during his trip to the East. The legend of the Garden, after all, was commonly believed to have existed by most people during the medieval period."

"As for Redmund, he did save our lives. He may be eccentric but he is a rich eccentric with a lot of resources. I don't think we could do this alone."

"I don't know, Alex. It's alluring to have a rich patron bankrolling your research, but you lose your independence. He says that we are free to leave at any time, but did you see all the security around this compound. I can't help but to feel like one of the doges — a well-cared-for prisoner." Ellie shook her head with reluctance. "I just don't trust him."

Ellie rubbed the balls of her hands against her eyes. She yawned uncontrollably, rose to her feet, and stretched her arms towards the ceiling. "I'm going to turn in. You coming?"

Alex peered up from the laptop that was resting on his knees for a moment. "I just want to check something before I go to sleep. You want me to walk you back?"

Ellie smiled. "I don't think it's necessary. I'm sure the guard outside the library will be happy to keep an eye on me."

30

Her face felt flushed as the door to the library slowly swung shut behind her.
The night air was cool and refreshing. She stood in front of the
doorway for a moment and peered at the guard stationed by the
library door. The man was dressed in a dark, fitted suit. A transparent wire ran alongside his neck and attached to an inconspicuous earpiece. *Ex-military, no doubt*, Ellie thought, staring briefly
at his tightly cropped blond hair and stone-faced grimace. She
nonchalantly bobbed her head and gave an uncomfortable smile.

"I'm going to turn in for the night," Ellie said, uncertain if the
explanation was necessary.

"Yes, ma'am. Goodnight," the guard replied without a hint of
emotion.

Ellie shrugged and strolled along the walkway leading back
to the house. Small iron pendant light fixtures suspended above
the walkway swayed in the breeze, creaking slightly and sending menacing shadows across her path. She glanced over her
shoulder and could see the guard watching her while talking into
his sleeve.

She left the walkway and began to walk along the grass bordering the rows of grapes. The sky was a brilliant black, lit only
by pinpoint stars and a crescent sliver of silver moon. She could
hear the wind rustle the vines. She breathed deeply the air and
sat down on the grass, drawing her knees close to her chest. Ellie
closed her eyes and tried to clear her mind, but the past always
had a way of sneaking up on her when times were most still.

The sunlight streamed into the room through the broken blinds. Her eyelids fluttered momentarily and lazily opened. She watched the dust float in the brilliant yellow light. The intramuscular injection of morphine left her dulled and content, floating on a warm narcotic tide. Ellie tried to focus her pinpoint pupils upon her hands but could only see huge wads of gauze wrapped around them like a pair of flippers. The white of the gauze was stained with a dull maroon.

The soldier arrived at her bedside with the stealth of a priest preparing to read the last rites. His young face appeared strained and uncomfortable as he held the camouflage cap tightly against his side.

"Ma'am? Dr. Griffin…ma'am," he muttered, his eyes trying to catch Ellie's. Her eyes rolled back and forth, finally settling on the soldier. She tried to talk but found her mouth unbearably dry and could only muster a nod.

"We, uh…have something for you. We were going through Dr. Russell's belonging and uh…ma'am…we believe that this is yours." The soldier's right hand shook as he explored his pocket and withdrew a gold ring with a square diamond fastened to it.

"Where?" Ellie's tongue stuck to her lips.

"It was in Dr. Russell's pocket."

"Mistake…" Ellie shook her head and breathed heavily.

The soldier tilted the ring and drew her attention to an inscription on the inner aspect of the band. "It says…'To my beloved, Eleanor, my timeless treasure.'"

Her eyes swelled. The back of her throat burned with bile.

The soldier froze with uncertainty, holding the ring between his thumb and index finger. He looked down at her mummy-wrapped hands. "I'm sorry, ma'am. We all are. I'll just set it down right here."

Ellie silently watched as the soldier placed the ring on the nightstand beside her mattress and quickly retreated to the door. She stared at the ring as the door clicked shut. The ring fragmented in a kaleidoscope of color through her tears.

Ellie wiped the wetness from her cheeks with the back of her hand. A soft pop in the distance helped focus her thoughts. She felt disoriented, having lost her sense of time. She pushed herself up, coughed into her fist, and walked back towards the house. Ellie climbed up an incline and found herself on the patio where earlier they had breakfast. She rounded the table and lifted the glass from the surface. The withered ball of brown that was the Resurrection plant was now a vibrant green plant. *Amazing*, Ellie thought and deposited it back on the table. As she backed away from it, her heel ran up against an object that sent her toppling backward. She caught the edge of the table at the last moment, preventing her from completely losing her footing.

She cursed under her breath and looked at the ground beneath her feet. A darkened form was stretched out on the stone surface. Ellie's heart galloped as she bent down. The burly man was dressed in the familiar dark suit of Clay's security service. A black hole was perfectly centered in his forehead, his eyes staring fixed into space. Ellie pulled herself closer to the table, her eyes darting about. She could see a wet spray of blood, brain matter, and bone on a wooden column beside the table. Ellie apprehensively peered out at the darkness of the vineyard. She could hear several faint pops in the direction of a security booth by the entrance to the complex. The lights flickered momentarily and suddenly went out, plunging the patio into darkness.

She froze with fright behind the table. *Alex!* Ellie thought with panic. She needed to find him. She crawled over to the body of the security guard and blindly reached out into the blackness, searching through the man's pocket. She came away with a set of keys with a small flashlight attached to them. She clicked on the flashlight and directed it into the palm of her hand, producing a red-orange glow. Ellie made for the walkway and stopped. She thought for a moment and rushed back to search under the man's coat. Her fingers found the edge of a leather holster, settled upon the grip of a lightweight pistol, and pulled it free. Having never held a gun before, she cradled it awkwardly in her hands before tightly gripping it. She once again made for the brick pathway.

She scampered across the walkway with the gun held by her side. The little moonlight there was delicately illuminated the poles that supported the canopy over the path. In the distance, she could make out the façade of the library and as she maneuvered closer to the door, a darkened form appeared to be sitting beside it. She scurried over to the body, clicked on the flashlight, and directed the beam at the man's face. The blond-haired security guard's eyes were rolled back in his sockets. Ellie panned the beam across the man's body, discovering a partially coagulated puddle of blood trailing away from the guard's chest.

A rapid burst of machine gun fire broke through the stillness and Ellie swung around. An explosion blew out windows from the house. Her nails clenched the grip of the gun. *I need to warn Alex,* Ellie thought frantically, her fingers finding the handle to the library door. As she attempted to pull it down, a hand suddenly reached out in the darkness and covered her mouth before she could scream. A vice-like arm wrapped around her torso and pinned her arms against her chest. The flashlight and keys fell onto the ground with the beam directed up. She was able to hold onto the gun and began to struggle, twisting her body. She drove the heel of her shoe hard on her attacker's foot and felt the grip momentarily lessen. Ellie let her body drop to the ground and found that she was able to escape the man's grasp. Spinning around she held the gun up and directed it at her attacker. The barrel shook in her hands.

She could hear the man curse and take a step towards her. Ellie responded with a flinch and tightened her grip on the gun. "Don't come any closer. I'll shoot."

"Dr. Griffin. Stick to the books. Guns aren't your thing, I'm afraid. Leave that to the experts." Jonas stepped into the light and snatched the gun from her hand with a quick slap. He held the gun up to her by the barrel. "Next time, take the safety off and don't hesitate if you mean to use it." Ellie trembled as Jonas slipped the gun into his waistband and then bent down to retrieve the keys and flashlight. He switched it off and tossed it into the darkness.

"This flashlight is going to get all of us killed. They have snipers," Jonas complained and turned to walk away.

All of us, Ellie thought. She hesitated by the door. Jonas turned around and peered at her impatiently. "You coming?"

Ellie scurried to his side and followed him into the darkness. Jonas silently crept across the grass until they reached the edge of the vineyard. She felt a sense of relief upon seeing Alex crouched behind a row of grape vines. Alex greeted her with a smile and embraced her.

"I thought they had gotten you," Alex exhaled.

"I thought the same," Ellie replied, momentarily burying her head in his chest. She looked sideways and could see Clay kneeling beside Alex. Clay's blue eyes were silver in the moonlight and strangely calm. He nodded to her briefly before conferring with Jonas in whispers. Jonas shook his head, slipped on night-vision goggles, and crawled to the edge of the vegetation and looked out into the darkness.

"I thought they would come for me, but not this soon," Clay muttered and shook his head back and forth. "They mustn't get these items." He motioned to a leather satchel slung over Alex's shoulder.

Jonas returned and pulled off the goggles. "We need to go now. Come on!"

They pushed further into the immense vineyard, their shoes digging into the soft soil as they ran along rows of grape vines. They cut across the aisles when an opening permitted and moved southeast away from the complex. Alex could just make out the roof of the library in the distance. A rustle ahead sent the four of them plummeting to the ground. Face down in the dirt, they could hear the sound of footsteps several rows away. Alex tried to place the sound, carefully lifted his face from the ground, and turned his head to the right. He could make out black boots through the twisted vines several rows away. The movement of the boots suddenly halted and he could hear the sound of a cartridge being loaded into a gun.

We've been seen! Ellie fought the desire to push herself up from the ground and run. The tendons in her wrist tensed in anticipation as her fingers dug into the soil.

With her cheek against the ground, she could see Jonas shake his head with disapproval. His hand gripped a sleek black gun by his head, ready to spring up and unleash a stream of bullets.

The boots started moving again towards the main house. They waited in the shadows as the footsteps finally faded away.

"That was close," Ellie said.

Jonas rose to a crouching position and drew them close as if in a huddle. He whispered with a look of displeasure. "The only way out of here is through the vineyard. Follow me. Move quickly and don't look back."

Before anyone could respond, Jonas had moved further into the vegetation. They struggled to keep up with him as he darted across rows, ducked under vines, and pushed into the darkness. The further they moved away from the house, the only sound they could hear was the crunch of their footsteps. After traveling for over fifteen minutes, they arrived at an overgrown stone outcropping.

Jonas pushed his hands through the weeds and drew them apart, revealing an entranceway to a cave. "This way," he whispered, motioning for each of them to enter. He took up the rear.

Alex and Ellie found themselves in complete blackness. They could hear Jonas curse and the sound of him searching desperately in the blackness. "Here it is!" A yellow beam from an oversized flashlight illuminated the interior of the cave.

"What is this place?" Ellie asked, her eyes exploring the stone walls.

"It's an ancient aqueduct from Roman times, a nice archeological prize to have on your property, but more importantly a conduit to safety in times of need," Clay responded with some pride.

"You've used this before?" Alex asked.

"I'm glad to say that I never had to, but it doesn't hurt to be prepared." Clay winked at them and turned to follow Jonas who had continued to push deeper and deeper into the tunnel.

Alex pulled the leather satchel snuggly against his chest, reached out into the darkness and gripped Ellie's hand. They walked side by side through the passageway to the sound of distant water droplets dripping and the squish of their shoes against ancient sediment.

"I'd say we escaped just in the nick of time." Clay's voice echoed as he ducked down to avoid hitting his head on a partially caved-in portion of the stone ceiling.

Alex mused upon what Ellie had said earlier about not trusting Clay. He couldn't agree more but as they traveled through the ancient aqueduct he could not help but feel a sense of camaraderie with the old man—a bonding based on the uneasy realization that for better or worse their fates appeared linked—they were all being hunted. They had stumbled upon something larger than each one of them. They were following in the footsteps of Polo. *There is no getting off this ride*, Alex thought and shuddered.

Ellie could feel Alex shiver and squeezed his hand in response. He turned to her and tried to muster up a brave smile. He felt responsible for getting her into this mess.

"I should have never called you," Alex muttered.

"Huh?" Ellie raised her eyebrows.

"That night I showed you what I had found on the box. Those

guys chasing us are the real deal. They have guns, explosives, and they are looking for us. They want to kill us."

"It's not your fault. The truth is that I haven't felt alive for a while: not since Iraq. This may sound sappy, but I don't think you can die twice. Something died within me in Mosul. Without you and *this*…" Ellie waved her hand. "…I think I would have stayed dead. You have nothing to apologize for."

"What happened in Iraq?" Alex tried to look into her eyes, but she turned away.

"Ask me some other time. Ask me something different." Ellie's hand slid from Alex's and she hugged herself. Alex dug his hands deeply into his pocket and walked in silence.

"What's the 'C' for?" Alex finally asked.

"Huh?" Ellie responded, squinting at him.

"The 'C' in 'ECG.' Eleanor C. Griffin."

"Oh." Ellie smirked. "Cleopatra."

Alex nodded and smiled in the blackness. *Of course*, he thought. They continued to push further and further into the aqueduct, following Jonas's dim light in the distance.

31

The blue Mercedes sat a small distance from the end of the aqueduct, hidden behind foliage and trees. Dusty and scratched, the car looked weathered, to say the least. Jonas eased the key he had found fastened to the visor into the ignition and turned it. The car initially screeched in protest, grunted several times, and began to vibrate.

"Like a kitten," Jonas smirked as he flipped the visor down and adjusted the rear-view mirror.

"More like a wounded tiger. I hope this car will make it to Verona," Clay responded as he attempted to wipe away grime from the passenger window with the sleeve of his jacket. The leather upholstery creaked as he settled into the passenger seat and turned to face Alex and Ellie in the backseat.

"That is where we are headed? Verona?" Clay asked.

"We think that is where Polo is leading us," Alex explained. "There is a church in Verona called the Church of San Proculus. It is near the Basilica of San Zeno on the outskirts of the city. The priest that prepared Polo's will was from that church."

"And the diamonds?" Clay extended the palm of his hand into the backseat. Alex could see Ellie give him a sideways look of distrust. Alex removed one from the box and placed it in the old man's palm. He watched as Clay held it up in the light. The jewel flickered brilliantly as he spun it between his thumb and index finger. Jonas's eyes opened wide with wonder…and perhaps something more. Alex squinted at the man.

"It's beautiful." Clay handed it back to Alex.

"What if this is Polo's secret? Maybe this is the treasure he was hiding," Jonas offered.

"There was a message in the box with the diamond that again referred to Saint Proculus," Alex answered. "Also we haven't found the third symbol, the circle with the dot in the middle. I think the diamond is another piece in the puzzle…"

"No!" Ellie interrupted.

Alex nearly dropped the diamond as he twirled around to find Ellie examining the contents of Alex's leather satchel. She had splayed out the contents of the bag upon the seat between them and finally displayed the empty bag.

"My notes…the laptop, they are not here!"

"Everything was so rushed. We couldn't take everything. We were lucky we got out of there with our lives," Clay responded.

Ellie looked at Alex with alarm. "My notes had everything we talked about. It had all of our research. We practically left them a map of our plans. They're going to quickly figure out what we know," Ellie wailed.

The car grew quiet as Jonas eased the stick shift into first gear and let the car roll forward. The vehicle roughly bumped up and down the uneven, unpaved path. He eased the car by small trees and bushes, allowing it to pick up speed as it neared the bottom of a small hill and the beginning of a paved road. As the tires contacted the pavement, Jonas' foot settled onto the accelerator. The car lurched forward and began to steadily pick of speed as it traveled along the provincial roads.

"Then, I suggest we get a move on if we hope to beat our friends to Verona," Jonas muttered as he focused on the road ahead.

32

The car rattled as it drove across the short bridge spanning the River Adige. Ellie stirred from her slumber and shielded her eyes from the sunlight. She could see Alex sitting next to her staring at a sketch he had made of the key symbol hidden on the bottom of the wooden box.

She watched in silence as he turned the symbol ninety degrees so that the key faced downward and rubbed his chin in thought.

Ellie yawned. "What is it?"

"This symbol bothers me. I can see that it looks like a key with the ridges at the end but I don't understand what the circle means." He traced the two intersecting lines. "It doesn't fit in with the other crosses."

"Maybe it's just trying to say that the diamonds in the box are the 'keys' to solving Polo's riddle."

Alex pushed the sketch aside as Jonas eased the car to the side of the road. The car idled beside a large stonewall. Ellie craned her head in an attempt to peer out the front windshield, in hopes of gaining her bearing.

"Is this it?" she asked. Alex pulled himself up and peered over

Clay's shoulder. Jonas and Clay were consulting a cell phone, which displayed a digital map of Verona. He watched as they zoomed up onto Regaste San Zeno, a road that paralleled for a stretch the River Adige as it wound its way through the city of Verona. Jonas panned through the map with the flick of his finger, exploring the area to the west of the river. An icon of a cross popped up a small distance from the Via Lega Veronese. He handed the phone back to Clay, pulled away from the curve without a word, and maneuvered through the streets of Verona. He finally stopped the car in a large outdoor parking area beside several oversized stone vessels filled with flowers.

"Now we are here," Jonas pronounced and shut off the engine. Glad to be free of the vibrations that shook the frame of the car during their travels, the four spilled out of the vehicle with an overwhelming feeling of relief. Ellie breathed deeply the unseasonably warm air and stared ahead at a large stone church.

The front of the church was disappointingly unattractive. The stone was a dreary cream-color that had been discolored by the elements through the centuries. A stone arch capped a bronze door composing the narthex of the church. Two stone lions flanked columns beside the entranceway. Above the arch was an elaborate window composed of twelve panes of glass arranged like petals of a flower.

"It's a rose window popularly found in Gothic architecture." Alex pointed to the window like a tour-guide. "They call it the Ruota della Fortuna—the wheel of fortune."

"Is this then the Church of San Procolo?" Clay asked as they walked towards the building.

"No. This is the Basilica San Zeno—the church dedicated to the patron saint of Verona."

Ellie could see a Romanesque bell tower to the right of the basilica and the remnants of an old Benedictine abbey to the left consisting of a brick tower and cloisters.

"I don't want to interrupt the history lesson, but let's not linger out in the open, mind you. Where is this Church of San Procolo?" Jonas asked gruffly, constantly scanning the area for any sign of trouble. Ellie's concern that her notes could have tipped off their pursuers to their location was not lost on Jonas who had surreptitiously slid an extra cartridge of bullets into his boot before leaving the car.

"I don't know. I've never been here before." Alex tentatively approached the entranceway. Ascending a small flight of stone stairs, he walked between the two crouching lion sculptures that flanked the porch of the church. The bronze doors were parted, revealing an ornate interior that belied the weathered and relatively understated exterior. Built in the shape of a Roman cross, the nave stretched away from them as they entered into the hall. Corinthian columns constructed out of alternating white and pink marble divided the nave into two long aisles. A staircase led to the presbytery housing the sarcophagi of Veronese saints that overlooked the grand hall. Steps led downward to the crypt where the body of Saint Zeno resided within an urn.

Ellie followed Alex as he explored the interior of the church while Clay lingered by a statue depicting Saint Zeno holding a fishing rod and his dangling catch. Jonas took up the rear, suspiciously eyeing visitors to the museum who dallied by the columns and looked their way.

"What do you think?" Ellie questioned.

"We need to find someone to ask where the Church of San Procolo is located."

Alex squeezed his body into a small group of tourists clustered around a baroque altar with a *Pieta* painted upon the wall. He could feel Ellie's body twist by several of the tourists and brush up against his back. As they neared the front of the group, the tour guide was entertaining the idea that the crypt of Saint Zeno was supposed to be the site of the marriage of Shakespeare's Romeo and Juliet. Several of the tourists smiled at the thought.

The guide raised a Union Jack flag on a stick over the heads of the clustered tourists in case one of her group had wandered off, and opened a nearby door.

"Now if you will follow me, we will be entering the adjacent cloisters." The tour guide held the door open as the members of her group filed past her and into the sunlight. She smiled painfully as if to fight a severe headache. Alex sidled up to her.

"Excuse me, where could I find the Church of San Procolo?"

"San Procolo? It's a delightful little church. But, it's not on the tour."

"Where could we find it?" Alex motioned to Ellie.

"Go out through the front door and make a left. You'll see it at the end of the fence."

Alex thanked her and drifted away from the assembly with Ellie following closely behind. They met Clay and Jonas within the central portion of the nave. Jonas appeared annoyed at the slow pace of their exploration of the complex. Alex waited until another group of tourists filtered into the main hall and passed by them.

"Alex, any luck on San Procolo?" Clay rubbed the palms of his hands together.

"Follow me."

Alex retraced his steps to the front of the church, squeezing through the oversized bronze doors, and back onto the stone porch. He quickly scampered down the short flight of stairs and walked backwards onto the grand piazza in front of the basilica. The bell tower loomed to the right of the basilica enclosed in a courtyard ringed by a wrought iron fence. Cyprus trees rose along the front of the courtyard but were dwarfed by the bell tower. As Alex's eyes drifted along the course of the fence, he could see a smaller building bordering the courtyard.

"I think we found the Church of San Procolo," Clay declared and patted Alex on the back.

They approached the smaller church. The façade of the Church of San Procolo was weathered with haphazardly alternating areas of exposed red stone and cream-colored tuff. There was a small narthex, which contrasted with the more elaborate narthex and porch of the nearby basilica. Two double mullioned windows flanked the stone archway that capped aged bronze doors. Above the archway was a window in the shape of an octagon. Unlike the Ruota della Fortuna on the façade of the basilica, the window on the Church of San Procolo was considerably less ornate and had only eight panes that symmetrically radiated out from a glass oculus in the center. Alex froze and stared at the window, prompting Clay to wring his hands with excitement.

"Yes, yes," Clay muttered as Alex reached into the leather satchel slung over his shoulder, removed the metallic flower piece, and held it up in the air. It hovered next to the window. It bore an uncanny resemblance.

"It's a sign, man!" Clay clapped happily, sending two cooing pigeons into flight and prompting a pedestrian to look their way.

Jonas unhappily grumbled at the attention garnered and scanned the piazza with concern. Clay lowered his voice, emitted a guilty smirk, and turned to Alex. "What do you think it means?"

"It's hard to say. This window had eight panes like the eight petals on this metallic artifact."

"Eight is an interesting number," Ellie added. "There are some who believe that the number eight has mystical significance. The Star of Bethlehem after all had eight points radiating from the center. The three magi from the East spotted the star that heralded the birth of the baby Jesus. This, of course, prompted their trip to Jerusalem where they gave gifts to Jesus. Others see the number eight as a sign of infinity or everlasting life."

"Let's move on," prompted Jonas as he edged Ellie towards the church.

"What is it?" Clay asked.

Jonas held his head down and lowered his voice. "We are being watched."

Ellie could not resist casually glancing back at the piazza.

"...the man walking with the camera near the tree and bench. He's trying to be inconspicuous. He was in the basilica with us, taking photos."

"He's probably just a tourist." Ellie seemed unconvinced. The man wore a Hard Rock Café tee-shirt, jeans, and white sneakers. She watched over her shoulder as he backed further away from the basilica and aimed his camera up at its façade.

"I'm telling you, he's not right. His camera was trained on us too often in the basilica. What tourist brings a camera with a telephoto lens into a building like the basilica?"

Ellie was quiet and peered at Alex. "Are they here?"

"He could be just a scout collecting intel on us while awaiting their arrival," Jonas surmised.

"Or maybe they're already here and are just waiting for us to do all the work for them," Alex said.

"Is it safe? Should we leave?" Ellie asked.

"Leave? When we are so close to solving the mystery?" Clay appeared appalled. "The only way is forward, my friends. The Polos never turned back. Neither will we." Clay turned his back to them and walked by three stone pylons that prevented vehicle traffic from entering the piazza. As he approached the bronze doorway, he looked back impatiently. Jonas reached under his jacket with his right hand, instinctively patted the grip of his pistol, and sighed.

"You coming?" he asked Ellie and Alex before following Clay.

"What do you think?" Ellie squinted at Alex. He gripped the metallic artifact in his hand and looked at the octagon window.

"The more I look at that window, the more it reminds me of something. It looks like a…"

"…a Greek cross," Ellie finished.

"Exactly. The aesthetic of this style of window has been thought to have been brought back to Europe from Arabic architectural style during the Crusades."

"From the East."

"I think Clay may be wrong." Alex pulled the strap of the satchel, bringing the bag against his chest, before slipping the artifact within it. He slid the satchel back until is rested against his right flank and began to walk towards the church. Ellie reached out and restrained his wrist.

"Wrong about what?"

Alex turned and looked into Ellie's blue eyes. "Wrong about being so close to solving the mystery. Something tells me that this is just the beginning."

"But the clues all seem to be directing us here. You said it yourself."

"Yes…directing us…but where. To Verona? To Europe?"

"To the east," Ellie nearly whispered. *And the LORD God planted a garden eastward in Eden.*

Alex nodded silently, allowing his gaze to drift from her brilliant eyes to above her right shoulder. He could see the man standing in the piazza slowly pan the telephoto lens from the basilica towards the Church of San Procolo. The lens sparkled in the sunlight.

33

The interior of the church was dark and considerably less ornate than the larger, neighboring basilica. An ethereal mix of yellows and whites streamed through the octagonal window and cast a wide circle of light upon the stone surface. The church appeared deserted as they quietly filed inside. Clay wandered around the nave examining frescoes depicting events from the New Testament.

"What exactly are we looking for?" Jonas gave Alex a sideways glance.

"I don't know." Alex found himself whispering the response, unwilling to disturb the unsettling silence that filled the church.

"Wonderful," Jonas groaned sarcastically.

"Look…we know that the notary of Marco Polo's last will and testament, John Giustiniani, was the priest of *this* church during Marco Polo's final years. We've recovered two symbols associated with *his* tabellionato. The message in the box also points to Saint Procolo…"

"Welcome, friends." The voice interrupted Alex and appeared to emanate from the darkness. Alex could detect out of the corner of his eye Jonas's hand slip under his coat in search of his weapon. They turned to see an old man dressed in a priestly vestment emerge from the shadows of the church. The man was diminutive in height with an anemic countenance that matched the white of his collar. His stooped frame only served to accentuate his feeble state.

"Welcome. This church does not see many tourists these days," the man wheezed. "They flock to the basilica but take little notice of this church at the edge of the piazza. This is truly a shame." The man shook his head and muttered, "Tsk, tsk."

"It's a beautiful church," Clay responded, having rejoined the group.

"Indeed. It is the oldest church in Verona." The priest smacked his lips and attempted to moisten his mouth. His hands shook from a resting tremor. He studied each of the visitors with a look of curiosity as if trying to make sense of the motley group before him—an elderly, aristocratic man, a brooding, muscular companion, and a young couple. "I am Father Fermo, the priest and curator of San Procolo."

"We are historians of sorts," Alex said, avoiding eye contact with Jonas. "We would love to hear more about this church."

The man smiled and Alex could detect a flicker of pleasure in his eyes. "Historians, you say? Si, of course…hear more. Where do we begin?" The priest closed his eyes as if asleep.

"How old is this church?" Ellie prompted.

The priest opened his eyes, cupped his hand over his ear, and leaned in. "How old you ask? Very old. The church dates back to sometime in the sixth or seventh century. No one knows for certain. The records have been lost long ago. This unfortunately is not the original church though. What I would give to see it in its original form! The church was destroyed by the great earthquake of 1117 and was subsequently rebuilt. It has been updated through the centuries, a new fresco here and there, but has remained fundamentally unchanged throughout much of the last millennia."

"It is as Polo might have seen it. Pretty amazing," Ellie whispered to Alex.

"What's that young lady, Polo?"

Ellie glanced at Alex who nodded his approval. "Is there any connection of this church to Marco Polo?" Ellie asked.

The priest tapped his index finger against his pink lips. "Marco Polo, the Venetian? No connection that I'm aware of, I'm afraid."

Clay pushed his body slightly between the priest and Ellie. "Father, have you heard of a priest named John Giustiniani?"

"Giustiniani, you say? I grew up with a Leonardo Giustiniani who became a priest. I haven't seen him since I was a child." The priest smiled.

"This priest was from the fourteenth century," Clay added.

"I may be old but not that old." Father Fermo chuckled. Alex could see Clay's shoulders sag.

"We need to explore the inside of this church," Ellie whispered through clenched teeth to Alex.

Alex tugged on the priest's sleeve.

"Father, if you are not too busy, we would really appreciate hearing more of your insight on this church."

"A tour...si, si a tour. I'm afraid it won't be long." He raised his arms. "You see it is a small church." The priest motioned for them to follow as he walked towards the back of the church. "There are only two parts—the nave and the crypt."

The crypt! Alex thought. *Not escaping eternal sin. What better place?*

Alex trotted next to the priest. "Could we see the crypt?"

The priest ushered them to follow him further into the church. He looked back as he walked and winked. "The tourists always want to see a crypt. Priceless frescoes? No, where are the dead bodies, they ask. A fascination with the grotesque, I suppose."

As they neared the back of the church, the ground became uneven. Careful inspection revealed that many of the stones were disturbed and piled high in the corner. Clay tripped suddenly, only to regain his footing at the last second, avoiding toppling into a larger hole.

"Mind your feet. It's the University. They bring their archeology students to tear up the church every now and then. They've found ancient burial grounds beneath the stones and portions of the original church." The priest looked away in thought. "Come to think of it, I haven't heard from them in a while. I wish they would come back and clean up their mess."

They reached a series of stone steps and descended into a small crypt. The walls of the staircase contained several carved-out graves emptied of their previous inhabitants. A Roman lead coffin sat on a pedestal within the crypt. There were two aisles with chairs, an altar, and an elaborate display of lit candles that flickered from an unseen draft and cast a reddish glow.

"Welcome to the crypt of San Procolo." Father Fermo stood to the side as the group entered the crypt and silently dispersed. Alex walked around the perimeter looking for any clue. The walls were constructed from a dark stone. There were iron sconces fastened to the walls, each with a single light bulb that provided a modicum of illumination. The walls were unadorned except for a gilded cross, secured to the wall opposite the stairs.

"Father, would John Giustiniani, the priest of San Procolo during the fourteenth century have been buried here?" Alex asked as his eyes scanned the interior of the crypt with frustration.

"I do not know this John Giustiniani, I'm afraid. Some were buried on the church property, I suppose. Others were buried in the place of their birth. The records have long since vanished. The crypt was reserved for men of great stature. The remains of San Procolo, himself, are beneath us. In those days, the elite of Verona paid a considerable fee to be interred here."

"Sounds like they didn't let just anyone into this place. Expensive real estate I suppose…" Jonas muttered.

Clay leaned in to Alex. "You see anything?"

"No," Alex replied as his eyes drifted across the interior of the room. He studied the ceiling, finding it to be soot-covered and claustrophobically low. "The lack of lighting doesn't help."

"Well, Alex. One thing this old fart realized many years ago is that anything worth achieving is never easy and what one is searching for is usually right in front of your eyes."

"That's a bit cliché, Redmund," Ellie teased.

"Its only cliché because it's true. Once when I was in the Amazon trekking with a bunch of botanist in search of a plant used by the indigenous people for centuries…"

Alex walked several feet away and dropped to a crouch position. The floor was constructed out of large square stones. A thick strip of mortar ran the length of the sides, securing the stones together. The surface of the stones, blackened with silver streak, rose and fell unevenly. Alex tilted his head and peered at Clay's shoes. Alex stood up and made his way to the altar. Father Fermo followed his movement with interest.

"May I?" Alex did not wait for the priest to answer. He reached out, gripped the large white candle by its base, and lifted it out of the golden candleholder.

Father Fermo looked perplexed as Alex held aloft the candle with the wax dripping down his wrist as he wove his way through the chairs and once again squatted near Clay's feet.

"…and that's how I was able to extract the essential oil, johimbo, that is the active ingredient in Clay Pharmaceutical's newest breast cancer drug, lactophyton." Clay peered down at his feet, surprised to see Alex examining the ground near his shoes. "Lose something?"

Alex ignored Clay and positioned the candle over the stone Clay was standing upon. Clay and Ellie responded by backing away. Alex shuffled forward on his knees, his fingers tightly gripped around the base of the candle. The flame flickered wildly as he neared the stone. He cupped his left hand in front of the flame to shield it from the unseen air escaping from the edges of the stone. The light settled on the stone's surface, revealing a series of silver symbols. "It's not right in front of our eyes," Alex announced. Clay and Ellie kneeled down beside Alex and examined the stone surface. "It's right under our feet."

"Polo." The name escaped Ellie's lips.

The symbols—three walking birds—were chiseled into the

stone. Weathered and trotted upon through the centuries, the stick-like avian images were faintly perceptible against the jagged, dark stone surface.

"What do we do?" Ellie whispered as the three of them huddled together and Jonas looked on from above. Alex peered back at the priest. Jonas had engaged the priest in a discussion on Ancient Rome's role in plumbing. Jonas feigned a scholarly demeanor. Between nods of agreement with what the priest was mumbling, he would periodically shoot the rest of the group a pained expression.

"We need to pry this stone up. We need to see what's under it. See this air?" Alex withdrew his left hand that had shielded the flame. The flame danced violently. "There is air coming from below the crypt. There has to be a void."

Ellie glanced back at the priest who had finished conversing with Jonas and was busy replacing the candle Alex had taken with a new one. She motioned towards the priest. "We can't just come in here with a backhoe and tear apart the place."

The group grew silent. Alex traced the edges of the stone, his fingers settling in a gap where the mortar had corroded and disappeared.

"Leave it to me." Clay rose to his feet and conferred with Jonas in the corner for a moment. Ellie could see Jonas nod his head in agreement and approach the priest.

"Father Fermo, we would like to make a donation to the church."

The priest's eyes widened with interest.

"A donation?"

"Dr. Clay would like to make a very generous donation. If we could move into the nave, we could discuss this further."

"Si, discuss...donation."

34

Ellie watched as Alex squeezed his fingers into the void separating the two adjacent stone slabs and fruitlessly pulled upwards with a grunt.

"It's pointless, Alex. You'll never be able to lift it."

They could hear footsteps on the stairs behind them. Clay and Jonas descended into the crypt with their arms full. Clay squatted down and placed several flashlights in a row. Beside the flashlights, he delicately deposited an old battery-powered lantern. Jonas followed with a bundle of sturdy pieces of wood and two black crowbars. Ellie panned around, expecting to see the priest hovering behind them.

"What happened? What did you do to Father Fermo?" Ellie asked suspiciously.

"That's awfully accusatory, Ellie. It seems that our pious priest is an agreeable soul. A hefty donation to support his Church of San Procolo and more importantly an even heftier donation to purchase a villa on the shores of Lake Como were enough to buy us the items before you and whatever time we need to tear up this place. I can assure you of one thing, privacy." Clay reached over and turned a knob on the lantern. The lantern emitted an insect-like buzz and bathed the crypt in a yellow glow. "Where do we begin?"

Alex surveyed the items resting on the ground and grimaced. "We need to free up the stone." He pantomimed a digging motion. "Get the bar into the crack and pry it upwards."

Jonas grabbed a crow bar, jabbed the straight end into the narrow opening, and pulled the fulcrum down. The muscles in his arms strained and his face turned purple as he struggled to elevate the stone.

"We need to loosen the mortar connecting this stone to the adjacent stones. Otherwise, it's useless," Ellie directed.

Alex retrieved the second metallic bar and brought the tapered straight end down against the edge of the corroded mortar. With repetitive stabs, he drove the end into the gray material and watched as it crumbled into a heap of curdled pieces. Jonas, upon seeing Alex's success, joined in at the far end of the stone and began to carve away at the mortar, revealing a black gap between the edges of the stone slabs.

After thirty tedious minutes of chipping away at the grout, Alex eased the last remnant of the clay-like material out of the gap and blew away the debris. He sunk back with exhaustion and dabbed at the sweat collecting on his forehead.

"Excellent job." Clay rose to his feet and patted Alex and Jonas on the back. "Now all we need is to pry up the stone."

"The stone probably weighs five-hundred pounds," Alex sighed.

"Then it's a good thing we have four people. Let's go," urged Clay with excitement.

"O.K." Alex pushed himself onto his knees and lifted the crow bar. He slid the end of the bar into the gap on the far end of the stone and watched as Jonas reciprocated on the opposite end.

"When the stone moves up, you need to slide in that piece of wood." Jonas directed Ellie towards the piece of lumber in the corner with a motion of his head.

Jonas shot Alex a fatigued look and nodded. They simultaneously pushed the handles of the bars downwards. The metal scraped against the stone surface, sending forth a deafening screech throughout the crypt. The stone initially resisted as unseen mortar cracked and broke away beneath it. The stone then slowly rose from a narrow stone ledge upon which it had rested for centuries. Ellie watched intently as Alex struggled to main-

tain his grip on the crow bar. His triceps quivered uncontrollably as the bar slipped from his sweaty palms, sending the stone
crashing back down with a bang. A cloud of dust wafted into the
air. Ellie coughed into her fist.

"Five-hundred pounds! I think it is a lot heavier than that. We
might just need that backhoe after all." Alex paced around the
room massaging the palms of his hand, which had turned a scarlet red. Jonas panted as he fixated on the stone with disappointment.

"Let's go, my boy. Do you need an old man to do a young man's
work?" Clay picked up the bar and replaced it into the gap. He
nodded to Jonas who, still panting, followed suit by slipping his
crow bar into the crevice. They began to push down. The stone
once again began to budge, rising slightly up in the air. Clay
groaned as he pushed down with all his might. The two men began to run out of steam and the ascent suddenly halted. The stone
bobbed up and down, threatening to drop. Alex ran to Clay's side,
slipped his hands next to the old man's, and joined in the effort.
The stone inched further off the ground. As it cleared the surface,
Ellie encouraged them to keep pushing. Just as the men could not
hold up the stone for a second longer, Ellie slid the wood underneath the stone and backed away. The three men eagerly relaxed
their grips on the bars and allowed the stone to settle onto the
piece of wood. The wood squealed uncomfortably but managed
to hold the slab of stone up.

Clay smiled painfully. "Just a couple of more pieces of wood
and I do believe we could squeeze through."

Alex looked at Jonas and grimaced. The metal bars were once
again wedged beneath the slab and the stone was slowly lifted off
the wood. Ellie rapidly slid additional pieces of wood underneath
the stone until the slab leaned precariously on the pile at nearly a
sixty-degree angle like a hatch partially swung opened.

"I think we're good," Ellie announced.

"Hand me the flashlight," Alex urged as he positioned himself prostrate and eased his body up to the hole. He looked with some concern at the stone slab perilously teetering on the pile of wood and shook off the thought of what might happen if the wood snapped. Flashlight in hand, he peered into the darkness beneath the stone and turned on the light. He panned the beam of light into the blackness, revealing a short drop onto a stone surface. Clay gripped his ankles as Alex swung his body over the edge and hung partially suspended. He could make out the far wall of a small room beneath them. Alex motioned with his right hand to be pulled up.

"What did you see?" Clay asked as he knelt down.

"Not a heck of a lot. There's a room below us. I can't see very far. There is a small drop, not too far."

Jonas wordlessly began to gather up the flashlights. The three of them looked up at him.

"Well, what are we waiting for?"

35

Alex was the first to descend into the darkness. Squatting next to the opening, he pivoted his torso and allowed his feet to slip through the gap. He wiggled his hips until half his body hung over the side and gripped the edges of the hole. Ellie knelt down next to him and tried to direct the beam of the flashlight into the abyss, without success. Alex gave her a 'here goes nothing look' and pushed his body backwards into the hole. He suspended himself momentarily as his knuckles turned to white. With a slight swinging motion, Alex released his grip, fell backwards, and disappeared into the darkness.

Ellie rushed to the hole and fumbled with the flashlight. "Alex!"

The beam of the flashlight bounced about as Ellie frantically searched for Alex. She could make out coarse stone walls and explored the ground below her, expecting to see Alex's body splayed out upon it. The floor was bare. "Alex!"

Suddenly the light caught the reflection of Alex's eyes. "I'm alright," he answered, shielding his eyes from the glare. He tussled his hair, sending dust into the air. "The drop is farther than I thought. Toss me a flashlight."

Ellie released the flashlight and watched as Alex caught it against his chest. She reached back and received another flashlight from Clay.

They waited in silence as Alex disappeared into the room. After several minutes, his face emerged from the hole.

"What do you see?" Clay asked, pushing Ellie aside. She gave him an annoyed glance.

"First thing is that there are stairs so no need to be all Tarzan-like," Alex squinted. "We need more lighting. It's hard to see what's down here."

Clay silently gathered the flashlights and handed Jonas the lantern. Clay prodded his assistant with the butt of the flashlight, driving it into the small of his back. "Let's get down there and see what Polo has left us."

Jonas helped assist Clay into the hole and Alex guided Clay's foot onto the hidden staircase. As Clay disappeared into the blackness, Ellie maneuvered towards the opening but was stopped by Jonas.

"I think it is best that one of us stay up here," Jonas commented.

"OK, stay up here," Ellie shot back and tried to break his grip on her arm.

"I don't think you understand. I'm going down and you're staying up here."

Ellie broke free and backed up as Jonas looked at her menacingly. He suddenly smiled at her. "No worries. It's a crypt. This is no place for a girl, anyway." Jonas turned away and descended down through the hole.

Ellie stood beside the opening in the ground, fuming. She looked at the stone resting on the pile of wood and gave the pile a kick for good measure. The stack did not budge. *'No place for a girl.' What an ass*, Ellie huffed to herself. *There's no way I'm staying up here.*

She slid her body along the ground until her feet dangled into the hole. She could feel her feet contact the edge of a step and gained her footing. As she carefully backed her way down the staircase, her flashlight caught the undersurface of the pile of wood above.

That pile better hold, she thought and took a deep breath in.

36

Jonas turned the dial on the lantern, bathing the room in a warm yellow glow. The room was configured in the shape of a rectangle. In the southwest corner of the room was the short flight of stone stairs they had descended. Up above, the stone ceiling was approximately eight feet off the ground. The walls were constructed of small stones of various shapes, sizes, and colors that were fastened together by gray mortar. The far wall had partially caved in over the centuries, with a lattice-array of crisscrossing cracks and holes.

Alex silently walked around the room, methodically directing his flashlight across the surface of the walls, examining the room for any sign of writing or symbols, any clue left behind by Polo. He came away disappointed by the monotony of the patterns on the walls. He directed the beam of the flashlight across the floor and found it to be constructed of tiles. Each one of the tiles was rectangular in shape and covered with a layer of dust and dirt collected through the ages. Alex bent down and wiped away the grime from one of the tiles.

"Gold," Ellie exhaled as she squatted beside him, marveling at the rich golden color of the tile.

Alex scratched at the surface of the tile with a fingernail and came away with gold dust upon his fingertip. He brought his finger to his lips and blew. A puff of yellow dust wafted into the air. They looked down upon the tile and found simple gray stone beneath the scratch.

"I guess it's not 24 karat gold. Not by a long shot," Ellie muttered and glanced at the hundred or so similar tiles that composed the floor.

Clay appeared agitated as he paced around the room. Ellie gave Alex a somber glance that encapsulated her academic assessment.

Alex lingered in a squatting position, bounced on his ankles for a moment, and then stood up in the center of the room. He swung around completely as the disappointing reality set in.

The room was empty.

37

"Empty. It's empty. After all this...empty," Clay wailed. He waved the flashlight in the air.

"We don't know if it was *always* empty," Alex mumbled, nervously tapping his index finger against his chin.

"Tomb-robbers?" Ellie asked. She had spent much of her archeological career confronted by the disappointment that followed the handiwork of tomb-robbers. How many times had she discovered a new excavation site only to discover the contents had long ago been looted? It made her irate.

"It's possible. This room has probably been here for centuries. I'm sure there was ample time to steal whatever items were in here."

"Maybe we're not in the right place, man," Jonas argued.

"You saw the Polo family insignia on the stone slab," Ellie countered.

Jonas cheeks twisted in anger. He brought his face close to Ellie's. His eyes opened wide. "What I saw was chicken scratch... chicken scratch! That's right! Scuffmarks from some tourist's shoes. No more!"

"It would be quite a coincidence that the scuffmarks happened to look like three birds walking in a row," Ellie shot back.

"I saw those marks. Could have been birds, could have been hippos, could have been Jesus, Father, and the Holy Ghost for all we know!" Spittle flew from the corners of Jonas's lips as he advanced menacingly towards Ellie, his face twisted and maniacal in the glare of the lights.

Alex jumped between Jonas and Ellie and lifted his hands in the air. "Look, everyone needs to calm down. We haven't eaten, or slept for that matter, for some time…let's just take a second to think about this. We need to be systematic and examine what we have before us. If you could just hand me the lantern, I'd like to take a better look at the room."

"Go ahead. It's all yours, Gandhi." Jonas grunted angrily and pushed the lantern forcefully into Alex's chest, sending him stumbling backwards onto the tile. He landed in a heap upon his back, the back of his head smacking against the hard tile. The impact sent the lantern flying from his hands. After clanging against the floor, the lantern light flickered and went out.

Alex's vision dimmed. Flashes of colors flickered in the blackness above him. As he blinked several times in an attempt to refocus, gravel fell from the ceiling and landed on his cheek. Alex reached up and brushed the grit away. A thin beam of light projected down from the ceiling, striking Alex in the center of his forehead.

Ellie flipped on the flashlight and rushed to Alex's side. Clay joined her and attempted to lift Alex to a sitting position. He resisted. "You O.K?"

"Flashlight," Alex urged. He wrested it from Ellie and directed it up towards the ceiling. Alex began to laugh.

Ellie studied him with concern. Had he gone mad? Did the fall knock something loose?

Alex smiled at Ellie and Clay and motioned towards the ceiling. Ellie and Clay followed the beam of light as it danced across the ceiling and finally settled on a rudimentary circle carved into the stone surface. In the center of the circle was a tiny chiseled hole that allowed a thin beam of light to pass through it from the crypt above. "It's the third symbol. It was right above us all the time."

38

Stop looking at me!

The dark eyes peeked out from rivulets of blood dripping from the crown of thorns.

Father Fermo swiveled his chair and averted his eyes from the large crucifix fastened to a wall in his office.

He was glad that the banging from the crypt had finally ceased. *What was that lot up to anyway with all that noise?* he wondered. It sounded like they were tearing up the place.

The priest guiltily peered up at Jesus. *I did it for the church! Please don't look at me that way. The church will be taken care of. That's all that matters in the end. And why not a little something for me? Have I not earned it after all these years of service?*

He closed his eyes and allowed his thoughts to drift to a sunny day as he floated along in a wooden boat on the placid waters of Lake Como. But something continued to nag him. His eyelids crept open. Through the slits, he could detect the penetrating glare of the statue.

Stop looking at me!

Father Fermo swung his chair completely around so that he faced the door to his office. He was startled to see two men standing in the doorway.

"I'm sorry, but the church is closed."

"Closed?" the shorter of the two men asked.

"Renovations," the priest replied and swallowed.

"I see." The shorter of the two men turned his back to the priest and shut the door to the office. He lingered for a moment staring at the wooden surface of the door. The corners of his lips curled tensely. "I'm sorry, Father Fermo but we are not here for the church."

39

Clay reached down and pulled Alex up from the ground. The muscles in Alex's back protested as he stretched. He glared at Jonas who shrugged and sat against the wall. Alex massaged the back of his head and detected a contusion developing.

"I must apologize for Jonas. He's always been a loose cannon. He can be very emotional. It's the Portuguese in him, I think." Clay frowned at the figure sulking against the wall.

Alex peered up at the circle carved into the ceiling. The edges of it were rough, as if a child had dipped a branch in wet cement. The hole in the center was nearly imperceptible if not for the rich yellow light streaming through it. Alex sized up the room they were in, placing it in the three-dimensional layout of the church.

"The hole must have been behind the altar, near the display of candles. The light must be from the candles above."

Clay craned his neck and looked up at the ceiling.

"Dirt must have loosened from the hole, allowing the light to pass through it."

"Do you think it is the third symbol?"

"Well, it sure looks a lot like it…a circle with a dot in the center." Alex pulled out a sketch of the three symbols from a paper in his pocket.

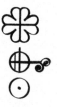

"What do you think it means?"

Alex held up a finger to silence him. He inspected the ceiling and then squatted down on the floor. Clay watched with intrigue as Alex brushed aside dirt from the surface of a tile and polished it with the sleeve of his shirt.

"Maybe the more appropriate question is not 'what does it mean' but 'what does it do?'"

"Well, what does it do?" Ellie wondered as a smirk appeared on Alex's face.

He reached out, grabbed Ellie's shoulders, and turned her body so she was facing the far end of the room. "Stay here and watch the floor." Alex retreated to the stairs and scampered up several steps. From the elevated perch, he surveyed the floor below him. "Everyone, please, turn off your flashlights."

One by one, the flashlights were shut off until the room was pitch black except for the thin beam of light traveling through the hole in the ceiling. Ellie gasped as the light settled on a single tile on the ground. The tile sparkled a luminous, golden glow that cast wave-like patterns across the walls.

Alex leapt from the stairs and ran over to the illuminated tile. As he kneeled down in front of it, the ethereal light reflected on his shirt and face. Clay crept along the floor and pushed his body close to Alex's side.

The tile, on first glance, looked like any one of the hundred or so seemingly identical gold tiles that composed the floor. Alex ran his fingernail across the surface and smiled as he pulled up his finger. He held his finger up to Ellie who could see that there was no gold paint on it like the other tile they had examined.

"You think it's real gold?" Clay raised his eyebrows and gave Alex a sideways glance.

The word 'gold' roused Jonas from his depression. He sprung to his feet and approached the two kneeling figures at the far end of the room.

Alex studied the tile closely, nearly allowing his nose to brush up against the surface. "I don't see any writing or symbols on the tile. It sure looks like all the other tiles, but it is different."

"What is it then?" Clay asked.

"What if it is a foundation stone?" Ellie chimed in.

"A what?" Jonas asked.

"A foundation stone. Throughout history, when a building was going to be constructed, a special stone was often placed within its foundation, thus a 'foundation stone.' It was mostly ceremonial in nature, often having an inscription on it or a blessing bestowed upon it. You know, the Grand Poobah would come out from the village and maybe sacrifice a sheep on it, sprinkle some holy water, or chant something. Sometimes it had a more important engineering role—it would serve as the first stone placed that would allow the builders to use it as a reference point for all the other stones. This was big with the Freemasons, who had a whole elaborate ritual associated with it. Most of the time the stone was positioned within the northeast corner and it was sometimes called a 'cornerstone' but not always. And sometimes things were hidden in it or under it."

"Hidden?" Jonas asked.

"Like a time capsule?" Clay followed.

"Yeah, something like that."

"Treasures?" Jonas mumbled with wide eyes.

Ellie sighed and gathered the group around her. She felt as if she was suddenly back at the university lecturing a class of undergraduates. "We talked before about the *Epic of Gilgamesh*, that marvelous, ancient Sumerian text which referenced a great Flood, magical gardens, and plants bestowing immortality long before the Judeo-Christian Bible. Well, the epic has a prologue that goes into detail how one could find the tablet of lapis lazuli upon which the tale of Gilgamesh's exploits was inscribed. In the prologue, it is stated that the tablets could be found under the *cornerstone* of the Eanna Temple in Uruk. If the cornerstone were removed, one would find a hidden copper box that contained the tablet. All I'm saying is what if this tile, this wonderful, golden tile, is the foundation stone of this church? What if Polo has led us to something hidden underneath it?"

"Yes, amazing." Clay stuttered. Alex smiled at Ellie who beamed back.

"We need to see if we can pull up this stone. Two in one day," Clay pronounced and disappeared into the darkness. He quickly returned with one of the crowbars they had previously used to pry up the stone slab that allowed for their descent. "I suppose this will have to do again."

40

The tip of the bar sunk deeply into the mortar. Alex had chipped away for nearly an hour and was finally battling the last of the stubborn cement. He maneuvered the bar in a circular motion, loosening the mortar and causing the tile to nearly float within the space he had carved out between it and the adjacent tiles. With a crack, the mortar was driven upwards and sent rattling across the floor.

"Supreme job!" Clay congratulated him with a paternalistic pat on the back. "Now let's see what's under that bugger."

He could feel the group close tightly in on him. Alex looked at each member of the eclectic team assembled with some uncertainty. What if there was nothing beneath the stone? He slipped the bar beyond the edge of the tile and pried it upwards. With a grating noise, the tile popped free of the surrounding stones. Ellie reached down and gripped the golden brick to her chest, surprised by the heaviness. They stared down at the rectangular void beneath the tile. The flashlight shook slightly in Alex's hands as he directed the light into the hole with tremulous anticipation. As he explored the blackened hole, he could make out the faint edge of a box.

"There's something down there!"

Alex extended his right arm deep into the void and searched blindly for the box. His fingers crept along the dank earth until he could feel the chill of metal against his fingertips. He stretched his arm to the limit as his shoulder ran up against the surrounding tile and prevented further exploration. Just as he was about to remove his hand from the hole and see if someone else in his party would have any better luck, his fingers were able to seize hold of a clasp. With a heave, he pulled his arm out of the space, clutching the box and set it upon the ground.

Ellie sunk to her knees, still tightly hugging the golden block to her chest.

The box was simple and unadorned. It was constructed out of dark, gray iron and had a clasp in the front of it. There was no lock, and Alex merely flipped the clasp upwards and silently lifted the lid back. Clay, eager to see the contents, leaned in excessively, blocking the light and causing Ellie to groan. She swatted him to the side with the backside of her hand.

With the flashlights trained intensely upon the interior of the box, they could see that the box contained a brown piece of leather that was folded snuggly upon itself. The leather covering was tied with a string made of horsehair. Alex reached into the box and carefully undid the knot of the string, allowing it to fall to the side. The four huddled closely together as Alex's fingers seized each end of the leather covering and delicately peeled them back. Beneath the leather was an eight-petaled metallic object seemingly identical to the one recovered from Dr. Gozzi behind the painting of the Black Doge.

"Wonderful. Now we have two of those 'things' that we don't have the foggiest clue what they are or what they are used for," Jonas complained.

Alex shook his head and attempted to shut out Jonas's comment. He lifted the metallic object, passed it to Clay, and suddenly froze. He stared down at the treasure that was beneath the artifact and gasped. Ellie edged closer to the box.

"Do you know what this is?" Alex flipped over the leather cover and could see the title written in Franco-Italian on the yellowed parchment. "I think we've found…"

Alex voice trailed off as his eyes were suddenly drawn to the opening in the crypt's floor from which they had descended into the subterranean lair. A shadow scampered across the hole, followed by a creaking noise.

"Quiet," Jonas urged as he held his index finger to his lips and directed the flashlight towards the opening above them. His eyes squinted and then popped open with alarm. He shot a severe look at Ellie. "You should have stayed upstairs!"

Jonas abruptly sprang up from a crouch and darted towards the stairs. He awkwardly leapt onto the first step of the stairs and stumbled upwards towards the opening. Having sensed the danger, Ellie followed closely behind, rushed to the bottom of the staircase, and peered upwards into the crypt above. She could see the heavy stone slab slowly levitate off the pile of wood.

Jonas thrust his hand up through the opening and planted the palm of his left hand flush against the undersurface of the stone. He froze as an inquisitive face studied them from the crypt.

The face was that of an elderly Asian man with black eyes and thickened, ruddy skin that appeared wind-burned. The man bent over with his hands on his knees and looked at Jonas and then Ellie with curiosity. When he finally spoke, it was in a heavily-accented English.

"And who do you think *you* are? Are *you* so deserving? This knowledge is not for you to possess." The man shook his head with apparent disappointment, glanced back into the crypt, and muttered something in a foreign language. Ellie tried to place it. It sounded Chinese but she wasn't certain. Ellie could make out a set of meaty fingers tightly gripping the edge of the perched stone slab. She followed the fingers back to a hulk-like form looming high above the hole. Ellie could only see up to the man's massive, bearlike chest.

The Asian man nodded to the enormous figure, who responded by heaving the stone further up. The pieces of wood were released from the weight of the stone and tumbled down the stairs into the room below. Jonas instinctively pushed upwards with his hand. He released the flashlight, which bounced down the steps with a rattle. Jonas withdrew his gun. He brought his shoulder to bear against the undersurface of the stone, planted his feet, and attempted to direct the barrel of the pistol through the gap.

The Asian man leaned in and uttered a ghostly whisper. "Now this will be your tomb, too." He nodded a final time to the figure holding up the stone.

"No!!!" Jonas shrieked and fruitlessly braced himself.

With a thunderous bang the stone fell, striking Jonas in the shoulder and sending him catapulting through the air and onto the ground below.

41

The thunderous crash of the stone falling echoed through the subterranean room. A thick cloud of dust wafted over Alex as he protectively flipped the lid on the box shut. The black dust coated the lenses of the flashlights, dimming the interior of the room. Somewhere in the fog, Alex could hear Ellie coughing uncontrollably. Clay crouched down beside Alex and shielded his nose and mouth with his shirt.

As the sound of the crash faded, Alex could hear groaning emanating from the corner of the room. Jonas rocked back and forth on his hips in a fetal position as he tightly clutched his left shoulder. His arm appeared unnaturally contorted. Clay scurried to the man's side and helped prop him up against the wall. Jonas grimaced in pain as he breathed rapidly through clenched teeth.

"It's dislocated. That bastard. He dislocated my shoulder." Tears welled up in the corner of Jonas's eyes.

"What do we do?" Clay asked with a look of horror.

"You're the doctor," Jonas barked back in pain.

"I'm not a clinician, I'm a researcher. I don't know the first things about dislocations." Clay frantically searched around the room for help. Alex shrugged. Ellie sighed and approached the two figures. She kneeled beside Jonas.

"I'll have you know that I have dislocated my shoulder nearly fifteen times. I actually stopped counting. It became somewhat of a party trick back at University. Lie on your back," she sighed.

Jonas looked at Ellie with uncertainty. Clay helped ease the injured man down on his back. Ellie gripped Jonas' wrist and lifted his arm vertically in the air, causing Jonas to grunt in protest. She pushed the tip of her shoe against his chest and roughly pulled upwards. Jonas's eyes opened wide and he growled in pain. With a swift motion, Ellie externally rotated his left shoulder, eliciting screams from the patient. A click reverberated through the room.

Jonas rocked back and forth, clutching his reduced shoulder, and whimpered pathetically. Ellie leaned in so her face was close to the injured man. "That felt good. How about for you? That was for Alex." She poked Jonas in the chest with her finger and stood up. She climbed up the stairs, wedged her small frame against the stone slab, and pushed up, to no avail.

Jonas pulled himself up to a sitting position as Clay steadied him. He glared at Ellie before speaking. "I don't want to state the obvious but we're trapped down here. It's not like we're caught in the lift and we're waiting for the firemen to come to rescue us. We are trapped as if no one is coming." Ellie looked at Jonas and shivered. She detected something in his eyes that she had not seen before from him—fear and surprise.

Ellie turned back and waved at Clay. "Hey, Redmund. Over here." The old man returned her gaze as if in a daze.

"Who were those guys? This doesn't make any sense. If the Order wants Polo's secret so bad, why would they lock us down here with it?"

Jonas began to speak and stopped.

Clay ran his fingers through his gray hair and came away with a fistful of dirt. "Agreed. It doesn't make sense."

"What if we yell?" Ellie pounded on the bottom of the stone. "Someone might hear us. Tourists…maybe that priest. Help! Help! We're trapped down here!"

"Save your breath, girl," Jonas spat out with venom. "Do you know how thick that stone is? Nobody is going to hear us."

Ellie smacked the bottom of the stone a final time, with frustration. She sat on the steps and put her head in her hands. She could feel the ceiling and walls close in on her and she fought the tide of claustrophobia lapping at her. *We're trapped in here! That man said this will be our tomb and he is right!* She abruptly lifted her head and fumbled for her bag. She plunged her hand into the bag and searched for her cell phone.

"What are you doing?" Clay inquired.

She ignored the old man, lifted the device out, and turned it on. The screen sprang to life.

No Service.

"Terrific," Ellie concluded and slipped the phone back in her bag.

Ellie rose to her feet and approached Alex who had carefully removed the text. "Hey Alex, I hate to admit it, but Jonas is right. We're in a bit of trouble here. Actually, a lot of trouble...." Her voice trailed off as her concerns momentarily drifted upon seeing the pages before her. "What is it?"

"I think it is a manuscript of Marco Polo's *Description of the World—Le Devisament Dou Monde.*"

"Could it be?" Clay rushed to Alex's side and kneeled beside him.

"Possibly."

"Possibly, what?" Jonas stumbled over, still clutching his shoulder.

"The original Polo manuscript, that's what!" Clay exclaimed. "It's a thing of legend. I've been searching for it for ages."

Clay nodded to Alex.

"OK. Here's the deal. After the Polos returned once and for all to Venice from their extensive travels through the East, Marco Polo led a surprising low-key and monotonous life. In fact, there are very few records of the man in the historical archives of the city—strange for such a celebrated man. He resurfaces many years later as a commander of a Venetian galley that gets captured by the Genoans during a sea battle. Marco Polo is imprisoned in a Genoese jail where he meets Rustichello, a Pisan author known for his tales of chivalry who had been previously captured during another battle. While in prison, the two collaborated in the creation of the *Description of the World.*

"Here's the mystery... the original manuscript vanished. As the handwritten versions of the *Description of the World* multiplied through the years, inevitably mistakes in transcription and translation were made—sections were accidentally, or intentionally for that matter, omitted or elaborated upon. So much was potentially altered, no one can be certain what was actually *in* the original manuscript. Hell, nobody is even sure what *language* the original text was written in...until, perhaps now."

They stared down at the text before them. The binding of the book was constructed from dark, brown leather. There was no writing on the front to identify what was inside. Alex flipped the manuscript open. Light brown calf-skin vellum lined the insides of the cover. Opposite the cover was a yellowed page of parchment with meticulously inked calligraphy.

"It's in Franco-Italian or Franco-Venetian, a literary language that was popular during the time of Marco Polo. It says *Description of the World, the Marvelous Journeys of the Greatest Traveler, the Noble Messer Polo, As Penned and Attested in 1298 from the Birth of Jesus Christ by Master Rustichello.*" The flashlight Alex was holding began to dim and flicker, the words on the page faded into the darkness. Alex shook the flashlight and tapped it against the palm of his hand to no avail.

"Wonderful," Jonas snorted. "Just wonderful. By my calculations we're down to just two working flashlights and from the looks of them I wouldn't be surprised if the batteries are from the Second World War."

"We'd still have the lantern if you hadn't thrown it at Alex and broke it," Ellie shot back.

"We wouldn't be locked down here if you stayed up there like I said! And by the way, I merely handed the lantern to him. It's not my fault if he couldn't hold onto it."

Clay spoke up. "O.K., everyone needs to relax and take a deep breath. First things first: let's try to conserve the batteries in the flashlights. We need to put our heads together and figure a way out of this predicament."

"Predicament?" Jonas sputtered. "Predicament? That's a bit of an understatement. We're about to become a permanent part of this crypt."

Ellie could feel her stomach churn—an odd gnawing of hunger and dismay. When was the last time she had eaten anything? She could not remember. Her fingertips tingled from the coldness of the crypt. She cupped her hands, brought them to her face, and exhaled hot air upon them. Rubbing her palms together, she hoped that the friction would restore warmth to her body. The cold dankness seemed to seep into her body, driving for the core, and making her bones ache. She could feel Alex's arm reach across her shoulder and bring her close. The warmth of his body felt soothing as she leaned against his shoulder. She felt exhausted, drained of all energy.

"Alex, how are we going to get out of here?" She closed her eyes.

"I don't know. We'll think of something."

As Ellie drifted off to sleep, she could hear Jonas mutter, "It would be ironic...that is, having to burn that manuscript to keep warm."

No one laughed.

42
Tomar, Portugal

*The man adjusted the cuffs of his shirt and looked out from his balcony over-*looking the city. A servant silently pushed aside the veneer drapes undulating in the wind and placed a glass of sparkling water with a lemon wedge upon a round table beside the railing. The man turned around, sat down in a chair beside the table, and placed his cellular phone upon the crisp, starched white linen adorning the tabletop.

"Thank you, Manuel."

The servant bowed slightly and retreated into the adjoining apartment, leaving the man to stare out at the rounded walls of the Convento de Cristo. Somewhere below, the buzz of a motor-bike competed with the honk of a car.

The cellular phone began to vibrate and inched its way across the table towards the edge. The man took a drink of water, delicately placed the crystal glass back upon the table, and lifted the phone before it plunged off the side.

"Yes, Mr. Haasbroek."

"My full team is positioned at the Church of San Procolo."

"Yes."

The South African seemed nervous. "They're gone."

"Gone, Mr. Haasbroek?"

"Vanished."

"Vanished?"

"We've performed a search of the church. The priest is dead in his office, bludgeoned to death. The rest of the church is empty."

"I thought you had surveillance?"

"I had a man monitoring the front of the church before we got there. They must have slipped out the back of the church before the rest of our team arrived."

The line grew silent. Haasbroek coughed and began to speak.

"My surveillance asset did capture images of two people who came and went from the church before the team arrived. I am sending the images to you right now."

The man looked down at the screen and could see a close up of two Asian men emerging from the church.

"You have disappointed me again." The man sighed. The days of the warrior-priests were over. It pained him to outsource the muscle, especially when there was not much brain to match. The line grew silent again. The man tapped the side of the glass and watched as the bubbles clung desperately to the sides before releasing and beginning their float to the surface.

"Mr. Haasbroek, organize your team and wait. They will resurface, and when they do, be ready."

"Sir, I do not wish to pry, but what are you not telling us. I'm sick of feeling like I'm part of some elaborate game."

"Mr. Haasbroek, do not disappoint me again." He disconnected the line and rose from the table. The pieces of the puzzle were all in play. He would need to confer with the rest of the Order.

The man pulled aside the curtains and entered the lavish apartment. How he enjoyed this small slice of heaven. It was a breath of fresh air from the enormity of his estates. He smiled at the Van Gogh and Picasso on the wall. They were divine after all. He did pay a steep price for them. Art theft was never cheap. But it was the unknown compendium piece to *The Mona Lisa* that always took his breath away. The blue sky was riveting and bold.

He paused and looked at the photo of the two Asian men on his phone.

Darkhad. Then the legends were true, after all.

43

Tap...Tap...Tap.

Ellie opened her eyes and was confronted by blackness. Disoriented, she found herself curled up with her head resting on her bag. Alex's jacket was slung over her like a blanket. She craned her neck in the direction of the tapping noise and could see the yellow glow of a flashlight and shadows.

Ellie raised her body from the frigid tile and pushed herself to her feet. Her legs felt rubbery as she neared the light. She reached the far wall in the room and found Clay directing the beam of the flashlight against the wall as Jonas stood beside it with arms crossed.

"What's going on?" Ellie asked groggily.

Alex ran his fingers along the jagged cracks and held his palm against a hole where several stones had fallen away. He could feel a cool breeze slip by his fingers. Lifting his foot, he drove the heel of his shoe into the wall and watched as a portion of the wall caved in, revealing a fist-sized hole. He peered back to see his three companions wide-mouthed.

"Did you know this all along?" Ellie asked.

"I had some suspicions. Verona is on the Via Gallica, an ancient Roman highway connecting the cities of Northern Italy. Off the Via Gallica are numerous Roman and Christian necropolises. It turns out that the city of Verona was built on such a necropolis. Something the priest said got me thinking. If my hunch is right, the Basilica of San Zeno and the Church of San Procolo were likely built over the Christian burial sites and if so there may be connecting catacombs. Grab our stuff, we're going through this wall."

Clay grinned slightly and mumbled under his breath. "He never ceases to amaze me."

The light danced upon the broken stone as Alex wedged his body through the hole and wiggled his torso free. He dropped a short distance into the neighboring room with a thud and scrambled to his feet. The room was little more than a cavity, a tight space with a partially caved in sloped stone ceiling and crumbling walls. He trained the flashlight into a carved out void in the wall, housing broken bone fragments. The light startled a rodent who darted from the hole and scampered quietly away.

"Great, an even smaller room," came from behind him.

Alex turned to see Jonas stick his head through the opening in the wall and pull himself into the room. Jonas squatted and turned back to assist Clay and then Ellie enter the room.

"This is cozy," Jonas complained. The four found themselves uncomfortably pressed against each other. Ellie shimmied her body to avoid being pressed up against Jonas's armpit, ducked under Alex's arm, and wedged herself into a void. "It's the first time I've been warm in hours."

Alex trained the light on the far wall and found a rectangular opening near the floor. He dropped to his knees and explored the gap. The aperture was man-made, carved out of the stone wall. The light revealed a dark passageway not much larger than a crawlspace. A cool breeze escaped from the opening and ran through his hair like iced fingers.

"There's an opening here. It's not very big but we should fit."

"It's going to be tight." Clay crouched down beside Alex and peered skeptically into the tunnel.

"We have no choice but to go forward."

Alex slung his parcel bag over his shoulder until it rested

against the small of his back. He subconsciously patted it for luck, hoping that the leather covered manuscript he had snuggly deposited for safe-keeping would finally emerge from its centuries-old grave. Dropping to his knees, he pushed the flashlight as far as he could into the tunnel. The walls were black and slimy. He slid his head into the space and squeezed the rest of his torso further in. Although he was only in a short distance, he suddenly felt fearfully alone—cut off from the rest of his team. Alex closed his eyes and fought the urge to scamper backwards like a crab. A faint howling noise rhythmically filled the passageway and the cold air stung his exposed face. Alex propped himself up on his elbows and lifted his body a short distance off the ground until the ceiling caused him to curve his neck downwards. He dug his shoes into the ground and pushed off. He propelled himself forward on his elbows, his hips twisting painfully with each movement. After a short distance, Alex contorted his neck and directed the beam of the flashlight back from where he came. He caught sight of Ellie's ashen face wedged into the tunnel behind him.

"Tell me you see a light at the end of this tunnel," Ellie groaned. She whimpered as a rat scurried across her back, up her neck, and got tangled in her hair before freeing itself and darting into the darkness.

Alex turned his head forward. The flashlight in front of him flickered momentarily. Alex sucked in his breath as the light dimmed and threatened to go out. He did not want to imagine what it would be like to navigate this tunnel in complete darkness. The prospect sent him pushing forward.

After some distance, the tunnel widened and split. The left passageway was blocked by a cave-in with a jagged array of stones filling the path. Alex squeezed into the tunnel to the right and suddenly found himself sliding down an embankment. He frantically attempted to halt his descent by digging the heel of his hands into the stone surface but the green grime coating it was too slippery. Alex's head flopped forward and collapsed the tripod support of his arms. He found himself sliding uncontrollably down the steep slope. His eyes widened with alarm as he quickly approached a narrow stone ledge that hovered over a larger room. His body struck the ledge hard. The impact sent his torso spinning until his hips flew out over the ledge and he found himself suspended precariously over the room below.

Alex's fingers dug into the stone ledge. His muscles ached as he forced himself to look below at the long drop onto the stone surface. The strap of his bag felt taut under his armpit. Alex looked up to find that his bag had fortuitously snagged a stony outcropping and was supporting him.

Thank you, Marco.

Alex struggled to pull himself back onto the ledge, gripping the leather strap with his right hand and the stone surface with his left. Muscles tensed, he swung his right leg up. His shoe caught the lip of the ledge and he used it as leverage to pull his body onto the stone surface. He lay for some time on his back, trying to catch his breath. He could see Ellie's face poke out from an opening in the wall above.

"You OK?"

"Just a little beat up." Alex pulled himself to a sitting position and looked up at Ellie. "Be careful, it's really slippery. You're going to need to go down feet first. I'll catch you."

Alex waited as Ellie's shoes dangled from the hole. She pushed her body backwards and slid down the embankment on her stomach until she found herself in Alex's embrace. Secure on the ledge, Ellie attempted to wipe the slime off the front of her blouse. The wet fabric stuck to her skin. She moved aside to allow Clay and Jonas to descend to the ledge.

"Now what?" Jonas asked as his flashlight explored the ceiling above, finding it to be a lattice-work of cracks.

"I would venture we go down," Clay responded, wiping the palms of his hands with a handkerchief before passing it to Ellie.

Alex walked along the stone ledge that ran along the perimeter of the room. A large break in the stone surface of the ledge produced a gap. With the help of the flashlight, he could see that jagged stones composed one of the walls.

"We climb down."

Alex let his foot dangle in the gap in the ledge. The tip of his shoe contacted a stone. He allowed his body to slip into the gap. Clutching the lip of the ledge, his other shoe found some footing on another rock. He slowly descended down into the room below.

Training the flashlight up, he could see his companions clustered by the gap.

"What do you see?" Clay asked.

Alex surveyed the room. The chamber was empty. The floor had a sandy bottom with rocks scattered upon it. There were faint frescoes painted on the walls, faded through the centuries. Alex could make out a youthful Jesus as shepherd tending over a flock of sheep.

"It may be an early Christian Church. It wasn't uncommon to have them underground during the time of Roman persecution."

"Just tell me there is an exit to this Church," Jonas urged.

Alex ignored the comment and let the light pan across the ground. A dull white object caught his attention and he squatted beside it.

"What do you see?" Clay asked as he scaled down the wall.

Alex reached out and grabbed a small handful of sand. He let the grains run through his fingers like a sieve until all that was left in the palm of his hand was a half-smoked cigarette.

"Cigarette." Alex held it up as Clay approached.

"Sorry. I don't smoke. It's a nasty vice."

"It's a cigarette."

"I don't get what you're trying to say."

"The early Christians didn't smoke."

"OK."

"Well, someone must have been in here. Possibly, recently."

Clay's eyes twinkled and he smiled broadly. "Which means that unless we find his skeleton here, there must be a way out of here!"

"Exactly."

The earthen and stone passageway leading from the subterranean church was narrow but tall. The four traveled in silence as the temperature continued to remain bitingly cool. Ellie could see frozen precipitation coating the walls and hear the sound of dripping water in the distance.

"I think we're near the river."

"Which river? The Nile? I feel like we've been walking forever," Jonas complained. The flashlight he was holding suddenly went out. He tapped it against the wall to no avail. "Looks like we're down to one flashlight."

"There's something up ahead," Alex announced as the passageway widened slightly. Along the side of the tunnel were barrels. The ground beneath their feet turned from dirt to cement. They reached a flight of stone steps that led to a wooden door in the ceiling. The wood was dilapidated with corroded planks eaten away or missing completely. Alex shined the light through the cracks and could see a room above. He pushed on the door but found it locked.

"Allow me." Jonas growled and not so delicately pushed Alex aside. Jonas leveled his good shoulder against the door. With a yell and a limited charge, his shoulder contacted the wood, splintering the planks, and sending the shards falling to the ground below. He continued to pound away at the door until he was able to pull himself through a hole into the room above. Alex, Clay, and Ellie followed.

The room was empty except for an ancient, vandalized kitchenette. Cigarette butts and hypodermic needles were strewn across the floor. Graffiti was sprayed across the walls. An old plaque proclaiming "Property of the Verona Water Authority" was covered over with a neon green peace sign. Ellie peered through a partially boarded up window and her heart quickened at the sight of the banks of the River Adige outside. Jonas initially tried the front door and found it locked. With a kick, the door cracked and opened. The sunlight was blinding. The four shielded their eyes with their hands and stumbled out like a group of drunkards dressed in tattered and soiled clothes.

Ellie sunk to her knees and pulled blades of grass from the ground.

Alex clung to his satchel and smiled as the river lapped serenely against the shore in front of him.

44

Ellie removed the plush white towel from the heating rack, tilted her head down, and loosely wrapped her hair. She leaned over the sink and with the ball of her hand wiped away the fog from the mirror. She peered at herself. The pink had finally returned to her cheeks but her lips remained chapped and red. She looked down at her naked body, running her fingers across the many bruises and bumps that dotted her skin. After the events of the prior days—the discovery of the Polo manuscript beneath the Church of San Procolo, the trek through the catacombs beneath Verona, and finally the flight from Verona aboard Clay's Learjet—the hot bath felt truly amazing. Clay had wanted to get far away from the forces hunting them, ultimately ordering his personal pilot to travel to Turin.

The five-star hotel was over-the-top in every way, from the exquisite dining to the large suites whose spacious balconies overlooked the city. To go from being trapped in a stone crypt to a life of luxury took some adjustment, but Ellie told herself that a girl could get used to it. She slipped the white robe on and cinched the belt tightly around her waist, looked one last time in the mirror, and opened the door. Steam escaped from the bathroom.

She walked barefoot on the carpet and stopped before the king sized bed. Laid out upon the duvet were an assortment of expensive Italian clothes meticulously organized in piles of shirts, pants, skirts, socks and stockings, and jackets. Although Ellie continued to be suspicious of the old man, she could not deny Clay's generosity. After fleeing from Verona with the muddied proverbial shirts on their backs, in Turin he had arranged for personal shoppers who canvassed the city and returned with new wardrobes for each of them.

Ellie sat down on the bed. Through a gap in the silk curtains, she could see the sun sinking below the cityscape, producing a muted silhouette of church steeples. She reached out and wrapped her fingers around the receiver of a gilded phone. Ellie had an urge to call Alex. She wondered what he would think about being asked if he wanted to come over. She immediately blushed with embarrassment. It seemed so collegiate but she could not deny her feelings. Perhaps it was the romantic ambience of the hotel or the excitement of the chase. She could not underestimate the bond two people could form in the face of adversity. She had found Alex to be compassionate, caring, smart, and strong. After Gordon, Ellie coped with his loss by creating an impenetrable shield that prevented any intimacy. All of this was unexpected as Alex had somehow disarmed her defenses. Though only a young graduate student, Alex possessed the very maturity and wisdom that made Ellie feel something she had not felt in ages…safe.

She smiled at the thought. Ellie lifted the receiver to her ear. Just then, a knock at the door startled her. She placed the receiver back on the cradle, sprung up from the bed, and made her way to the door.

Ellie leaned in and placed her eye to the peephole. She grinned upon seeing Alex nervously waiting by the door.

She opened the door. Ellie nearly laughed upon seeing Alex. He was dressed in a black jacket adorned with bright silver zippers that served no practical purpose, crisscrossing the fabric in a pattern that could only be admired by the critics at a fashion show.

"Don't say a word," Alex warned. "I don't think my personal shopper, Italo, and I have the same taste in clothing. Don't worry, I'm told my brown jacket is being dry cleaned as we speak."

"I think it looks…" Ellie smirked.

"Not a word," Alex brought his index finger up to silence her.

"What brings you to these parts," Ellie asked coyly.

Alex appeared to suddenly realize that Ellie was dressed in a robe with her hair bundled in a towel. "I'm sorry, but I couldn't wait to come by…may I?" He motioned to come in. Ellie nodded and moved aside.

Alex entered like a whirlwind. "I've been looking through the manuscript and I'm frustrated."

"Oh, the manuscript," Ellie replied with disappointment and closed the door. "You're not the only one frustrated," she mumbled out of the side of her mouth.

"I think we need to brainstorm on it. I hope you don't mind, I asked Redmund and Jonas to come by."

"They're coming here?"

"Yes. Sorry. I should have checked with you first." He paused and looked at her in her robe. A flash of confusion passed across his face. "You probably will want to change, huh? They'll be here any second."

Ellie swung around and angrily grabbed several of the garments on the bed. As she stalked away from Alex, he could hear her mumble under her breath, "Men!"

45

"You're stuck." Clay rose from the chair and paced around Ellie's suite. He was dressed in a dapper blue blazer with a collared shirt, slacks, and Bruno Magli shoes. In his left hand was a fine porcelain saucer upon which rested a small espresso cup. Clay would periodically lift the cup to his lips and take a sip. Jonas hovered in the background, leaning against a dresser. He still appeared to be nursing his shoulder. Ellie sat in a pastel colored upholstered chair with legs and arms coolly crossed. Her hair was still damp and tussled.

"I think that is a little harsh, Redmund," Alex answered. He had cleared off an antique wooden desk in the corner, removing a leather-covered book containing descriptions of the amenities provided by the hotel, magazines about the city of Turin, and a pile of hotel stationary. The manuscript was delicately laid out upon the desk behind Alex. He swiveled in the chair and looked at Clay. "I'm not an expert in the field. I'm just a graduate student. Let's not forget that. Besides that, I'm certainly not a linguist. This manuscript is written in a hybrid language not used anymore—it's a mixture of French and Italian. Foreign languages aren't my strong suits, especially Franco-Venetian."

He looked around the room and did not sense any sympathy.

"You said this is the original Polo manuscript. Unless I am forgetting. Maybe the freezing temperature in the crypt might have made me delirious," Jonas teased.

"I *think* it is the original manu…" Alex held up his hands. "Listen…hear me out. There are many versions of Marco Polo's

Description of the World. Redmund, you know this better than anyone through your own searches. Most Polo scholars divide the manuscripts into three principal categories. Category A includes a series of manuscripts that most scholars believe to be the closest to the original manuscript. Some of these manuscripts are written in French, others in Venetian or Tuscan, others in Czech or Gaelic. Category B includes manuscripts with material that is not found in the A versions and may have been added later or suppressed for some reason from the early versions. The third category contains a single manuscript known as the 'F' version. It is the oldest known copy of Polo's *Description of the World.* It is an early fourteenth-century manuscript written in Franco-Venetian known as *The Book of Wonders,* kept at the Bibliothèque Nationale in Paris. If my suspicion is correct, I believe that this manuscript predates the 'F' version. It may be within its *own* category. It may be the source text for all other manuscripts."

"Sounds like we need an expert on the manuscripts, someone who can make sense of the text," Clay voiced aloud. "Who knows what secrets are within it? I think there is only one person who can truly help us. We need Bertrand Foucault."

Alex raised his eyebrows.

"Bertrand Foucault has written the most definitive translation of the 'F' version. I bought a limited edition facsimile of *The Book of Wonders* many years ago annotated by Foucault. He's done some work for me in the past. If anyone can help us with this manuscript, it's him. Pack up your things, we're going to Paris."

46

With the press of a button, the massive white screen silently elevated, disap-
pearing into the ceiling. The final slide from his presentation, the stylized logo of the Bibliothèque Nationale de France—*BnF*—lingered on the purple, velvet-clad wall. Dr. Bertrand Foucault slipped on his silver spectacles, positioned them low on the bridge of his nose, and inspected the illuminated control panel on the podium.

"Yoyons voir," he muttered under his breath and randomly flipped a switch. Feedback screeched through the auditorium. "No...no." The professor quickly toggled the switch back to its prior position and glanced into the darkness of the vast hall. He pressed a square neon blue button. The lights along the periphery of the auditorium dimmed and went out, plunging the room into complete darkness. He was greeted by mischievous whistles and clapping. "Parfait."

"Professeur, pardon."

Dr. Foucault was relieved to find his teaching assistant at the side of the podium. The student wordlessly leaned across the podium and proceeded to click a series of buttons with the confidence and effortlessness of a seasoned concert pianist. The lights of the auditorium grew brighter with a crescendo and the final slide disappeared from the wall.

"Merci, Thomas, merci."

The teaching assistant merely nodded, having performed the same task numerous times before at Foucault's lectures. He just wished the old man would finally learn how to use the system. He slung his bag over his shoulder and waved. "Au revoir, Professeur."

Dr. Foucault gathered his papers and arranged them in a small pile before sliding them into a leather briefcase.

"Dr. Foucault. One more question."

An American? The voice was familiar. Dr. Foucault looked up from his bag and scanned the interior of the room. He could see students filing out of the auditorium. As a group of laughing students squeezed through a row towards the aisle, he could see four individuals who remained seated in the back row of the auditorium. He shielded his eyes from the glare of the lights and attempted to make out the source of the plea.

"Oui, monsieur."

"You said that the most influential Italian book of the fourteenth century was Dante's *Divine Comedy*. What about Marco Polo's *Description of the World*?"

Dr. Foucault allowed the corners of his mouth to curl ever so slightly upwards into a smirk.

"You, better than anyone, should realize that it was written in 1298. It loses by a technicality, I'm afraid, Dr. Clay. What brings you to the City of Lights?"

"You."

47

Dr. Foucault hurriedly ushered the motley foursome into a small conference room down the hall from the Scalle Ovale. He suspiciously looked back down the corridor before pulling the door shut and locking it.

"This is all very unexpected, Redmund. Still looking for your white whale?"

"Until my last dying breath, Bertrand. It's been a while. It has to be what… fifteen years? You've certainly moved up in the world since then. There are even rumors that you are on the short list for running this monstrosity, the Bibliothèque Nationale."

"Rumors, innuendo, the muttering of fools, I'm afraid." Dr. Foucault removed his glasses and cleaned them with a handkerchief from his pocket. "I'm perfectly content to continue with my research and teaching."

"I suppose introductions are in order. I would like to introduce Dr. Eleanor Griffin, daughter of Harold Griffin and a very accomplished scholar in her own right, I might add." Ellie smiled and extended her hand. Dr. Foucault accepted it and shook it with a faint nod. "This here is Alexander Stone, not quite a doctor of philosophy, but you'll find him to be a precocious soul—he's quite gifted really." Alex quickly seized the professor's hand and shook it. "And you may remember Jonas."

"The muscle," Dr. Foucault tersely summarized. Jonas gave forth a smug smile, crossed his arms, and puffed out his chest as if to appear even more intimidating.

Ellie sized up Dr. Foucault. He seemed to be the French version of any number of academics back at Oxford, down to the mossy green Tweed jacket with suede brown elbow pads, vaguely unkempt gray beard, and messy hair.

He looked curiously at Ellie and Alex.

"Let me guess. Dr. Clay has you convinced that the great Venetian traveler, Marco Polo, died with an earth-shattering secret—so monumental it has been hidden for centuries awaiting discovery. What was it—everlasting life, the Garden of Eden, magical trees, and all that nonsense?"

When summarized in that fashion, the sheer ridiculous nature of their expedition caused Ellie to blush and look guiltily at Alex. The expressions on Ellie and Alex's faces made the professor chuckle. "I can postulate from your expressions that our modern-day Ponce de Leon has sold you on his quest for the legendary fourth part of Polo's manuscript. As someone who sunk five long years into Redmund's fantasies with nothing to show for it, I would caution you to shake off his spell."

"Fourth part?" Alex interrupted. He cast a confused glance at Clay, who simply ignored it.

Clay approached Dr. Foucault, put his hands on his shoulders, and peered into his eyes. "Bertrand. We found it." An enormous grin spread across Clay's face. "After all these years of searching, we found it."

"It?"

"It, man! The original manuscript!"

The professor backed away with a ghostly pallor. He pulled aside a chair and sat down with exhaustion. "I don't believe it." He suddenly sprung to his feet and looked around the room with agitation. "Where? How?"

"Bertrand, we are here because we need your help…and your confidence. I must request the highest level of discretion in this matter."

The professor grew impatient as he searched around the room

with his eyes for any sign of the manuscript. "Oui…of course… discreet. You can trust me. I must see it."

Clay silently nodded to Alex. Alex casually strolled over to the long conference table in the center of the room and deposited his satchel upon it. He carefully reached into the bag and withdrew the leather-bound volume. He retreated slightly from the table to allow the professor to squeeze his rotund form past a series of chairs. The professor stood before the text with a look of religious awe. He wet his lips with his tongue and with tremulous hands delicately lifted the cover. His eyes opened wide as he explored the pages.

"Can you translate it?" Ellie asked and immediately wished she had not.

The professor paused and gave Ellie a glance tinged with annoyance. "Translate? But of course. It's Franco-Venetian. I translated the oldest known version of Monsieur Polo's travels, *The Book of Wonders*, also written in this vernacular. All I need is some time. You leave it with me and I will not only translate it but verify its authenticity."

"Unfortunately, that won't be possible. I must insist that this manuscript not leave our sight. This is non-negotiable. I hope you do not take it personally."

"Not to be trusted, why take it personally?"

"Yes, I am sorry. There is another matter. It has become apparent that there are those who are keen to discover Polo's secret, so keen that they will take any measure to achieve their goals."

"Redmund, what are you saying?"

"Just that if you agree to help us, you are taking a risk. You could be a target."

"A target? From who? A bunch of bifocaled academics?"

Jonas placed the balls of his hands on the edge of the table beside Dr. Foucault and leaned in. "Professor, I'm afraid that these are not academics hurling pretentious criticisms at you. These are

killers who will stop at nothing to get their fingers on this manuscript."

"Collectors?" Dr. Foucault asked with confusion.

"So to speak. We've been a step ahead of them so far. The
quicker we can have this manuscript translated, the better."

"It's not something one can do well quickly," the professor protested.

"I know but these are extenuating circumstances. You'll have a
capable team assisting you. I have been pleasantly impressed by
the outstanding capabilities of our two stars, Ellie and Alex."

"I think you are asking for a lot," the professor complained.

"Yes, yes, but if I didn't think you could do it, we wouldn't
be here."

48

"*Next page. 'Now to Kublai Khan. He is of the Imperial lineage being de-scended from Genghis Khan, the first sovereign of the Mongols.'*"

Ellie listened as Dr. Foucault read from the manuscript, inter-mittently pausing to formulate the most accurate translation into English. The professor stared at the text with a palpable intensity in the shadows of the darkened Scalle Ovale. The library had long since closed its doors to the general public and they had the vast and elegant reading room to themselves. Alex, functioning as a scribe, frantically transcribed the professor's translation upon a white piece of paper. Behind them, Ellie could hear rhythmic snoring and she turned around to find Jonas slumped over in a plush leather armchair. Clay sat silently across the table, listening to Dr. Foucault's reading of the text.

"What did you mean by the missing fourth book?" Ellie asked, breaking the professor's train of thought.

He sighed and pushed the text slightly away from him. The professor removed his glasses, placed them on the table, and rubbed his eyes with fatigue. "I guess this is as good a time as any to take a break." He lifted his glasses off the table, huffed on the lenses, and wiped them with his handkerchief before placing them back on. "When Marco Polo and Rustichello collaborated in creating *The Description of the World*, the account was divided into parts or books."

Dr. Foucault reached out and lifted the manuscript off the ta-ble and positioned it between Ellie and Alex. He carefully flipped through the pages until he arrived at the beginning of the manuscript. Ellie stared down at the beautifully written text—block-like and written perfectly straight as if perched on an invisible line. The letters were predominately written in a crisp black ink with the ink of some of the letters appearing to be contaminated with golden flecks. She had earlier noted the exquisite penmanship of Rustichello and wondered aloud how a prisoner in a jail had the capability of crafting a text of such beauty. Alex was quick to explain that her image of a sordid jail cell was likely far from the reality of Polo and Rustichello's incarceration. He explained that their confinement was more akin to house arrest for nobility.

Dr. Foucault continued. "The narrative begins with the prologue that serves as a concise summary of the Polo family's adventures, first describing Marco Polo's uncle and father's initial trip to the East and later their return to the court of Kublai Khan with a young Marco Polo in tow. It of course ends with their voyage back to Venice after many years in the service of the Great Khan. It touches on the core features of the story to follow, without all the details that will be fleshed out in the remainder of the work. The prologue, however, leaves us with a mystery of sorts."

The professor pointed to the first page of the manuscript. "The work begins with the famous introduction: *Emperors, Kings, Dukes, Marquis, Counts, Knights and people of all levels of study who desire to obtain knowledge of all the varied races of mankind and the diversities of all the great regions of the World, take these **Books** and have them read*. Livres not livre, books not book."

"The remainder of the narrative is divided into three 'books.' The first book follows the Polo family's voyage from Armenia across the Silk Road into the heartland of the Mongol Empire. The first book concludes with the Polos arrival at the grand summer court of Kublai Khan at Shang-tu or Xanadu for all you fans of Samuel Taylor Coleridge. The second book provides a glimpse into the customs of the Mongols and their conquered lands to the East such as China or Cathay. The third book deals with the

Polos's trip through exotic Southeast Asia—the islands of Java, Madagascar, and Zanzibar—and India. The book concludes with the Polos making their way back to Venice."

"Now if you look further in the prologue you find the following: '*Confined to a prison in Genoa, Messer Polo caused Messer Rustichello of Pisa, who was also imprisoned, to write of his travails. He divided it into four books.*' Four books. Thus arises the mystery of the legendary fourth book."

"I've seen versions of *The Description of the World* that have a fourth book. It has material on Turkey and Russia..." Alex offered.

Dr. Foucault interjected, "...and random vignettes of military battles amongst the Mongol tribes. It is true that some later versions have added material and wrapped them up into a fourth book. Go back to these versions and note the asterisk next to them, questioning if they are indeed a part of the original manuscript. Read them over again and you will be left with the creeping realization that they are fragments of text, patch-worked together like a quilt. It will be apparent that they were added later.

"I for one believe there was a fourth book. I do not believe that when Rustichello '*divided it into four books*' that this was a typographical error. You could see how a scribe producing a copy of the work might find only three books and omit the line or change it to '*divided it into three books*' or something like that. You could also see how later scribes embellished the work with a hodgepodge of information on Mongol military tactics within a new fourth book. For most, I imagine, the assumption was that there were only ever three books."

"What if Rustichello considered the prologue to be the first book?" Ellie asked.

"Smart girl. It is a legitimate question but I think it is unlikely that this is the case. The first book after all is labeled as such and comes after the prologue." The room grew silent, interrupted by the wavelike ebb and wane of Jonas's snores. "Now I said that many assumed that there were only ever three books. Many, but not everybody. There were those that searched in vain for older and older versions of the text in hopes of discovering this fourth book."

"Marin Falier?" Ellie asked.

"Probably the most famous of searchers. There were those whose imaginations ran wild. What was in the fourth book? To some this mystery became an obsession." Dr. Foucault paused and glanced up at Clay who smiled. "We know that Marco Polo remained under the service of Kublai Khan for seventeen years but know little of what occurred during that period of time." Dr. Foucault flipped through the pages and read: '*From this point on, Messer Marco Polo worked in the service of the Great Khan for some seventeen years. He continually came and went, from here to there, often on secret missions. And sometimes he traveled for private matters, often with the consent of the Great Khan…and thus it came to be that Messer Marco Polo obtained knowledge of a great number of countries and cultures of the World more than any other man…*' Could the fourth book reveal more about what Marco Polo did during those seventeen years?"

"Why keep it a secret?" Ellie asked. "Why write a fourth book if you intend on keeping it a secret? If he had found something so great, why all the subterfuge? Marco Polo certainly doesn't seem like the humbles of souls—after all, he claimed to be the most knowledgeable man on earth. It would seem that he would be overjoyed to scream to the rest of the world about his accomplishments."

"He had his reasons," Clay answered.

"And what reasons were they?" Ellie inquired.

"I don't know."

"For someone with so little answers, Redmund, you are quite the zealot when it comes to Polo."

"I believe in Marco Polo."

"Yes, exactly. You believe in Marco Polo. You believe that he found the Garden of Eden and the Tree of Life and all that. You've brought us all on this quest with you. Sure it is alluring, but what do you expect to do with all this knowledge if we are even able to crack Polo's code?" Ellie barely realized her voice had raised, causing Jonas to gurgle and stir from his sleep. Jonas looked around the room glassy-eyed.

"Cure the world."

"Oh, that's all," Dr. Foucault muttered and nonchalantly returned to the text.

49

"There you have it."

Alex's hand ached as the pen slipped from his fingers and rolled across the table. A callous along the outside of his middle finger throbbed from where the pen rested against it while he wrote. He felt utterly spent, so tired that the roots of his hair hurt. They had been working non-stop to translate the text. Alex glanced at his watch. It was four in the morning.

Alex looked over at the professor who let his face flop into the cradle of his palms. The room was silent. He could see Ellie sleeping on the floor with her head perched up on a small pile of books. In the darkness, he spotted Clay passed out in a chair, his legs propped upon the ledge of a bookcase. Jonas sat upon the leather chair facing their backs. He seemed to be watching them until Alex realized Jonas's eyes were also closed.

"There's no fourth book," Dr. Foucault pronounced. "In all, this version is very similar to the copy within this library—the so-called *Book of Wonders*—except for some minor differences. Bear in mind, though, this was a ridiculously quick submersion into the manuscript—probably a record translation. We should contact one of those World Record organizations. I could have missed something."

"This is so disappointing," Alex complained. "I thought for certain that there would be something in it that hasn't seen the light of day for centuries. I really thought we were in uncharted territory."

"I warned you not to get wrapped up in Redmund's fantasy world." The professor motioned to the old man in the corner.

"From your whole lecture on the fourth book of Polo, I pegged you as a true believer."

"Let's just say that, I'm a bit of an agnostic."

Alex smiled and withdrew a crumpled piece of paper from his pocket. He read it again for the thousandth time.

"What's that?" asked the professor.

Alex looked down at the paper and passed it to the professor.

"It's an inscription that we obtained that we think was left by Marco Polo."

"Let's see…" The professor leaned over and positioned the slip of paper under the light.

Adam's Staff
Eastward Go
Illuminated Path
Where King Interred

Alex could detect a faint twinkle flicker in the professor's eyes. "We think that 'Adam's staff' refers to the Tree of Life and 'Eastward Go' the general direction in which the Garden of Eden would reside for a Westerner. The 'Illuminated Path' and 'Where King Interred' aren't exactly clear to us."

The professor remained silent. His eyes left the paper and tracked along the pages of the manuscript. He reached out and picked up the text off the table and tilted it slightly in the light before putting it down. He smiled at Alex and handed the crumpled paper back to him.

"Can't say that anything immediately comes to mind, I'm afraid."

The professor looked around the room at the sleeping forms and back at Alex. He tapped his index finger against his chin.

"Yes. Now that I think of it, there is a critical work written by Sergio Palma on Gnostic teachings that refers to an 'Illuminated Path' of some sort that was popular with Nestorian Christians during Polo's time. The book is up on the second floor. We should go get it."

Alex looked back at Jonas. Saliva was collecting at the corner of his mouth.

"Oh let them sleep. We'll just run up and look for the book," Foucault said jovially and patted Alex on the back.

Alex shrugged and rose from his chair. Dr. Foucault smiled warmly at Alex. "You might as well bring the manuscript. We might have need of it while we are up there looking for sources. It would be a shame to have to keep running down. Plus, I wouldn't trust it with these narcoleptics."

Alex laughed and slid the manuscript into his leather satchel. He followed the professor to the elevator, clutching the satchel tightly to his flank. As the doors of the elevator shut, he could see Jonas stir slightly and once again drift off to sleep.

50

The sleek, modern elevator door had scarcely closed when Dr. Foucault gently tugged at Alex's elbow.

"It is this way," he uttered, his voice hoarse from hours of translating.

Alex glanced around. The second floor was dark. They walked down a long corridor that ran beside the aisles and aisles of bookcases. As they advanced, florescent energy-saving light bulbs triggered by motion-detectors sprung to life, giving forth a greenish glow.

"You said you worked for Redmund for five years," Alex commented as they strolled along the corridor.

"Oui. Five years or so."

"If you don't mind me asking, what happened at the end of those five years?"

"I had already completed a critical edition of the earliest known version of Marco Polo's travels when Redmund Clay contacted me. I was a hotshot young researcher ready to turn heads in the world of academia. Probably very much like you. As you are well aware, Polo's accounts went by many names throughout history— *Description of the World, The Travels of Marco Polo, Il Milione, The Book of Wonders.* I imagine that the earliest French version had the title *The Book of Wonders* for a reason. Polo's stories were thought by many people at the time to be, at best, the product of an overactive imagination and, at worst, a complete hoax. We now know that Polo's descriptions of Mongolian and Chinese cultures are simply too accurate and detailed to be a work of fiction. When I read Polo's narrative, I couldn't suppress the feeling that there was a sense of 'wonder' for a lack of a better word in the work. It was not that I felt that subjects were being fabricated but...how can I explain it to you? It was the feeling when you sense something is not right and the hairs stand up on the back of your neck."

The professor stopped. "My father died when I was very small, dropped dead in his bedroom. My mother never went into that bedroom again and so it was left intact just like it was on the day he died. I remember sneaking into the room one day and looking around. It was exactly as I remembered it, but there was something big missing—my father."

He waved his hand dramatically. "Thus leading to the hair standing on the back of one's neck." He looked at Alex with a grimace, frustrated by his ambiguity. "Alex, when I read Marco Polo's work I wasn't struck by what was present but by the feeling of omission. It seemed like such an incomplete work. When I came upon the rumors of a fourth book, it just made sense."

Dr. Foucault, satisfied with his explanation, began to move on, followed closely by Alex.

"One day, I got a knock at my office door and in walked Redmund Clay. Now I had my head too far up the bindings of books to know who the heck THE Redmund Clay was at the time. He said he was intrigued by my views on Marco Polo and was embarking on a grand endeavor to find the original manuscript. He needed an assistant to advise him on purchases of texts and he was willing to compensate quite generously for my services. For a poor academic, this was like Christmas and my birthday colliding. I accepted the position and worked for five years for Redmund."

"What ended your relationship?" Alex wondered.

"You must understand that Redmund Clay is a true believer."

"And you?"

"I want to believe. It's not the same. His head is in the clouds and in the end, mine is a bit closer to earth. I desired a new direction in life."

Alex was about to dissect the professor's ambiguous answer when Dr. Foucault stopped at a computer monitor resting on a thin platform jutting out from the wall. "Here we are. We'll just access the library's computer cataloguing network and see if we can locate this work."

Alex watched as the professor typed on the keyboard with a single finger, slowly navigating through the library's system. Dr. Foucault was able to locate a book by Sergio Palma entitled *Gnosis and the Nestorians*. He removed a piece of paper from a holder and a tiny pencil, wrote down the call number, and handed it to Alex. "Here's the number. That aisle is down at the far end of the corridor on the left. Why don't you look for it? I'll continue to look through the library catalogue for anything else on this 'Illuminated Path.' The professor smiled at Alex and gave him another fatherly pat on the back.

Alex strolled down the corridor, the leather satchel loosely bumping against his side. He sighed and adjusted the strap slightly. He glanced down at the call number—DL354.20. Scanning the ends of the aisles, he was able to locate a range of call-numbers designating the collections confined to the two long sets of bookcases in each aisle. As he neared the end of the corridor, Alex finally located the aisle containing the volume. As he stepped into the aisle, small lights hanging from the ceiling turned on. He peered back down the corridor but could not see the professor.

Alex examined the bindings of the books. He could hear the professor's voice in the distance. "You know, we are not too different, Alex—you and me. At least a younger me." Alex smiled and kneeled down—DL353.80...DL353.90...DL354.10. He stared down at DL354.20—*Gnosis and the Nestorians*. Alex laid the leather satchel upon the floor and slipped the brown covered volume from the rack. The book was thick and heavy. Alex flipped open the book and found the binding tight.

Somewhere he could hear the professor's voice again. "Yes, we're very much alike and different. You wouldn't find me digging through crypts. Not with my claustrophobia."

Alex looked down at the book and froze. Suddenly the lights went off, plunging the floor into darkness.

"Goodness, the lights just went off. Leave it to the French to screw up the electricity. Stay where you are, Alex. I'll come to you."

Alex's hands ran across the floor in the blackness, seizing the strap of the leather satchel in one hand and the book in the other. He flipped open the satchel and his fingers probed the inside until they found the leather bound manuscript inside. He felt along the bookcase for a space.

Alex pulled himself to a standing position and slipped the leather satchel over his shoulder. Running his hands across the bookcase, he made his way blindly back towards the corridor.

"Dr. Foucault, we never told you where we found the manuscript." Alex listened for a response, but found none. He poked his head out from the aisle and tried to look down the darkened corridor.

He was greeted by the intense beam of light.

"Alex, I talk too much."

Blinded, Alex attempted to stagger back but bumped up against a bookcase. He tried to duck but was too late. The crack of the pole hit just above his left ear, dropping him to his knees. He knelt upright for a moment, mechanically grasping for the leather satchel, before teetering forward and collapsing in a heap.

51

Dr. Foucault swung his Peugeot into the parking space and bolted from his car. Soon he would have an Alfa Romeo, he thought. He took the steps to his apartment building two at a time, pausing by the landing to take a final look at the street below. The buzz of delivery vans was becoming more numerous as Paris began to awaken. He surveyed the area suspiciously. Satisfied that he had not been followed, he opened the front door and stepped inside.

The professor walked past the mailboxes and pressed the button for the antiquated elevator. The elevator descended to a score of squeals and creeks. He slid aside the metal grate, entered the elevator, and pressed three. He waited impatiently for the door to slowly close. The elevator began its slow ascent to the third floor. He could feel his heart race. A bead of sweat slid down the side of his temple.

He nearly ruined it. That Alex had bought the story up until the very end. He was particularly impressed by the story he had told to Alex about his father. Wouldn't he be surprised to know that his father was very much alive—a drunk living in Marseilles who beat his wife and left his only son to a life of poverty. He did tell the truth about at least one thing—his head was a bit closer to earth than Redmund's.

The elevator halted its ascent. Dr. Foucault waited as the door slid open. He pulled aside the metal grate with a screech. He carefully peered down the hallway and found it empty. Clutching the leather satchel, he silently crept towards his door at the end of the hallway. The clang of a door's lock being undone caused him to jump back.

An elderly woman wearing a hairnet and curlers opened a door across from his and poked her head out. She was holding a black and white cat against the front of her pink robe.

The professor brought his right hand against his heart with relief. He could feel the sputter of his heart dissipate.

"Good morning, professor."

"Good morning, Ms. Pelican."

"I found your cat wandering the halls."

The professor looked at the cat with confusion. He impatiently slid the key into the keyhole of his door. "Thank you, Ms. Pelican. Hugo must have slipped out…probably when the cleaners came."

The old lady lifted the cat in the air. The feline's hind legs spread out with uncertainty.

Dr. Foucault wiped his forehead with his sleeve and turned back to the lady. "Ms. Pelican, would you be so kind as to watch Hugo for me."

"Are you going on a trip? A conference?"

"Oui, oui, a conference. I will be gone for a short period of time. I would be very grateful."

The old lady held aloft the cat and wrinkled her nose. "I would be delighted, professor. I have been so lonely and Hugo is such a wonderful companion."

"Thank you, Ms. Pelican."

The woman retreated to her apartment and shut the door. He could hear the click-clack of the locking of her many locks. He turned the key and pushed his door open.

The apartment was as he had left it. He paced around the apartment nervously, popping his head into his small kitchenette and finding the plates positioned as they had been left yesterday morning. The professor slid the leather satchel from his shoulder and placed it on his desk by the window. He scurried to his bed, bent down, and looked under it. He found it empty. *I am being paranoid*, he thought. Hugo's escape from his apartment had unnerved him. The cleaners usually came on Wednesday and it was Tuesday. Had she followed him out the door when he had left for work?

He darted over to the closet and removed a small suitcase and plopped it on the edge of his mattress. He scurried over to his dresser and removed socks and underwear. He tossed the items into the empty suitcase and removed several shirts and pants from his closet. Returning to the suitcase, he quickly squeezed in the clothing. *No time to fold*, he thought as he tried to focus his thinking. *Passport*. He ran to his desk and removed the passport from a drawer and shook out a piece of paper. He then slid the passport into the inner pocket of his jacket and stood by his desk, overlooking the satchel.

Dr. Foucault lifted the receiver of his phone and dialed the number on the paper. He waited as a distant sounding ring echoed through the receiver. He looked out of the window at the empty street below. The sun was peeking out over the buildings in the distance.

"Hello, Dr. Foucault." The voice was ghostly.

The professor's hands found the fastener on the satchel. He snapped it open and slid his hand slightly in. His fingers brushed up against the text.

"I have the manuscript."

"Where are you?"

"My apartment."

"Stay where you are, I am sending a team to collect you." The line grew silent for a moment. "Have you found the fourth book?"

"It's in my hands…" The professor gripped the edge of the text and pulled away with alarm. The receiver nearly slipped from his shoulder as he turned the satchel over and shook the text out onto his desk.

"Merde."

"What is it?"

A beeping noise was transmitted over the phone line and threatened to interrupt his thoughts. He stared down at the book in a daze. The beeps continued. "One moment..." muttered the professor as he looked down upon the street below. He pressed the call waiting button.

"Oui."

"Dr. Foucault?"

"Oui"

"Dr. Bertrand Foucault?"

The explosion shook the apartment building, sending glass showering down upon the parked Peugeot. Smoke billowed out of the window into the springtime Parisian air, followed by pieces of paper floating serenely down to the street below.

52

Solomon Haasbroek leaned against a black streetlight and inconspicuously looked over the hood of a parked car at the commotion across the street. The wail of the green and white ambulance had finally ceased, but the flashing lights continued to pulsate. A fire-truck was positioned at an angle, blocking traffic along the street while police milled about, casting glances at the apartment building's façade while they shielded their eyes. The third floor window overlooking the street was little more than a giant chasm with black soot staining the margins of the irregular hole. Gray smoke continued to waft into the air.

A tap on his back caused Haasbroek to turn. Ox nodded and handed him his phone.

"It's for you, chief."

Haasbroek spat on the ground and brought the phone to his ear.

"Howzit?"

"What happened?"

"It appears that someone got to your professor before we could secure him—blew him and his apartment to smithereens. It's still smoldering." Haasbroek paused and watched as police wearing white space-age jumpsuits carefully navigated down the front stairs of the apartment building, carrying a black body-bag on a stretcher towards the waiting ambulance. Haasbroek turned away and brought the phone angrily back to his ear. "Look, I've about had it with this mission. The money's good but I don't like being in the dark. Just what the hell is going on here, after all? I've felt played from the beginning and I don't like it."

"Mr. Haasbroek, we have been in search for an ancient text that I am afraid is now lost forever. Your disappointment cannot rival mine on this matter."

"Who keeps screwing with us?"

"A group whose purpose is to ensure that it is never found. I'm afraid they have finally succeeded." It became very hard to hear the man.

"I'm having trouble hearing you," Hassbroek barked into the phone as he pushed the phone against his right ear and covered the left ear with the palm of his hand.

"I...have...go...find Redmund...Cl...Clay." The phone went dead.

The man stared down at the crashing waves against the stone walls of Cape Sagres. The wind blew ferociously across the promontory. Behind him he could hear the blades of a helicopter and turned to see it land a short distance away. He began to walk towards the simple white chapel of Nossa Senhora da Graca. They had a lot to discuss after the events of this morning. All was lost unless... He hated to have to rely on the competition. He would know soon enough.

53

"Alex! Alex!"

Alex stirred. He sensed the flicker of lights turning on as his eyelids slowly parted. His cheek rested on the cool tile floor of the library

"He's here!"

Alex was helped to a sitting position. His head wobbled slightly on his neck as he inched his body back until it rested up against a bookcase. Ellie leaned over and tilted his neck to get a better view of the bloodied gash across his left temple. She sighed.

"Good thing I have such a hard skull." Alex tried to laugh but found his jaw stiff and painful. He could hear the pitter-pat of feet running down the corridor. He turned to see Clay and Jonas gathered at the end of the aisle. Jonas had his gun by his side.

"Where is Foucault?" Jonas asked.

"He's not who we think he is. He clocked me with a pole or something and took off." Alex rubbed his hand against his temple and winced.

"Where's the manuscript? Is it safe? Is it secure? Where's your bag?" Clay sputtered with alarm. He bent down to peered down the aisle.

Alex looked around him. "My bag's gone."

Clay drew Jonas close to him. "You need to track down the professor before it's too late." Jonas looked in Clay's eyes, nodded, and made to leave.

"Wait. DL354.20." Alex muttered under his breath.

"What?" Clay responded.

"Check the shelves. Check the call number." Alex motioned to the bookcase in front of him.

Clay squatted and began to examine the spines of the volumes within the bookcase. When he reached the call number, he paused. The number was skipped but in its place was the leather-bound manuscript. He smiled and withdrew it from its hiding place.

"How did you…what made you…?" Clay could not finish.

"I had just enough time to make a switch."

"What does Foucault have?" Ellie asked.

"Some book *Gnosis and the Nestorians*. He's in for a big surprise."

"We need to get out of here before this library opens," Jonas suggested.

Clay and Ellie helped Alex up to a standing position. He balanced unsteadily, supported by the two. Alex looked first at Clay and then Ellie. "Foucault saw something in the text that made him try to steal it. The good news is that I think I know what it was."

54

Ellie pulled the door to the bathroom shut and locked it behind her. Alex glanced at the scratched mirror over the sink. *I look like hell,* Alex thought. The hair on the left side of his head was matted down by dry blood while the rest of his hair was wildly messy. Dark circles had formed under his eyes and his skin seemed drained of any color.

"You look like crap," Ellie announced while she ran a paper-towel under the faucet of the sink.

"You think?"

"You have to stop hitting your head against hard objects," she smiled and brought the wet towel up against Alex's left forehead. He winced at the touch of the cool pressure.

"Don't be such a baby." She continued to dab at the blood, tossing paper towel after paper towel into the garbage can until Alex was left with a large bruise across his left temple.

He looked Ellie in her eyes and feigned machismo. "How do I look?"

"Like you lost a fight..." she laughed. "...really, really badly but you're still my hero." Ellie leaned in and kissed Alex. The small of his back contacted the edge of the sink and he let his hands run down her back and settle on her hips.

An impatient knock at the door caused them to suddenly stop kissing.

Jonas's voice boomed from beyond the door. "We have to go, kids."

Ellie sighed in Alex's arms and nuzzled her head into his chest. "I really hate that guy."

Alex leaned down and kissed her again before opening the door. Jonas stood by the door wearing sunglasses. Behind him they could see the bustle of activity in the café.

Jonas wordlessly handed his cellphone to Alex. Alex and Ellie peered down at the LCD. The mobile internet was connected to the English version of *Le Monde*. There was a photo of a burning apartment building surrounded by emergency vehicles. The headline read:

*****Breaking News:** Explosion in Paris. Police are at the scene of a suspicious explosion at a residential apartment complex on Rue de Dame. There have been reports of a single fatality. As a result, there has been a precautionary evacuation of the surrounding buildings. There have been unconfirmed reports that Dr. Bertrand Foucault, lecturer and researcher at the Bibliothèque Nationale de Paris, was pronounced dead at the scene. The anti-terror services have been dispatched to the location. Stay tuned*****Breaking News.**

Alex handed the phone back to Jonas in a daze. What was going on?

"We need to leave Paris now. Get your croissants to go."

55

The Hawker 850 jet rocked back and forth as it pierced the gray clouds. Alex slid the manuscript onto the table and inched his body forward so that his backside was nearly perched on the edge of the plush chair. Ellie sat across the table and watched as Alex delicately opened the text and tilted it slightly.

"Well, I hope you are not going to keep us in suspense for much longer." Clay gripped the headrest of Alex's chair and fought to steady himself as the plane vibrated. He brought a crystal glass of scotch to his lips and struggled to take a sip without spilling the contents.

The plane began to settle out as Jonas emerged from the cockpit and slumped down in a chair towards the rear of the plane.

"We've issued a flight-plan under a dummy company. It should be a short trip to England. Any progress on the manuscript?"

All eyes drifted to Alex.

"It all goes back to the riddle we found with Ellie's wooden box from Mosul:

Adam's Staff
Eastward Go
Illuminated Path
Where King Interred

"We've already discussed the significance of 'Adam's Staff' and its relationship to the mythology surrounding the Tree of Life and immortality. 'Eastward Go' seems to substantiate this premise in that, as Ellie noted, the Bible places the Garden of Eden eastward and Marco Polo's travels were to the East. What hasn't been clear is the meaning of 'Illuminated Path.' What do you think about when you hear the word illuminated?"

"I think of brightening something with light," Clay answered.

"Yes," Alex responded.

"When I think of 'illuminated' I tend to see it more as making something clearer. Enlightening someone either intellectually or spiritually," Ellie added.

"These are both true and I don't think these two definitions were lost on Polo. After all, he has wanted us to 'see the light' all along. But there is another way of thinking about the word 'illuminated' that is at the root of Polo's gift to the Western world: his book."

Clay gripped his glass tightly. "I'm afraid you lost me."

"When Marco Polo and Rustichello wrote *The Description of the World*, they did so in a world that had yet to be affected by Gutenberg's invention of the printing press. Books were hand-written. These texts were then copied by hand and re-copied and on and on. The life of a scribe may have been tedious but it was far from mechanical. There was a fair amount of art to being a scribe."

"An illuminated manuscript!" Ellie exclaimed.

Alex smiled broadly. "Yes."

Clay interjected, "When I think of illuminated manuscripts (and believe me when I say I have purchased quite a few in my day), I imagine texts with elaborate drawings. I think of medieval monks hunched over in tiny cubicles crafting manuscripts with fancy, gilded letters on each page."

"That's true but all 'illuminated' means is to make a manuscript 'brilliant.' It often involves decorating it with gold."

"The flecks of gold!" Ellie nearly stood up. "I saw it but I thought it was a contaminant in the ink. I didn't think much of it."

As if on cue, the plane rolled slightly to the left and dazzling sunlight filled the interior of the plane's cabin, bathing the pages of the manuscript in luminous yellow light. Several of the letters on the page gave forth a golden sparkle.

"Amazing," Clay exhaled.

"What does it mean?" Jonas asked.

"Ellie do you have some paper and a pen?"

Ellie retrieved a magazine from a holder beside her chair, searched for a page with little print, and ripped it out. She withdrew a pen from her pocket and straightened out the paper on the table before her.

"Let's see." Alex placed his finger beneath the first golden letter. "…L…" He found the next golden letter, "…I…" and continued: "…B…R…E…Q…U…A…T…T…U…O…R."

"Libre Quattuor! It's 'Book Four' in Latin! We've had in our hands the fourth book of *The Description of the World* all along. The fourth book is hidden within the text! What better place to hide it! It was what Foucault realized and why he was determined to steal the manuscript!" Alex exclaimed.

"You did it, my boy! You did it again!" Clay patted Alex roughly on the back. "Do you realize what you have done? Drinks for everyone! Jonas, get us that special Champagne I've kept in the refrigerator just for such a moment."

"This is incredible!" Ellie concurred. "It's as if we are about to hear the lost voice of Marco Polo—something that hasn't been heard in centuries."

"But searched for, mind you, at great cost," Clay soberly added.

"Other than Polo and Rustichello, we may be the only people who have laid our eyes knowingly on it," Alex added.

"Enough with the gloating…we have a lot of work to still do." Clay smiled widely. "Well, maybe just a little sip of Champagne first."

56

Ellie's fingers searched through the yellowed pages of the manuscript. The tip of her index fingers finally settled on the next golden letter.

"A," she announced and paused to allow Alex the opportunity to jot down the letter upon a piece of paper set before him. He read through the last several letters and drew an oblique line after the 'A.'

"This is not easy," Alex concluded, running his hands through his hair. "I never appreciated punctuation in my life until now. It's hard to tell where a word ends and another begins. Marco certainly hasn't made this easy for us."

"Well, if it was easy then it probably wouldn't be worth it," Ellie answered.

Alex glanced at Ellie sideways and formed a mischievous grin. "Eleanor Cleopatra Griffin, are you becoming a believer?"

"I'll believe it when I'm standing in the Garden of Eden itself. This could be the biggest hoax in history." Ellie flipped the page over. "There's only one more page."

"Thank God for that."

They were exhausted. It seemed like ages ago since the jet had touched down upon the remote private runway somewhere in the English countryside. The plane was quickly directed into a hangar at the edge of the runway. A chauffeured Rolls Royce arrived and spirited them off to an isolated cottage. Clay assured them that no one knew he owned the cottage, that the property had been surreptitiously purchased through one of Clay's numerous shell companies. They would have all the time and quiet necessary to decipher the contents of Polo's fourth book.

The cottage was constructed out of dark gray stone and was dotted with small windows that only provided a modicum of light. It was nestled in the woods near a quaint brook. The surrounding forest was at once menacing and strangely serene, a dark and lush wilderness overgrown with fuzzy moss and shaded by towering oak trees that created a canopy of green that blocked the sunlight. The rays of light that were able to penetrate the thick canopy streamed down with a heavenly glow upon the ground. Ellie could imagine Robin Hood and his troupe of Merry Men gallivanting through the woods as they fought to right social and economic inequalities. She pushed the drapes aside and peered out at the woods. Ellie could see Clay and Jonas strolling through the forest in the dying minutes of dusk. They suddenly stopped and faced each other and appeared to be engaged in a serious discussion. Clay shook his head and walked off into the woods leaving Jonas behind.

"...the next one."

Ellie slowly broke the trance and let the drape flop back. "What? I'm sorry. Just day-dreaming."

"What's the next one?"

Ellie sat up straight on the leather chair and looked down at the text resting upon her crossed legs.

"What was the last letter?"

"A."

Ellie searched the page for the golden letter. Her index finger stopped at the 'A' momentarily and then continued to run across each line until she came across the next golden letter. "E."

Alex nodded and transcribed the letter onto the paper. He studied the page before him.

Ellie rubbed her eyes and looked around the study. The room was elegant and refined. A stone fireplace was at the far end of the room. The wood, exceptionally dry, popped and crackled wildly, sending small embers alight which floated serenely in the air, only to burn a brilliant red when they contacted the metallic wire mesh strung across the hearth. The walls of the study were filled with leather-bound books. There was even an oak ladder that was perched against the bookcase that could be moved across an unseen metallic railing. Alex was hunched over a wooden desk while Ellie sunk further into the leather chair.

"Next letter."

Ellie searched for an additional golden letter. After finding none on the rest of the page, she turned it over to find a blank sheet and the leather cover beside it. She withdrew her finger from the manuscript and silently closed the volume.

"That's it."

Alex brought the tip of his pen against the surface of the paper and inked in an exceptionally large black period beside the last letter for good measure. He looked out tiredly across the top of the desk, finding papers haphazardly lying across the surface. He reached out and gathered the numbered papers, created a pile, and proceeded to tap them against the desk until they were tidy.

"Now the real work starts," Alex muttered. He studied the papers before him. Alex had painstakingly written in rows of black block print the golden letters that Ellie had read from the manuscript. Pencil was used to position slashes between letters that appeared to delineate the end of one word and the beginning of another. Perched above each of these words was the likely English translation from Latin. There were many words that were crossed out and rewritten. Others merely had frustrated question marks perched atop the letters. Alex sighed. *It is certainly a work in progress.*

Ellie yawned and stretched.

Alex looked at her with bloodshot eyes.

"You look exhausted," he said.

"Thanks. You don't look so hot yourself. Maybe we should tackle it tomorrow morning."

"You might as well turn in for the night," Alex mumbled, his eyes fixed on the papers.

"What about you?"

"I don't think I'm going to be able to sleep until I figure this out." He rubbed his chin as he turned over each paper. "I've skipped over a lot of words that I couldn't immediately translate. To be honest, I'm not entirely sure that I've separated all the words appropriately. There are a lot of permutations. Meanings change if you're off by one letter. Some of these words have multiple meanings. All I can say is thank God I took Latin. My parents thought it was such a waste of time—*Alex, take Spanish, there's a useful language. Half of America will be speaking it when you are older.* I took Latin, go figure. Some 'Dead Language,' huh?"

Ellie smiled and yawned again.

"If it's OK, I think I'll keep you company. All that medieval armor in my room gives me the creeps. I feel like the knights' eyes keep following me."

"If you pull the arm, a secret passage opens."

"The way things have been going lately, I wouldn't be surprised."

Alex laughed and returned to the pages of transcription before him.

"I guess the best thing to do is start from the beginning." Alex positioned a blank sheet of paper to his right and began to neatly write. *"Libre Quattuor...Book Four...Is eram dum ego...It was while I..."*

Alex stopped and looked across the desk at Ellie. She had drifted off to sleep, clutching the manuscript tightly to her chest. Alex could see the text rise and fall with each breath. He smiled, rose from his chair, and teased the text from her grasp. She stirred with each tug, resisting, but he was finally able to free it from her hands. He set the volume down on a side table and drew a wool blanket across her sleeping form. He learned over and kissed her forehead. Ellie mumbled something incomprehensible in her sleep.

Alex searched the bookcase in the orange glow of the fireplace and withdrew a Latin dictionary from a shelf. He returned to the desk and spread out the papers before him.

Marco, it's time to give up your secrets.

57

Alex pushed the door open and peered into the kitchen. Jonas noisily rum-
maged through a cabinet in search of jam while Clay held aloft a
porcelain saucer and cup as he watered a hanging plant.

"It's done," Alex croaked. Clay and Jonas froze and looked
back at him with curiosity.

Alex's mouth was parched and his eyes burned in the light. He
felt vaguely nauseated and hungry at the same time. The muscles
in his legs were heavy and seemed to pulsate a dull ache that
reached the small of his back. He caught his reflection in the
stainless steel toaster oven and grimaced. He could see the imprint of a pen on his right cheek where it came to rest when he
had finally fallen asleep, face down on the desktop.

"Done?" Clay grinned excitedly. "Already?"

Before he could answer, the opposite door opened and Ellie
bounced energetically into the kitchen cradling a hot cup of tea
and a scone. She handed them to Alex.

"Here, take this. It will make you feel much better."

Alex looked down at the cup. His nose crinkled at the sight of
its cloudy contents. "There's milk in this tea."

"Is there another way of drinking tea? Surely, not. I'll turn you
into a proper Englishman, yet."

Alex slid the papers onto the kitchen table and plopped down
roughly on the wooden chair. The saucer shook in his hands and
Ellie helped to direct it onto the tabletop. He took a bite of the
cranberry scone and a sip of tea. He could feel the hot liquid coat

his stomach, warming him from the inside out. The sugary and tart scone helped revive him. "Thanks."

Clay grabbed the chair opposite Alex and pulled it closely to him. "Well, let's get on with it. What does it say? Is it fantastic? Is it all we have dreamed?"

Alex lifted the cup to his lips, took another sip, and swallowed. All eyes were trained on him as he set the cup back down.

"It's the most fantastic thing I have ever read."

58

Alex arranged the pages before him and cleared his throat. *So this is how John the Baptist felt when delivering the Sermon on the Mount.* Clay pinched his top lip between his thumb and index finger and waited for Alex to speak.

Book Four

It was while I was under the tutelage of the most magnificent and all-powerful Khan of the Tartars, Kublai Khan, that many wonders were revealed to me. Writing from this prison in the year of our Lord 1298, and with the cannon fire and death from the battle from which I was captured still repeating in my sleep, I find myself a Westerner coated with the dust of the East. There are days that I have lost and not spoken of. There are lands that I have seen and remain undisturbed. These are dangerous and wonderful places. I dare not speak of them for the cost is too great, as the reader will come to understand. But I cannot forget them because like the cannon fire, they are in my dreams, haunting me with every breath. And to my very human fault, I cannot simply bury them. I beseech the reader to bear my burden carefully for what I speak of are secret journeys. But this world is foreign to the reader and as such preparation is necessary.

For my fellow traveler, I, Messer Marco Polo, leave this fact: the life of the supreme and most revered King of the Tartars, Genghis Khan, has passed into legend. It is said that men like Genghis Khan do not die. He rose as a boy from poverty to unite the Tartars and create an Empire through blood and power. His lands were vast and his authority unquestioned. He conquered the Idol-worshippers to the East until the water stopped him (some said that he could rule the fish in the sea if he chose to). He stretched into the dark lands of the North where the feral people lived and into the lands of those who worship Mohammed. Those who resisted were destroyed. He commanded reverence. And so it is said that men such as Genghis Khan do not die.

A tale is told that when Genghis Khan was old and gray, he embarked on his greatest campaign of all. He sought to conquer death itself. To do so, he summoned the Idol-worshipper, Ch'ang-ch'un, a wise man from the captured land of Cathay who was rumored to know the secret for everlasting life. Ch'ang-ch'un traveled for four years and experienced much hardship to finally meet with Genghis Khan. To the Great Khan's dismay, the wise man denied the existence of such an elixir of immortality. He advised Genghis Khan if he wanted to achieve a long life he would have to abstain from habits of debauchery such as hunting, fornication, and intoxication. The all-powerful ruler replied that this was not the Tartar way and sent Ch'ang-ch'un away.

The Great Khan was much dismayed that everlasting life remained elusive. In all the lands that he conquered he questioned the wise men from various faiths. A priest and follower of Nestorius told Genghis Khan of a garden created by the Lord in the East where there was a Tree of Life whose oil would grant immortality. The garden was in Eden and was protected by cherubim with flaming swords who guarded the entrance to paradise. When asked how one could find such a garden the priest said that it was not for man to know and was reserved for the righteous.

For the conqueror of much of the known world, Genghis Khan found this to be a challenge and omen. One cold night on the steppes, he called four of his most accomplished soldiers into his yurt. By torch light, he told these soldiers of this wonderful paradise and a tree that offered immortality. He commanded them to embark on a mission to find this garden so that their master could live forever. The soldiers traveled in four directions and scoured the world for this paradise. Time passed and none of the soldiers returned from this quest and the Great Khan grew weary with age. He gathered his closest and most trusted council together and ordered that if such a place were found after he had died, that his body should be brought to this place and buried beneath this magical tree. His soul would become one with the tree, the land, and the heavens. Before he died, he decreed that this place be kept a secret and protected for eternity.

It has been whispered that just after Genghis Khan died in his sleep, one of the soldiers emerged from the wilderness of the world. The man was thin and weak. His eyes were wide and wild, having been consumed by a troubled mind. Upon learning that his master had died, the soldier fatally collapsed, succumbed by the sorrow of this loss. Before he passed, he revealed the location of the garden as his master had desired and left this world with a final clue: the sky has fallen...lift it to enter.

The body of the Great Khan was transported in secret to this location. It is rumored that all those souls unfortunate to cross the path of this somber procession were slain. Such care was undertaken to ensure that the burial site would remain hidden that the bearers of the body were put to the sword until only a small group of the most faithful followers of the Great Khan remained and knew the location. Even the horses that bore the body were killed to prevent them from returning to the site. These followers pledged their lives and the lives of their descendants to the protection of this holy site.

Having an unending curiosity, I, Messer Polo, embarked on a journey of my own to discover that place where life began and life ended. I traveled to the ends of the Khan's lands in search of the garden. I listened to the diverse inhabitants of the Empire and tread carefully through myths and legends. I hung the golden piazza around my neck and bore the weight of it in order to be provided passage and provisions through lands off limits. And after years of searching, I finally approached the gates of the Garden and saw the flaming eyes of the cherubim. I stopped. The fiery sword of the guardians would strike down those that trespass. The Garden was only for the righteous. I thought what a twist of fate for the Great Khan to journey so far only to return to the Endless Sky.

I traveled back to the court of Kublai Khan with fragments of my journey hidden in my clothing and constructed a map in secret to the garden. But with time, there were shadows in the court who stirred. They held true power and were those whom suspicions were greeted with the edge of a sharpened blade or poisoned tip of an arrow. I don't know how it was that I survived that time. The Lord himself must have interceded on my behalf to prevent my slaughter.

During a trip to Kara-Khoto on behalf of my master, Kublai Khan, a chance encounter with a white monk traveling in a caravan provided an opportunity. He was from a Camaldolese monastery on San Michele and as fortune had it he was a map-maker himself. I told him of my voyage and prayed for his confidence. He agreed to take the map and keep this knowledge safe within the walls of his order.

As the death of Kublai Khan neared, an occasion arose to leave the land of the Tartars and the court of the Khan. When I returned to Venice, the secret of the garden burned inside of me. May the Lord forgive me; I could not confide this knowledge to His Holiness in Rome. I would be responsible for a calamity worse than the Crusades. Take heed of Merv.

The map-makers will remember the path when the world is finally filled in. It is as constant and elemental as the winds that guide the sails and blow across the plains eastward...always eastward.

59

The kitchen was silent as Alex finished reading and placed the handwritten translation upon the table. The stainless steel teaspoon that was resting precariously on the edge of the saucer jiggled slightly, cutting through the heavy silence like a wind-chime. Alex glanced at the faces of his colleagues and found them stone-faced, as if soaking in by osmosis the significance of what they had just heard.

A thunderous clap broke the solitude and all eyes turned to Clay.

"I knew it! I knew it all along. Polo found it. Who's the crazy one now?"

"Jury's still out, Redmund," Ellie cynically replied. "It all sounds a bit like a fairy tale to me, as if Marco was reading too many tales of King Arthur or Alexandrian romances. It doesn't seem we are any closer to figuring out where this so-called Garden of Eden is located. After all this, Marco couldn't be a little more specific? I mean we were nearly entombed for eternity trying to get a hold of this fourth book and we're left with another mystery. Where do we go from here?"

"We find this map, of course." Clay tapped his finger on the table for emphasis. The teaspoon finally toppled off the saucer with a clang.

"Oh, that's all. And how do you plan on doing that?"

"That's what you two are here for," Jonas challenged.

Alex remained silent as the three began to argue. He reached for a piece of paper and turned it over, exposing the blank side. He withdrew a pen from his pocket and traced out the symbol:

"It's beginning to make sense."

The three continued to quarrel.

"It's beginning to make sense," Alex repeated in a louder voice. The three stopped their debate and turned to Alex. They looked down at the symbol with confusion.

"What makes sense, Alex," Ellie asked softly, her face flushed.

"What do you think of when you see this symbol?"

"It looks like a key to me."

"I would have to agree with you. We need to put it in the context of where it was found. It was hidden at the bottom of the box Ellie found in Mosul, the one with the diamonds."

Ellie reached into Alex's leather satchel, removed the box, and placed it before them. Alex picked it up and showed it to each of them.

"What has confused me for so long is the cross associated with the key. It seemed incomplete, as if someone forgot to extend the horizontal beam of the cross to the left. But what if it was never meant to be a cross? If you turn the symbol on its side…" Alex flipped the paper ninety degrees until it was lying vertically.

"It's a symbol for a TO-map."

"A what map?" Jonas asked.

"A T…O…map. During medieval times, the world was depicted as a circle…an 'O.' Alex made a ring with his index finger and thumb. All humanity was contained within this circle. To provide some organization a 'T' was placed within the circle to act as a partition. The major rivers of the world composed the arms of the

'T.' The rivers were the Don, Mediterranean, and Nile. Above the horizontal portion of the 'T' was the Eastern world. To the left was the north, the right was the south, and the bottom was the Western world."

Alex drew out a diagram of the TO map.

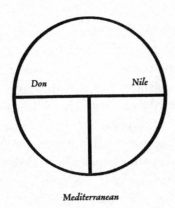

Mediterranean

"This was how the world was depicted at the time of Polo. We've been searching for a map all along. The map is the key! It has always been the strangest thing about Marco Polo's *Description of the World*. Here is a man that spent much of his life traveling throughout the world...a man who brags about his knowledge of the diverse lands and there's not one map in his account. Every map one sees in a volume of the *Description of the World* is a product of an editor piecing together his travels through his writings. Many historians have postulated that there must have been a map but none has ever been found."

"Why keep it a secret for so long? I just don't understand the danger of releasing the details?" Jonas pulled up a chair beside Alex and sat down.

"He spelled it out in the fourth book."

"I must have missed it."

A branch rattled against the window. Alex thought of how best to start.

"Let's take a step back, a step back to the time of Genghis Khan. Before Genghis Khan united the tribes of the steppes…"

Jonas held up his hand. "I think you're going to have to give us the 'Idiots-version' of Genghis Khan, starting with what are the steppes."

"OK, fair enough. We are talking about Central Asia. You know, the 'stans. Places like Kazakhstan, Uzbekistan and also Mongolia. The steppes are the plains of Central Asia. They are vast landscapes, usually grasslands where few trees live, and the temperatures can fluctuate wildly from very hot to brutally cold. Nomadic tribes lived on these steppes, hunting for scarce resources and fighting amongst themselves. They were fierce warriors hardened by the elements. They were hopelessly divided, fractured by petty squabbles and jealousies. That was until a boy named Temüjin rose out of poverty to unite the tribes of the steppes.

"He became Genghis Khan or 'oceanic sovereign' and ruled with an iron grip. His people were the Mongols. Interestingly, many in the West referred to the Mongols as the Tartars after the name of a small tribe called the Tartas, who Genghis Khan subjugated. It was also a nice play on words, because Tartarus was the Greek version of Hell. Typically outnumbered, Genghis Khan was a master military strategist and led his people to vicious victories over far numerous opponents. Within a quarter of a century, the Mongols conquered more land than the Romans did in three to four centuries. Think of that for a second—in only twenty-five years. They were so powerful that the Western world shuddered in their armor at the threat of meeting the Mongols in battle. Many in the West felt that the rise of the Mongols spelled the beginning of the end for humanity and that the Mongols were surely the minions of Satan.

"Like most things, however, it was never that simple. Although they were a people who delighted in war, Genghis Khan also served to create an Empire of relative peace and stability in a land used to chaos. It was, after all, during precisely this time that the Silk Road flourished and commerce bloomed between the West and the East. The Mongol rule enabled caravans to travel safely along these routes. Indeed, it was what allowed the Polos to travel as freely as they did.

"Now, let's imagine that the Garden of Eden had been found. It would be wondrous to be sure. Now imagine that it was located in enemy territory. Not just any enemy, but the most fearsome warriors this world has ever known. These warriors, after all, decimated the celebrated Templar knights of Georgia. Now imagine if the body of Genghis Khan were buried within this sanctified soil—the minion of the Devil within the land of creation. Psychologically, this could threaten the foundation of the Judeo-Christian faith—how could God allow such a sacrilege to persist? Then imagine the clamor to reclaim this land—a call not unlike that of the Crusades to free Jerusalem. How many Christians and Muslims were slaughtered during those campaigns? Keep in mind that the Mongols routed the powerful Muslim armies. Surely the Christians could be defeated easily. If Marco Polo had transmitted this information to the Pope, who knows what this world would look like today?"

"What did he mean by 'Take heed of Merv'?" Ellie asked.

"Merv." Alex grew quiet and nearly bowed his head. "Merv *was* the largest city in the world in the twelfth century, a virtual oasis within Central Asia…that was until it came up against the Mongol onslaught. In the early thirteenth century, the city of Merv boasted vast libraries, mosques, palaces, and observatories. It was a very prideful city and so when a small group of Mongols probed the perimeter of the city, they were captured, paraded within the walls of the city, and executed. Genghis Khan was not one to be disrespected. He returned with a larger force and quickly subdued the city. The artisans of the city were spared and made into slaves while the rest of the inhabitants were summarily killed. It is said that each Mongol soldier was responsible for the massacre of three to four hundred citizens. In fact, a noted cleric gave an account that a total of one million three hundred thousand people were slaughtered over a mere thirteen-day period of time."

"One million three hundred thousand people? That's crazy," Ellie responded with her hand on her mouth.

"They literally wiped Merv off the planet. Look for it now. You won't find much left."

"I'm beginning to see Polo's point of view," Jonas acknowledged.

Clay began to pace around the kitchen. He leaned over a center island and ducked his head to avoid copper pans hanging from the ceiling from iron hooks.

"Well, we've established why dear old Marco decided to keep this all a secret but how do we find this map of his. It does not appear that we have much to fear from Genghis Khan or his troops now that he is long gone."

"He gave the map to a Camaldolese monk," Alex responded.

"Never heard of a Camaldolese monk." Jonas scratched his head.

"It's some sort of monastic sect. I'll have to research it," Alex announced.

"Polo didn't just say 'monk,' he said 'white monk," Ellie added.

"I think that's how it would be translated. It's strange...the wording. Redmund, do you have internet access."

"What am I, a barbarian?"

"I take it that is a yes." Next to the key symbol, Alex wrote *Camaldolese* and *white monk*. "I guess we have some more research to do."

"Why not go in?" Ellie wondered aloud.

"What's that?" Alex asked.

"If Polo was at the gates of the Garden, why not take the final step? How could he resist?"

"It says in the fourth book that he didn't feel righteous," Alex responded and put down his pen.

Ellie looked at each of the members of their group. She kept silent but could tell that they were all asking themselves the same thing.

Am I righteous enough?

60

Ellie reached out and tilted the monitor of the laptop computer until she was satisfied.

"Is that O.K. for everyone?"

Jonas and Clay nodded as they inched their chairs closer to Alex, nearly pinning his chair against the desk. Alex glanced back over his shoulder with annoyance and shuffled his chair back and forth to create a pocket of wiggle-room. Ellie swiveled her hips along the edge of the desk, perched herself on the corner, and leaned in.

Alex's fingers explored the plastic of the keyboard and typed "Calmaldolese" into the search engine. A new screen appeared, listing numerous sites. He toggled through the hits and finally settled on an online Encyclopedia of Catholicism. His eyes scanned through the content of the site, sifting through pages of minutiae.

"It says here that the Calmaldolese are a small sect of the Benedictine monastic order. The sect was founded in the eleventh century by an Italian monk named St. Romuald who was attempting to bridge the world of the hermit with the more community-focused world of monastic living—the coenobitic and eremitical. According to legend, St. Romuald was searching for a location to found a new hermitage in central Italy when he stumbled upon a count named Maldolus. Maldolus, it seems, had fortuitously fallen asleep in one of his fields and had a miraculous vision of monks dressed in white habits climbing up a ladder into the heavens."

"White monks!" Clay exclaimed.

"So it seems. This count decided to donate a portion of his land to St. Romuald and aided in the construction of a new hermitage called Campus Maldoli in honor of its patron. This came to be known simply as Camaldoli and the sect eventually adopted the name Camaldoles. It says here that there are several congregations of Camaldolese still in existence, including small congregations in Italy, Brazil, Poland, India, France, and even the United States."

"What about during Marco Polo's time?" Ellie asked.

"Good question. There were essentially two congregations at that time from what I gather. The first was the mother ship — the Holy Hermitage near Arezzo, Italy, not far from where Maldolus had his fateful vision. The second was a congregation in Murano, Italy. It was founded in the early thirteenth century and consisted of a monastery on the island of San Michele between Venice and Murano. It would have been the one that Marco Polo would have been most familiar with as it can be seen from the banks of Venice."

"This is a wonderful history lesson but I'm not sure how this is helping us." Jonas frowned severely. "How are we supposed to figure out which monk Polo gave the map to?"

"What do you expect, 'X' marks the spot?" Ellie shot back.

"That would be nice, wouldn't it, my dear?" Jonas smirked.

"Is there anything on that site that talks about cartography, map-making?" Clay tapped his finger against the LED screen, temporarily distorting the image and leaving behind a smudge. Alex grumbled as he attempted to rub away the fingerprint with his shirt sleeve.

"Let's see…why don't we try "Camaldolese and map…""

A list of sites popped up on the screen.

"What's this?" The first site was a link to JSTOR and referenced a "mappae mundi by Camaldoles Fra. Mauro." Alex clicked on the listing and was directed to the JSTOR site. He could see an image of the cover of the journal, *Imago Mundi.*

"What's a mappae mundi?" Jonas asked.

Alex twirled back. "It's from Latin. *Mappa* translates to cloth and *Mundi* to world. Roughly it is 'cloth of the world' or better 'map of the world.' It's a term that came about sometime in the ninth century and is used in academic circles to describe medieval maps."

"And this JSTOR site?" Jonas added.

"JSTOR is short for *Journal Storage*," Ellie answered. "It's an online system of archiving journals so that there will be a single database available to universities across the world." She looked at Alex. "Do you need a login?"

"No, I'll just access it through my account at the Met." Alex quickly brought up the Metropolitan Museum of Art's website, navigated through the library portal, and finally connected to JSTOR after typing in his login ID. A digitized image of the article on Fra. Mauro appeared from the journal *Imago Mundi.* The article, written in 1955, analyzed the role of Fra. Mauro in medieval cartography."

"Who's this Fra. Mauro?" asked Jonas.

"Friar Mauro was a Camaldolese monk who lived in the monastery of San Michel in the late fifteenth century. He was a famous cartographer who is credited with creating what many academics view as the crowning mappe mundi of medieval cartography."

"Maybe he's the monk Polo gave the map to." Jonas tried to pull the laptop away from Alex. Alex gripped it tightly and heaved it from the man's grip.

"Unlikely. Fra. Mauro lived over one hundred years after the death of Marco Polo."

The room descended into silence. Clay huffed at being frustrated by another impasse. *Nothing is easy with Polo,* he thought.

"Alex, why don't we go to the Monastery of San Michele?" Ellie asked. "We know from Marco's fourth book that the monk who acquired the map came from that monastery. There must be records, archives in the monastery, that may shed light on the members of the sect who may have been in the East at the time of Polo. It may take a lot of digging but it could lead to something."

"The only thing it would probably lead to is a dead end," Alex replied.

"That's a bit harsh." Ellie was taken aback.

"Literally, *a dead end*. The monastery doesn't exist anymore. In fact, the Island of San Michele often goes by a different name now—Cemetery Island. When Napoleon's forces conquered Venice, he ordered that dead bodies from Venice be buried on the Island of San Michele. There's not much more there than graves."

Ellie reached out and swung the laptop monitor shut with a snap. "Well, I can tell when we've hit a wall. But, if we're looking for a map, I know just the right person to help us out and the good news is, she's in London."

"I'm a bit wary of involving, how should I put it, another third party into this search. Bertrand Foucault was such a disappointment," Clay protested.

"Maryanne Hunter is no Bertrand Foucault. I can vouch for her discreetness and if I must be honest, I trust her more than I trust you."

"Ah, at least you're honest." Clay smiled.

Through the curtains of the window in the study, Alex could see the driver standing beside the Rolls Royce. Jonas lingered by the side of the car, as Ellie slid into the back seat.

"Here's a little gift," Clay said.

Alex glanced over his shoulder and could see Clay standing by the door holding a brown leather satchel.

"It was my father's from the second World War. He was an

intelligence officer for the U.S. Army. As a child I used to take it with me to school and brag to the other kids that my father used it to transport secret papers behind enemy lines. I'm not sure if it was close to being true but it was always greeted by awe by my peers. Well, anyway. We've lost your old bag, so here's a new one. It's the least I can do."

Alex reached out and accepted the satchel. The bag was constructed out of brown leather that was weathered and faded. Two sturdy straps were attached with nickel buckles to the bag.

"And one thing more," Clay muttered and walked over to the desk. He bent down and opened the lowest drawer and removed a transparent bag. Clay retrieved the leather bound book of *The Description of the World* and slid it into the bag. He ran his fingers across the top of the bag and sealed it. He clicked a button on the end of the bag. A sucking noise was emitted by a miniaturized device fastened to the bag. Alex watched as the air within bag was quickly evacuated, leaving the transparent coat to tightly hug the book.

"It's an archival storage bag. It's guaranteed to protect what's inside from the outside elements. If we are going to be adventuring, we do need to protect Polo's original text."

Clay held up the book in its casing and brought it to Alex. Alex opened his bag and allowed Clay to place the book into it.

"Thanks," Alex said as he slipped the straps over his shoulder. He adjusted the buckles until the bag hung comfortably against his flank.

The beep of a horn caused Clay to push aside the curtains and peer outside. He could see Jonas leaning into the driver's side of the car as he honked the horn.

Clay turned back and smiled at Alex.

"It sounds like we are being summoned. Jonas can be so impatient."

61

"Eleanor, it is so good to see you." The gray-haired woman rose from her desk and warmly embraced Ellie. She broke off the hug and backed Ellie slightly away, still gripping her hands tightly. The woman studied Ellie and smiled. "Let me just look at you. I can see your father in you."

Ellie blushed and hugged the woman a second time. She had not been in Maryanne Hunter's office at the Royal Society of Cartography since she was a child, but nothing had seemed to change, down to the African mask adorning the wall to the black-and-white photo of a younger Maryanne donning a parka at a base station at the foot of Mount Everest. The bookcases along the walls were filled to the brim with leather-bound volumes, and cylinders containing maps were piled high in the corners of the room. Ellie motioned to her three colleagues who had followed her into the office and introduced each in turn.

"Maryanne, I would be lying to you if I told you I've come here on a social visit. The truth is that I...*we* need your help...and your discretion."

The elderly woman seemed initially surprised, but responded with a firm nod. "Yes, of course, dear. Anything for you. I do hope you are not in any trouble," she said, glancing suspiciously at Jonas and then back at Ellie. Ellie doubted very much that Maryanne believed for a second that Jonas was a Yale doctoral candidate, but she did not question Ellie's assertion.

Ellie tried to deliver a comforting smile. "No trouble at all, really. We are, how shall I put it, in an academic bind of sorts. I think that if anyone can help us, it is you.

"As you know, it is such binds that I love to unravel. But before we begin, tea anyone?"

62

*Solomon Haasbroek leaned over Martin's shoulder as he typed upon the key-*board. A long list of numbers ran across the screen. The muscles in his neck felt tense. His men were beginning to become distracted as their prey failed to resurface. *Inaction is debilitating for a military unit,* he thought as he reminisced on prior failed missions. Just when he was beginning to succumb to despair himself…a break. These amateurs were getting sloppy.

Martin smiled and pointed at the screen. "There it is commander. Someone recently accessed Stone's museum account and logged in under his name to this journal site."

Solomon bent down and examined the screen.

"What was he looking at?"

Martin clicked several more keys and brought up an article on Fra. Mauro from an academic journal.

"This."

"Good. Let's see if our patron has anything to say about this." Solomon gave Martin a firm slap on the back.

63

*Maryanne Hunter listened silently as Ellie explained that they were search-*ing for a map that Marco Polo may have given to a Camaldolese monk during his travels to the East. Ellie had intentionally left out how they had come to acquire the knowledge of the existence of such a map. She was grateful that Maryanne sensed that this subject was off limits and did not press her for more information.

"Well, that is an interesting request…a very interesting request indeed."The elderly woman's hands shook slightly as she brought a porcelain teacup to her lips and took a dainty sip. "Marco Polo never produced a map…" She placed the cup down on the saucer with a clang.

Ellie could hear Clay suck in air through his pursed lips with disappointment. Maryanne gave a mischievous smile.

"…that is, unless you believe in the legends."

"What legends?" Ellie inched her chair closer to Maryanne. The woman looked at each of her guests and nearly whispered to her audience like an elementary school teacher reading a ghost story aloud.

"You'll love this. Gather around. One of the greatest periods of cartography coincided with what is today known as the 'Age of Exploration.' It was a time of great curiosity in which the world beyond the Western boundaries appeared to be a vast and empty canvas—a tabula rasa waiting to be inked in once and for all. We, of course, know that the world outside the West was always there after all. It didn't necessarily *need* to be discovered…it's all a bit ethnocentric of us in the West to use the term 'discover.'" Maryanne paused as if lost in her own thought and smiled with embarrassment. "I'm sorry, you'll have to ignore some of the ranting of an old-fashioned liberal. During that time, explorers probed the coastlines and sketched out the promontories and gulfs, providing the pieces of the larger jigsaw puzzle. The 'Age of Exploration' was a dynamic time and owed a lot to the accomplishments of Marco Polo.

"Polo, you see, was a true pioneer. His travels were primarily overland, fraught with danger from man and nature. His writings about the East helped fill in what was between the lines. One wonders whether Christopher Columbus would have ever contemplated sailing to China without the magical work of Marco Polo. We know today that Columbus prized more than anything his well-worn copy of Polo's *Description of the World*.

"In the world of cartography, however, Marco Polo is somewhat of an enigma — a frustrating mystery to those like me who study the history of map-making. He is one of the greatest travelers in history, yet there is no map of his voyages, nothing to hold in one's hand, unroll, and say 'this here is the world as Marco Polo saw it.' He traveled through unfamiliar lands and undoubtedly used maps to navigate the terrain and yet none have survived to this day."

"What are these legends you speak of?" Ellie probed.

Maryanne smiled and shook her head slightly. "That curiosity...so much like your dear father. I said that Marco Polo never produced a map. That is unless you believe Ramusio's accounts, and unfortunately few have throughout history."

"Who's Ramusio?" Ellie asked the question on everyone's mind.

"John Baptist Ramusio. He was the first person to serve as the unofficial biographer of Marco Polo. Mind you, he wrote approximately two centuries *after* the death of Polo. Facts have a tendency of being altered or lost entirely after such a long gap in time. Thus, much of the information provided in his biography of

Marco Polo is circumspect, felt to be more fiction than fact. He has been discredited by a fair number of historians through the years. But Eleanor, as you know, I have a tendency to root for the underdog and have found it hard to completely dismiss Ramusio.

"One of the things Ramusio wrote about was the legacy of Marco Polo. He wrote about the popularity of *The Description of the World* in Italy after Polo's death and how the book was chained to Rialto Bridge in Venice so that the general populace could read from it. He also wrote about an interesting connection of Marco Polo to medieval cartography."

Maryanne rose form her chair and walked over to an old, gray metal file cabinet pushed against the wall. With a screech, she pulled out the top drawer and slipped on the glasses that were dangling from her neck. The four watched with interest as Maryanne's head nearly disappeared into the drawer as she flipped through the files as if playing an ancient instrument. She would intermittently pause at a file and peer inside before moving on. After searching for several minutes, they could hear her utter 'bloody good' and pull a folder from the drawer. Maryanne returned to the desk and allowed the file to flip open, revealing a yellowed paper with faded black print from an old typewriter.

"This is an excerpt from Ramusio's *Navigationi et Viaggi*:

It remains for me to repeat certain things regarding this book that I heard repeatedly when young from the very learned and reverend Don Paolo Orlandino of Florence, a very good friend of mine and a fine cosmographer, who was Prior of the Camoldese monastery of Santo Michele on Murano near Venice and told me that he had heard these things from other friars in his monastery. And this regards how that fine illuminated world map on parchment, which can still be seen in a large cabinet alongside the choir of their monastery, was by one of the brothers of the monastery, who took great delight in the study of cosmography, diligently drawn and copied from a most beautiful and very old nautical map and a world map that had been brought from Cathay by the most honourable Messer Marco Polo and his father...it is clear that the said world map was undoubtedly drawn from that of Messer Marco Polo...

"The Fra. Mauro map?" Alex asked. "Are you saying that Fra. Mauro copied a map from Marco Polo?"

"I'm lost," Jonas protested.

Maryanne delicately slipped the yellowed paper back into the folder, closed it, and pushed it gently aside.

"Fra. Mauro is arguably one of the most celebrated and influential medieval cartographers. His map of the world is a work of art. We know that he was a bit of a recluse, rarely leaving the walls of the monastery of San Michele. He was also a ravenous collector of information on the outside world—he was quite a character. Mauro was an avid reader of travel tales. He also had a passion for collecting maps, particularly those of sailors searching for routes to the East. He ultimately became a very accomplished cartographer—this without ever truly traveling himself. I have always felt that Fra. Mauro was a lost soul born far before his time. What he would have done with the internet!

"Anyhow, in the early to mid-fifteenth century, King Alfonso V of Portugal commissioned Mauro to create a mappe mundi. The map was ultimately completed in 1459 but was destroyed before it could reach its destination. He was asked to create a second one but unfortunately died before he could complete it.

Alex nearly stood up. "Could Polo's map have been incorporated into Fra. Mauro's map?"

Maryanne shrugged. "We know that the monastery's library had quite a collection of maps collected through the ages. It would be truly divine if it was still standing."

"How is this going to help us, man," Clay moaned. "The first map was destroyed and the second wasn't completed."

"Oh, I never said the map wasn't completed. I said that *Fra. Mauro* never completed it. It was indeed finished. It just happened to be finished by another mapmaker."

"Who was this map-maker?" Ellie asked.

"His name was Andrea Bianco."

"Who?" Alex prompted with raised eyebrows.

"Andrea Bianco, a quite accomplished cartographer in his own right. Unlike Mauro he was a seasoned traveler, a Venetian sailor. He also had long familial ties to the monastery at San Michele that went back to the beginning of the order. I think I have an image of one of his works…" Maryanne disappeared beneath her desk. They could hear shuffling and the sound of a box moving against the hardwood floor. Suddenly they could see an old slide projector levitate into the air above the desk like a feat of legerdemain, held aloft by unseen hands. With a thud the projector was deposited onto the desk. Maryanne's head popped up, her gray hair in disarray. "…right here." She unzipped a case containing pages of slides housed in small plastic sleeves. They watched as she flipped on the slide projector. The machine shot out an antique yellow beam against the far wall, exposing a truly alarming amount of dust floating in her office. Jonas found himself reflexively coughing at the sight.

"Let's see…" Maryanne's fingers marched across the sleeves like the legs of a spider before finally stopping. She brought the sleeve close to her eyes so she could make out the miniscule writing on the edge of the slide's cardboard frame. "Oh, here it is! You'll have to excuse the slides. I can be a bit old-fashioned and set in my ways. The students these days don't know from slides. Everything is computers, computers." The fan clicked on and Maryanne raised her voice to battle the noise from the machine. She rose to her feet and approached the projected image upon the wall.

"This is a mappe mundi—a world map—created by Andrea Bianco from 1436."

The image was of a large circle of water. In the center was an irregularly shaped land mass with several waterways carved into the land like jagged cracks.

"It's relatively primitive when compared to the more elaborate Fra. Mauro map, but it's got a lot of the basic elements." Maryanne pointed to various portions of the map. "In this map, the Eastern world is positioned at the top of the map. In the upper left is Asia. The bottom left is Europe. To the right is Africa. Jerusalem is in the center. It's got many Biblical references, as was common in medieval times." She pointed to an irregular promontory at the top left of the landmass where a castle was etched in. "This is the Land of Gog and Magog. Separating the Land of Gog and Magog from the rest of the world is Alexander's Wall." Her fingers drifted to a peninsula extending nearly straight up from the top of the landmass. "No depiction of the Eastern World would be complete without an image of the Earthly Paradise with Adam and Eve, the Tree of Life, and the four rivers flowing from it."

Ellie squinted and could see two naked forms standing beside a tree. Next to the Earthly Paradise was a primitive sketch of a building.

"What's that next to the Garden of Eden?" Ellie asked.

"What's that, dear?"

Ellie rose and pointed to the structure. Her finger cast a dark shadow across the image.

"Oh that! That is an image of the Hospice of Saint Macarius. He was a monk who was warned by an angel at sword-point that the Garden of Eden was inaccessible to man. It has been taken by many to be Bianco's warning that the Earthly Paradise was off limits to mankind."

Maryanne ejected the slide and placed it atop the projector. She removed a second slide from a sleeve and slipped it into the projector. Another map was projected onto the wall. Like the

Bianco map, the world was depicted as a circle of water. There was an elaborate landmass of linked continents occupying much of the world. Waterways, lakes, and seas dotted the landmasses while gulfs and bays created jagged coastlines. Extensive notations filled the map, and images of castles and cities were painted upon the landmasses.

"Now this is the Fra. Mauro map. It's significantly more complex and elaborate. Unlike Bianco's earlier map, the Eastern World is not at the top of the map but is at the bottom of the map, not unlike Arabic maps. It has China, Europe, Africa, and the Middle East. There are annotations throughout the map that give a brief description of various locales throughout the world. It's like a map-meets-book and as such one can see the fingerprint of Marco Polo on it."

"Where is the Garden of Eden on this map?" Clay inquired.

"That is a great question. Unlike many other maps, Earthly Paradise is drawn outside the inhabited earth." Maryanne pointed to an illustration in the bottom right corner of the map, beyond the circle containing the inhabited earth. "The map contains a long discussion of different views on the existence of the Garden of Eden that includes folks like Augustine, Peter Lombard, Albert the Great, and Bede. The final view presented is that the Garden of Eden does indeed exist somewhere in the East, but that it was inaccessible to man."

Alex stood up and approached the image projected onto the wall. He leaned in to see the blurry image of Eden. There was a circle with a perimeter of Byzantine castle walls. In the center was a green area containing Adam, Eve, a man Alex presumed was God, and the Tree of the Knowledge of Good and Evil. A single angel appeared to guard the entrance into Eden with a sword. From the circle sprung four rivers that drained into a mountainous and desolate surrounding area.

"It seems like a lot of effort to duck the question of where the

Garden of Eden is located," Alex added. He stared at the image before him in silence. "Dr. Hunter, could you show me that slide of Bianco's map again."

"Surely."

Maryanne switched slides and projected Bianco's earlier map onto the wall.

Clay frowned and looked at Alex with curiosity. Alex had a finger outstretched and appeared to be counting.

"What is it, man?" Clay whispered to Alex.

Alex shrugged him off and continued to count.

"Dr. Hunter, what are those lines?"

"Sorry?"

"The lines crisscrossing the map." Alex left his seat and traced out a series of lines emanating like spokes on a wheel from Jerusalem to the periphery of the map.

"Oh those. They are navigational lines. Remember, all these maps preceded the discovery of longitude and latitude. That didn't come around until the era of scientific cartography in the mid-seventeenth to early eighteenth century. Before that, many ships were lost at sea without the certainty of longitude and latitude. What you see here are essentially rhumb lines or loxodromes—courses of constant bearing. They are based on the winds. Many medieval maps employed the use of wind roses or compass roses to delineate space. These lines on Bianco's map simply create an eight-pointed compass rose."

"Eight points," Alex echoed.

Maryanne withdrew the slide from the projector and returned the slide of the Fra. Mauro map. She pointed to a series of eight-pointed stars positioned primarily along the periphery of the map, like asterisks.

"These are good examples of compass or wind roses. Eight points for each of the winds: tramontana, Greco, levante, sirocco, ostro, libeccio, ponente, and maestro."

"Of course," Alex smiled broadly.

Clay looked at him and laughed before jovially smacking Jonas in the shoulder. "He's done it again! Clay turned back to Alex with a suddenly serious look. "You have done it, haven't you?"

"I'm not certain, but I have a hunch."

"A hunch is good. What is it then?" Clay urged.

Alex turned to Maryanne.

"You said that this cartographer was likely the man that completed what is known as the Fra. Mauro map? The one Ramusio said was derived from a map of the East from Marco Polo."

"Yes. If you believe Ramusio." Maryanne answered with a look of uncertainty bordering on apprehension.

"You also said that this cartographer had familial ties to the Camaldolese since its inception?"

"Yes."

"And what was this cartographer's name again?"

"Andrean Bianco."

"Bianco. I don't believe that Marco Polo was referring to the color of a habit when he referred to giving the map to a 'white monk.' I think Polo was telling us a name—a family name. Bianco is White in Italian! What if Polo's map was in the possession of the Bianco family all along and the Fra. Mauro's map is the final product of this knowledge?"

"I would say that was incredible!" Clay exclaimed.

"As would I," chimed in Maryanne.

Alex looked around the room and caught Ellie's eyes. They were beaming with pride and excitement.

"And even better, I think I might have figured out how to decipher the map. Where is this map now?"

Maryanne looked at the image of the Fra. Mauro map upon the wall one more time before flipping off the projector. The fan continued to whirl. "It's housed at the Biblioteca Marciana in Venice."

"Venice," Alex repeated as if in a stupor.

"You have to be kidding. It was right in front of us all along," Ellie muttered.

64

Ellie apprehensively glanced over her shoulder and could see the Byzantine façade of the Doge's Palace lit by moonlight across the piazzetta. Although it had been the scene of a heart-pounding pursuit little over a week ago, the building now seemed dreamlike against the wisp-like, plum-colored clouds that stretched out across the sky—stripped of its menacing air. She fought a wave of fatigue that crept up on her unexpectedly and threatened to submerge her thoughts in a morass of tiredness. Ellie brought her hand to her mouth and painfully yawned into her fist. Behind her she could hear Jonas speaking to Alex in the dark. She inched along the northern side of the Biblioteca Nazionale Marciana, keeping to the shadows as the water of the Venetian lagoon lapped at the stone supports.

Back in Venice, she thought incredulously. *Back to where Bernardo was murdered.* She was thankful that the police barriers and crime-scene tape had been removed. It was difficult enough to be back in the city that claimed such an important person in her life. A visual reminder of the murder would be all the more painful—the wound was too fresh. She imagined that the bureaucrats of Venice must have lobbied hard to have the crime swept under the rug. The suggestion that the City of Romance was unsafe could have a stunting effect on the summer tourist season.

"Here we go," Jonas announced under his breath as he stopped in front of an inconspicuous metal door. The weathered portal was thin and tall. Unmarked and without a handle, the door was barely noticeable unless someone was intentionally seeking it out.

Jonas leaned against the metallic surface and pushed it open with a slight creak. He smiled as the door swung back, revealing a darkened stairwell. He whispered proudly, "The crazy thing is that it didn't even take a big bribe to get the maintenance guy to leave the door open for us. I told him that I was from the tabloids, looking to photograph the scene of Gozzi's final gasp."

Ellie's fingers tightened into a fist. Alex reached out in the darkness and restrained her hand.

"What about security," Clay asked as he glanced back along the waterfront, studying the long shadow cast by a passing boat.

"Two words: Italian security. It's an oxymoron. The truth of the matter is that anyone could probably walk off the street or the piazza and stroll away with a museum piece. I would be more worried about the guy who buffs the floor (who incidentally is having a drink at his favorite bar and will be there for the next couple of hours). Trust me. We will have the library to ourselves." Jonas gave a smug smile and ushered them through the door with a theatrical bow.

The darkened stairwell was dank, lit only by the moonlight streaming through a tiny window perched high above. Ellie squeezed through the doorway and allowed the door to snap shut behind them.

They stood in the stairwell for a moment and tried to gain their bearings.

"Where to?" Ellie asked.

"Don't look at me," Jonas responded. He pointed to Alex. "Ask the professor."

Alex flipped on a flashlight and shined it down on the most recent volume of Acquisitions and Exhibits at the Biblioteca Nazionale Marciana. He turned the pages as if it were an old-fashioned flipbook and stopped at a schematic of the floorplan of the library. Small numbers were positioned within the rooms. Alex found the legend and located the number corresponding to Fra

Mauro's map. He gripped the corner of the page, bent it down, and closed the book.

"OK, I know where the map is," Alex whispered.

Jonas pulled out a second flashlight and tapped the end against the palm of his hand. "I would like to make a suggestion if I might. Let's try to keep the flashlights off if possible. I've cleared out the library for us but I don't want some tourist alerting the carabinieri to strange lights bouncing around through the library late at night. It might call attention to us and we want to be as invisible as possible."

"Agreed," Alex answered and turned off the flashlight. "We need to make our way through the main portion of the library towards the Museo Correr that is connected to this building. Follow me."

Alex led them up a short flight of stairs and paused at a door at the end of a landing. He slowly pushed open the door and poked his head out. He could see the darkened interior of the library. Alex waited and listened for any sound of movement from the room. Satisfied that they were alone, he trudged into the adjacent room, followed by Clay, Ellie, and Jonas.

The room was elegantly decorated with gilded walls and ceilings and an intricately checkered white-and-black marble floor. Alex moved deliberately across the room and stopped beside a large globe perched atop a wooden frame and housed within a glass display case. The globe was illuminated and the four huddled by it as Alex reopened the book with the schematic and identified where they were. He wordlessly traced his finger along a path through connecting rooms until his finger reached the asterisk against which he tapped his finger several times. His colleagues knowingly nodded and Alex slipped the book into his satchel.

Alex quickly exited the cavernous room and took the first right. The library was eerily still as he wove through room after room, breezing by glass cabinets with artifacts and artwork. After several minutes of searching marked by the occasional misstep, reconsultation with the schematic of the library, and the need to double-back, the group finally arrived at a stairwell at the far end of the library near a connection to the Museo Correr. Alex stopped and looked down at the book with confusion.

"What is it?" Clay whispered with concern.

"It should be somewhere here, at least according to this schematic," Alex responded, glancing up and down the stairwell.

"It's a weird place to place a map of such importance," Jonas muttered and proceeded to lean against the wall. "How old is that book you have…" He nearly lost his footing as his body partially disappeared behind a set of red velvet drapes hanging loosely across the wall. Clay reached out and steadied Jonas.

Ellie grabbed a portion of the drape and took a peak behind it before letting it flop back. She placed the palm of her hand against Jonas's chest and not so gently directed him back and away from the drapes. She reached out and took hold of each free end of the drapes and with a sweeping motion pulled them aside.

"It looks like Jonas can be useful after all," Ellie announced and took a step back to admire their find.

Beneath a long metal rod from which the velvet drapes were suspended was the Fra. Mauro map. The map was set in a partially gilded, wooden square frame. In each of the four corners of the map were circles. In the top left corner were thirteen concentric circles surrounding the earth, which was positioned like the pupil of an eye. The circular layers represented the elements of water, air, fire, the planetary spheres, the heaven of the fixed stars, the crystalline heaven, and the empyrean. In the top right corner was a second set of concentric circles that explained the influence of the moon on the oceanic tides. In the bottom right corner was a circle divided by three horizontal lines depicting the climatic zones of the earth. Finally, in the bottom left corner was the illustration of the Garden of Eden that they had previously seen in Dr. Hunter's office. The Garden of Eden was enclosed within a circle of fire and guarded by a cherub. Within the square frame was a second round frame that surrounded the map of the inhabitable world. The round frame looked like a perfect ring of golden snakeskin.

"We've found it," Clay announced with a smile. "The Fra. Mauro Map."

65

Solomon loaded a magazine into his pistol and looked at the old man with interest.

"It's good to finally meet the 'Man Behind the Curtain' after all this time. I was beginning to think that you were just a voice at the other end of the phone." Solomon smiled sarcastically. He leaned against the stone column and studied the empty Piazza San Marco.

The man shifted his body in the shadows and responded with a subdued smile. "I assure you, Mr. Haasbroek, that I am very much flesh and blood, to a fault."

The cell phone in Solomon's shirt pocket vibrated and he looked away from the old man. He retrieved it and brought it to his ear. His eyes remained trained on the courtyard ahead.

"Howzit." Solomon listened for a moment and hung up. "O.K. It's time to go."

Solomon glanced back at the man as he slipped the phone back into his pocket and slid the gun into its holster. "It appears that we are moments away from delivering to you what you ordered. What these guys have must be pretty precious for you to be paying what you are."

"I assure you, Mr. Haasbroek, it is priceless." The man slipped out of the shadows so that his face was partially illuminated by the lights around the Piazza.

"Well, priceless or not, we're about to reach the endgame." Solomon spat on the ground and ushered the man to follow him.

As Solomon turned to go, he could hear the man say, "That's where you are wrong. This is just the beginning. Now the true search starts."

66

*Clay and Jonas trained the beams of their flashlights up at the map, reveal-*ing its intricate details. They could see a jigsaw arrangement of land masses crisscrossed by rivers and dotted with elaborate depictions of palaces and cities. White caravels sailed across majestic, blue seas and tiny notations were crammed across the canvas like the ranting of a madman.

"It's beautiful," Ellie sighed.

Alex removed a book from his satchel that Maryanne had given him before they had departed from London. The book was an analysis of the Fra Mauro map and had a detailed reproduction of the map with a dissection of the notations and locations illustrated on the map. He placed the book on the floor and folded the binding back. Alex rummaged through his satchel and removed the wooden box and two metallic roses.

Clay glanced up at the map again and then back down at the cross-legged Alex. He watched as Alex held up the slender key and slid it into the hidden keyhole in the wooden box to open it. The two diamonds sparkled wondrously as they reflected and refracted the light of the flashlights.

"Well, I for one am dying to hear your thoughts at this moment, Alex," Clay urged.

Alex removed each of the two diamonds from the box and handed them to Ellie. She delicately cupped the precious gems in her hands and observed Alex studying the two metallic roses.

"It didn't make sense to me until Dr. Hunter explained the significance of the eight lines crisscrossing Andrea Bianco's map. They were rhumb lines, loxodromes, navigational markers placed on a map by cartographers to help direct travelers during medieval times. Then I thought of what Marco Polo wrote at the end of his fourth book:

The mapmakers will remember the path when the world is finally filled in. It is as constant and elemental as the winds that guide the sails and blow across the plains eastward...always eastward.

"*It is as constant and elemental as the* **winds**. Polo was giving us a clue to solving the puzzle."

Alex held aloft the two metallic roses. "I think these two artifacts are compass roses or wind roses."

Ellie knelt down by his side, her eyes opened wide.

"Constants...yes, like the Tower of the Winds."

"What's that?" Clay queried.

"The Tower of the Winds is an octagonal marble tower in Athens that was built before the time of Christ. It was dedicated to the eight wind deities — the constants."

Alex nodded his head in agreement and rose to his feet. He turned to Clay and explained. "Since ancient times, wind has been viewed as a constant, a way in which man could help order the world around him. If necessary, it could be used to denote directionality for travel. The directions of the winds could be arranged to correspond to the cardinal directions — north, south, east, and west. Sometimes maps would employ the bare minimum of direction, four winds, and consequently four points — like the points of a compass. Most, however, would use eight winds. These winds had names."

Alex traced on his palm with the tip of his index finger to illustrate his point. "Tramontana — north, Greco — northeast, levante — east, sirocco — southeast, ostro — south, libeccio — southwest, ponente — west, and maestro — northwest. The symbol of the eight winds was the 'wind rose' because it resembled the petals of a rose. Over time the wind directions and cardinal directions became synonymous and many just called it a 'compass rose.' Sometimes maps would have wind roses with more than eight winds. There were on occasion sixteen winds as is seen with a wind compass formed around an obelisk in St. Peter's Square. Other maps would even have thirty-two-point compass roses. Sailors who could recite all thirty-two directions of such a compass rose were said to be able to 'box the compass.' At the time of Marco Polo, a map would either have a four or eight-point compass rose."

"If those things are wind roses then what do we do with them and why are there two identical wind roses?" Ellie asked Alex as she helped him to rise to his feet.

"Firstly, they are not identical." Alex turned the metal roses over, revealing the flat back side of the artifacts. "There is writing on the back of each. This first one says in Latin: "the First footsteps." The second one says: "the center of the world." As for what do they do...Ellie could you please hand to me those two diamonds?"

Ellie gave each of the diamonds to Alex as the four huddled closely together. Alex grasped the first diamond between his index finger and thumb and positioned it in the middle of the metal rose. With a gentle push, the diamond snapped into the center of the rose. Alex subsequently held aloft the second diamond and pressed it into the middle of the second metal rose.

"You asked me why Polo left two wind roses. It came to me when Dr. Hunter was discussing the importance of longitude and latitude. Think of GPS—global positioning systems. If you know longitude and latitude, then you are never truly lost. You always know precisely where you are in the world (at least in a two-dimensional sense). Of course you would need a third coordinate for elevation if you want to be a purist, but you get the point. I think that by having two wind roses, Marco Polo left to the Bianco family a way to triangulate a location without utilizing longitude and latitude. I believe that this information was safeguarded by the Bianco family through the years. What was it that Polo said?

"The mapmakers will remember the path when the world is finally filled in.

"I believe this location has been hidden in this map."

"Amazing!" Clay exclaimed.

"Well, how does it work?" Jonas asked.

Alex was stopped by the sound of a gun safety and a deep voice bellowing from behind them.

"Yes, Mr. Stone, tell us, how does it work?"

67

Five men dressed in black quickly crept up the stairs with guns drawn. Ellie looked at Alex with alarm as the threatening figures formed a perimeter around the four of them. She reached out blindly, her fingers momentarily probing the air until they brushed against Alex's hand. She gripped his hand tightly and shot a severe glare at Jonas whose eyes darted around as if trying to identify a possible exit.

"Trust me,' you said. 'We will have the library to ourselves,'" Ellie uttered with venom.

Jonas turned back with an equally severe look. "It's your friend, Hunter. She gave us up."

"Never. She wouldn't."

Clay stood tall and looked at the scene before him with a look of frustration and despair. "Quit it you two."

They were trapped.

The men formed a semicircle around them and continued to train their semiautomatic weapons at their prisoners. Suddenly two of the armed men moved aside to allow a tall man in black to pass through their perimeter. He sauntered with a swagger of confidence, carrying a gun loosely at his side. Ellie immediately recognized him as the man from the chase through the Doge's Palace and shuddered at the memory of him standing at the top of the marble staircase as they fled from the palace into the courtyard beyond.

The man was handsome, with tightly cropped blond hair and stubble across his cheeks and chin. His pupils were like black pearls, and when he finally halted in front of Jonas he assumed a stiff posture that exposed his military background. He nonchalantly raised his pistol, pressed the barrel against Jonas's left temple, and smiled. When he spoke, his South African accent belied a twinge of Afrikaans streaked through it. Jonas could feel the cool tip of the barrel pressed against his skin and instinctively raised his hands to surrender.

"Before we become more familiar, would you be so kind as to hand over the pistol in your waistband? And while you are at it, the revolver in your boot."

Jonas reached into his waistband with his right hand and pulled out the gun. He held it up by the grip and dropped it into the South African's hand. The man promptly passed it over his shoulder to one of his waiting men. Jonas motioned to his boot for permission to bend down. The leader nodded his approval and Jonas knelt down as the man leveled the barrel of his pistol against the back of his head. Alex watched as Jonas pulled out a small revolver from the top of his right boot. He handed it to the man and rose to his feet with a look of defeat.

"Well done." The man examined the small revolver, shrugged, and slipped it into his waistband. "You've been a hard bunch of monkeys to catch, but in the end, here we are."

"What do you want from us?" Ellie asked.

"Don't act so innocent, girl. Do you always creep around old libraries in the dark of night? I'd say that you must have caught the scent of something important. I have a patron willing to pay a generous fee for what you know."

"You're wasting your time," Clay growled back.

"I'm not so sure, Dr. Clay." The man raised his gun and pointed it at the chest of Clay. "Are you willing to bet your life on it?"

"That's enough, Mr. Haasbroek. Put the gun away. We can discuss this in a more civil fashion, surely."

The voice in heavily accented English came from behind the

armed men, and Alex craned his neck to identify the source. He could see a tall, thin man impeccably dressed in a black suit weave through the cordon of men and approach Clay. The man appeared to be in his late sixties and had thinning hair that was slicked back across his head. As he walked, his expensive shoes tapped against the marble floor.

"Dr. Clay, I have followed your pursuit of Eden for some time. I must commend you on enlisting such capable help in deciphering this mystery. We couldn't have done a better job ourselves. Foremost, I admire your unbridled persistence. It is a shame that we have become, unwittingly, such adversaries. This is coming most sincerely from one passionate collector to another. I would like to introduce myself. You may call me Phillip."

"This was never about collecting," Clay responded. "We are not talking about some antique vase or a bucket of ancient trinkets. This search is about reclaiming what we have lost and the promise of improving the world with that knowledge. You would seek to keep this knowledge in the hands of the few."

"Do not lecture me about motives. You know nothing of us."

"I know that the Order of Christ has been searching for the Garden of Eden for centuries and has been driven mad by it. The Order has had little compunction about using the sword to reach this destination. It is precisely from these people that Marco Polo hid the path."

"The Order of Christ," the old man repeated with a smile of amusement. "We do not like to go by this name any longer. This Order's day has come and gone, diluted by centuries of patronage—reduced to an honorary degree bestowed upon people who have no understanding of the significance of this honor. We are the descendants of a visionary—Prince Henry the Navigator—who understood that there are powers and secrets hidden in the ancient world that could be unlocked through exploration. I am just one member of an organization of individuals—lawyers, politicians, bankers, academics—linked by a desire to uncover the wisdom of the ancient world…and what better knowledge to possess than the single thing that has eluded mankind since the fall—eternal life. If others must lose their lives so we can obtain this, then so be it. There are many souls that have invested their time and money in this venture, people who are betting that before they exhale their final breath, the secret Polo so selfishly hid will be finally revealed. I am here to ensure that this happens. Do not underestimate our power."

The old man looked away from Clay and peered at Alex with intensity. "My apologies, Mr. Stone. I interrupted your very insightful explanation on the use of wind roses to decipher the Fra Mauro map. I must insist that you continue."

Alex caught a glare from Clay and then looked at the armed men around him. "I'm sorry but that's it. That's all I have, I'm stuck. I haven't figured out the rest. Maybe with some time…"

The well-dressed man nodded to the South African commander. Solomon raised his gun and directed the barrel at Alex's chest. "Listen to the man and do what he asks." He lowered the barrel and aimed it at Alex's right knee. "I'm an impatient man except when it comes to torture. Then I'm an exceptionally patient man. Let's say we start with the knees. You can still use that big brain of yours in a wheel-chair."

Ellie cast Alex a frantic glare. "Tell him what he wants, Alex, for God's-sake."

"Someone seems to care about your ability to walk around the university campus. Listen to the lady, Alex, she can tell you what I did to her last boyfriend back in Iraq."

Ellie felt bile shoot up her esophagus and the muscles in her neck tighten, sending pain across her chest. The explosives, the ambush! They were searching for the box all along! Ellie and Gordon were pawns in this game and this brute took Gordon away from her. She felt bitterness for Clay for exposing Gordon to this danger. This bitterness was quickly subsumed by hatred for Gordon's killer.

"I can see it all making sense to you. Leaving the C4 for you guys back in Mosul was a nice touch, but helping to alert the insurgents to your position was, if I might say so myself, brilliant. I must admit, had I known you were in possession of the box, I might have been a bit gentler, but fate has a strange way of working itself out." Solomon smiled devilishly. Ellie sprung forward, but was restrained by Alex.

"You sadistic son-of-a-bitch!"

"O.K., O.K." Alex pleaded and settled Ellie down. He tried to organize his thoughts. "Give me a second." He looked into Ellie's eyes and tried to calm her down. "Ellie, I need your help. I need you to focus." Alex could see the rage begin to drain from her cheeks although her hands still trembled.

"Where did we leave off? Two wind roses and triangulation of a single point I believe," the old man offered.

Alex backed away from the Fra Mauro map to examine it from a different vantage point. He lifted up the metallic roses and reread the inscriptions on the back of each. "The inscriptions on the back of the wind roses have to be clues to where they should be placed. I'm just not sure what they mean."

"What does it say again, Alex?" Ellie sidled up beside Alex and looked up at the map.

"It says: the First footstep."

"First footstep…" Ellie repeated. "Maybe it refers to Marco Polo's point of departure. He, after all, was a traveler. The Polo family crest has three birds *walking*. It could be Venice. Where is it on the map?"

"It's a good thought. It could be figurative in nature. After all, the Polos left Venice by boat. I don't know, though. Directions on the map are reversed. The top is south, the bottom north. The right of the map is east and the left is west." Alex approached the map and pointed to an elongated landmass extending to the right of the map. "This is Europe, which would make this upside boot-shaped structure protruding into the Mediterranean Sea, Italy." Alex seemed dissatisfied and looked down at the inscription again: the First footstep.

"There is something odd about this clue. Everything is in lower case except the word 'First' is capitalized. Why capitalize it?"

"You capitalize to designate something as being important," Ellie offered.

"Is it a name? Is Polo pulling another 'White Monk' trick?" Clay asked.

Alex bit at his lip. He repeated 'the First footstep' over and over in his head in hopes of seizing upon any inkling of what Polo was hinting at.

"Riddles and more riddles. He's like the Sphinx, Polo," Ellie muttered.

"What do you mean?" Alex wondered.

"Oh nothing. It's just that Polo can't just spell it out. You always have to jump through a hurdle with him. It reminds me of story of the Riddle of the Sphinx that my father used to tell me when I was a young girl."

"How did it go?" Alex asked.

"You know from Sophocles's *Oedipus Rex*, the part when Oedipus encounters the Sphinx who demands that he answer a riddle before being allowed to pass?"

"What was the riddle?"

"Which creature in the morning goes on four feet, in the afternoon on two feet, and by night on three feet...the answer of course is man—crawling as a baby, walking on two feet as an adult, and finally, in old age with a cane."

"That's it. You're a genius!" Alex exclaimed. "It's Biblical. Who had the first footsteps of man? Who was the first man?"

"Adam," Clay answered.

"Exactly. Marco left the clue to the first wind rose marker in his writing. After he left the service of Kublai Khan, he and his family sailed back by way of the Far East, India, and Ceylon, now known as Sri Lanka. One of the sites he writes about is called Adam's Peak. It is a mountain in central Sri Lanka. Some people have felt that it is the actual location of the Garden of Eden. On the mountain there is a boulder with an indentation that appears to be that of a footprint. This 'footprint' is considered sacred by several religions. Many Buddhists believe that it is the footprint of Buddha while some Hindus believe that it is the footprint of the god Shiva. There are some Muslims and Christians who believe that this is the first footprint of Adam as he left the Garden of Eden."

"The *First* footstep," Clay repeated in awe.

Alex darted over to the book on the Fra Mauro Map. The mercenaries' guns followed his sudden movement. He searched the index for Sri Lanka and was able to locate a number corresponding to a location on the map. Returning to his feet he approached the map again and pointed to a triangular shaped island in the left upper quadrant of the inhabited earth. Under the island was written 'Saylam.'

"It's there. That's Ceylon or Saylam or as it is known today, Sri Lanka. In the middle of the island is Adam's Peak."

"Is this Eden then?" asked Clay.

"No this is just the first marker," Alex answered

"Well-done," applauded the well-dressed man. "One down. What does the inscription on the second wind rose say?"

Alex turned over the second wind rose.

"It says…'the center of the world.' Alex interweaved his hands behind his back and studied the map hanging on the wall. He bit at his lip and began to pace before stopping momentarily in front of Ellie. She caught his eyes. He seemed to be trying to communicate something to her. She squinted, trying to decipher the message. Alex moved on. *What is he up to?* she wondered.

After several minutes, Alex stopped pacing and addressed the audience around him. "If you look at the Fra Mauro map you will notice that there are eight wind roses arranged along the periphery of the inhabited portions of the world." He pointed to symbols that appeared like asterisks within circles, each with eight lines radiating from the center like rays of the sun or spokes on a wheel. "These wind roses denote the cardinal positions. If you draw lines from each of these wind roses, they all intersect in the middle of the map. This is what Polo is referring to as 'the center of the world.'"

"Now Mr. Stone, I was pleased with you up until this point, but I am not a mere dilettante in the field and I do not appreciate being led astray. Mr. Haasbroek, our young colleague many need a little refocusing of his thoughts."

Solomon smiled and directed the gun at Ellie.

Alex raised his hands with alarm. "O.K. I get the point. Just put the gun down."

Phillip nodded to Solomon, who responded by lowering the barrel of the gun.

"The center of the word in medieval times was Jerusalem. It was typically in the center of the map. However, the Fra Mauro map is noteworthy for the fact that it was displaced westward. People have argued that this was done when it became obvious from years of exploration that the Eastern world was vast compared with the West. This certainly makes sense, but now one wonders if Bianco moved Jerusalem westward for another reason. If you look closely at the Fra Mauro map you can see a ninth symbol of a wind rose at the edge of the Mediterranean Sea." Alex pointed to the symbol. "That's Jerusalem...the eternal center of the world."

"Now that wasn't so bad. Was it?" asked Phillip. "I imagine

you've already figured out how to use the wind roses or are we going to play this game again?"

Alex turned to Clay and Jonas. "I need your help." They nodded silently and clustered around him.

Alex selected the metallic wind rose with the inscription "the center of the world" and handed it to Clay. Alex then passed the second wind rose with the inscription "the First footstep" to Jonas.

"Jonas, I need you to place the wind rose I gave you against Adam's Peak on the map." He waited as Jonas slid the metallic artifact across the canvas until it rested in the center of the triangular island of Saylam. Alex then turned to Clay and directed him to the right of the canvas. "I need you to place the second wind rose on Jerusalem." Clay nodded and positioned the wind rose on the location of the Holy City.

Alex took several steps back from the map. He could see the faintest flicker at the edges of the petals that composed each of the wind roses.

"Now what?" Jonas asked as he impatiently held aloft the wind rose.

"We need light. Directed light." Alex bent down and retrieved the two flashlights resting on the floor. He handed one to Ellie and kept the other for himself. He walked up to Jonas and lifted the flashlight until it was level with the diamond in the center of the wind rose. His finger found the switch on the flashlight and he pushed it forward. The diamond in the center twinkled brilliantly as the light was focused on it. Suddenly, eight thin beams of bluish light shot out from the ends of each of the petals, cutting across the canvas.

"Ellie, you need to do the same with Redmund's wind rose," Alex urged, his eyes ablaze with wonder.

Ellie excitedly flipped out the flashlight and brought it up to the center of the wind rose. This time eight rays of yellow light emanated from the tips of the rose petals. The two sets of lines crisscrossed the canvass, meeting at several points. The points in which the beams contacted were green except for a single point.

"Amazing," Alex gasped.

In the lower portion of the map, one of the points in which the lines intersected glowed a brilliant crimson color.

"X marks the spot," Alex could not help but say.

68

"What do you see?" Clay asked as he twisted his neck and tried to get distance from the map while still holding the wind compass flush against the surface of the canvas.

Alex approached the glowing red dot and tried to place it within the context of the depiction of the world. It was located towards the bottom of the map and left of center.

Alex traced out the landmasses with his finger while intermittently glancing back at his audience. He could see several of the armed mercenaries allow their guns to lower slightly as they looked on in wonder.

He started at the far left of the map. "This is Java." He pointed to an island at the edge of the map. "Remember, in this map, left is east and right is west, up is south and down is north. If you move to the right or west, you hit China." His finger ran just above the surface of the map and paused at a large area of land. "If you go further west you hit the Ganges River." His finger followed the serpentine river as it cut into South Asia. "Beyond it to the west is India. Now if you go down or north, you are into the western portions of China." Alex's finger stopped at the red dot. "This location is between Asia and what the map refers to as Scythia."

"Scythia?" Clay asked.

Ellie stepped up and spoke.

"It's an area named after a nomadic people in the eighth century B.C. called the Scythians. Herodotus wrote about them. When people talk about Scythia they usually are thinking of what some would call Eurasia."

"Or Central Asia," Alex added. "The wind roses are directing us to a place deep in the heart of Mongolia."

"Intriguing," muttered Phillip.

Alex drew closer to the map and examined the red spot projecting on the canvas. It was on a portion of the map that was devoid of any symbol or writing. He brought his face so close to the surface of the map that his nose nearly brushed up against it. He could see the surface of the map that was illuminated red was irregular, bubbled, with a faint, nearly imperceptible web of cracks, like a break in a car's windshield. As he studied the latticework of cracks, he could see that a small, irregular piece of paint had fallen away, revealing the original white canvas upon which the map was painted.

"What's this?" he whispered.

He nearly gasped at the sight of a portion of black writing seemingly tattooed upon the white canvas.

"There's something underneath this map!" Alex exclaimed. Ellie and Phillip surged forward towards the spot. Phillip pushed Ellie and Alex aside and examined the surface of the map.

"Yes," the old man hissed and looked back at Alex with maniacal eyes. Phillip ran his finger across the rough surface of the map and wedged the tip of a fingernail under the flaking paint. He scratched at the surface, sending tiny flecks of brown floating to the floor.

"What are you doing?" Alex protested and advanced towards the man.

Suddenly Phillip swung around, removed a short blade from his pocket, and held it up in the air.

"Whoa!" Alex jumped back with his hands defensively raised.

"Don't worry, Mr. Stone. It's not meant for you." Phillip smirked, bent down, and slid the tip of the blade behind a raised portion of the paint. He proceeded to flick off the paint layer.

"You're going to destroy the map, for God's-sake! Stop. It's a priceless piece of history! We could have the map radiographed to see what is underneath that coat of paint. It's been done many times before to see if an artist painted over any earlier work. It won't harm the map. The technology is out there."

Phillip turned back to Alex with a look of impatience. "And how do you suppose we do that? Should we inform the board of the Biblioteca Nazionale Marciana that we intend on wheeling in a ton of high-tech imaging equipment so we could spend months analyzing the x-rays? I appreciate your concern, but this is far quicker."

Alex took a small step backward and bowed his head slightly. He felt a profound sense of guilt as he watched the old man pick at the map. But he could not help but acknowledge that despite his desire to preserve this historical piece, his heart yearned to see what was beneath the paint.

Phillip paused, looked back at Alex, and squinted. He placed the knife on the floor and then turned and glanced at Clay, Ellie, and Jonas. "When I reveal what is behind here, I will be asking you to join me for the final journey. My motive will be simple: I still believe you can help me. You will all say yes, not that you will have a choice. You will try to convince yourself that your decision to join me was about self-preservation but in your hearts, you will know that this is not true. You will come because you cannot bear to not see this through to the end, whatever the costs."

The old man smiled, revealing perfectly white teeth, lifted the blade from the ground, and wiped it on his sleeve. He returned to picking and peeling away paint until he was left with a square-foot of exposed white canvas. In the center, written in black and stained into the underlying fabric, were a series of symbols. The symbols were written vertically and consisted of several columns.

Jonas slipped the wind rose into his pocket. "Looks like chicken-scratch to me."

Ellie bent over and examined the symbols. "It's strange. It almost looks like Sanskrit, but it's not. It has elements of Arabic with the cursive appearance but it's not. It's vertically oriented like Chinese but it is most certainly not Chinese." She bit her lip.

"It's Uyghur," Phillip stated matter-of-factly. "Or at least an Uyghur-derived script. It might be more accurate to say that it is Mongolian. The Mongols conquered the Naimans—a Turkish people living on the steppes. A man by the name of Tata-Tonga who was captured helped adapt the written language of his people to the Mongol culture, which did not have a written language. You are right that it is written vertically and left to right for that matter."

"What does it say?" Alex asked.

The old man smiled broadly. "It says: Sacred Kaldun, Where Eden Lies."

"What does it mean?" asked Jonas.

Phillip held his blade up to the exposed canvas and with a stab drove the tip of the knife into it. With a sawing motion he cut away a swatch of canvas containing the message. A gaping black hole was left in the map. Alex looked down at the hole with dismay.

Phillip silently folded the piece of canvas and finally looked up.

"It means we are going on a trip. All of us."

MONGOLIA

69

The Toyota truck suddenly lurched forward with a squeal like a wounded animal. Ellie backed away and watched the tires, glistening with a layer of shiny mud, fruitlessly spin. Globs of detritus from the forest floor were spat into the air as the rear chassis of the vehicle wiggled back and forth. One of the mercenaries, a bespectacled young man who looked like he belonged in an office cubical rather than trudging through the wilderness with soldiers of fortune, whom Ellie learned was named Martin, leaned his head out of the driver's side window, shrugged, and turned off the ignition.

"It's for shit, Sir," he barked out the window.

He emerged from the cabin, smoking a cigarette, and promptly plopped his boots into the thick, black mud.

"Fantastic," she could hear him complain as he waded through the slime.

Ellie swatted at a horse fly that had settled upon the nape of her neck and peered back at Alex who was perched atop the gnarled, exposed root of a tree. He pulled out a water bottle, took a drink, and wiped his mouth with his sleeve. The stubble on his face and unkempt hair told volumes of the ordeal to date. Ellie could feel warm sweat trickle down her shirt and settle in the small of her back. The fabric of her shirt clung tightly to her as she bent down to retrieve her bottle of water. She wordlessly climbed up the short embankment and sat down next to Alex.

They sat side by side in silence and watched as the two other jeeps maneuvered in front of the truck trapped in the mud. They could see Phillip emerge from the lead jeep. He was dressed in an olive-colored tee shirt and khaki pants and wore a handkerchief loosely around his neck. He stood by the front of the jeep and stretched out a map across the hood, securing each end with a water bottle. He motioned for Solomon and the Mongolian guide to join him. As they conferred by the front of the jeep, members of Solomon's team began to remove cables to hook up to the immobilized truck. They moved matter-of-factly, having performed the same task five times previously. The remote wilderness of Mongolia had proven to be a formidable opponent, confronting them with a dearth of paved roads and a plethora of impassable paths. One fateful turn of the wheel onto an unseen patch of mud hidden beneath a blanket of leaves could spell disaster.

Your mission is cursed. That was what the old Mongolian shaman had said shortly after their arrival at Möngönmorit, a small town at the northeast corner of the aimag or province of Töv. The man was rumored by locals to be the most capable guide into the Khan Khentii Strictly Protected Area that straddled central and eastern Mongolia. They had found him cooking over an open fire beside a rundown, wooden cabin on the steppes. Dressed in a flannel shirt, loose-fitting pants, and a floppy white hat, the man had squatted by an iron pot, mixing a turbid stew with a long spoon. He glanced up from his task and looked at his visitors suspiciously through his right eye, the left eye having long ago become clouded white by a cataract. The young Mongolian man who had brought the group out to the cabin to see the shaman looked embarrassed as he translated Phillip's request for a guide to travel to Burkhan Khaldum—the Sacred Hill—deep in the heart of the Khentii mountain range.

The old man had continued to stir the stew and listened without interruption. When he finally spoke, his voice was raspy and raw, a suitable match for the windblown skin of his face. The young Mongolian hesitated and then translated with a look of apprehension.

"I know why you are here. I know more than you would think. This had all been foretold. First the Soviets came here with their tanks and sealed off this area. They with their Mongolian cronies destroyed the monasteries and slaughtered the monks. They tried to destroy our spirit, but failed. What were they afraid of, I ask you? Then one day, poof...they left. They could not kill a spirit of a people that has soaked into the grasslands, mixed with the rivers, and has become one with the trees, the stars, the sky. Now you come after all this time from the West with money and seek to pay for these secrets. You, too, will fail. Money means nothing here." He looked up at Phillip and pointed his thin finger menacingly his way. "Beware what you seek under the Eternal Sky for it does not belong to you. Your mission is cursed." The old man had spat on the dirt ground and went back to stirring the pot as if he was alone once again.

Phillips eyes blazed with rage. He bent down, gripped the man's shirt sleeve, and tugged several times. "Are you Darkhad? Darkhad?"

The shaman pulled his shirt from Phillip's grip, smiled at him, and resumed cooking.

Phillip stood up with a look of disgust and walked over to Solomon. Phillip leaned in and whispered something in Solomon's ear. Solomon nodded and walked over to the old man. He suddenly reached down and grabbed the diminutive man by his collar and violently dragged him to his feet. Without a word, Solomon slipped a gun from his waistband, pressed the barrel against the man's forehead, and fired. A spray of blood, shards of skull, and brain matter diffused across the blue sky. Solomon let the limp form crumple to the ground in a heap. He spat onto the man.

"Let this be a warning to the Darkhad," Solomon bellowed. As if in response, the wind across the grassland began to pick up. He angrily directed the gun towards the young Mongolian man who stood twisting the brim of his hat nervously in his hands. The man winced at the sight of the weapon, expecting to be struck down as well.

"Ogdon?"

"Ogdi…but …you can call me…Jimmie," the man said nervously.

"Well, Jimmie. This is your lucky day. You just got yourself a job. How would you like to take us to this holy mountain?"

A screech interrupted Alex's thought process. Instead of the jeep pulling the truck out of the mud, the motor of the jeep sputtered wildly. Smoke began to waft from the hood of the jeep as the vehicle began to slip and slide backwards until its bumper contacted the truck and its rear wheels sunk deep into the mud.

They could see Phillip slam the ball of his hand upon the jeep's hood in frustration. Solomon looked on stoically as one of his men popped open the hood. The jeep belched out a long cloud of gray smoke that wafted into the cloudless sky. Alex could see the smoke clear the tops of the tree and wondered how far the smoke could be seen. *Will it bring help?* he wondered to himself.

"We could try to hitch the last jeep up, but it's risky," Solomon said to Phillip as he took a step back to avoid getting a face full of smoke. "If that vehicle goes down, then it's a long hike back to Möngönmorit. 'You can call me Jimmie' was right, we should have brought horses. This terrain is no good for vehicles. We could send someone back for help."

"And wait for him? We will camp here and set out on foot tomorrow. Nothing is going to stop us from reaching Burkham Khaldun."

This mission is cursed, Alex repeated in his head with a mix of foreboding and promise.

70

The damp wood hissed violently when it was dumped onto the fire pit. Steam escaped and floated into the night air. Ellie pulled the windbreaker tightly against her body and huddled closer to Alex. The temperature had dropped precipitously after the sun set, and the vivid purple of dusk was replaced by the blackness of night. If she was not so chilled to the bone, she might have thought of the massive night sky that loomed above as a thing of beauty. Far away from the lights of any city, the sky teemed with an infinite number of brilliant stars. It was overwhelming and humbling.

No wonder the Mongols worshipped the Eternal Sky as a god, Ellie thought as she hooked her arm around Alex's elbow, shivered, and drew him even closer.

Clay approached them with a can of beans, which he delicately cupped in his hands to keep warm. A single spoon awkwardly stuck out of the top of the can.

"It's lukewarm at best, I'm afraid," he announced and handed the can to Ellie who quickly spooned a portion of the brown beans into her mouth. They were strangely mushy and flavorless.

Jonas arrived with a second can of beans. He let himself flop down upon the ground and wrapped a blanket around his body. He blew on his hands several times and ran his palms back and forth against each other, hoping that the friction would warm his numbed fingertips.

"Are we close to Eden? It sure doesn't feel like paradise here." Jonas could see his breath before him as he spoke. "I thought we would be in a warmer place—somewhere like the Middle East."

"It's a reasonable point," Alex answered, took a bite of the beans, and passed the can back to Ellie. "Ellie, you know more about this subject than anyone."

Ellie raised another spoonful of beans to her mouth and plopped them on her tongue. She chewed the soft legumes for a moment, swallowed, and reached for her water. Ellie could not believe that here she was in the Mongolian wilderness, about to lecture on Eden. But somehow, the switch to her professor-mode was reassuring and familiar.

"It's complicated. The idea of 'Eden' is something that predated the Bible—the vision of a magical land free of death and disease. Almost every culture has some otherworld to aspire towards. We are biased of course by the hegemony of a Judeo-Christian faith. Whether you believe that Moses penned the Bible or not, there is little debate that it was written from the perspective of a middle-easterner. What would 'paradise' be to a person who lived in the desert anyway? It would be a land that was lush, green—a place where water was plentiful and food readily available. What emerges is an image of the prototypical garden.

"The word 'paradise' originally comes from the Persian word 'apiri-daeza' that roughly translates to an orchard bounded by a wall. Now the origin of the word 'Eden' is even more interesting. In Hebrew it translates to 'delight.' It probably comes from a Sumerian word 'E. din' that means an open expanse of nature—a great plains or, in other words, steppes.

"Imagine, however, you lived in the jungles of Brazil where you are surrounded by tropical vegetation and plentitude of rainfall. Your idea of paradise or Eden may be very different than someone living in the desert."

"The Bible, however, is fairly specific about Eden," Clay challenged. "It talks about certain rivers running through it."

Ellie paused before speaking, waiting for one of Solomon's men to return from the perimeter of their encampment. The man slung his rifle across his back and warmed his hands against the fire.

"What the Bible says was that God planted a garden in the eastern portion of Eden. It says that there was a river that flowed out of Eden—a single source—that divided into four separate rivers. These rivers were the Pishon, Gihon, Tigris, and Euphrates Rivers. Now a lot of scholarship has been devoted to these rivers through the centuries. In particular, there has been great debate over what rivers were called Pishon and Gihon. Titus Flavius Josephus, the first century Jewish historian, postulated that the Pishon corresponded to the Ganges River and the Gihon to the Nile. This was the dominant view for centuries amongst scholars and religious figures. As for the Tigris and Euphrates…they exist to this day, running through Iraq. Researchers who have been consumed with identifying possible locations for Eden have not surprisingly centered their attention on the Middle East. Utilizing satellite imagery to identify dried riverbeds, a recent view places Eden somewhere in current-day Iran. Others have argued that Eden is now underwater, somewhere off the coast of Saudi Arabia.

"Names can be a serious problem in the Bible. As a historical piece of work, the Bible doesn't pass much muster. It is full of inconsistencies. It is not surprising that certain names, locations, and times may be off. But mostly I, and others, have wondered whether cultures within the Middle East co-opted prior legends and dressed them up in their own familiar garb."

"What do you mean?" Clay asked.

"Let's take the myth of paradise with four rivers flowing from it. Now think how limited travel must have been in Biblical times. If you went a couple of miles, this probably seemed like a universe away. What they knew about the world was local. There was no 'world history' in those days. All 'world history' was inevitably 'local history.' If there was a tale of four rivers, then it seems reasonable that people may assign these rivers familiar names. Thus, there is no reason to think that the Euphrates River in the Bible is the same Euphrates River we know today. Which came first? It's a chicken-versus-egg game. Maybe people settled near a river whose cycles of flooding created a rich environment for planting. It was paradise to those who lived near it and consequently this extraordinary river must be the Euphrates River of the Bible. The name sticks and the rest is history. And then there's the whole Flood thing."

Clay put down his can and leaned in with interest. "What Flood thing?"

"Well if you want to believe in the Bible—I mean truly *believe* in the truthfulness of the Bible and accept that there was indeed an Eden with a magical garden within it then you would be obligated to accept the historical reality of a Great Flood. In the Bible, Adam and Eve are expelled from Eden and humanity continues to putt-putt along in sin and decadence until God one day has had enough of his vile creation and decides it is time to wipe the slate clean and start over. He commands Noah to build an ark and proceeds to essentially kill off his creation with a massive Flood. It's kind of ironic when you think that paradise was centered around a land with abundant water and now humanity is being drowned in this life-giving liquid. The Great Flood changes everything. Every river, mountain, plain, valley, anthill that existed before it was altered forever. After the Flood, Eden could be anywhere or nowhere." Ellie glanced around at the dark camp and hugged her body tightly. "This place is as good as any, I suppose."

"I still think it's awfully cold for Eden," Jonas complained and drew the blanket taut against his body.

The fire crackled and popped. Ellie could see Phillip emerge from a tent erected near the back of his jeep. He looked their way as he engaged in a seemingly intense conversation with Solomon. He held in his left hand a satellite phone that glowed neon blue.

"What's this Darkhad thing all about?" Ellie asked to no particular person. The question seemed to float in the air. Ellie shivered at the image of the old Mongolian shaman lying lifeless upon the steppes, his blood slowly seeping into the soil.

"It's a thing of legend," Alex responded quietly. "It goes back to the death of Genghis Khan. As Marco Polo mentioned in the fourth book, when Genghis Khan died, he was buried in secret. Great lengths were taken to hide the location of his burial site. After he passed on, a devoted tribe of Mongols dedicated themselves and their progeny to protecting Genghis' final resting place. These people were known as the Darkhad. It seems that it was precisely these people who Marco Polo feared so much and who contributed to his early departure from his service to Kublai Khan. They may also explain why he never chose to return to the East. Whether such a group still exists is a question we may see answered."

"Well it sure seemed to spook dear Phillip," Jonas said, and motioned to the man trying to speak into the phone. Phillip scowled with displeasure.

Ellie brought her knees to her chest. She thought back to their near imprisonment in the crypt beneath San Proculo and the menacing Asian man's final words before he sent the slab of stone tumbling down... *This will be your tomb*. She entertained bringing up the episode, looked at her weary colleagues, and thought better of it. Ellie caught a glimpse into Alex's eyes and immediately felt ice cold. For the first time she saw true fear in his eyes.

71

Alex stirred to the sound of the front of the tent unzipping. He could hear Ellie moan beside him as he strained to lift his head off the frozen ground. He struggled to wiggle his body out of the sleeping bag enough to prop himself up on his elbows. Alex could see one of Solomon's men in a wool hat duck his head into the tent and scowl.

"We're moving out in five. Pack up your gear."

Before Alex could look at his watch the man was gone. The front of the tent was left undone. A biting, frigid wind began to blow into the tent, making it that much harder for Alex and Ellie to extricate themselves from the relative warmth of their sleeping bags. Ellie's neck was stiff and she swallowed several times in an attempt to rid her mouth of a metallic taste. She winced in response to a pounding from her temples and prayed that someone had brewed a pot of coffee.

"What's this all about?" Ellie sighed as she made her way on her knees towards the opening in the tent.

They crawled out of the tent to find the camp alive with activity. Solomon's men were busy removing crates and boxes from the backs of the vehicles and taking inventory of the contents. Alex could see one of the mercenaries, a hulk named Ox, remove sophisticated weaponry one by one from a crate. He examined each gun like a lost love, cradling the weapon delicately, initiating its laser sighting, and eventually slapping in an ammunition cartridge after he was satisfied that it was in prime condition. The man proceeded to hand out the weapons to the rest of the men in his team. Each member grabbed a weapon and slung it over his shoulder. They collected extra ammunition and slid the cartridges into weapon belts strapped across their bodies.

"Looks like we're going to war," Clay said nonchalantly as he sidled up beside Alex and Ellie. He awkwardly balanced three cups of black coffee in tin mugs. Alex and Ellie thanked him and accepted the mugs. They looked at the heavily armed men with curiosity.

"What's going on?" Alex asked.

"It appears that our dear commander, Phillip, has decided that we will proceed on foot to Burkhan Kaldun. He's even more impatient than me."

Alex took a sip of the coffee and found it unbearably bitter. He wiped his lips with his sleeve.

"We don't even know what we are looking for. If we believe Polo's account that Genghis Khan was buried in the Garden of Eden, all we know is that it is at Burkhan Kaldun. There have been several expeditions in this area looking for Genghis Khan's burial site that have been unsuccessful. I'm not sure how we are going to be any more successful," Alex complained.

"Well, it appears that Phillip has considerable faith in your talents, as do I. He truly expects you to sort this all out."

"It's expecting a bit too much," Alex bemoaned. He could see Solomon begin to fill a backpack full of blocks of clay-colored explosives. Solomon began to zip up the bag and glanced back, catching Alex's eye. He smiled.

"What's that for?" Alex asked.

"Insurance," he muttered and stood up.

Solomon climbed onto the hood of one of the jeeps and waved for everyone to gather around. In a booming voice he explained that they were going to leave the camp and travel by foot towards this 'Holy Hill.'

"Our computer genius, Martin, has drawn the short straw and

is going to be staying at the campsite. He is going to guard the vehicles, monitor the progress of our expedition, and organize help if it is needed…which it won't be."

Martin leaned against the vehicle and gave a faint-hearted salute with just his index finger. He lit a cigarette and took a long puff. "I'll be thinking of you guys while I'm sitting on my ass and you're humping up a freakin' mountain."

72

Incessant chirping permeated the forest as the light of the late afternoon struggled to penetrate through the canopy of trees. They had been trudging through the overgrown wilderness for several hours since leaving the campsite behind. Jimmie, the Mongolian guide, took the lead scanning the scenery ahead and occasionally stopping to squat beside an animal footprint. Solomon's mercenaries fanned out, forming a loose perimeter around the party, carefully monitoring the woodlands surrounding them for the slightest sound. The forest seemed menacing and strangely 'alive'. The passage of wind through the trees gave the appearance that the forest was inhaling and exhaling. The soldiers remained disciplined and focused on their task, training their guns periodically into the woods in response to the rustle of Tibetan snowcocks frolicking through the thicket.

Static suddenly cut through the tranquility, prompting a hidden falcon to alight off a branch and flap across the sky. Solomon held up the two-way radio to his mouth and toggled the dial to select channel seven.

"Howzit, Martin?" Solomon asked and watched as Phillip fiddled with the satellite phone beside him. There was silence for several seconds and then static crackled out of the radio receiver.

"Perfect, Sir. It's like a freakin' safari out here. I've seen elk and even a nasty old boar…but not much else. How's things out in the shit?"

"Fairly similar. We'll keep you updated…and Martin, try not to treat this like a vacation. Keep sharp. The sat phone is on the fritz—we can't get a signal out here. I hate to say it but you're our lifeline to the outside world."

"Affirmative. Let me know how I can help…and Sir? Watch out for the bears."

"You too, Martin." Solomon clicked off the radio and handed it to one of his soldiers who slipped it into his backpack. "Hey, Jimmie! How much farther?" he barked.

The guide ignored Solomon and continued to walk in silence. He carried himself with an almost mournful carriage, his hands buried deep in the pockets of his jacket and his shoulders hunched forward. He looked miserable.

Alex quickened his pace and maneuvered beside Jimmie. He matched the man's walking cadence and continued trotting beside him in silence for several minutes. The guide appeared to barely take notice of Alex and remained focused on the forest ahead. When Jimmie finally spoke he did so softly, almost inaudibly, without glancing at Alex.

"You're not with them are you? …You, the girl, that old man, and the man that always seemed pissed off at something."

"You must mean Jonas. Yes. How should I put it? We are here against our will."

"Like me. But you are eager to see what secret Burkhan Khaldun holds?"

"Yes."

The guide nodded and grew silent once again.

Alex picked up a stick and swatted at the ground. "What is so special about this place?"

"Burkhan Khaldun?"

"Yes."

"It is the heart of the Mongol people. It is blessed. It has been and always will be. When Genghis Khan went to pray, it was there he preferred to go where he was closest to the spirits of the world—the gazriin ezen…the nature spirits. There is a life force that pulsates from the Khentii mountains. When you climb it, you look down upon the vast lands of the Mongols and feel centered and fixed to the earth. You understand that life flows down these peaks like the three rivers — the Onon to the east, the Tula to the west, and the Kherlen to the south. People have come from far away in search of the tomb of Genghis Khan — the Japanese, the Russians, the Americans. They have all failed. It does not want to be found. They are grave robbers. They would like to do to us what was done to the pyramids of Egypt"

"But it isn't gold or treasures that we are seeking."

"Then what is it?"

Alex thought for a moment and realized how ridiculous it sounded in his head. "Life. Everlasting life." He nearly winced from embarrassment.

The guide turned and looked at him for the first time. "If the great Khan couldn't achieve this, what makes you think this blessing is for you? Everlasting life?" The man emitted a short chuckle. "You Westerners have your heads in the clouds. You always want to take the short cut." Alex's face became flush with embarrassment.

"These are sacred sites and must not be trespassed. This is madness." The guide leaned in slightly and whispered. "I tell you this because I believe that in the end man has free will. We are being followed. We have been from the beginning. The Darkhad will not allow this sacrilege to occur. In the end the life that you seek will only beget death. Hear me out, this will all end badly."

Alex did not know how to respond to this warning and slowed the pace of his walking. The guide pulled away, leaving Alex behind. Ellie approached Alex and hesitated at the sight of horror on his face.

"What is it, Alex? What did he say?"

"We need to get out of here...and soon." Alex could see that Jimmie had stopped at the edge of a bank of trees. The group began to collect around the guide. Beyond the tree line was a valley and beyond that several large hills.

The guide pointed across the valley at the hills looming in the distance. "That is the Khan Khenti and the bald ridge is the Burkhan Khaldun—the Sacred Hill."

"That's my boy, Jimmie!" Solomon congratulated the guide with a powerful slap on the back.

"How much farther to it?" asked Phillip as he looked at his watch and at the darkening sky. Already the temperature had dropped considerably from the hot afternoon.

"Less than a day hike."

"Then we'll set up camp here and leave early tomorrow for it."

73

Martin propped his feet upon the dashboard of the jeep and rolled up the window slightly. It was beginning to get cold again. He zipped his jacket until it was snug. *This place sucks,* he complained to himself and took a long puff from his cigarette before flicking it out of the window. He reached across the passenger seat, retrieved his battered laptop computer, and slid it onto the dashboard. He clicked the release and bent the screen back until it stood upright. The battery light blinked incessantly. He searched for any satellite signal but was disappointed to find that he was in a dead-zone.

Why am I not surprised? he asked himself with dismay.

As he went to fold the screen down he caught a faint reflection of a shadowy figure scamper behind him.

What the...

He sunk down into his seat. His fingers first sought out the two-way radio. He gripped it for a moment, before pushing it aside to find the grip of his gun. Martin clutched it tightly to his chest. He peered into the rearview mirror and could see only the forest behind him. The door squeaked as he slowly opened it. He waited and listened. The woods around him were still.

Too still.

74

"What did he say?" Ellie whispered to Alex as Clay and Jonas squeezed in beside them. She could see the Mongolian guide sitting sadly beside the blazing fire.

"He gave me a warning. He said the Darkhad were coming and when they find us it will be best not to be counted among Phillip's crew. They will do everything possible to prevent the tomb of Genghis Khan from being disturbed. They'll kill us all."

An ominous howl echoed through the forest, sending a chill up Ellie's spine.

"What should we do? We can't just leave. Solomon's men are ready to shoot us if we try to escape and even if we were lucky enough to evade them, we're in the middle of nowhere."

"If we could just get some distance between us and Solomon's men, then maybe we could find some help. Maybe we'll find a group of hikers who could aid us. Who knows? Solomon's men guard the campsite in shifts. There's usually a short period of time when the two shifts are making small talk. I say we wait for the right opportunity and slip away into the forest."

"When?" Ellie asked.

"As soon as possible…tonight."

"Do you know what would happen if they caught us?" Jonas asked.

"I'm afraid it would be the same outcome if we stay."

"What about the Garden, Alex? We are so close." Clay's eyes appeared wet in the moonlight. "Could you turn your back on it? We're walking in the final footsteps of Marco Polo."

"Redmund, is it worth our lives?"

"Let me answer that question with another question. Would you be willing to risk your life for the opportunity to save millions of others? If this tree has one-tenth the powers it could have, it could be the greatest medicinal discovery this world has ever seen. If it could be analyzed and its properties distilled into base components it could revolutionize the treatment of the greatest scourges of the earth. Think of it Alex... AIDS, cancer, malaria: cured. I must ask you to reconsider your plan to leave." Clay leaned over and squeezed Alex's shoulder a bit too hard. He looked him in the eye. "We need your help, Alex, to take us over the threshold."

"*We...us...*what are you talking about?" Ellie protested. She watched as Jonas swept aside part of the blanket that was wrapped around him. She could see that he was holding a pistol in his lap.

"How did you? What is going on here?" Alex tried to stand but was restrained by Clay's hand. Alex could see Solomon and Phillip watching them from across the camp.

"Listen to me, Alex. Don't do anything stupid. You are a smart boy but you lack a perspective you gain from age and experience. This is too important to turn our backs on. I *cannot* let you. We..." Alex again tried to stand and was forced back down again by Clay's grip on his shoulder. "...*we* have made a deal. At the end of this you two will go free."

"In exchange for what?" Alex pulled his shoulder away from Clay with a twist. His face was flush with anger from the betrayal.

"In exchange for you taking us the final step."

"And if I don't."

"Don't talk like that, Alex. You've seen what these men are capable of. They'll kill you. They'll probably threaten to kill Ellie first as leverage. They'll kill Jonas and me, too. We're not exactly in a position of bargaining. Jonas and I have been given the job of seeing that you succeed."

"You said that we must prevent the Order from finding the secret of Polo at all costs," Alex protested despondently.

"Let's be a little realistic now. Look around you. Whether you like it or not, they will get the information from you. I'm trying to do what's best for everyone in the end. I'm sorry that you feel betrayed, but the equation changed at the library."

Ellie glared at Clay, her fist clenched tightly until her knuckles shined white in the moonlight.

The howls of a pack of wolves erupted from somewhere deep in the forest.

Alex could only think of what the guide had said.

This will all end badly.

75

"*Martin, are you there?*" *Solomon spoke into the radio and released the but-*
ton. Only static returned. *Something's wrong,* he thought. An
uneasy sensation gnawed within him as he turned to Ox and
slapped the radio into his beefy chest. "Keep trying to reach him."
Solomon instinctively patted the grip of his gun within its holster.
He surveyed the area.

They had emerged from the forest into a relatively flat and open
area. Up ahead he could see the Khentii mountain range tower
over the pine trees. It felt good to finally emerge from the dark
forest, but as he twirled around he suddenly felt exposed. Gone
was the cover of the forest canopy, the deep green of the leaves, the
long trunks of the trees. To make matters worse, the brutal sun beat
down on them, sapping their energy. He could see members of the
party appear wilted as their pace slowed through the high grass.

Ellie's legs felt heavy as she pushed through the grass. Her
toes were blistered and bleeding from the hike. She gave Alex
a sideways glance. He was looking at a copy of the Fra Mauro
map that Maryanne Hunter had given them before they departed from London. He had turned to a page showing a magnified
view of the bottom left corner of the map—the depiction of the
Garden of Eden. She could see the circle surrounded by a ring
of fire with a cherub guarding the entrance. In the center was
the figure of God addressing Adam and Eve as they stood by a
tree and a body of water. From this single source of water flowed
the four rivers that spilled out towards a mountainous landscape.
Alex looked up above the tree line and back at the paper.

"What do you see?" Ellie asked. In the distance she could hear the faint sound of branches snapping. She twirled around and could see Solomon's men scatter. Several of the men crouched with their guns trained at the forest behind them. Others dropped into a prone position, disappearing beneath the tall grass with their rifles drawn. Solomon dropped to one knee, pulled out his pistol, and waited. The rest of the party instinctively crouched down with tensed anticipation of the unknown. Ellie could feel her heart race as the sound emanating from the forest continued to grow louder and louder. She tried to place it. What was at first the sound of breaking branches was beginning to sound like a rumbling thunder.

"What is that?" Alex whispered. He could see Jonas slip out his pistol.

Suddenly a darkened form burst from the edge of the forest and madly galloped into the open area. Ox's finger curled around the trigger as the barrel of his gun followed the unexpected form of a horse darting across the grassland.

Solomon rose to his feet. He looked at the racing form incredulously and then turned pale as a ghost. "Hold your fire!" he screamed and began to approach the crazed beast. He looked back at his men. "Watch the forest in case it's a diversion." The horse had stopped and began to pace nervously back and forth, snorting and raising its legs. As Solomon approached, he could feel his throat tighten. Slung over the horse's back was Martin's lifeless body. Blood dripped from Martin's neck, staining the side of the horse. Martin's hands and legs were tied.

Solomon found himself walking towards the horse as if in a trance, his gun trained on the creature. With a screech, the horse reared up on its hind legs and kicked out its front legs in the air. Martin's body slid off the horse's back and tumbled onto the ground. The horse snorted once more and began to gallop away.

Solomon followed the course of the horse with his gun until it disappeared into the forest. The field was quiet once again.

Phillip stood up and approached Solomon, who stared down at the lifeless corpse. Martin's eyes were opened and appeared focused on the sky above.

"My God, it's one of your men," Phillip said.

Solomon dropped to his knees, bent over, and ran his hand over Martin's eyes, closing the lids forever. He could feel rage surge through his body as he clutched his pistol even tighter.

"It's a warning."

Solomon looked around him to see who said it. He could see Alex, Ellie, Clay, and Jonas slowly rising out of the high grass. He scanned the grassland further. His eyes settled on the Mongolian guide who sat cross-legged on the ground, staring at the forest behind them.

"It's a warning," the guide repeated ominously.

Solomon sprung to his feet and slipped his pistol back in his holster. He approached the guide whose back remained facing him. "Is this the work of the Darkhad? Well, they'll have to bring more than this. I've seen a lot worse...I've done a lot worse myself...so...get your ass up and guide us up that hill."

The guide was unfazed. He continued to sit cross-legged, gazing at the woods. "I'm not going any further. You're on your own."

Solomon made a fist as he stood over the guide. "Jimmie, I'm not asking you. I'm telling you that you are going to get off your ass and take us up that hill or I'm going to put a bullet in..."

The guide's movement was as unexpected as it was quick. Alex watched as the man twirled around and reached up, grabbing Solomon's gun from his holster. Momentarily stunned by the guide's quickness, Solomon pulled out a second pistol from his waistband and pointed it at the guide. Solomon's men instantly responded by leveling their weapons in the air and surrounding Jimmie.

The guide stood up and began to back away from Solomon.

"Jimmie, don't do anything stupid," Solomon commanded as he directed his gun at the man's chest.

The guide shook his head sadly. "You just don't understand… do you? You don't understand a single thing." In a completely fluid motion, the man lifted the gun, pressed it against the side of his head, and pulled the trigger.

Alex jumped at the deafening sound of the gunshot. He could see the man's body drop to the ground like it was made of lead. Solomon looked down at the body with a look of confusion, nudging the man's torso with the tip of his boot.

Ox lowered his rifle and stood over the dead man's body. All he could say was, "Did that just happen?"

Solomon glared at Phillip. "Well, I hope your golden boy can lead us the rest of the way…and quickly."

Alex could feel his heart race.

76

"Where do we go from here?" asked Phillip as he paced behind Alex.

Alex stared up at the bald ridge of Burkhan Khaldun. It seemed strangely unimpressive, a mere rolling heap of earth composing only a portion of the Khentii mountain range. A small amount of snow covered the ridge, even in the Mongolian spring. It was not to say it lacked beauty—the green and beige was lost partially in the mist, seamlessly blending with the expansive blue sky above it. It was, however, somehow anticlimactic, an anti-Everest. He found it hard to believe they were in the antechamber of Eden.

He looked down again at the copy of the Fra Mauro's map. It did not make sense. Marco Polo went through all this trouble hiding the location of the Garden and all they were left with was Mongolia…and Burkhan Khaldun. Could not he have been more specific? After all, he said in the secret Fourth Book that he 'approached the gates of the garden and saw the flaming sword of the cherubs.'

Where was this? There has to be a final clue, Alex thought. He ran his fingers through his hair with frustration. *I can't do this*, he thought, feeling the stress diffuse through his body. He peered at Ellie beside him and tried to muster a reassuring smile. *It's too much responsibility.*

Ellie pointed at the blown-up image of the Garden of Eden from the Fra Mauro. "You seem to be focused on this picture. What is it?"

"I don't know. I really don't."

"You feel it in your gut that it's important, don't you?"

Alex nodded.

"Well, then it probably is," she said and looked over his shoulder again at the image. "What does the writing say above the image?"

Alex looked at small writing meticulously written in several lines over the image of the Garden of Eden. "It's a short discourse on the existence of the Garden of Eden. It discusses different views that were commonly cited during the medieval period such as from the works of St. Augustine and Albertus Magnus. I've read through it a million times and it doesn't seem too informative."

"Let's start from the beginning. What does it say?" Ellie asked.

Alex placed his finger beneath the top line of Italian text. "It says…first there's the title of the discourse… 'The Location of the Earthly Paradise.' It goes on to say… 'The Paradise of Delights does not only have a spiritual meaning; it is also a real…'" Alex paused.

"What is it?" Ellie asked, wide-eyed.

"…it is also a real place on the earth…" Alex finished and brought his hands together as if in prayer. "It can't be." He smiled broadly.

"What can't be?" Ellie sprung to her feet.

"I can't believe I didn't think of it earlier. You're amazing."

Alex waited as the rest of the group began to gather around him. Both Phillip and Clay looked at him with excited anticipation.

"Where is it?" asked Phillip.

Alex grabbed Ellie's hand and directed it at the bald ridge of Burkhan Khaldun. He held up the image of the Garden of Eden from the Fra Mauro map in his other hand. "Bianco painted Burkhan Khaldun onto the map. The location was never hidden. It was always in front of our eyes." He released Ellie's hand and pointed up at the ridge. "Burkhan Khaldun is relatively free of significant vegetation, especially trees. But look at the western edge of it."

Clay looked intensely at the ridge ahead and squinted.

"Now look at the picture from the map." Alex ran his finger across the mountainous area outside of Eden. He counted four trees that were placed on the barren mountain depicted on the map. "I need a knife."

Alex looked at Phillip with impatience. The man slid his hand into his pocket and handed over his blade. He watched as Alex folded it open and placed the tip of the blade against each tree. He poked holes through the paper at the location of each of the four trees and held the paper up once again.

"My God," Phillip gasped as the four trees in the distance filled the holes perfectly.

Alex pulled his body back from the paper while holding it up and found the location of the entrance to the Garden of Eden where a cherub stood holding aloft a burning sword. "That would make the entrance to the Garden right about…" He brought the tip against the paper once again and pushed it through with a pop. The hole revealed a relatively prosaic outcropping of stone in the distance. "…here."

The group stood dumbfounded as they stared up at Burkhan Khaldun.

"And another thing…based on this picture from the map, I think the tomb of Genghis Khan and the Garden of Eden for that matter are underground. I guess the world did change quite a bit since creation."

The group looked up at the edge of Burkhan Khaldun in awe as Alex folded the paper, flipped the knife shut, and slid both into the pocket of his pants.

77

Clay paused for a moment to catch his breath. He could see that the outcrop- ping was not much further. Jonas slung his arm around his shoulder and assisted him up the increasingly steep slope. Clay tried to pick up the pace as the rest of the group neared the outcropping ahead. When he finally arrived on the barren area, he slumped down and looked upon the vast green of the Mongolian heartland below them. His jacket flapped loudly in the cold breeze, which vigorously blew across the Khenti mountain range. His face felt numb, his lips frozen.

Solomon surveyed the area. They were standing on a flat area approximately halfway up Burkhan Khaldun, along the western slope. The ground was covered with yellowed grass and prickly weeds.

"I'm not sure what I was expecting, but this isn't it," Solomon announced and took a long drink of water.

Ellie paced around the outcropping as she channeled her knowledge of numerous previous archeological digs. She had worked with the philosophy that *if it was easy to see, then it would have been discovered long ago.* Ellie squatted onto the heels of her boots and attempted to shield her face from the biting wind. The tip of her nose was red and wet and she wiped at it with her windbreaker. She reached down and dug her fingernails into the soil, coming away with a handful of light brown dirt. She shuffled the soil in her hand like a pair of dice before tossing it away. As the wind caught the grains of dirt, out of the corner of her eye, she detected a gray structure slightly protruding out of the ground. She rose to her feet and looked around her to see if anybody else had seen it. She found the rest of the crew content to take a breather. Ellie approached the gray structure and kneeled in front of it.

The stone was light gray and triangular in configuration, like the top of an obelisk. There were no markings on it, just the pits and crevices wrought by the harsh weather. She ran her hand across the rough surface and drove her fingers into the soil beside it. Ellie began to pull away chunks of hard soil, revealing more and more of the stone structure. Blood began to drip from around her cuticles and she hesitated a moment, afraid of damaging the edges of where her skin graft was sewn into her native skin.

"What is it?" asked Alex as he bent down beside her.

"Help me expose the base of this stone," she requested.

Alex began to dig along the edges of the stone until it was freed up. He stopped upon discovering that the pyramidal stone rested upon another layer of gray stones.

"Hey, I think we found something here!" Ellie announced.

Within seconds, the group rushed behind them

"There are stones beneath the ground. From the pattern, I would bet that this is not a natural phenomenon." Ellie looked up at Phillip, then Clay. "Someone or some people placed these stones here…and buried them."

Solomon looked at Phillip, who eagerly nodded. Solomon swung around and addressed his men. "O.K., don't just stand there gawking. Grab your shovels and start digging!" he barked.

The men removed foldable shovels from their backpacks, that were typically used to dig foxholes or fill sandbags, and drove the tips of the shovels deep into the firm soil. They feverishly tore away at the earth, revealing more and more stones placed in ever increasing square-shaped layers. Not before long they had found the furthest edges of the stones. The stones were stacked upon each other, forming a pyramidal shaped pile.

"It looks like an ovoo," Ellie said. "It's a cairn—a stack of rocks that were placed to denote an important location, sometimes a burial site or a place of religious significance. It has different meaning for different cultures. I believe the Mongolians used them in shamanistic services to worship the sky, the mountains, or the forests. Some New-Age people place them in areas that possess special metaphysical properties, like a vortex. But ovoos are supposed to be above the surface to be seen. I've never heard of an ovoo that is buried. It's weird."

The bigger question is what does it mark?" Phillip asked.

"Or what's beneath it," Alex added.

"Yes…beneath it," Clay echoed.

"We need to move these stones," Phillip commanded. Solomon motioned to his men who began to remove stones from the pile and toss them aside. As stone after stone was pulled from the cairn, the men found themselves in an ever-expanding pit surrounded by earthen walls. They continued to lift up the stones, passing them to the surface like a water brigade at a fire. Finally, the men arrived at a single large slab of stone in the shape of a square. Several of the men hopped down into the pit and gripped the edges of the stone. With loud grunts they were able to lift it, revealing a final dirt layer beneath it. In the center was a hole, and blackness beyond it.

Phillip peered over the edge into the pit and could see the men standing curiously beside the hole.

One of the men wiped sweat from his brow, looked up, and said, "We found something at the bottom."

"I'll say," Phillip replied with a smile. *That's an understatement.* "Let's see what's in this rabbit hole." He glanced at Solomon. "Grab some lights—I think we found the entrance."

78

*Solomon squatted by the edge of the hole and directed the beam of the flash-*light into it. The light penetrated a short distance and then was swallowed by the darkness.

"What do you see?" asked Phillip as he leaned over Solomon's shoulder in an attempt to get a better vantage point.

"Not too much," Solomon mumbled under his breath. He mustered up some saliva, spat into the hole, and listened. After several seconds, he could hear a muffled splat return. Solomon reached into his jacket pocket, withdrew a clear plastic stick, and bent it until it made a snapping noise. After shaking it vigorously, the stick glowed neon green. Solomon tossed it into the hole and watched as it dropped into the blackness and rattled to a stop. Below him, he could see the stick resting on the ground of a passageway, surrounded by a small green halo.

He looked back up at the figures gathered around him and tapped the end of the flashlight against the palm of his hand.

"There's a bit of a drop…not too far." He glanced up at Pieter. "Grab some rope and secure your end. We're going to have to climb down."

Solomon stood up and brushed the dirt from his pants. "Here's the plan. We are going down into this pit. But first things first…I'm leading this operation." He turned and looked Phillip in the eye. "No disrespect, Sir…you've been very generous…but as long as those savages are running around carving up my men, I'm calling the shots. Understood?"

Phillip gave a wry smile. "We are all in your capable hands, Commander."

Solomon flicked on the flashlight and shined it at Jonas, Alex, Ellie, and Clay. "You're coming with us, and don't get any creative ideas. Our dear patron may want to keep you around a little bit longer, but I'm not so convinced that you are of any further use to us."

He took inventory of his squad. The loss of Martin was devastating. He was the computer genius, but what Solomon most needed now were men with good intuition and muscle. He had it in the remaining four members of his team. He looked at the heavily armed men and weighed his options.

"I'm leaving you two here to watch the entrance." He nodded to two of the youngest members of his outfit, Bryce and Fredrick. "Watch each other's back. Remember what those animals did to Martin. The Darkhad have played their hands too early. They've lost the element of surprise. Stay sharp and if you see anybody coming this way, take them down. I don't care if it's a park ranger or a little green alien. Just shoot."

The men nodded silently and tried to hide their apprehension about being left on the desolate perch to face an unseen enemy. Solomon watched as they climbed up onto the outcropping and disappeared from view. He patted Ox on the back and winked at Pieter. "You two are coming with me." Solomon bent down and unzipped the side of his backpack enough to reveal the Sentex explosives and a number of intricate timer mechanisms within it before zipping the bag up and slinging it over his shoulder.

"Ox, you lead the way," Solomon ordered and watched as the bear-like man gripped the rope suspended into the hole. With a grunt, Ox began to climb down into the darkness. Within several seconds the rope relaxed and Solomon peered into the hole. He could see the bald man holding up the green stick.

"Ready when you are," Ox bellowed with a smile.

Alex felt unsettled as Solomon motioned with his flashlight for the rest to queue up by the rope.

Solomon bit his fingernail as Alex dangled his feet into the hole and seized the rope. He reached down and tightly gripped Alex's wrist for a moment.

"Professor, this better be worth all the trouble," Solomon muttered.

Alex caught a glimpse of Clay as he began to wiggle awkwardly down the rope. He could see a twinkle in Clay's eye and could almost read his mind — *we are walking in the footsteps of Polo...all the way to the gates of Paradise.*

Ellie looked up at the sky above her as her boots swung free of the rope. A thick fog was settling over the mountainside and she struggled to see the blue sky through the gray mist. She dug her fingernails into the rope and steadied herself. She could hear the wind howl a final time — an eerie wail of deep foreboding, a banshee's scream. She tried to shake off a growing sense of uneasiness the further she descended along the rope. She had never felt out of place on an archeological dig, but as her feet made contact with the hard ground below she realized what bothered her most. *Here they were...trespassers...interlopers.*

She blindly reached in front of her and walked forward like a lumbering zombie. She bumped up against Clay's back. She could see up ahead in the darkness the bouncing beam of a flashlight. As her eyes adjusted to the darkness, she realized that they had entered a long dank tunnel that was carved deep into the side of Burkhan Khaldun. Despite the light provided by the two flashlights, the tunnel remained disquietingly dark and still. She took a deep breath and found the air stale and cold — tomblike. Ellie drew her jacket tightly against her body in a fruitless attempt to ward off the cold. She could see her breath float in front of her face and drift away.

Phillip shined the flashlight along the ceiling and walls of the tunnel and paused upon spotting an unlit torch resting in an iron holder fastened to the wall. He pulled the torch free with a vigorous tug and withdrew a small metallic lighter from the pocket of his pants. With the snap of the lighter, a blue flame danced in front of him as he struggled to light the torch. With a whoosh, the torch ignited, filling the tunnel with a flickering orange and red light.

"Nice torch. Now I feel like a real explorer, china—a real Alan Quartermain," Solomon said as he released his hold of the rope and stepped into the tunnel.

Ellie examined her surroundings more closely. They were in a stone-walled tunnel that was at least ten meters across. The ceiling loomed high above, nearly twenty meters. The walls were gray and monotonous in the dark but gave off an incandescent sparkle when the light hit them.

Phillip held aloft the torch and advanced further into the tunnel while Ox cautiously trained his gun ahead. Alex ran his finger across the surface of the wall and pulled away. The stone was cold and damp.

"Look at this!" Phillip urged.

The group gathered around him as he waved the torch in front of a portion of the wall.

"It's some kind of writing."

Ellie pushed forward until she was next to Phillip. Etched into the stone surface was an assortment of symbols. Lines, arrows, circles, and pictograms filled the wall from floor to ceiling.

"I don't recognize the language," Ellie announced. She pointed at the symbols. "It has elements of cuneiform, but it's a totally different language. This is amazing. Cuneiform is one of the oldest known forms of written human expression in the world. The Sumerians were writing cuneiform back in 3000 B.C." She turned to Alex, her eyes filled with excitement. "What if this predates cuneiform? This could be from a culture that preceded the Sumerians. This could be the greatest linguistic finding since… since…the Rosetta Stone? We need to study this."

"There'll be time enough for that. This is not why we are here," Phillip impatiently answered, and waved the torch in the air.

Alex walked along the wall and knelt down. "This is interesting." He focused on a series of images painted across the bottom of the wall. It seemed to tell the story of a man wounded in battle who is found by his comrades. Two men appeared to lift the injured man into the air, carry him to the base of a giant tree, and prop him up against the tree. They retrieve a white leaf, which is ground up in a bowl and feed it to the wounded man. The final image showed the man hunting, apparently healed and whole once again.

"I get the story, but it's no apple," Jonas said.

"That's what Adam and Eve ate from the *Tree of Knowledge*. You're getting your trees of the Bible mixed up," Clay scolded. "This is the healing tree…the Tree of Life." He turned to Alex, glowing. "Alex, we are so close. I can feel it in my bones." Clay patted Alex on the back and left him kneeling by the wall. Alex glanced back at Clay and wondered if the man was not crazy after all.

"We need to keep moving," Phillip urged and advanced further down the tunnel, leaving Ellie, exasperated, behind. As the light gradually faded from the walls, the carvings were swallowed piecemeal by the darkness.

"Just a little bit longer," Ellie protested.

Alex rose and followed Phillip down into the shadowy tunnel. With each step forward, Phillip's torch illuminated farther and farther into the passage ahead. He could see the man pause and lift the torch high in the air.

"Uh…Ellie…you may just want to pace yourself," Alex nearly whispered.

"What's that?" Ellie replied. She shook her head back and forth, displeased with the group's willingness to simply pass by the intricate carvings in the wall. Ellie pushed past Alex and stopped.

"Take a look for yourself," Alex muttered behind her as if in a trance.

"Wow," was all Ellie could muster.

The walls and ceilings of the tunnel were completely covered with writing. Though at first overwhelming, it soon became clear as they neared the wall that the writing etched into the stone surface consisted of four repeating pictograms.

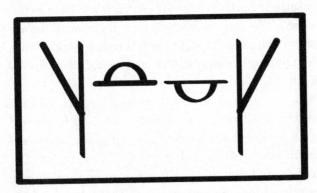

"What does it mean?" asked Phillip. He looked at Ellie. She frowned.

"I'm sorry. I just don't know. It's obviously a word of some importance. Maybe it's a meditative word or a blessing."

"Or a curse," Jonas snickered.

Phillip slowly advanced down the tunnel, peering up at the ceiling and down along the walls. The writing was so intricate and uniform it reminded him of an Arabesque mosaic. As the flame of the torch flickered back and forth, the dark edges of the etching appeared fluid, as if ripples in water drifting to and fro. He felt giddy at the sight, turned back to the rest of the group, and walked backwards for several steps.

"It makes you feel like you are in the presence of God himself," Phillip said with a queasy-looking smile.

"If these etchings are as old as they appear, you might want to say gods," Ellie responded. "Monotheism is a relatively new phenomenon. Much of human history was polytheistic and much more was simply animistic. Everyday objects of nature had souls and spirits—rocks, rivers, mountains… trees. Worship was not necessarily directed at a single being but at life-forces that occupied all parts of this earth."

Alex thought of what the Mongolian guide had said about the significance of Burkhan Khaldun—that it was close to the *spirit of the world*. As Alex walked through the tunnel, the writings seemed to swirl. He felt that he was traveling back in time, back to the beginning of things as they once were. *Is this what Polo felt?* he wondered.

"Well, I for one am not ready to worship a rock," Phillip responded with a chuckle and turned around. As he pivoted, two twisted faces stared back at him from out of the blackness.

Phillip jumped back with a startle, knocking into Ox who sent off a round from his gun into the ground with a ping. The sound echoed throughout the tunnel. Phillip regained his composure as the light from the torch flickered back and forth in his shaking hand.

"Oh for Christ-sakes," Solomon wailed. He walked by Phillip and snatched the torch from his trembling hands. "They're a bunch of statues, you baby. They're not going to bite you."

He held up the torch to reveal two stone statues at the end of the tunnel. The two statues were nearly seven feet tall and framed each side of a door-like rectangular slab of stone like mirror images. The statues were of bull-like creatures reared up on their hind legs as if in anger. Stone wings sprouted from each side of the torso of the beasts and shot up towards the ceiling of the tunnel like tongues of fire. The hands appeared hoofed like those of a horse. The hand closest to the center of the tunnel held aloft an unlit torch. The hands closest to the wall were fused to the stone surface like a bas-relief.

Solomon brought the torch closer to the face of one of the statues. The face was strangely human-like but contorted and grotesque like a gargoyle.

"It's the Cherubim," Ellie whispered.

"These are the feared guardians of the Garden of Eden…stone statues?" Phillip asked incredulously.

"I thought cherubs were those cute little baby angels. These guys are pretty ugly if you ask me." Jonas squinted at the statue closest to him.

"It's a common misconception, I'm afraid," Ellie answered. "Those fat baby angels who seem to float weightlessly are actually called putti. In the Bible, the Cherubim are the guardians of the gates of the Garden of Eden. After Adam and Eve were banished from the Garden of Eden, God placed the Cherubim at the gates to prevent humanity from re-entering. They are not meant to be cute or cuddly. They are powerful beings whose purpose is to act as a deterrent. Of course there is some historical basis for Cherubim in the Bible. The idea of the Cherub likely comes from ancient storm gods — forces of nature…powerful beings who were entrusted to protect a sacred site."

"Like an alarm system," Solomon responded.

"…of Biblical proportions," Clay added and peered at the statues suspiciously.

Ellie pointed to each of the statues flanking the end of the tunnel. "The way the statues are positioned, it calls to mind the *shedu* of the Sumerians — bull-like creatures with wings that were placed beside entranceways in palaces and houses to protect what was inside from…"

"From what?" Solomon asked.

"…intruders," Ellie replied with a distracted look. She squatted and examined the ground in front of the statues. There were small diamond-like gems fastened into the stone surface of the ground. They glistened in the light of the torch.

"This is it!" Phillip exclaimed. "This is the end of the tunnel. We need to open that door." He walked across the square on the ground and approached the far end of the tunnel. The stone slab was taller than a man and appeared to be constructed of white marble with green veins running through it. Phillip pushed his shoulder against it and grunted. He placed the palms of his hands against the surface of the marble and tried to pull it aside like a sliding door. Alex watched as the back of his neck turned beet-red.

Solomon sighed, looked at Ox, and flicked his head in the direction of the laboring man. "Ox, see if you can get that thing open, will you?"

Alex watched as Ox slipped his semi-automatic gun from around his shoulder, leaned it against the base of one of the statues, and clapped his hands together like a weightlifter. He walked between the Cherubim and tapped Phillip on the shoulder.

"Please, Sir. Step aside," he bellowed and motioned for the older man to back away. Phillip nodded and walked back to the group mumbling, "…it's not budging."

"Ox, how about more light?" Solomon asked rhetorically and approached the statues, holding the torch high in the air. He tilted the torch and brought the flame up against each of the dry torches held by the Cherubim. The end of the tunnel was suddenly illuminated in a fierce light.

Ox began to push against the marble slab. They could hear a strange sizzle, followed by a whooshing noise. Solomon held up his hand to silence the group.

"Do you hear that? Ox, are you doing that?" Solomon asked. Ox looked back, shrugged, and leaned further into the marble slab.

The whooshing noise grew louder. Alex reached out, grabbed

Ellie's wrist, and tentatively took a step back. The flames dancing atop the torches held in the hands of the Cherubim lit up the faces of the stone beasts. The eyes of the statues glowed a brilliant scarlet and sparkled like jewels. Beyond the sound of the whooshing noise, he could hear something that sounded like a rope stretching taut. With a sense of panic, he thought back to what Polo had written in the fourth book: *I finally approached the gates of the garden and saw the flaming eyes of the cherubs. I stopped... the fiery sword...*

"Wait! Stop!" Alex blurted out just as the Cherubim's eyes appeared to pulsate a blinding red light.

Suddenly a screech erupted from each of the statues. Alex could see two crescent blades shoot out from each wall, slice through the flames of the torches held by each Cherubim, and nearly instantaneously retract into the opposite wall. Ox's body remained upright for a moment before crashing to the floor. His decapitated head rolled backwards and settled between Phillip's legs. Phillip jumped back in disgust. Ellie nervously peered at an irregular spot of red that was left on the white marble door.

"Holy shit!" Solomon exclaimed and placed his hands on his knees as if out of breath. He looked at the headless body slumped awkwardly against the far wall.

Phillip turned around in stunned silence and looked at the rest of the group with horror. A spray of blood speckled his face. He frantically wiped away the blood with the back of his hand.

Solomon held up his right hand and regained his composure. "Calm down everyone," he softly murmured. "Everyone just calm down!" he roared. He tentatively approached Ox's head resting between the two Cherubim. With the tip of his boot against Ox's right ear, he flicked the head aside. The head bounced over to the side of the tunnel, wobbled for a moment, and finally settled against the wall. Ox's eyes remained opened and fixed in surprise. Solomon drove his fist against the wall in frustration.

"What do we do now?" Phillip asked.

Solomon glared at Alex. "Well, there has to be a way past these Cherubim. How do we do it, Professor?"

Alex peered at Ox's headless body and apprehensively swallowed. His throat was painfully dry.

"I don't know," Alex replied.

"What do you mean you 'don't know'?"

"I mean, I don't know."

Solomon looked away in anger. Phillip tapped Solomon on the shoulder. "You have explosives, don't you? Can't you blow apart that door?"

Solomon slapped the wall with the palm of his hand. "See this wall? These walls are made of Kimberlite. I happen to know a few things about it. My father ran a diamond mine back in Kimberly. Crack through this in the wrong way with explosives and you'll release natural gas and then boom! If we are lucky, we may just cave in part of the tunnel. At worst we could be shot out of this tunnel like a cork. That said, I may be willing to take the risk if the Professor can't figure this one out."

Ellie gripped Alex's hand. "I'm not too eager to test the explosive thing out. There has to be a way to open that door. We can figure this out." She looked into Alex's eyes with determination.

"You two start figuring it out then," Solomon commanded. He turned to Pieter. "Go check on Bryce and Frederick outside, will you? Make sure they're alright. This could take a while."

79

Pieter slung the gun over his shoulder and pulled on the rope to make sure it was secure. Satisfied, he jumped a short distance, gripped the rope, and dug the heel of his boots against a knot formed in the rope. He shimmed his body quickly up and peered at the hole looming above. The fog that was just beginning to roll across the side of the mountain when they had first descended was now significantly thicker. *Bryce and Frederick must be having a hell of a time seeing anything in this soup. They must be scared shitless*, Pieter thought as he pulled himself the final way over the lip of the hole. With a quick motion, he sprang to his feet and slipped the gun from his shoulder.

The excavated pit was eerily still. He called out to his compatriots and listened intently, but no answer was returned. He could feel the muscles in the back of his neck tense in response to the silence. *This is not good.* He climbed slowly out of the pit and onto the outcropping. The mist was disorienting. He immediately felt lost in the monotonous gray haze and struggled to see one foot ahead of him.

"Bryce...Frederick? You guys alright?"

Pieter trudged cautiously forward, the barrel of his gun blindly trained ahead into the mist. The wind began to whistle and as it died down, he could hear a soft flapping noise. As the fog momentarily began to dissipate in front of him, Pieter could see a long, silver spear driven into the hard ground of Burkhan Khaldun. An array of horsehair was tied to the shaft of the Spirit Banner, and he watched as the hair flapped back and forth. He slowly maneuvered around the spear as the air before him darkened once again. His index finger curled around the trigger of his gun as he moved carefully across the outcropping in silence. The tip of his boot suddenly struck a soft object and he squatted beside it, his gun braced against his flank, ready to fire. The mist floated above the ground, and as he lowered his body towards the surface the air became clearer. He could see the twisted forms of Bryce and Frederick splayed out side-by-side on the ground before him. He reached out and ran his fingers across their necks and found them pulseless and cold.

"Shit," Pieter muttered as his heart began to race. He struggled to regain his composure. Pieter rose to his feet and began to back away from the bodies of the two men. He continued to point his gun straight ahead as he carefully walked backwards in the direction of the pit from which he came. He stopped to listen for a moment and could hear the rattle of movement along the mountain slope.

A burst of wind appeared to catch the fog and swirl it upwards. He could see the deep blue sky peak out from the gray mist. As his eyes settled on the clearing fog, he observed as many as fifty men spread out along the side of the mountain. They were dressed similar to that of the slain shaman—flannel shirts, loose pants, and wool hats. He caught the eye of the Mongolian man closest to him who frowned and reached for his waistband. Pieter crouched and pulled the trigger of his gun. The rat-tat of the semi-automatic echoed across the outcropping and he could see the man clutch his chest and stagger backwards. The other men quickly scattered and Pieter took the opportunity to retreat back towards the pit as he unloaded several other bullets blindly into the mist.

A loud crack erupted from the fog as Pieter felt a searing pain shoot through his abdomen. The force of the bullet sent him stumbling backwards to the edge of the pit. His foot slipped over the edge and he found himself sliding uncontrollably down the dirt slope on his stomach. Pieter landed at the base of the pit in a heap and struggled to crawl to the hole leading into the tunnel. His hands began to tremble as he fought to grip the rope. He could hear above him a blood-curling battle cry. With a grunt he forced himself over the threshold of the hole and tried to seize the rope. Weakened, his fingers slipped and he was sent falling into the blackness below.

80

Ellie stared up at the repeating pictograms carved into the ceiling and walls. She frowned and ran her hands through her oily hair. When was the last time she had washed it? She could not remember.

"Can you decipher it?" Clay asked.

"I don't even know what civilization wrote it. Most ancient scripts can be deciphered in two ways. The first is if subsequent existent scripts contain elements of the ancestral script. The second way is if you are fortunate to have an ancient text that has multiple languages. That was the way Henry Rawlinson helped decipher cuneiform from a trilingual inscription of Darius the Great at Behistun in Iran. It was in Old Persian, Elamite, and Babylonian. As far as I can tell, this is a bunch of symbols that could have only specific meanings to some ancient culture."

"So it could be saying anything."

"Yes and no. When I approach pictograms, it is sometimes best to take them for what they are. When I look at those four symbols, I think they were chosen for a specific purpose. Look at the two in the middle. There is a semicircle perched atop a line. It looks like a sun rising over the horizon. The one next to it is the opposite. The sun has set. It is a common motif in ancient languages. It's the cycle of the day...the cycle of life if you will... birth to death. Some cultures like the Mayans worshiped the Sun as a god. Others were consumed with the stages of the Moon. It was a way to account for the natural order. If you bring these two symbols together you get a complete circle. Now if you take the two symbols on the ends and join them..."

"It's a tree!" Clay exhaled.

"This goes back to what I said earlier. Most of human history was not lived in a Monotheistic mindset. Just think about Ancient Rome and Greece. There were multiple gods. Some were more major gods than others, but there was no single supreme being. If you go back further, many cultures found gods and spirits in the everyday—the sun, moon, sky, rocks, and trees. Many of these beliefs persist to this day. Tengerism or Shamanism is still practiced here in Mongolia. We would like to believe that there have been dark ages in religion, that mankind was unwittingly led astray in the infancy of humankind…that the Monotheism of today is the unavoidable end to man's quest for spirituality.

"It reminds me of a question I asked my father when I was a little girl. It was along the lines of 'do dogs go to heaven.' I had learned about cavemen in school. I remember sitting in church, turning to my father, and asking if there are any cavemen in heaven. Jesus had not come—there was no such thing as Christianity, Judaism, or Islam. He said that if they were good people then they would be in heaven with or without the teachings of Jesus. I sat there thinking about all the eons that passed by in which people roamed the earth, never going to Church or taking Communion, never reading from the Torah or reciting the Koran. I thought, how strange. I have come to realize that this is all an evolution. I believe that this could be 'cradle of humanity' of sorts—a glimpse into an ancient culture from which the great religions of today took root—the most basic yet all-encompassing view on spirituality."

Solomon stopped pacing for a moment to blurt out, "That's all very Kumbaya. Just get the door open, will you?"

Ellie glared back at Solomon and was about to cast an insult his way when the sound of footsteps stopped her. Solomon quickly glanced at Jonas. "You still got that gun on you?" Jonas nodded and pulled the pistol from the small of his back. Solomon leaned against the wall and trained his pistol at a figure awkwardly staggering forward.

"Don't shoot," Pieter urged as he stumbled and collapsed on the ground. Solomon darted to his side and waved Phillip over to provide light from his torch. Solomon reached over and turned the man on his back. Pieter's face was ashen white and his breathing was rapid and shallow. He was clutching his abdomen. As Solomon pried Pieter's hands from his abdomen, he found that the man's shirt was saturated with blood. The bullet hole had entered through the epigastric region and exited through his right flank.

"What happened?" Solomon asked.

Pieter looked at him as if he was seeing a stranger.

"Pieter, what happened?" Solomon asked again with a stern voice.

Pieter raised his head slightly off the ground and whispered. "They're dead. Bryce…Frederick. They're DEAD! There's too many of them. They are all over the place." Pieter was overtaken by a coughing fit, which sprayed red arterial blood into the air and left blood at the corners of his mouth. His lips were dusky. He drew Solomon closer bringing Solomon's ear to his mouth and whispered: "They are coming. You need to get out of here."

Solomon could feel the man's grip of his shirt loosen. He turned his head and slowly laid Pieter's lifeless body back on the ground.

Phillip held up the torch and looked down at Solomon. "Commander, I'm afraid we are getting a little thinned out here."

Solomon ignored the comment and rose to his feet. He drew his gun and leveled it at Alex and Ellie. "I'm going to tell you this once more and only once. Get that door open and get it open NOW! Otherwise we are all dead."

Solomon swung around and knelt beside his knapsack. He gripped the zipper and opened the bag. He removed the clay-like blocks of Semtex and made a pile beside the wall of the tunnel. Solomon began to unspool a long length of wire and stripped the ends with a blade, exposing the uncoated wire.

Ellie looked down at him incredulously. "What are you doing? Have you forgotten what you said?"

Solomon glared at her as he began placing the explosives along the walls of the tunnel. "I know what I said and I know what this stuff does. Just get that door open."

Alex bit his fingernail as he stared at the marble door. Ellie gave him a concerned glance as she watched Solomon arranging the final touches on the explosives. Jonas defensively drew his weapon and pointed it down the tunnel.

"In the fourth book Polo says that the soldier Genghis Khan sent out in search of the Garden of Eden told the Khan's staff where the location was and gave them a clue: *the sky has fallen…lift it up to enter.*" Alex looked up at the ceiling again and studied the writing.

"What does it mean that the 'sky has fallen?'" Clay asked as he sidled up beside them.

"I'm not sure, but in the Mongolian culture, the sky was the most important of the spirits. They worshiped the Eternal Sky above all else. If the sky had indeed fallen, I imagine this must have been something calamitous."

"The whole natural world would be out of order," Ellie added.

"You needed to 'lift the sky up to enter' if you follow the clue," Alex said.

"Well how do we do that?" Phillip chimed in as he peered down the darkened tunnel apprehensively.

"I don't know," Alex responded.

"I'm losing faith in your golden boy, Redmund," Phillip growled. He stopped as a loud warrior cry echoed through the tunnel. "We are going to get slaughtered here."

The primeval cry pierced through Ellie's body as she stared down at Pieter's motionless corpse with dread. She followed the coagulating blood draining from his wound onto the stone floor. In spots it covered the small gems incorporated into the stone ground and seeped into crevices. Ellie suddenly felt nauseated and weak. She backed away and squatted against the wall to settle her breathing. Across the ground she could see a multitude of gems flicker in the torchlight like tiny stars. *Stars!*

Ellie sprung to her feet.

"Alex, look at the ground! See the jewels built into the stone. They look like stars." She pulled Alex, Clay, and Phillip back towards the wall to provide a better vantage point. "The world is upside down...the sky is on the ground."

"The sky has fallen!" Clay exclaimed.

"This is the clue to open the door," Ellie announced.

Clay backed further away from the Cherubim and surveyed the celestial scene. "I've been a bit of an amateur astronomer since my father bought me a telescope as a child. This looks like a map of the stars. There's Pleiades." He pointed to seven gems arrayed across the floor.

"The Seven Sisters. They're mentioned in Homer's *Iliad* and *Odyssey*," Ellie responded. "This makes sense. The stars are a part of almost all ancient cultures. They are fixed entities...predictable. And better yet, they have stories about them. They peer down from the great unknown. What better way to leave a clue."

"Well, how do we 'lift it up'?" Phillip asked impatiently.

Alex peered up at the ceiling. Ellie was quiet and bit her lip.

"What if we are looking for a constellation or a star?" Alex mumbled.

Ellie smiled broadly. "That's it! In certain ancient cultures, particularly shamanistic cultures, the stars had spirits associated with them. Some of these spirits played distinct roles. The polar stars were felt to keep the sky up! We need to find Polaris... the North Star!"

All eyes moved to Clay who held up both hands as if to ask for some time to examine the celestial map. "O.K...let me think for a moment." He walked back and forth, pointed at various gems and mumbled to himself. "We need to first find the Big Dipper. It's a part of Ursa Major." Clay frowned, frustrated by his close vantage point, and continued to move further down the tunnel until his back hit up against one of the stone Cherubs. He looked up at it with a mix of apprehension and opportunity. He stepped up on the statue's feet and climbed up until his arm was slung over one of the wings of the beast.

"Be careful," Ellie warned, expecting the sharp blades to suddenly slice through the air.

"This is better," Clay muttered and surveyed the star map beneath him. Alex watched as the man appeared to be connecting stars in the air with his index finger. "O.K. There are seven stars in the Big Dipper—three for the handle and four for the cup. By my estimation, Ellie you are standing on the handle."

Ellie blushed and moved aside.

"Now if I am remembering correctly, there are two pointer stars within the constellation. They are stars that direct you to another star or constellation. If you draw a line from the two stars that make up the part of the cup furthest from the handle..." He connected the two stars with his index finger and continued to extend the point of his finger away from it. Ellie watched as his finger traveled between the two Cherubim behind him and settled on the headless body of Ox.

"From my calculations, the North Star is well…under him." Clay slipped off the statue and back onto the ground.

Solomon looked over his shoulder while toggling through a rectangular transmitter.

"Great job. Who's going?" Solomon anxiously asked. They could hear footsteps in the distance.

"I'll go," Alex said. Ellie cast him a look of concern.

"Alex, it's suicide," she wailed.

"It's the only way out of this. What other choice do we have?" Ellie reached out her hand and caught the tip of his fingers. She tried to pull him back towards her but his fingers slipped through her grasp. He peered back at her and smiled. "I'm going to be alright."

"That's what all the important people in my life think," she moaned.

"This is going to be different."

Ellie watched as Alex adjusted the strap on his leather satchel until it rested on his back, crouched down in front of the two Cherubim, and finally placed his body prostate on the ground. Using his arms and knees, he began to pull himself along the floor between the two statues. He nervously glanced up at the stone figures but found them frozen. As he neared Ox's torso, he could see the bloodstain on the marble door and swallowed. Somewhere behind him he could hear a chant in a foreign tongue fill the tunnel with foreboding. Alex pulled himself alongside the muscular body, reached out, and gripped Ox's shoulders. He tried to push the body aside but was unsuccessful. Alex could feel his heart pound in the depths of his chest cavity as he slowly propped himself up on his knees. He slid his boot out, wedged the tip of the boot and his fingers underneath the man's right shoulder, and pushed up with all his might.

He could hear the sound of a rope tightening.

"Alex!" Ellie gasped with horror.

Suddenly there was the sound of a twang. The crescent blade sprung out of the wall with a screech. He could feel a hot breeze across his right ear and a tug at his shoulder. The leather satchel slid off his back and onto the floor. He caught the cleanly cut edge of the leather strap and stared at it with amazement.

"You O.K.?" Ellie anxiously asked.

Alex could feel the hairs on the back of his neck sprout up. "I'm OK. It missed me by..." He stared down at the strap. "...by a couple of millimeters. Redmund, I'm sorry about your father's bag."

Alex fought the desire to crawl back to the rest of the group and resumed his task of trying the push the heavy body up. With several painful pushes, he gradually elevated the man's right side until the torso was resting completely on its left side. A final heave sent the body toppling over. Beneath the man's body was a circular diamond. His fingers probed the edges and found it loose. He rocked the gem back and forth until it popped out and revealed a hole dug into the stone surface. Alex slipped two fingers into the hole and was able to seize a golden ring attached to a cable.

From the darkness of the tunnel he could hear a voice boom in accented English: "This is a holy place. Do not disturb the gazriim ezen. Stop now and you will die with honor."

Alex gripped the ring tightly and pulled it out of the hole. As he pulled, he began to meet considerable resistance from the cable. He braced his feet against the marble door and continued to tug as hard as he could. Sweat rolled down the nape of his neck as the golden ring dug into his knuckle. With a creak, the cable gradually released. He could hear a loud knocking noise. He released the cord and could feel the tunnel begin to rumble. Ever so slowly the marble slab began to shake and slide aside. A roaring noise filled the tunnel as the door opened and wind blew across Alex's face. Alex felt heat on his face as he squinted at what was before him. A wall of fire filled the opening.

81

"Oh my God," Ellie whispered. *The end of the tunnel was filled with a bril-*liant red glow as flames leaped into the air as if a luminous curtain were draped over the opening. "It's the ring of fire surrounding the Garden of Eden! The legends are true."

Jonas leaned against the wall and continued to train his gun down into the blackness of the tunnel from which they had entered. The sound of chanting was growing louder and louder. He glanced back momentarily, mesmerized by the fiery spectacle behind him. When he returned to his defensive stance, he could see a Mongolian man creep out of the shadows clutching an AK-47. Jonas dropped to his knee and pulled the trigger. The man gave a startled cry and was sent spinning backwards. His AK-47 discharged erratically, sending rounds ricocheting throughout the tunnel. Solomon ducked as a bullet struck the hoof of one of the Cherubim behind him.

"Son of a…" Solomon cursed and grabbed Ox's discarded machine gun. He quickly advanced down the tunnel and peppered the area in front of him.

Ellie crouched down and wiggled her way to Alex's side. She lifted her head and peered into the flames and down at the palms of her hands. "What do we do? We'll be burnt alive." She covered her head as a bullet whizzed by, flicking aside several strands of hair and sending slivers of stone showering down upon her. Behind her she could hear Jonas and Solomon returning a long stream of deafening firepower.

Alex attempted to shield her with his body as the firing intensified. He reached over and tried to pull Ox's torso behind them as a barrier. "It's either that or get shot." He looked back and could see Phillip several yards away, crouching behind Solomon as the ping of the bullets bounced off the ground at his feet.

"Do you hear something?" Alex asked.

Ellie fought to try and push the sounds of gunfire to the back of her mind. She could hear a strange whirling noise.

"I hear it." She placed her ear against the ground. "It's coming from somewhere close. I think it's under the ground." As she rested her ear against the cool stone, her eyes opened wide at the sight of the cable quickly retracting into the ground.

"Alex...it's the cable!" she exclaimed. Alex lunged for the golden ring but was too late as it and the cable disappeared into the dark recess of the hole. He quickly plunged his fingers into the opening, explored the emptiness, and pulled them out with disappointment. He shook his head.

"I can't reach the cable. It's..." Alex paused mid-thought. He could feel the ground beneath him begin to shake. There was a deafening screech as the marble door began to slide slowly across.

"The door's closing!" Ellie screamed.

Alex crawled forward, pressed the palms of his hands against the marble, and tried to stop the door from sliding. Unable to stop the door from moving, he slumped down beside Ellie.

"We need to go through," Alex urged.

Jonas peered back nervously. At that moment a series of gunshots echoed throughout the tunnel. Jonas could feel a bolt of heat shoot through the middle of his abdomen. He staggered back and managed to fire off several shots blindly into the darkness ahead. He reached out wildly and found the stone wall while attempting to steady himself. His legs felt unbearably heavy and numb. Although he did everything in his power to will them to keep retreating backwards, his legs buckled uncontrollably under him, leaving him to gracelessly slide down the wall and onto the ground.

"Jonas!" Clay screamed. He weaved and bobbed across from the far side of the tunnel through a hail of bullets. Clay nearly slid across the ground and ended up by Jonas's side. He found the man propped up against the wall clutching his abdomen as he tried unsuccessfully to staunch a brisk bleed from the entrance site. His legs were flopped and folded awkwardly in front of him.

"Jonas! You're OK." He looked around the room for help but found only chaos. Clay reached across Jonas's shoulder and attempted to move him back towards the Cherubim. "We need to get you out of here."

Jonas pushed Clay's arm away and looked back at the closing door behind him with urgency. "Boss, I'm not going anywhere. I can't move my legs. You need to go before that door closes forever." Jonas grimaced through the pain, reached out, and grabbed Clay's wrist. "If you don't go now, all this won't be worth anything. You hear me? All this searching will be for nothing. You're so close. I would have loved to see it, but it's not meant to be."

Clay hesitated but Jonas looked away and pushed him back. Jonas leveled his pistol and pulled the trigger. A Mongolian fighter lurking in the shadows crumpled to the ground.

"Go, for God's-sake!"

Clay looked at him sadly, nodded, and retreated towards Alex and Ellie. As he maneuvered back to the far end of the tunnel he could hear Jonas mutter, "The truth is I didn't believe you. I thought you were a crazy man. What do I know? Who's the crazy one now?" Jonas emitted a pained laugh.

Clay crouched beside Alex and Ellie, his eyes wet and red.

"Jonas?" Ellie asked.

Clay looked straight into the dancing flames and answered without looking at either of them. The door was nearly half closed. "He's not coming."

"Not coming?"

"It's time for us to go," Clay responded and pulled himself

to a standing position. Ellie and Alex winced, expecting the unseen blades to shoot out of the walls and cut the erect figure in half. None came. Clay took his first step forward. His body appeared strangely black against the reddish flames. He paused for a moment in front of the fiery wall and extended his hand quickly into it. He smiled, took a final step forward, and disappeared.

Phillip watched as Clay passed through the portal. He pounded on Solomon's shoulder. "We need to make for the door," Phillip screamed over the blasts and gunfire. Solomon backed up and unleashed another furious round of machine gunfire ahead. He looked back at the door, now nearly three-quarters closed.

Alex reached out, cupped Ellie's head between his hands, and kissed her. She looked at him and smiled.

"Just in case that's my last chance for doing that," Alex mumbled under his breath.

Ellie and Alex pushed forward on their hands and knees towards the opening. Suddenly two hands reached out from the fire, grabbed each of their hands, and pulled them through the portal. They closed their eyes and braced themselves for the heat, which never came.

"Solomon, it's closing!" Phillip wailed.

"We'll make it," Solomon responded, grabbed the old man's shirt, and pulled him forcefully back towards the door. Solomon kept his attention on the advancing Darkhad, letting loose a stream of bullets as the two figures made for the door. As they neared the two Cherubim, a series of gunshots echoed through the tunnel. The first bullet struck Solomon in the left chest, loosening his grip on Phillip, and sending him staggering into one of the stone statues. He clung to the beast's hoof and gritted his teeth as the heat of the bullet seared his muscles, tore through his lung, and broke apart bone. The second bullet struck Phillip in his calf, ripping apart his Achilles tendon and leaving him splayed out on the ground, moaning.

Solomon gritted his teeth and wheezed, looked down at the hobbled man writhing in agony, and then at the nearly closed door behind him. Phillip lifted his torso off the ground and caught Solomon's eyes.

"Solomon, don't leave me," he pleaded.

Solomon looked away and stumbled towards the portal.

Phillip's eyes were filled with rage and despair.

"Don't leave me! I hired you! I hired you...." Phillip pulled his body across the ground. "...to help me!"

Solomon stopped for a moment, glanced back at Phillip, and muttered without expression. "You didn't hire me to be an angel."

Phillip pounded the ground with his fist as Solomon slipped through, just as the door slid shut with a final bang.

Phillip continued to pull his body forward as the gunshots began to die down and the tunnel became quiet. With grunts of pain, he reached the base of the closed door. His fingers explored the hole in the ground but he could not find the cable Alex had pulled. He forced himself up to his knees as the blood pooled around him on the stone floor. He planted his palms upon the marble and pulled himself to a standing position in front of the door. Standing with his weight precariously perched on his one good foot, Phillip began to pound on the door as Jonas chuckled behind him.

"Give it up," Jonas mumbled as he searched through his pockets for a cigarette.

"I need to see it! I need to see Eden! I need to see it!" Phillip cried. He continued to strike the door until his hands were raw. He wailed so loud that he did not even hear the tightening of the rope, the snap of its release, and the pair of blades hurtling through the air and striking him down.

Solomon stumbled forward and collapsed in a heap. He tried to catch his breath and pushed the pleuritic pain to the back of his mind. His fingers explored his pants pocket and retrieved the small rectangular transmitter. With the flip of a switch, the device glowed green. He held his finger for a moment over the button.

Jonas held the unlit cigarette in his hand. He looked longingly at the lit torches held by the Cherubim. *What I would give for a lighter at this moment.* He could see that the tunnel ahead was alive with movement as Mongolian men advanced cautiously, holding aloft their AK-47s. They stopped with fear upon discovering the intricate array of explosives wired across the tunnel. The men began to talk rapidly. *Doesn't matter what language you speak; fear is universal,* Jonas thought. He could hear panic as the men quickly attempted to retreat back down the tunnel.

Jonas looked at the explosives and then down at his useless legs.

"Oh, hell."

The explosion ripped through the tunnel, cracking through the Kimberlite, and releasing pent up natural gas. The walls and ceiling fractured and fell in. A luminous fireball shot through the tunnel, incinerating all who were left inside and sending a plume of smoke and fire erupting out of the side of the mountain and across the Eternal Sky.

82

It was the sound of rushing water that immediately struck Ellie as she emerged from the chaos of the tunnel. The roaring and churning overwhelmed her senses, penetrating deep into her head until she was left feeling intoxicated and unbalanced. She kept her eyes closed and breathed deeply the moist air, finding it imbued with an organic fragrance that conjured up a swamp bog.

Ellie slowly opened her eyes and apprehensively looked down at her forearms, expecting them to be charred and blackened. She was relieved to find them unscathed, despite her trip through the wall of fire. She blinked several times and tried to shake off the reddish tint that seemed burned onto her retina. As the scarlet veil slowly lifted, she was greeted by a scene of awesome serenity that made the hairs on her arms stand on end and her skin tingle.

"My God, Ellie. Is this it? Is this Eden?" whispered Alex. His hand blindly explored the air until he was able to locate her hand, seize it, and caress it softly.

"It's beautiful," Ellie replied with amazement.

They found themselves standing upon an earthen walkway that ran along the perimeter of a perfectly circular chamber carved deep into the mountainside. The cavity stretched nearly fifty stories into the air and was capped by a luminous dome of rock that sparkled blue.

"How is this possible?" Ellie wondered. "It's so... so light... all this way underground."

Alex looked along the edge of the walkway and discovered a long thin trough dug into the ground. As he peered into the trough, Alex could see an oily, iridescent liquid filling the trench from which red flames leapt a short distance into the air. The light of the fire was magnified a thousand-fold by a seemingly infinite number of small ruby-colored gems encrusted into the stone wall. Alex released Ellie's hand, walked a short distance to the wall, and extended his hand. He hesitated for a moment before placing the palm of his hand upon the surface of the gems. They felt cool to the touch.

"It was all an illusion," Alex announced.

Ellie gave him an inquisitive look.

"The fire," Alex said and motioned in the direction from which they had passed through the door. The reflected and refracted light produced the appearance of a wall of fire when, in reality, the true flames lapped less than an inch off the ground. Alex surveyed the periphery of the chamber and could see that this subterfuge of lighting created the appearance of a menacing ring of fire encircling the room.

"What else isn't as it seems, I wonder," Ellie asked skeptically. She looked up along the walls of the chamber and could see that above the layer of ruby-colored gems was an endless assortment of jagged, silvery jewels that were mirror-like and coated the walls. The light reflected by these gems was astronomical, serving to fill the vast interior with a white glow.

"We found it. I told you it was true!" Clay exclaimed.

The old man had advanced halfway across an earthen bridge. He peered up with his right hand perched atop his forehead like a visor.

There were four identical bridges that arched their way across a large body of water and connected the outer circular walkway to an island in the center of the chamber. The bridges were evenly spaced within the room, like hands and legs of a cross, or the directions of a compass. Arising from the middle of the island was a massive green tree that reached high up towards the top of the chamber.

Alex and Ellie stepped onto one of the bridges as if in a daze and walked slowly towards the central island. The ground was soft and velvety beneath their boots, and they looked down to see green moss covering the earthen bridge. They stopped and peered over the edge of the bridge and could see the water churn violently beneath them as if agitated by some unseen force. The water had a vaguely neon green hue.

As they neared the island, they could see that the green of the tree was actually from an extensive network of green vines that emerged from the water and wound its way up along the exposed roots of the tree, covering the trunk like a rich beard and creeping up the seemingly endless number of branches stretching into the air. The ivy ultimately hung from the branches like a rich, emerald canopy.

Alex inspected the tree even more closely and found that beneath the covering of vines, chalk white bark peaked out. Had it not been for the lush green vines draping its frame, the tree would have appeared ghostly.

Clay moved across the island and stopped beside the base of the tree.

The trunk of the tree was elevated off the ground and appeared to levitate as if it was supported by a series of massive, twisted, and gnarled roots that spread out across the island like tentacles. Before diving into the ground and disappearing beneath the surface, the roots crisscrossed, producing a cave-like void beneath the base of the tree. A green glow pulsated within the space.

"What's this?" Clay asked as he carefully maneuvered between the roots.

Beneath the tree and enclosed by the cage created by the roots was a human form perched atop a wooden platform. The body appeared to be that of an aged man of Mongolian ancestry with a tightly trimmed gray beard. He was dressed in armor constructed of hardened leather and iron. A purple silk vest peaked out from under the armor. He clutched a large bow across his chest. The body seemed to glow green.

"Polo was right. The legends are true," Alex nearly whispered from behind Clay. "It's the body of Genghis Khan."

Ellie ducked under a horizontal root and pushed her way into the space enclosed by the canopy of roots. "It's not possible." She approached the figure, carefully walking alongside the funeral platform. "There's no embalming here, but he looks completely preserved. It's as if he died yesterday. Genghis Khan died in the thirteenth century. I've dug up my fair share of dead people, even a couple of mummies, and I can tell you that it isn't pretty. Does this look like a person who died over seven hundred years ago? Is this some kind of hoax?"

Clay twirled around. "It's the tree!" He extended his arms in opposite directions. "It's this place!" He smiled. "There's life here. Don't you feel it? There is a force. I feel it in my body."

"Now you're sounding crazy again," Ellie responded. "I didn't peg you as a new-ager, Redmund. The tree didn't seem to raise him from the dead."

"This isn't a place of *miracles*, Ellie. You should know this better than anyone. This is the place where the *tales* of miracles began. What if the myths passed down through the eons, including the story of Genesis from the Bible, were mankind's attempt to explain what seemed unexplainable—a tree that appears to give life. I am a man of science first and foremost and I believe that there is an explanation for what is occurring here. I believe that this needs to be studied, starting with this tree."

"You mean a tree that seems to be able to grow underground… without sunlight?" Alex asked.

"Yes. Extraordinary isn't it?" Clay responded with wide eyes.

Alex watched as Clay looked up at the base of the tree's trunk. Alex bent down and looked under the wooden funeral platform and could see the pulsating green light.

"Alex, where are you going?" Ellie asked as she watched Alex crouch down and wiggle his way into a tight space beneath the platform. In the center of the island beneath the platform was a circular hole like an oculus from which a green glow would periodically emanate like the beats of a heart. As he crept on his hands and knees towards the opening in the ground, Alex could hear a continuous roar like the sound of a monstrous waterfall. He maneuvered towards the edge of the opening and peered down. He could see a whirlpool of water violently swirling beneath him. White caps speckled the surface of the water. Beneath the dark blue of the water, he could see a green light pulsate like a giant strobe light.

Alex could feel Ellie's body move beside his. She held his arm as she looked down into the tumultuous water.

"What is it?" she asked.

Alex turned to Ellie. Her face was green in the glow of the water.

"What if this is the 'single source?'"

"What are you saying, Alex?"

"I'm saying what if this is the fountain that gives rise to the four rivers of Eden? Think of it. From the center of this chamber there are four sections demarcated by the bridges. What if these are four underground waterways? This could be where the legend of the four rivers of Eden originated."

"What's that green light and what's producing that whirlpool?" Ellie asked.

"The four rivers…yes…yes…the four rivers. It makes perfect sense," Clay muttered as he peered under the platform. "It's all very interesting, but there seems to be a problem with the tree. A very serious problem, I'm afraid."

"What problem?" Alex asked.

83

"The vines: they are killing this tree," Clay announced as the three looked up at the rich layer of ivy coating the trunk. "They are like parasites twisting their way across the trunk, winding their way up the branches, strangling them as they go. It may be a beautiful sight but I'm afraid what is left is little more than a carcass wrapped in a suit of vines. It's really quite tragic."

"I would have expected you to be more upset," Alex noted as he examined where a large root next to him plunged down below the water's edge and disappeared into the darkness.

"In the face of adversity, there is always hope. Do you remember the drawing on the tunnel wall?"

"The one depicting the injured warrior?" Ellie offered.

"The very same. The mortally injured man is carried to a tree and is fed a leaf...*a white leaf*...and lo and behold he is healed."

"I remember it," Ellie responded.

Clay pointed up towards a point midway up the tree. Ellie squinted and strained to try and identify what he was attempting to illustrate. She could see the rich and luxurious green canopy of vines draping over the tree with the glint of white branches peeking out. Her eyes darted about and finally settled on a short branch that arose directly off the main trunk. Snakelike vines were wound tightly around the branch. Off the tip of the branch was a single white leaf.

"Unless your eyes are better than mine, I can only see one white leaf. In this leaf I see hope," Clay solemnly pronounced.

Alex sized up the distance to the leaf and gave Clay a skeptical sideways glance.

"Redmund, it's quite a climb."

"I may be old but nothing is keeping me from getting my fingers on that leaf," Clay announced with determination.

"I wouldn't be so sure."

The voice was raspy and shallow, causing the three to turn around suddenly. Perched atop one of the bridges was Solomon. Like an apparition, he staggered forward across the bridge, clutching his chest. His breathing was labored and perspiration dotted his forehead. He leveled his gun at them as he unsteadily positioned his body next to the tree. The gun shook in his tremulous hand and he glanced down at it with embarrassment. He gave a quick look up at the single white leaf hanging from the branch.

"You know that there isn't a chance in hell that you are laying your hands on that leaf so you can look at it under some microscope. I don't imagine you have much sympathy for me, but I think I'm in need of more immediate help." He lifted his hand from the side of his chest. A wheezing noise was emitted as blood and air escaped from a jagged hole between his ribs. "Now I would send one of you monkeys up there for me but frankly, I don't trust a single one of you buggers enough not to chomp on it yourself." He thrust the gun in Clay's face. "Back up, old man, or I'll drop you right in front of your precious tree."

Clay raised up his hands and backed away, frightened by the maniacal glint in the man's eyes. "Solomon, please. This is more important than you or me."

"Maybe you...not me," Solomon responded and slipped the gun into the back of his waistband. He swung his leg over a root, straddled it, and shimmed up it until his body was flush against the massive trunk. Clay watched helplessly below and pleaded. "Solomon! It can't be wasted! It's the last one! Think about what you are doing!"

Solomon grunted in disgust at the man's idealism and reached out to seize a handful of the vines winding across the trunk. He gripped them, pulled down, and found them to be as strong as a rope. Satisfied that they could hold his weight, Solomon took a short leap and clung to the trunk. He immediately dug his boots into the rough surface of the white bark beneath the ivy and was pleased to find that it provided a suitable foothold.

His breathing grew increasingly rapid and painful with each series of advancement up the trunk. He glanced over his shoulder and could see the three figures below staring up at him anxiously. *My lung's collapsed. My chest cavity is filling with blood. I'll be dead in no time unless that crazy fool is right about that leaf,* Solomon thought and grimaced. He shook off any doubt of his success. *I've been through worse. I've survived it all. I will survive this.*

Solomon emitted a bestial roar as he fought the searing pain shooting through his chest and into his shoulders. He continued to stoically pull himself up along the vines as he ignored the warm trail of blood running briskly down his flank and dripping onto the island below. He pressed his torso tightly against the trunk of the tree and paused to catch his breath. The sensation seemed as innocuous as it was unexpected, a faint tickle across the portion of his abdomen left uncovered by his torn shirt. When the tickle did not cease, he inquisitively peered down at the itching spot. He was more than a little surprised to see that the vines pressed against his torso appeared to wiggle and twist.

I'm going crazy. I'm losing too much blood, Solomon thought.

He felt a wave of urgency sweep across his body. He dug his boots even more forcefully into the bark and propelled himself up farther. Solomon smiled at the sight of the white leaf nearly two yards above him. His biceps tensed as he gripped the vines. Then suddenly, he froze. He could hear a subtle hissing noise. The vines began to squirm wildly beneath his body, producing the hissing sound as they rubbed back and forth against the bark. He pulled his left hand away as a vine began to wind its way around his wrist. An intense pain shot through his hand and he looked down in horror as a violaceous welt was left where the vine had been attached. Solomon kicked away at the vines beneath his feet and scurried up. At first the burning in his skin was mild, but as he continued to climb up the tree he could feel an intense heat spread across his exposed forearms. He looked down with alarm as red splotches quickly appeared on his skin and his arms began to swell dramatically. He teetered for a moment as the scorching heat began to travel through his entire body.

The vines! They're poisonous!

He clung desperately to a branch as his skin began to bubble and crack. Large fluid-filled blisters and boils began to form across his body. The slightest contact would disrupt the thin, translucent membrane of the blister leading to the expulsion of cloudy fluid. Solomon gave forth a blood-curling shriek at the sight of his skin peeling off in long sheets.

He felt his grip slip and he reached out at the last moment to catch a thick branch under his armpit. He stood awkwardly for a moment propped against the branch with his boots pressed against the trunk of the tree. His breathing continued to grow more rapid and shallow. His throat began to burn and narrow as the mucosal lining grew edematous and bubbled. He struggled to stay focused, but found the world around him growing increasingly dim. Solomon hung limply and whimpered as his eyelids began to swell dramatically and his vision narrowed. He peered up through the slits between his eyelids and could see the white leaf hanging less than a yard away. Solomon reached out and could see his hand float in front of him as if it was not a part of his body. He could feel his body slipping forward and screamed out in horror as the skin from his armpit peeled off. He reached out wildly a final time, catching the vines under his elbows. With a snap, he could hear the vines tear away from the tree, sending him tumbling uncontrollably towards the ground below.

84

Ellie turned away at the sight of the man lying contorted in a heap at the edge of the island. Solomon lay motionless, his body swollen and red, his facial features barely recognizable from the inflammation. Ellie had hated this man, despised him for killing the people she had loved...Gordon...Bernard. She could remember the indifference in his eyes as he dispatched the Mongolian shaman with the flick of the finger. She wished him dead. But now that he was dead, she felt strangely empty.

"That was certainly unexpected," Clay muttered behind her. The man clearly had no desire to mourn such a villain.

Alex knelt beside Solomon and peered at the swollen mess that constituted his neck.

"Tell me you're not thinking about feeling for a pulse. He could be contagious. Look at him! Whatever those vines seem to secrete is poisonous. I wouldn't go near him," Ellie urged.

Alex sighed. "I wouldn't even know where to feel for a pulse."

Clay paced around the island in thought, periodically peering up at the white leaf suspended from the branch above.

"It's quite extraordinary. These vines seem to be alive. They are actually *responsive* to stimuli. Now we've all heard of carnivorous plants like the Venus Fly-Trap or Pitcher plants, but this is in a new category entirely. These vines are quick...reactive. It's almost as if they are protecting the tree."

"I thought you said they are killing the tree," Ellie responded.

"Maybe a little bit of both," Clay mumbled as he distractively tapped his index finger against his lips. "A symbiotic relationship perhaps. The vines gain nutrients and the tree…protection. There's a fine line between life and death, I suppose. If the vines get a little too rambunctious, they might overwhelm their sustainer. It does produce a difficult problem."

"What problem?" Alex asked suspiciously.

"The problem of retrieving that white leaf, of course."

"You're not thinking about trying to get that leaf?" Ellie asked with exasperation. She motioned to the gelatinous form of Solomon. "Look what happened to him, for God's-sake."

Clay looked down at Solomon and made a sour face. "It's certainly a problem."

"That's an understatement!" Ellie replied and threw up her hands.

"I just need to think this out," Clay mumbled and walked away.

Ellie looked at Alex and rolled her eyes. "The man's crazy. Even if there is a miracle and he is able to get that leaf, Solomon blew the tunnel. There is one entrance into Eden…one entrance! He caved in any chance of us getting out of here."

Alex glanced back at the door. Jagged cracks ran across the tilted marble slab with large fragments of stone missing and scattered upon the ground beyond it. Through the openings, Alex could see a wall of stones created by the explosion, blocking the tunnel. *She's right*, Alex thought. *We're trapped*. He looked up at the tree towering above and beyond it the vivid blue dome. *Trapped in paradise*.

"Is that what you are worried about?" Clay interjected midpace. "I'm disappointed in you two. I would have figured that you would have solved that problem long before me."

Ellie and Alex peered at him inquisitively.

Clay pointed to the destroyed door from which they had entered. "It is true that there is one *entrance* to Eden." He looked down at the agitated water wafting against the island and held up four fingers. "There are, however, *four rivers* that leave Eden.

Four rivers supplied by a single source. Alex, you said it yourself."
He pointed to each of the four waterways neatly divided by the
earthen bridges. "One...two...three...four. Four rivers!"

Alex knelt down at the edge of the island and stared across
the water. He could see the water stretch away from the island
toward the walls that constituted the perimeter of the chamber.
Beneath the circular walkway from which they had trod before
crossing the bridge, there was a curved archway that rose above
the surface of the water. The opening was completely black. Alex
moved quickly across the island, periodically crouching to gaze
across each of the waterways, finding a total of four openings
carved into the stone walls.

"Redmund may be right. There seems to be four canals and
the water seems to be funneling out through those passageways."

"It has to be the way out," Clay responded as he circled the
trunk of the tree, stepping over some roots and weaving under
others. He stopped on the far side of the tree where Solomon
had clung desperately to the tree before toppling helplessly to the
ground. The white of the bark shone brightly where the coat of
vines had been ripped away as Solomon fell.

Ellie hugged herself. The neon green-tinged water gurgled
violently and swirled. "I don't know how eager I am to jump
into that water, but I'm not too fond of spending an eternity in
this cave."

"Prometheus," Clay mumbled under his breath.

"What's that?" Alex asked as he placed his finger into the water
and found it warm.

"Prometheus...stealer of fire from the Gods. That's how I'd
like to be remembered," Clay grunted.

Alex twirled around with alarm.

"Redmund. What are you doing?"

Alex and Ellie turned to see Clay standing on a root before
the trunk of the tree. They darted towards the tree just as Clay's

fingers dug into the exposed bark, pulling himself up off the root.

"It's suicide!" Ellie exclaimed. "There's got to be a better way."

Clay turned back as he clung to the trunk. "I've thought it out. None of us will return to this place. And I refuse to believe that all of this has been in vain. My entire life has been leading to this moment. It is what I have been searching for. This is my decision." He pushed off with his boot propelling himself upwards. His fingers dug deeply into the bark until his fingers bled. He looked up along the trunk and could see a path of white. He continued to pull himself up, gripping the rough bark. Clay's pulse quickened at the sight of vines twisting and slithering forward, beginning to fill in the region of the bark left uncovered by Solomon's ill-fated attempt.

"Redmund!" Ellie cried at the image of the vines spreading towards the man. She could see his foot slip off the bark. He hugged the trunk for a moment, regained his composure, and secured his footing again.

I need to keep moving, he thought as the vines began to thrash.

Clay clawed his way upwards. He could feel vines brush against his clothes. He swung his body away from their advance but found that the vines were spreading from all directions. He frantically looked upwards, his eyes searching through the green canopy, until they settled upon the lone white leaf extending from the ivy-covered branch. His heart quickened upon seeing that the branch was little more than three yards away. He continued to pull himself upwards as sweat collected along the palms of his hands. Just then, his spirits were dashed at the sight of the vines twisting across the trunk above him until the white bark ahead was covered by a thick coat of green. He stopped his ascent and looked down at the figures of Ellie and Alex.

"Come down. It's not too late," Ellie wailed.

If it were easy, then it wouldn't be worth it, Clay told himself with a grimace. He grunted, reached out with his right hand, and seized a handful of the vines. He could feel heat scorch his palms. Clay tensed his biceps and pulled himself further up the tree. The pain grew more and more excruciating as he advanced hand over hand, pulling the vines. He struggled to free his legs as the vines encircled them. Kicking them off, he cried out as he forced himself to keep moving farther up. The skin along his abdomen felt raw and his hands, now purple and red, pulsated sharp, stabbing pain. He could see the branch with the white leaf an arm's length away. Reaching out, he attempted to grab hold of the branch. A vine sprung forward and quickly wrapped itself around his wrist. He screamed in pain as the skin was seared beneath it. Focused on the white leaf, he continued to extend the arm until the vine broke away with a snap, leaving a deep, red laceration across the back of his wrist. He nearly fainted at the sight of two bones visible through the jagged cut.

His hand grabbed the branch. He gritted his teeth as he fought to maintain a grip on the branch as his hands became increasingly clumsy due to the swelling. With all the strength he could muster, he pulled himself above the branch, and then allowed his torso to flop down on it. He hugged the massive branch and continued to pull himself across it with jerking movements. The skin along his cheek blistered and cracked. He breathed shallowly through his teeth as he forced himself to ignore the pain and struggled slowly ahead. As his breathing became more labored and his eyelids swelled, he pulled himself the final distance and gripped the branch tightly. He fought to open his eyes and sighed at the image of the white leaf hanging before him like a mystical image. His hands shook uncontrollably as he reached out and clutched the stem of the leaf. With a yank, the stem broke.

So simple looking, he thought and awkwardly slipped the leaf into his shirt pocket. With a groan, he dug his thighs into the branch and began to back up until he reached the trunk again.

The vines had grown even thicker around the trunk and he fought to free himself from their entanglement as he descended. Weakened and overwhelmed by pain, he tried to control his descent, to no avail. He slid erratically towards the ground, breaking through the tentacles of vegetation that sought to encase him. With a thud, he painfully landed upon the root of the tree from which he had climbed. As he slipped off the root, he could see the vines twist wildly above him.

85

Clay struggled to prop up his body with his elbow. His eyelids slowly opened, exposing glassy dark pupils set against an injected sclera. He fought to remain conscious as the world around him swirled in a blur of colors. He reached blindly into the pocket of his shirt.

"My God, Alex," Ellie said. She turned away in horror and fell into Alex's arms. Clay was a puffy mess. His face was raw from where the venomous poison of the vines had made contact, leaving behind pockmarked and torn blisters leaking a bloody ooze down his cheeks and onto his chin.

Alex kneeled at the injured man's feet and sighed at the state before him. "Redmund, what have you done?"

Clay's eyes rolled back in his head as his hand blindly explored the pocket of his shirt. The movement of his fingers were excruciatingly painful and clumsy from the swelling. He removed the leaf. The leaf was diamond shaped and ash-white with raised veins running through it. The top surface was glossy, which contrasted with the dull surface of the back. The stem was torn from where Clay had freed it from the branch. A clear fluid slowly dripped from the frayed tip of the stem and ran along Clay's macerated forearm. Alex looked on with amazement as the sappy fluid left behind a trail of healing. The inflammation affecting the forearm had retreated from the path of the sap, leaving behind a smooth and unbroken layer of skin.

"Your arm…it's being healed."

Clay's head wobbled on his neck as he attempted to look down at his forearm.

The bang of the gunshot startled Alex. A shower of fragments of wood flew through the air as the bullet impacted the far side of the root nearest them.

"Alex!" Ellie screamed and pulled him backwards just as a second bullet whizzed by his head and ricocheted off the ground. As Alex tumbled back against Ellie, he could see Clay's face suddenly contort with pain as the bullet struck him with a thud in his torso. Clay grunted and clutched the leaf even more tightly as a pool of blood began to appear by his flank and spread out along the ground.

"Lea...ffff. Th...th...lea....fff." The voice was guttural and barely recognizable as human. Alex could see beyond the roots of the tree the ghastly form of Solomon staggering forward with uncoordinated movements. His pistol was held loosely in his bear-like paws with the shaft of the gun pointed down at an awkward angle. Alex pulled Ellie forward and maneuvered her behind the root just as Solomon raised the pistol again and unleashed another bullet that impacted just in front of Ellie's feet. She found herself diving forward through a cloud of dust stirred up by the bullet and scampering behind the protective shield of the overgrown root. Alex ducked and weaved as another bullet cut through the air in his direction and created a splash in the water behind him. He slid in beside Ellie, pushed himself close to the root, and peered at the lumbering form of Solomon approaching them.

"He's lost his mind. He's going to kill us all!" Ellie exclaimed, her eyes wide with fear.

Alex's heart raced as he looked back for any possible escape. He was startled to see the spot where Clay had been lying now empty. He followed the trail of blood across the ground towards the water's edge and could see the wounded man slowly pulling himself by his elbows forward. Clay stopped with exhaustion and reached out towards the leather satchel Alex had previously left haphazardly upon the edge of the island.

"He'll shoot us down if we try to run. We'll be an easy target," Alex said as his finger dove into the back pocket of his pants.

Ellie glanced down inquisitively as Alex found the handle of Phillip's switchblade and pulled it free.

"What are you thinking about doing?"

Alex reached out and cupped his hands along both sides of her head and brought her close to him. Their foreheads nearly touched.

"Look, Ellie, promise me when I get up. you will run. If things go horribly wrong, jump into the water and take your chances with the canal. Redmund may be right about it."

"What are you going to do?" she asked apprehensively, fixated on the glistening steel of the opened switchblade.

"Just do it, please," Alex urged. He could see Solomon's legs framed by the cage-like array of roots. He tightened his grip on Ellie's head and kissed her. He could taste the brininess of a tear that had run across her cheek and collected along the folds of her lips.

Before she could protest, Alex sprung up from behind the roots, leaped over the largest one, and lurched forward. Solomon flinched with surprise and wavered on his feet before raising his gun. Before the man could fire, Alex lunged forward, driving the tip of the blade into Solomon's left flank. Solomon winced from the pain and responded by grabbing Alex's wrist. Alex cried out as his skin burned. He fought to free his wrist from the man's grasp. Solomon raised his gun and brought it down hard against the side of Alex's head, sending him staggering backwards. Alex tried to stay on his feet but tripped over a root and tumbled to the ground.

Solomon grimaced as he gripped the handle of the switchblade and pulled it free from his flank. Alex tried to crawl back but ran up against the gnarled roots as they dove into the ground. Solomon took several wobbly steps forward, holding the blade in his hand. With a flick of the wrist he tossed the blade aside, sending it clanging in the distance.

Alex watched as Solomon's eyelids parted. He lifted his gun into the air, and pointed it down at Alex.

"No!" Ellie wailed as she leapt over the roots and charged Solomon. Solomon turned to his left and responded by striking her with his elbow, sending her stumbling to the ground.

Alex wiped away blood from his temple and took advantage of the distraction to groggily push himself onto his knees. His eyes were drawn to the island behind Solomon. He could see that the vines that had been previously limited to encasing the tree had propagated, extending from the surrounding water, and covering the ground in a thick coat of green. The vines twisted upon the soil, inching closer towards them.

Solomon wheezed, looked in the direction of Clay, and leveled the gun at Alex a second time. Alex closed his eyes and braced himself.

The pained scream caused Alex to open his eyes. A series of vines had wrapped themselves around Solomon's ankle. The man tried to pull his leg free but the vines were too strong. He fell to one knee. The vines swarmed up his leg, encircled his waist, and pulled him backwards into a prone position. Solomon cried out as his skin was further seared. The ivy continued to cover his body, running up his neck, embalming him in a wrap of green. Alex looked into Solomon's eyes and could see in them the fear of one who is facing a certain and painful death. He took a final deep breath, inhaling the caustic poison deep into his lungs, burning his airway, before the green second skin wound its way across his head, and sealed him in a deadly cocoon.

86

Clay reached into the satchel. Behind him he could hear the sound of gunshots reverberate through the chamber, followed by the commotion of a struggle. He felt increasingly weak as the blood drained from his side. Inside the satchel, his fingers awkwardly probed the inside until he found what he was seeking. Clay clutched it to his chest and rolled onto his back. A curious clanging noise attracted his attention and he peered back to see an opened switchblade close by. He pulled himself towards the weapon and seized it in his swollen hand. He tried to take a deep breath and focus his thoughts, if for one more crystalline moment.

There is still work to be done.

87

Alex scampered towards Ellie and found her crumpled on the ground, nursing a bloodied lip. He quickly reached out, grabbed her hand, and nervously looked back over his shoulder. The island was alive. The vines wiggled and twisted as they spread out across the ground towards them.

"I'm sorry I wasn't much help," Ellie muttered, momentarily resisting Alex's pulling. She could see a mound of green where Solomon had fallen. Ellie's eyes darted about as the vines surged forward. The animated vegetation wrapped across the earthen bridges and began to climb the walls.

"Alex, the vines..."

"I know. We need to move. We don't have much time. We need to get to Redmund."

They maneuvered through the maze of roots and fled across the island towards Clay, pursued by the ever-advancing vines. Alex and Ellie found the man prostate upon the ground near the water's edge. Alex grabbed Clay's shoulder and turned him over. Clay moaned. His inflamed eyelids slowly opened and stared at them. His arms were tightly wrapped around Polo's book. Blood was smeared across the transparent protective covering. The man's breathing was shallow and labored.

"Where's the leaf?" Ellie asked urgently. She frantically looked back as the vines, winding their way across the roots, rapidly converged on them. "You need to eat it. Redmund, you're going to die if you don't. Where is it?"

Clay dug his elbows into the ground and pushed his torso

up. He attempted to speak but only a raspy grunt was produced. Clay stubbornly shook his head back and forth as froth spewed from his mouth. He looked to his right and saw the advancing toxic vegetation. Clay gripped the book even tighter in his hands before pushing it into Alex's chest. He appeared to be trying to talk once again and Alex leaned in. A guttural sound escaped. "Boo…book." Alex looked down at the book with confusion. Clay pushed him away. "Ggg…go."

Alex could feel Ellie tugging forcefully at the back of his shirt.

"We're in trouble," Ellie cried frantically. They were surrounded on three sides by the vines. She looked over her shoulder and saw a quickly eroding path towards the water. "What should we do?"

Alex turned back to her and held the book against his chest. "We need to get to the water. It's our only chance."

They ran hand in hand as the deadly vegetation rapidly encroached on the pathway to safety. As they neared the water's edge, the vines dashed across the unaffected corridor. Ellie dug her fingernails into Alex's palm as they ran full speed at the barrier of vines that had maneuvered to block their escape.

"Redmund had better been right about this. Jump!" Alex urged.

The two leapt just as the vines overwhelmed the surface of the island beneath them. As they looked down, they could see the water bubble violently beneath them.

88

The water churned as they plunged into it. Alex clung uneasily to the book as he fought his way through the rough surface. He could see Ellie bobbing up and down as she attempted to keep her head above the surface of the water. As the chamber continued to darken, the water periodically assumed a vivid green hue. Alex tried to swim towards Ellie but found his strokes limited by his hold upon the book. He began to slowly drift away from her.

"There's a current!" Alex shouted above the rush of water.

"Something's pulling me down!" Ellie gurgled after swallowing a mouth-full of the warm water.

"We need to stay together."

"I'm trying!" Ellie wailed and frantically tried to swim towards Alex. She suddenly began to swirl around as if caught in a vortex. Ellie battled to keep her head above the chop but an unseen force yanked her down like an ant fighting the suction of a drain. "Alex!" she cried out before vanishing beneath the surface.

"Ellie!"

Alex tried to fight his way to the spot where Ellie had submerged. He labored, casting stroke after stroke through the water with his right hand while holding the book tightly to his chest with his left hand. Despite expending considerable energy, he was dismayed to find that he had not moved a significant distance. *Ellie!* Alex looked down at the book sealed within its protective covering and released it. It rose to the surface and bobbed behind him. He dove into the water and swam with unfettered strokes towards the location from which Ellie had disappeared.

As he neared the spot, Alex felt a powerful pull grasp his lower body. He struggled to maintain control but found himself spinning wildly. He was pulled underwater for a moment but fought to resurface. Alex tried to tread water as the waves crashed into his face. He peered down into the green water, hoping he could see Ellie. He could feel a sense of hopelessness overwhelm him. Alex dove down into the water and was immediately gripped by an undertow that spun him around and sent him hurtling backwards under the water in a circular motion. His eyes opened wide underwater as he struggled to hold his breath. He could see the shadowy form of one of the earthen bridges pass overhead as he rapidly catapulted within the whirlpool. Alex tumbled uncontrollably head over heels within the strong current. As he twisted his body he could see the source of the intense green light pulsating under water. A volcanic crater seemed to stretch infinitely under the surface as if it arose from the center of the earth itself. Green light and bubbles periodically erupted from the conical opening of the massive structure. He could feel the pull towards the center lessen. The tree's roots and vines crisscrossed through the water like a net around the structure, ultimately clinging to its side and disappearing into the dark depths of the water. As Alex rounded the formation, he realized that he was being driven towards it as he was caught within the centripetal force of the whirlpool. He struggled to release himself from the pull, but was helpless. Air escaped from his nose and he watched with alarm as the bubbles shot up to the surface. His lung's burned and his vision began to dim.

Just as Alex was losing consciousness, his movement was suddenly halted and he was pulled up. As he broke though the surface of the water, Alex coughed uncontrollably. Frothy water shot from his nose. Ellie held his shirt tightly as she clung desperately to a tree root. She helped Alex gain a grasp of the root.

Alex limply wrapped his arm around the root as the waves pummeled his face. He struggled to maintain a grip.

"I don't know how much longer I can hold," Ellie groaned, her voice raspy and pained.

"We have to get free of this whirlpool," Alex yelled over the roar of the water. "We need to get to one of those canals." He looked back and could see an arched opening in one of the far walls.

"The pull is too strong," Ellie responded, overwhelmed by a coughing fit brought on by swallowing a mouthful of water.

"There's something under the water..." Alex said.

"I saw it for a moment," Ellie interjected, her face flush from coughing. Another pulsation of green light was released from beneath the water. Ellie's face assumed the green color until it faded.

"I think it is producing the pull. It periodically gives off that green light and when it does it seems that the suction it is producing is momentarily relieved. It may give us time to get far enough away from it."

"I can feel it," Ellie added as she sensed the whirlpool weaken just as another beam of green light was released.

"I think if we can time it just right we could get free of it. Do you have a watch?"

Ellie motioned to the wrist of her hand clutching the root.

"Thank God I got the waterproof one." Ellie tried to smile but found her jaw uncomfortably stiff.

Alex peered at the watch and waited until the next episode in which the green light was emitted. When it finally came, he did his best to concentrate on the second hand as the waves crashed around him. After several minutes, he turned to Ellie.

"It seems regular. It comes every 90 seconds or so. The light lasts for twelve seconds. Every six minutes it seems that the light lasts for about twenty-four seconds. I vote for holding on to this root until we can take advantage of the six-minute cycle. It will give us our best chance."

Ellie cast Alex a skeptical look. "I don't doubt your mathematics but do you really think we could swim far enough away in twenty-four seconds before we are sucked back?"

"I don't know. But I think we should go before the six-minute mark and take advantage of the current before breaking free."

"Like a sling-shot?" She smiled at Alex. "Alex Stone, I would have never in my wildest dreams have pegged you as a physicist. I'm proud of you."

"Let's wait to see if it actually works before you start congratulating me." He looked back at her watch. "Now, we need to make sure that we can identify the six-minute mark."

Alex clung to the root as he counted the releases of the green light. He counted aloud the length of each episode, identifying the ones that lasted twelve seconds and those that last twenty-four seconds. Satisfied that he had done so, they waited as a new cycle started.

Alex floated face to face with Ellie and tried to give her a reassuring smile. The water glowed green. Staring at each other in silence, they bobbed up and down as the water rushed by them.

"Are you ready? The next one is in ninety seconds. This one should last twenty-four seconds. The way I figure it is if we leave ten seconds early we could get a boost from the current."

Ellie nodded silently and looked towards the far wall. Alex concentrated on her watch.

"That's thirty seconds…" Alex muttered.

Ellie could see an object being tossed back and forth behind Alex's back. She strained to see what it was.

"Ellie, hold still," Alex protested. "I need to see your watch." Ellie bit her lip and tried to keep her arm still. "…ok that's sixty seconds. We are letting go in twenty seconds. We need to swim like hell towards the wall."

Ellie could see Marco Polo's book emerge from the chop and begin to rapidly float their way.

"Alex, Polo's book!"

Alex remained focused on Ellie's watch and did not look back. "Forget about the book."

Ellie extended her arm out and watched helplessly as the book was just out of her reach. Straining even further, her fingertips just brushed the binding. Ellie released her grip on the root.

"Ellie, it's too early!" Alex wailed.

Ellie was immediately ripped from the root. She was able to grab hold of the book but was whipped around the island.

Alex looked on helplessly as she was dragged away.

"Oh great!" Alex pushed off from the root and followed Ellie as she spun uncontrollably in the water passing beneath an earthen bridge. He could feel the downward pull and frantically splashed to remain afloat.

"Try swimming towards the wall!" Alex urged as he attempted to break free of the whirlpool.

Suddenly the room was filled once again with the luminous green light. They could feel the downward and centripetal tug lessen. Alex floated into Ellie and grabbed the book from her hand. With all his might, he threw it as far as he could towards the far wall.

"Swim!" he screamed.

Alex and Ellie cut through the water with powerful strokes, taking advantage of the relatively placidity of the water. Alex counted in his head, frustrated by the precious seconds lost by Ellie's rash action. "...fifteen...sixteen...seventeen..."

"Keep going!" Alex spat out between strokes, his voice barely audible over the splashes.

"...nineteen...twenty..."

Ellie's heart raced and her arms burned as the lactic acid built up within her muscles.

"...twenty-two...twenty-three..."

Alex stretched as far as he could for the final stoke, propelling himself towards the far wall.

"…twenty-four…"

The room dimmed again as the green light subsided. Alex and Ellie could feel a gentle pull at their feet as they continued to swim towards the far wall. As they neared the wall, the water became considerably more still. They could see Polo's book bobbing up and down in the water. Alex doggy-paddled to the book, reached out, and retrieved it. He began to tread water as his heart pounded ferociously in his chest. Ellie panted beside him.

"Congratulations," was the only thing Ellie could spit out as she struggled desperately to catch her breath.

Alex looked at the arched opening in the wall in front of them. The archway was simple and unadorned, naturally carved out of the stone wall. Peering into the underground canal, all he could see was blackness.

As they neared the opening, they could feel the current of the water funneling into the canal. Alex gripped the book even tighter and looked at Ellie with surprise.

"Not again," Alex moaned as they were driven rapidly towards the tunnel.

Ellie reached up in a futile attempt to halt their progress by grabbing hold of the stone archway. She found the surface to be smooth and wet as her hands slipped off.

Alex looked uneasily into the darkness as they were swept into the underground waterway.

Clay lay on his back and crossed his arms over his chest. His body felt lighter now that the burden had been finally removed. He opened his eyes and could see the magical tree loom high above him. The vines had climbed high up the gem-encrusted walls of the chamber and were moving rapidly across the blue dome. The vast cavity progressively darkened as the reflective crystals were covered beneath the abundant vegetation.

It's being reclaimed, Clay thought and closed his eyes once again. *The impurities are being purged.*

He could feel an intense burning flaring up along his ankles and spreading like a molten rod towards his knees. He grimaced as the vines wound their way up his body, and across his neck, cinching tightly around it. The chamber continued to dim. Clay gasped for air and fought an overwhelming impulse to panic. He controlled his breathing, forcing himself to take smaller tidal volumes. He opened his eyes just as the vines began to wind their way across his nose.

The chamber had been finally plunged into darkness. A green light shot up from the center of the island, basking the tree in an otherworldly glow. Just then he watched as the vines began to retreat slowly from the tree. As they pulled back, he witnessed sparkling buds appear all along the branches. Clay watched as at an impossibly fast pace the luminous buds cracked opened and sent out shoots. The shoots opened to reveal diamond-shaped leaves.

Not death. Rebirth.

Clay closed his eyes a final time with a smile as the vines enclosed his head.

Alex clung to Ellie as they passed under the archway into the blackness of the canal. Although the current was strong, it was relatively free of significant eddy currents and turbulence. The two floated straight ahead, able to keep their heads above the surface with relative ease.

The sensation of floating in the darkness was unsettling and disembodying. They reached out blindly in hopes of seizing a fixed object to both halt their movement and to ground themselves to the earth again. The temperature of both the water and the ambient air had dropped precipitously since leaving the large chamber, and Ellie's teeth began to chatter uncontrollably.

"I'm frrrr…eezing," she complained.

"We're in some kind of underground river," Alex said as his eyes slowly adjusted to the darkness. He tried to focus on a flickering object in the distance.

"There's a light. Maybe it's a way out," Alex motioned in front of them.

As they continued to float along with the current, they could see that the light was produced by a number of luminescent stalactites that appeared to drip down from the ceiling of the tunnel. The rock formations were made of frosted and variably colored mineral deposits that gave forth a brilliant palate of colors. Pink, blue, and yellow hues reflected off the surface of the water.

"They're so beautiful," Ellie uttered and reached up to touch the irregular tip of one of the stalactites. The rock formation was slimy and left a blue residue on her fingers.

The pastel light produced by the mineral deposits helped define the interior of the tunnel further. They were in a moderately large subterranean cave filled nearly halfway up with water. The tunnel's walls appeared shiny and black like obsidian.

Alex propelled his body towards the wall and ran his hand across it, finding the surface completely smooth and devoid of any imperfection that would allow him to secure a grip. As he continued to float alongside the wall, the black stone appeared to absorb the pastel colors produced by the stalactites, swirling and mixing stunningly beneath the surface.

"Alex, look."

Alex turned to see that the underground canal was emptying into a vast chamber that was cistern-like. The stalactites that appeared to drop down from the ceiling high above were accompanied by enormous stalagmites emerging from the depths of the water. Several of these rock formations joined each other to form wondrous, multicolored columns dividing the expansive body of water. The walls were rich in mineral deposits that appeared to drip down like ghostly wax.

The water beneath them glowed a vibrant mixture of oranges, reds, blues, and greens as they continued to float along with the gentle current. Alex could see that the colors were from coral that was coating irregular shaped rocks at the bottom of the body of water. He could see tiny ethereal fish swim by, their flesh transparent and eyes opaque.

"What is this place?" Ellie asked, her jaw agape.

"It's magical," Alex replied as he was able to grab hold of one of the columns. Ellie floated beside him and was also able to secure a grip on the large column.

Ellie shivered as she looked down into the crystal clear water at the astonishing symphony of colors that filled the underwater world beneath their feet. She panned her eyes across the magnificent mineral deposits and rock formations that formed this natural cathedral. She smiled at the realization that the source of the shiver was not a sensation of coldness but a feeling of profound humility in the face of something larger than her life. She felt humbled and blessed.

"I wonder how many…if anybody has seen this." Ellie laughed as a rainbow colored fish darted across her stomach.

"Gazriin ezen," Alex responded.

"What's that?"

"It's what the guide mentioned. Nature spirits…life force. There is an energy here. Do you feel it?"

Ellie cleared her mind. She felt her skin tingle and the center of her body pulsate warmth. "I feel something. I mean I'm skeptical of all that kumbayah stuff. I'm the first person to stick my nose up at those people buying healing crystals and magnets with powers, but it makes you think. We've built up such elaborate systems to explain the mysteries of the world. We take communion; kneel six times a day after call to prayer; read through the Torah—all things that help us figure out where we came from, who we are, and where we are going. Then you find yourself in this place one day. It's a world untouched by man. Wars happened, people were born and died, prophets came and went, and this existed, isolated all that time. If the scientists are right and we crawled out of some primordial ooze, then maybe this is it. It's as good as any. This place, the rocks, the water, the tree, all seem as alive as us. I feel like I am beginning to appreciate what the guide meant about the spirits in nature."

"Gee, Ellie, if I didn't know any better, I'd say you've finally found religion." Alex grinned at her and then peered up at the ceiling. "It does make you think," Alex muttered distractedly.

Ellie gave him a sideways glance and squinted. "What's that?"

"I was thinking about what you said about languages and their roots in pre-existing cultures."

"Huh?"

"Gazriin ezen…Ezen….Eden." The two were silent as they

listened to the water lap against the column. "It's probably just a coincidence," Alex said and looked away. He could see the flow of the water traveling towards a tunnel at the opposite side from which they had entered. Alex looked back at Ellie and smiled. "What do you say we see if we can return to the rest of the cursed civilization of mankind?"

Ellie looked apprehensively at the narrow tunnel. "Well, we can't stay here forever, I suppose."

91

*Releasing their hold upon the stone column, the current propelled them to-*wards a small opening in the wall at the far end of the chamber. Alex took several strokes and arrived at the side of the passage. Holding the rough stone surface tightly, he could feel his feet float towards the entrance. He reached out and linked arms with Ellie while maintaining a grip on the Polo book. He tried to look into the opening but found it completely black.

"What do you think?" Ellie asked, her face taut and stiff from the cold.

"It's hard to say. The current seems to be emptying into this opening. I think we've committed ourselves to seeing this to the end. I'm not sure if there is much choice."

"Well I guess we should get a move on then," Ellie replied and separated from Alex. She was quickly propelled into the tight opening. Alex followed closely behind.

The passageway was completely dark. As the two reached out, they could feel that the wall and ceiling were within arm's length. They could detect a smooth stone surface beneath them that had been polished by eons of water rushing over it.

Ellie's hand extended back and found Alex's.

"I think we're in some type of tube," she said, hearing her voice echo repeatedly. Ellie could detect a subtle change in the angle of inclination as they slid along. Their speed began to gradually increase as the passageway sloped downward. They continued to descend in the darkness until the canal appeared to plateau and they were left floating serenely for several minutes.

The drop was unexpected in the darkness. The passageway suddenly sloped at an acute angle and they were sent sliding uncontrollably down at a rapid pace. Ellie's hold on Alex was broken as they shot down through the tube, finally splashing at the bottom.

Ellie coughed and spat out ingested water as she tried to gain her bearings. The passage remained utterly dark, heightening her uncertainty and fear.

"You alright?" Alex asked from somewhere behind her.

"I think," Ellie rubbed her head. During the tumble she had struck it on something and was left with a dull ache along the right side of her temple.

Ellie kicked out her feet but could not detect a bottom to the water-filled chamber. She panicked at the realization that the level of water reached high towards the ceiling. Ellie treaded water and reached up, running her fingers along the stone ceiling.

"We're running out of air," she moaned as she struggled to keep her mouth above the surface. She could feel Alex fighting to do the same. As the rush of the water continued to push them along, they began to hear a deafening noise. A monstrous roar filled the canal.

"What's that?" Ellie asked with alarm.

"That can't be good," Alex responded as the rush of the water suddenly seized them. They found themselves unexpectedly submerged in the black water. Tumbling head over heels, they were bombarded by turbulent waves. Kicking wildly, the two were disoriented as they attempted to swim towards the surface. The roar above was dulled underwater. Alex grabbed hold of Ellie's shirt, allowed himself to float for an instant, and then darted upward. They broke through the surface of the water, gasping for air. The two were met once again by a bone-shaking roar. They were whisked through the water, bouncing up and down as the rapids grabbed hold of them. Unable to see, they were sent crashing into submerged rocks. Ellie and Alex grunted in pain with each impact against the boulders, trying their best to shield their heads. Alex cried out in pain as the side of his chest struck something hard. Hearing ribs crack, he winced, nearly releasing the book.

The thunderous and continuous sound continued to grow louder as they were tossed about uncontrollably.

"What is that noise?" Ellie cried out as she tried to keep her head afloat while nursing a bruise along her hip.

Fear shot through Alex.

"We need to swim back," Alex screamed and fruitlessly attempted several strokes. The full force of the rapids spun him around. He stared into the darkness ahead with horror as water sprayed across his face. "It's a waterf...."

Alex was the first to go over the waterfall. He could feel his stomach drop as he fell feet first into the watery abyss. The plunge seemed endless, punctuated by Ellie's screams. The impact upon the surface below was unforgiving and devastating. A piercing screech echoed in his ears as he sluggishly tried to free himself from a watery grave. Water pounded upon him like seismic waves, hitting his head with concussive blows. He reached up helplessly as his body seemed to float in slow motion. His lungs burned as they begged for air. As he neared the surface he gasped deeply but was greeted only by more water.

92

Alex stirred to the sensation of movement. He slowly opened his eyes and could see mud and grass. He twisted his face and was left with a glob of brown mud clinging to his chin and cheek. Alex coughed and cried out as a searing pain shot through his chest. The coughing led to vomiting of water. He could feel himself being lifted roughly by the back of his shirt and he moaned as the broken ribs rubbed back and forth against each other. Alex's lower body felt heavy and disconcertedly disconnected. He was chilled to the point of numbness.

As he was lifted up, the images came in flashes—grass along the ground, rocks, boots walking—as he waxed in and out of consciousness. Above him, he could hear people speaking in a foreign tongue. His eyes rolled back in his head as he was tossed onto the ground.

He awoke to a person slapping his cheek. His eyelids parted just enough to see an Asian man squatting in front of him with a cigarette dangling loosely out of the side of his mouth. Alex could see the strap of an AK-47 slung across his chest. The man was gaunt, unshaven, and coated in dirt. He stared at Alex with a mixture of amusement and curiosity.

"Hello, hello," the man said through pursed lips as he tried to keep the cigarette from falling out. Alex's head bobbed up and down as he vacillated between consciousness and unconsciousness. The man reached out and gripped Alex's hair, forcing his head upright. With his other hand he drew Alex's eyelids open. Alex's eyes rolled back and forth, unable to focus. The man tried to catch Alex's attention.

"You lucky man…or unlucky." The man cackled and took a drag of his cigarette. "We see."

The man reached back and displayed a black hood. He propped Alex up and placed it over his head.

The world went dark once again.

The light was blinding as the hood was removed. Alex scrunched his eyelids closed. He moaned as his hands immediately went to the site of his broken ribs. Slowly he forced his eyelids open as the beams of light shot through his eyeballs like daggers. He found himself in a fetal position. As he tried to straighten out his stiffened frame, his body screamed in protest. His heart leapt upon seeing Ellie also curled up in a ball on the ground across from him. She groaned as she attempted to push her body up.

"Alex," she whispered upon seeing him. Her face was bruised and battered from the rapids. Her lips were dusky and cracked. A large cut ran down the center of her lower lip and was covered by dried blood. Her blond hair was matted and damp with dirt and leaves twisted into it.

"Are you OK?" Alex asked. His voice was raspy and barely audible.

"I don't know," she croaked.

Alex grimaced as he pushed his torso up by his elbows. He looked around at their surroundings.

They were in a circular tent with a wooden lattice-frame covered with felt. The interior was sparsely decorated with a small wooden table in the center and a single chair behind it.

"Where are we?" Ellie asked.

Behind them, the front of the yurt was suddenly pulled aside.

They turned to see three Mongolian men walk in. In the center was an older man dressed in loose-fitting pants and a flannel-shirt. He was holding Marco Polo's book. Beside him walked two younger men holding AK-47s loosely at their sides. Alex and Ellie scampered back at the sight of the guns. The two armed men barely looked at Alex and Ellie before tossing wool blankets at each of them. Alex and Ellie caught the blankets and looked down at them with confusion.

The older man motioned to Alex and Ellie.

"Please. The blankets…you must be freezing," the man said in mildly accented English. Alex and Ellie snuggly wrapped the blankets around their body and sat upright.

Two short women stealthily entered the tent carrying steaming pots. They wordlessly knelt by Alex and Ellie and deposited the containers beside them before retreating to the opening of the tent and disappearing.

"Eat. Please. You must be hungry," said the man and motioned with his fingers to his mouth.

The older man uttered something in Mongolian to the two armed men who nodded, marched out of the tent, and sealed the entrance.

Alex and Ellie peered down into the bowls to see a turbid brown stew with circles of opaque fat collecting at the surface of the liquid. Steam wafted up through the air. Ellie leaned in and sniffed it tentatively, finding it pungent. She felt unbearably weak from hunger and reached out to grip a metal spoon leaning on the lip of the bowl. The muscles in her arms were fatigued and burned with even the subtlest movement. Ellie apprehensively stirred the contents within the bowl finding unidentifiable root vegetables, bone, and gray meat within. Ellie looked across at Alex who shrugged and brought the spoon to his mouth. Ellie followed suit. She scooped a small amount of the greasy liquid, brought it to her mouth, blew on it, and finally swallowed. The stew had the flavor of boiled meat desperately in need of salt. The warm fluid, however, did wonders restoring heat to her body's frigid core. With each mouthful of the mystery meal, she could feel her strength returning.

The old man looked at each one of them, cleared his throat, and sat down behind the simple, wooden table. He turned the dial on an oil lamp, filling the small room with a rich yellow light. He pulled out a pair of spectacles from a pocket of his shirt, huffed on the glass, and rubbed them with the sleeve of his shirt. The man unfolded the glasses and slid them along the bridge of his nose. He cleared his throat for a second time, positioned the book on the table before him, and opened it.

The man studied the book like a scholar, in silence. A smile periodically spread across his face. Satisfied, the man flipped the book closed, pushed it slightly forward on the table, and leaned back with his arms crossed tightly across his chest.

"They said that they found you along the river bank clutching this book like it was a baby....or a treasure," the man said and pointed towards Alex. He smiled.

Riverbank, Alex thought and tried to recall the events that brought him to this tent. He could remember the tremendous roar of the waterfall, a wall of mist, and a free-fall that seemed to last forever. Then the world went blank. *How did we end up here?* he wondered.

"You are both a long way from home, Alexander Stone and Eleanor Griffin."

Ellie cast Alex a look of surprise.

"Don't be so shocked. We know all about you two. We've been following your adventure for some time—following it with interest and concern. A fair number of my men were lost trying to prevent your party from achieving your goal."

"You're Darkhad?" Alex asked despondently. His heart sank upon realizing the company in which they found themselves. *We're doomed*, Alex thought.

"Yes. We are the protectors of the legacy of Genghis Khan and much more. You see, this land you have treaded upon is sacred. It has been since the beginning of time—before mankind crawled upon the surface. It was something the great Khan realized and embraced. He left us with the task of preserving this. Everything that man has and is was given to him by the earth and the spirits that inhabit it."

"Why not share it with the rest of the world?" Ellie asked.

"Genghis Khan was a warrior-king. He knew the necessities of war and violence because at heart he knew the depravity of man. He saw it first-hand around him and bristled at the notion that man could ever be trusted with something so pure, so fragile. It would be destroyed and the magic lost forever. It is a life-force that gave birth to us and may restore us once again when the time is right. And for that we are blessed and should be thankful."

"So you intend to keep it hidden?" Ellie countered.

"Mankind is not ready for the true power that lies at the heart of Burkhan Kaldun. One day, perhaps. And besides, your companions have done quite a lot to insure this by sealing the one entrance."

"They were not our companions," Alex replied earnestly.

The old man nodded and pulled Polo's book back along the table. He opened the text again and proceeded to flip through the pages once again. The man raised the book by its spine, let the pages fan out, and shook it. He subsequently snapped it shut with a thud, looked down at it, and handed it to Alex.

Alex rose to his feet and accepted the book with a look of sheer befuddlement.

"When you leave this tent, travel through the pines at the edge of the steppes. You will come to a river. Follow the riverbank south for five kilometers and you will find a small town. From this town you will be able to leave this place and return to your homes."

Alex looked across at Ellie who stared back at him in disbelief. *That's it?* he wondered to himself.

"Why are you doing this?" Alex asked.

"Although there are some in my tribe who seethe with anger and would like nothing more than revenge for the loss of their comrades and your trespassing on holy ground, I do not believe that your intentions were with malice."

"But we've seen it…I mean, we know the location. What would prevent us from returning with a larger team and excavating machines," Ellie blurted out, immediately regretting opening her mouth. What was she saying? *Just shut up and leave like the man offered*, she thought and reprimanded herself for her stupidity.

The old man laughed. "The fact that you would ask that tells all. True, such knowledge is dangerous. I believe that you have the sense and understanding that it is necessary to leave such a place undisturbed. And take heed, we Darkhad are always vigilant…always. Do not test us. And be sure that we will follow your careers closely."

"The book?" Alex added.

"Ah yes, the book…Marco Polo's original manuscript. Why would I allow it to ever leave this place? Why would I not toss it straight into the fire and be done with it once and for all? Why take the chance that some bright academic like you might connect the dots and decipher the fourth book encoded within its pages?

"Let me tell you a final tale before you go." The man stiffened his posture in his chair. Ellie looked at the old man and found him strangely professorial.

"There once was a man named Qaidu who was born in the Hentiyn Nuruu—the Kentei Mountains—to the howl of the Blue-Gray Wolf. Genghis Khan had passed from this world and the Mongol empire was in the midst of a power vacuum that was ultimately filled by Kublai Khan. Qaidu was a simple man who led a relatively prosaic early life until he began to suffer from frequent and debilitating spells that would leave him incapacitated for periods of time. You see, Qaidu was Darkhad and he was proud of being a member of this tribe that was entrusted to care for the legacy of Genghis Kahn. But, as his illness became more noticeable, members of his family and tribe began to believe that he was possessed by evil spirits. A shaman even portended that he would bring down destruction on the Darkhad. As a result, poor Qaidu, was ostracized from the people he had grown up with and forced to live a life of loneliness.

"So it was that one fateful day while hunting alone in the woods of the Kentei Mountains, Qaidu suddenly saw flashes of lights shoot across the sky like falling stars. These brilliant colors mixed and merged until they consumed his sight and left him stricken dumb upon the forest floor. He lay unconscious on the cold earth for some time before the fog that had clouded his mind lifted, leaving him exhausted and spent. When he finally reopened his eyes, he was surprised to find himself beside a raging fire in the middle of the woods. He looked at his surroundings and nearly jumped at the site of a bloodied carcass of a wolf with an arrow sticking out of its hide beside him. There was a majestic horse tied to a nearby tree. Beside the fire sat a man wearing a patchwork fur coat and his face hidden in the shadows of a hood.

"Startled, Qaidu demanded to know who this man was. The stranger beside the fire removed his hood and looked at Qaidu.

"'I'm the man who saved your life,' the stranger answered in perfect Mongolian. Qaidu was astonished to see that the stranger was a white man. 'I see that you are finally up.'

"'Am I dead?' Qaidu asked the apparition as he looked down upon the carcass of the wolf a second time.

"The man smiled and said,"Not unless I am, too. You had a spell and I have watched over you until you returned to this world. It is dangerous to hunt alone out here.'

"'You are alone,' Qaidu pointed out.

"'That is true,' the stranger agreed. 'I am on a mission and I'm never truly alone with this...' The man opened his coat to reveal the golden piazza of Kublai Khan hanging from around his neck. 'It is heavy but it is worth the weight.'

"'Piazza.' Qaidu had heard of such things. He stared at the stranger. 'I have seen you before. I have seen you in my visions. You have come from far away. You will take me away from this place'

"'I am Marco Polo. I have come from far away.'

"Polo explained to Qaidu that the Christian Apostle, Paul, had also suffered from spells. He told how Paul had a vision on the road to Damascus of a resurrected Jesus. Polo explained how Jesus had died for mankind's sins and how Paul was not initially a believer in Jesus until he was struck by his vision.

"'Are you Jesus?' Qaidu asked.

"Polo laughed. 'No, I'm simply a man. No more, no less.'

"Polo explained to Qaidu that he was on a journey to discover a land called Eden where there existed a magical garden, which had a tree providing immortality. He had searched far and wide through the vast lands of the Khanate in hopes of finding this place but had only come across vague rumors and whispers of its existence. His voyage had led him to the base of the Kentei Mountains but no further. He was lost. Qaidu listened quietly as the mysterious foreigner wove his tale of wonder.

"Qaidu was a conflicted soul. He felt loyalty to his tribe but felt indebted to this strange white man who had saved his life and protected him in his time of need while the Darkhad had abandoned him. But above all, he had seen this man in visions when the world would go black and he knew that his life was leading to this day. Qaidu made the fateful decision to reveal to the stranger that he knew where this Garden could be found.

"In the light of a half moon and to the howl of the wolves, the two ascended Burkhan Khaldum and entered the secret passage.

Qaidu never spoke of what happened as they approached to gates of paradise. As the two traveled down the mountainside, Qaidu realized that his life now, for better or worse, was inextricably linked to that of Marco Polo. So it was that when Polo fled the Khanate, Qaidu joined him and had adventures of his own in the Western World."

"Qaidu is Peter? Peter…Marco Polo's 'slave.' The one from his will!" Ellie exclaimed.

The old man nodded. "Qaidu was hardly a slave in Polo's eyes, but a friend. In Venice, how else could you describe this Mongolian man? Qaidu, now Peter, remained a conflicted soul, not unlike Marco Polo. He was untethered. As Polo had become increasingly Easternized through the years, Qaidu became increasingly Westernized. What is that saying that is so popular in the West? They were ships passing each other in the night.

"As Qaidu aged, the spells became less frequent and he settled into his life in Venice. Qaidu watched as Polo crafted his manuscript with Rustichello and imbedded the contents of the fourth book within the text. Before Marco Polo died, he summoned his friend to his bedside and asked him to keep the book safe to ensure that there will be a path back to paradise. After Marco Polo died, Qaidu ultimately left Venice and returned to his homeland. He eventually married and was able to reintegrate into the Darkhad. His wife gave birth to many children who passed on Qaidu's secret of betrayal and his promise to Polo to keep the book safe. It is a burden that I hold tightly to my heart."

"You're a descendant of Qaidu…of Peter, aren't you?" Alex asked incredulously.

The old man nodded. "The final descendent of Qaidu…the bearer of many secrets." The man grew silent and rose from his chair. He paced around the room and stopped suddenly with his back to Ellie and Alex. "There is one thing more. You asked me why I am giving you this book. Several years ago, I too began to be overtaken by spells. At first it was just short episodes of muddling of my mind. I would stare into space blinking for no reason, no reason at all. Then the spells became longer. Later they started with flashes of color, loss of consciousness, and…visions. I cannot explain it any better but to say that *I need to give you this book*. I know this because I feel that I have seen this before. Now I know how Qaidu felt upon seeing Marco Polo in the forest. In my visions, we are here in this tent and I give you this book. You leave and I feel at peace with my decision. I don't know how better to explain it. I don't know what purpose this book will serve, but this is my decision."

Ellie looked at Alex and shrugged.

"Go," said the man without turning.

Alex motioned to the entrance of the tent. Ellie leaned into him and whispered. "What do we do?"

Alex clutched the book to his chest. "Let's go," he whispered back.

The two slipped through the opening in the tent and were blinded by the sunlight. The two guards watched them as they staggered forward. Alex pointed to pine trees in the distance. They began their long walk.

Alex stared at the exposed radiator and listened as it wheezed and popped. He reflexively rubbed his hand alongside the right side of his chest. He could still feel a twinge of ripping pain with each deep breath and felt strangely relieved by the sensation—it was a reminder that all that had happened was not a thing of dreams. Once again squirreled away in his miniscule office buried within the basement of the Metropolitan Museum of Arts, Alex felt increasingly disconnected with the events that had occurred over a month ago. He looked down at the newspaper folded in half on his lap. Clay Pharmaceutical stocks had plummeted on the news that Redmund Clay remained missing.

The ring of the phone startled Alex. He searched under journals splayed out on his workbench and was finally able to locate the receiver.

"Hello."

"Alex, is that you? Finally." Dr. Graham sounded exasperated. "Where have you been? Things have been crazy here. I had to cancel the lecture on the Black Death. You haven't touched the material I left for you on my desk. This is very unlike you, Alex. Frankly, I expect more from you. You came to me with impeccable recommendations and now this. How's the Crucifix Exhibit progressing?"

"Dr. Graham, I'm going to have to get back to you on that one. I'm a bit tied up for the moment. I need to go." Alex listened for a moment and relished the sound of stunned silence before Graham blurted out, "Wait! Wait!" Alex smiled and hung up the receiver.

The door to the office made a grating sound as it was pushed open. Ellie popped her head in. The bruising along her cheekbone had faded and she looked stunningly beautiful again.

"Hey you." She wiggled her way into the room and leaned over to kiss Alex. He clung to her for a while. "Well, I've had discussions with several museums and institutes and I'm convinced we will find a good home for Marco Polo's original manuscript. I've made it a prerequisite that the collection be named after Bernardo."

Alex peered at his desk and could see the book sitting upon it.

"Well, we did lose the box with the diamonds, Polo's last will, and the piece of Fra Mauro's map that Phillip cut out," Alex responded. "I suppose we owe it to posterity to see that at least one historical artifact is preserved."

"We did the best we could under the circumstances. Hell, we're lucky we got out alive." Ellie glanced down at the folded newspaper and frowned. "You know, Alex, this will open a lot of doors for you. Actually, both of us. The world of academia is wide open to you with our discovery of the Polo's original manuscript. You can finally say, 'Screw you, Graham.' I know you've been dying to all this time. You could pick where you want to go. I'm voting for somewhere in New York City, not too far away from me." Ellie smiled mischievously. She paused upon seeing a look of pain across Alex's face. "What is it?"

"I keep seeing Redmund's face as he pushed the book into me. It's haunting. Everything went wrong so fast. I just don't understand why he didn't try to eat the leaf."

Ellie rubbed Alex's shoulder. "I don't think we'll ever know for certain. I do know that he was acutely aware at how much the book meant to you."

Alex leaned back and sighed. He twirled around in his chair

and stretched his neck backwards. He felt completely exhausted and closed his eyes. He had not slept well since their return to New York. *How could he?* Alex asked himself. He could not stop replaying the events of that day. Alex slowly opened his eyes and could see the top of the book. He followed the binding of the text and froze.

Alex sprung out of his chair and seized the book. Ellie jumped back and watched as he frantically flipped opened the book to the blank cover page. His fingers explored the edges of the parchment glued to the back of the leather cover. At the top of the parchment was a nearly imperceptible slit.

"Look at this," Alex mumbled under his breath.

He gripped the cover and pinched his fingers allowing the parchment to pucker slightly. The slit opened, exposing a gap between the parchment and the leather cover. He maneuvered the opening into the light and shook his head.

"Ellie, hand me those tweezers."

His hand shook as he slid the tips of the tweezers through the opening and secured the object. With the tweezers delicately clasped around the object, he slid it onto the surface of his desk and took a step back.

The white leaf was luminous.

"My God, Alex. He did it." Ellie could feel her eyes well up with tears.

"He knew that we would have made him eat the leaf. This was the only way he thought that the leaf could have any chance of reaching the rest of the world," Alex added.

They stood in silence staring at the leaf until Ellie finally asked, "What do we do with it?"

Alex looked at Ellie and then down at the newspaper article.

"I think we should do what Redmund would have wanted us to do."

Ellie's hand found Alex's and squeezed it tight.

EPILOGUE

Dr. Carol Fife placed her thumb upon the biometric fingerprint reader and waited impatiently as the glass door clicked and slid aside. She rushed through the opening as she struggled to get her left arm through the sleeve of her starched, white lab coat. Dr. Fife nodded to the security guard stationed behind the closed-circuit monitor and continued down the long dimly-lit hallway. She could see Anne, one of her laboratory technicians, waiting by the door to her lab clutching a clipboard tightly to her chest.

"Did you check it?" Dr. Fife tersely inquired as she whizzed by the technician into the enormous lab.

"Yes, Dr. Fife. Multiple times. The data is reproducible," the technician responded and tried to keep up. "It's amazing. It's like a miracle."

Dr. Fife looked back at the young girl and snickered. "There's nothing miraculous about science." She had been a researcher long enough that her wildly unkempt research hair had turned from a dull brown to a shock of gray. She had been here before, confronted by the promise of a breakthrough in her field, ultimately to be let down. Such was the life of a researcher. It was a life she had devoted over fifty years to. *Science can be a bitch*, she thought.

Dr. Fife rummaged through the pile of data forming an unstable tower upon her workbench and found her glasses. She snatched the clipboard from Anne and studied the numbers spat out by the computer.

"This can't be," she muttered.

"It's what I thought," replied Anne. "That's why I ran the study again…and again. Dr. Fife, the results were identical."

"I need to see…see for myself," mumbled Dr. Fife as she stood up and walked in a trance over to the door at the far end of the laboratory. Dr. Fife threw off her lab coat and hung it on a peg beside the door. She slipped a blue paper jumpsuit over her clothes and pulled the hood over her hair, feeling the elastic dig into her forehead. Beside her Anne was matching the ritual and handed a surgical mask to her mentor.

Dr. Fife pressed her thumb against the reader and waited impatiently until a light beside the door's handle changed from red to green. She gripped the handle, opened the door, and entered the antechamber leading into the isolation room. She could hear a clunk followed by the whooshing noise of the ventilation system kicking in. The scientist waited as Anne pulled shut the door from which they had entered. After a lag, the panel beside the second inner door read: **Seal Complete.** With a whirl, the second glass door slid aside.

Long fluorescent bulbs set into the ceiling suddenly sprung to life, illuminating the isolation chamber. The room consisted of several long black counters, enormous refrigerator and freezer units, and work areas under metallic hoods that provided continuous positive pressure ventilation.

As the two advanced beside a wall of cages, chimpanzees grunted, squealed, and shook the metallic frames.

"It's over here," Anne urged and directed Dr. Fife to a workbench beneath a hood.

Dr. Fife sat down upon a stool and popped her head under the hood. The ventilation system hummed. She could see a small metal cage on the table with white lab mice scurrying about. In the corner of the work area were several test tubes lined up in a row within holders. The tubes were labeled "WhiteLeaf5" and contained clear fluid.

The leaf defied scientific logic. The cells that composed it were primitive and were absent of chlorophyll, the green pigment within plants that allowed them to harness energy from the sun. The cells that constituted the white leaf had a prototypical mitochondrial organelle vaguely similar to those that could be found in animal cells. They were able to successfully extract the oil from the leaf and break it down into its constituent elements. The molecular framework was one she had never seen before.

Confident that they had isolated a pure form of the oil, animal trials had been initiated. They had genetically bred mice to develop rhadomyosarcomas, an aggressive tumor of the musculature that was fatal and left the animals physically deformed with balled up tumors pushing up through the skin. These mice were the first to receive doses of the oil.

Dr. Fife looked again at the healthy mice scampering around the cage.

"Where are the mice from the trial?" Dr. Fife asked with a tinge of annoyance.

Anne poked her head under the hood beside the doctor. "That's just it. That's what I'm trying to say. *These* are the mice from the trial. These are the mice with the altered gene. They're supposed to have cancer and look at them!"

Dr. Fife stared at the animals in disbelief. They looked as if they had just been purchased from a pet store. "There must be some mistake."

"I sacrificed several of the mice and did a complete histological analysis. Here's one of the slides." Anne pushed the microscope towards Dr. Fife.

The doctor's arthritic hands trembled as she adjusted the focus dial and brought her glasses up against the eyepieces. She could see the normal repeating pattern of red, striated muscle cells. There were no cancerous cells.

"Dr. Fife, it's amazing. The slides are all normal! I ran an immunoassay and it was normal. The radioactive markers for the cancer genes didn't light up a single thing. It's like these mice never had cancer."

The doctor sat in silence, clutching the focus dials on the microscope and fixated upon the vials of the clear oil. She pushed herself from the work area and backed away.

"Run the tests again," Dr. Fife muttered as she retreated in a daze for the door.

"Again?" asked Anne.

Dr. Fife triggered the release to the door and backed into the antechamber. Her fingertips tingled.

"Run the tests again!" she barked. "This time with the chimps!"

She waited for the second door to open while she tried to catch her breath. The red light finally switched to green and she grabbed the handle and bolted into the lab. She ripped off the surgical mask, leaned her body against the wall, and shut her eyes.

After a minute, she wandered across the lab until she reached the long window looking down upon the parking lot of the Clay Pharmaceutical research building she had worked at for most of her research life. She rested her forehead against the cold glass of the window. Her hand slipped under her blouse and she rubbed her fingertips across the side of her left breast. *I can't feel it*, she thought.

The mammogram had picked it up—a spiculated mass with microcalcifications. The biopsy had confirmed the diagnosis of invasive ductal carcinoma—breast cancer. The MRI of the brain that followed answered why she was having headaches for the last several months. Pea sized metastases were scattered through her brain like buckshot. The oncologist was brutally honest with her prognosis. *Is there anything that you have been meaning to do?* he had asked.

The coolness of the glass against her skin felt soothing. Below, people navigated their way through the parking lot, unaware of what the next days could bring.

Stay focused, she told herself. *Be analytical. Be a scientist.*

She couldn't stop her body from trembling.

It's a miracle.

Acknowledgements

This novel was a long time in the making. Along the way I have incurred a debt of gratitude to people who have steered me in the right direction. Henry Morrison, Natasha Haines, John Hiehle, M.D., and Katie Crawford all offered advice at important moments. Beth Cohen helped design my webpage and create a platform for this social media neophyte.

I am grateful for the team at Deeds Publishing: Bob Babcock, Ashley Clarke, Matt King, and Mark Babcock all believed in my manuscript and helped get it to this stage.

I am eternally grateful to my amazing children, Benjamin, Sophie, and Vivienne, who tolerated impromptu retreats to my study as I hastily logged a thought before it escaped my mind. Their constant curiosity and spirit inspires me daily. And I would be remiss to overlook George, my faithful, furry companion, whose sleeping presence comforted me while I typed late at night.

Finally, I thank my wife, Sara Byala. From travels abroad and library visits to proofreading and re-proofreading drafts of the manuscript, her belief in this project has never waivered. I could not have done this without her. She is at the heart of this—and all—journeys.

About the Author

Chad Brecher was born in Long Island, New York, in 1972, the youngest of three sons. From an early age, two things captivated him: science and literature. After studying to become a physician (attaining degrees from Brown University and Brown University School of Medicine, and later training at Harvard Medical School and Johns Hopkins Medical Center), he settled with his family in suburban Philadelphia. There, he completed his debut novel, *The Lost Book of Wonders*. Brecher continues to write in his free time, working on a sequel to *The Lost Book of Wonders* and additional projects.

CPSIA information can be obtained
at www.ICGtesting.com
Printed in the USA
BVOW03s2156120717
489208BV00001B/44/P